THE HOMECOMING

m.c. merrill

Unbated Productions
UP
www.unbated.com

THE HOMECOMING

Copyright 2005 Marc Merrill

ISBN 0-9770699-0-7

Printed in the USA

Published by
Unbated Productions
1522 Walnut St.
Yankton SD, 57078
www.unbated.com

Cover art copyright: Unbated Productions. All rights reserved.

All rights reserved. No part of this book may be reproduced or transmitted in any form by any means, electronic or mechanical, including photocopy, recording, or by any information storage and retrieval system, without written permission of the Publisher, except where permitted by law.

ISBN 0-9770699-0-7

AUTHOR'S NOTE

Like all "based upon" novels, *The Homecoming* takes certain dramatic license with plot and character. The murder of Tammy Haas and the times that preceded and followed are real, but many of the places and events were altered to fit the narrative. Many actual names have been used, while pseudonyms have been used for others. At times, more than one character has been combined or invented to serve the story. I have also taken certain creative license with precise quotes. A storyteller cannot recreate reality, but can only take the facts at hand and shape them into a fictional work. The body of information on this case is quite sprawling and available to the general public in newspaper archives and court records. Be assured, my intention in veering from what many would consider traditional nonfiction was simply to better blaze bright the light of truth into a darkness that has loomed over my hometown for well over a decade.

For Tammy

…my angel, my muse…

THE
HOMECOMING

PART I

DENIAL

CHAPTER ONE

GRIEF WAS WHAT we called the hill that morning as we crawled up through the dew-dripped razor wire. It seemed a fitting enough name, not because of the lactic acid pumping through our legs, every muscle rebelling, the last of our adrenaline sapped hours ago, nor because we were so numb that we could no longer feel the cuts opened and bleeding across our bellies and our arms. We were well accustomed to the physical rigors of the mission. Grief was a rather simple name, perhaps the best we could come up with on brains starved seventy-two hours of sleep. I suppose, in the end, we called it grief because this one last crawl was the big thank-you-very-much that would end a night-long forced march through the thickest, nastiest, wettest, most bug-infested stretch of swamp Fort Benning had to offer, a dozen dirty recruits elbow-crawling upward, weapons tucked under our chins, the stench of Chattahoochee backwater gone to mildew on our web belts, on our chin straps, on our bootlaces, on our blood-stained, three-day worn festering-rancid GI olive-drab socks, every last one of us with only one thing on our minds...

Almost home.

Grief was a good name because every time we thought we had reached the top, another little saddle would open to our front revealing a few hundred meters more of dick-in-the-sand crawling to go. As if kicked in the head, it occurred to me just then, so I had to whisper it back to the boys: "Another good name would have been Wild Goose, because I'm getting the feeling—"

Suddenly—movement dead ahead!

The business end of my M16 blurred a rousing little dance and darting little shadow demons flitted about my periphery. I needed to get a drop on what was coming at us, but the more I tried to focus, the more my vision bled. I thought I heard a gunshot ring out, and I thought I felt the warmth of blood, and for a few moments, all I could make out were spectacular reds. My insides had just unfolded out—I was sure of it.

But then again, I was still able to consider the situation. I had just turned nineteen, developed rashes in some very delicate places, a knee too swollen for my tastes, and a twitch in my lower back that wouldn't go away. I blinked and shook my mind free of the blood-dance. The sun was shining. We were within a hillcrest of completing our mission. Something had just moved through the brush to our immediate front.

I rallied my strength and crawled forward twenty feet. It was the curvature of enemy Kevlar, a helmet poking up from the short grass—I was almost certain that was what had moved—there one moment, gone the next. Had we crawled upon the opposing force unseen? Highly unlikely. I reached the crest of a little ridge, pushed a mound of sand aside, and confirmed my second suspicion. My Bravo Team leader Freddy Reyes closed the distance to receive my intelligence report. "Turtle."

"Say again?" Reyes' voice came up the slope.

"Turtle," I whispered.

Reyes crawled up next to me and we watched as the enemy helmet rose up on four feet and made lazy away.

YOU KEEP HER cradled in your arms, high and dry, right at your chin. You do this to keep the sand from grinding its way into her trigger assembly and down her barrel. Carrying her like this adds an extra moment of hesitation, the extra moment it takes to get her shouldered, a moment that could mean the difference between life and death, a moment worth waiting, and a risk worth taking if it means saving you from a weapon malfunction. You give her the respect you would give a lady, because she is your life.

THE REALITY WAS none of us had ever once tasted true grief.

WE HAD JUST crossed paths with the turtle and were so close to the top I could feel it coming. The smell was talc—anti-fungal foot powder maybe, used to soothe chafing thighs, and gun oil too. The air stilled just enough so that we could hear the sound of a red-cockaded woodpecker tapping, gently rapping in the distance, and just beneath the sound of all that tapping, the careful, slow click of an M16 safety rising into the firing position.

White of our eyes—we had dropped our guard and crawled right into an ambush! So there we were, popping to our feet, blasting each other down. We had the sun behind us. They had the numbers. Third Squad, First Platoon, Charlie Company, First of the Fiftieth doing everything we could to kill First, Second, and Fourth Squads of Charlie Company, First of the Fiftieth (our dear comrades on any other occasion) fire spitting from our barrels, clutching our chests, stumbling, tumbling down through the sand, death acted so casually, fourteen seconds of raging close-combat machine-gun fire—and that was that—five hours of planning, sixty-seven hours of humping through the most miserable shit you could possibly imagine, a crawl up a hill we called Grief, and only one thought as the smoke cleared...

Almost home.

DRILL SERGEANT ECCLES was the foul-mouthed son of a Baptist minister, a black man capable of stringing together curses with such precision and cleverness that art was the only word for it. Eccles had been shadowing us along the way, monitoring our progress, but somewhere up the hill, about a half-hour ago, our radioman heard him receive a cryptic radio message telling him to switch to a secret radio channel. The last we heard from Eccles was the chirp of his radio, and then just as suddenly as he was there, he was gone. Eccles was an old Pathfinder with about twenty years under his belt, two in combat. He was a master of the vanishing act.

THE WINNERS WERE basking in the sun. The losers—those whose MILES gear sounded their demise—were gathering up spent ammo. That was the state of affairs when Drill Sergeant Eccles reappeared, rolling up the hill in the back of the Charlie Company cargo transport. Riding with Eccles were the Company Commander, First Sergeant, XO, and Battalion Chaplain.

"Company Attention," somebody shouted and we all leapt to our feet.

Eccles wasted no time with formalities. "Private Merrill, front and center." It wasn't the first time I had been called front and center for an ass chewing, but it was the first time it happened with command staff present. In other words, the ***gravitas*** of face-time with all this Brass was not lost on me.

The salute I snapped woke something biting in my shoulder. A piece of paper was passed from the Battalion Chaplain to the First Sergeant to the Company Commander. The Company Commander took a half-step sideways, unfolded the scrap of paper, read it to himself, and then stepped back at me, this time a bit too close for my taste, close enough that I knew he was a smoker of cheap cigarettes and a drinker of Dayquil by the bottle. "Private Merrill, this message comes from the Red Cross," he said.

I made myself rigid right then and there.

"You can stand at ease, son," he said and without missing a beat read, "Private Merrill, your father requests your presence due to the death of Tamara Ann Haas, reported missing September 19, 1992, body discovered in Nebraska Ravine, September 23, 1992." As he finished reading, a wind barely felt caught that little scrap of paper and tore it from his hand. There was fumbling among the four and then the Captain had it back in hand. "Confirmed by Local Newspaper, September 24th, 1992. Chaplain Fry notified."

I just stood there stupidly.

"Collect your rifle and ruck and we'll get you to the rear," Eccles said. "Further arrangements will be made from there."

Disappeared, a ravine, her body found...

I turned sideways left and sideways right.

"What are you looking for, Private?" Eccles said.

"My rifle, Drill Sergeant."

"On your shoulder, son," Eccles said.

He was right—it was exactly where I had slung it, upon my left shoulder, but even as I cradled it down, I couldn't feel it. I couldn't feel anything. Eccles held out his hand and I surrendered my weapon to him. Ten minutes ago, all I wanted was any excuse to go home. Now, my wish was granted and I hated myself for it.

AS I BUMPED along in the back of the Humvee, Fort Benning shrunk to a blur of meaningless green. Maybe it was the lack of sleep—that's why I felt this emptiness, this utter and indescribable self-hatred. I liked the blurring, the slipping of reality, my guts falling from the inside out.

"You were close to her?"

It was First Sergeant asking, but I didn't recognize his voice. First Sergeants bark, but this particular First Sergeant, at this particular moment, as the wind whipped around us, bore a rare and gentle humanity.

"I'm sorry, First Sergeant?"

"You were close to her?"

I didn't know how to respond to that.

"We have a liaison office that'll help you book tickets for your flight home," First Sergeant said. "Some leave paperwork for you to sign. We'll have to do some fudging. Emergency leave only gets granted for the loss of a spouse or child." And then First Sergeant just stared off into the green for the rest of the ride, and then finally, as we rolled up to the barracks, he offered me a handshake, and as I took it, he tucked into my nail-bitten, grime-scabbed fingers the little scrap of paper that had fifteen minutes earlier carried the message I was only now starting to fathom...

Tammy was dead.

ALONE AND UNDER the fiery mists of the gang showers of the Charlie Company barracks, I sank to my knees, my body releasing all that it had been holding. "There's nothing more for me to do," I said again and again. "There's nothing more for me to do."

THEY SAY SOLDIERS dying on the battlefield cry out for their mothers. I didn't know if that was true or not. The phone rang and rang and all I could do was rest my head against the cradle, the cool of the keypads at my fingers. The great empty space whispering through me was growing wider, its weight becoming unbearable. I was standing at the phone islands just east of the parade field. The standing order was only five minutes on the phone on Sundays (a privilege earned.) There was always a line behind you and the noise was sometimes so much that you had to plug your free ear to hear anything at all. You dialed fast and prayed that she would answer and when she didn't answer, your heart would break. It would be another week, if you were lucky, before you got another chance. You would pen her letters every night and send them off like prayers into the unknown. You would dial again the next week, your skill at rationalizing unanswered prayers growing. You would hope against hope, and then finally, after twenty rings, you'd give up and use the last of those precious few minutes to call Mom or Dad.

"What happened?" was all I could ask her and my mother tried to explain...something about how she knew, just knew that something like this was coming...something about how this was her worst nightmare...something about how she didn't see Tammy at the Homecoming game...how they tried to reach me...how the newspapers weren't reporting anything new...how she looked so happy the last time they saw her...and then my mom began to sob...and she kept sobbing...and kept sobbing...

"Mom, is Dad home?"

...and she kept sobbing...

"He isn't dead too?" I asked.

There was a long, cold silence.

"The Army booked me tickets home," I finally said. "It's a red-eye. I won't be able to get into Omaha until 0330 tomorrow."

"Three-thirty in the morning?" she asked. "Down in Omaha?"

"Should I try to rent a car from the airport to get me—?"

"Just let us handle that part," she said.

"You won't forget?"

Again, she started sobbing.

"You won't forget?" I said more firmly to plant it in her memory.

"We won't forget, of course, we won't," she said.

She wanted to talk some more. She wanted to know how I was doing, how I was feeling. I made an excuse about how there were people behind me waiting for the phone, even though there was nobody in sight. She told me to fly safely. I told her I wouldn't be in charge of the plane and then hung up.

THE BOOM-BOOM brothers, Meriwether, Brokedick, and the rest of the boys arrived late that night to find me busy mopping the mess-hall floor. Technically, I was on leave already, but my flight wouldn't depart for another eighteen hours. On my slow walk back to the barracks from the phones, a Bravo Company Drill Instructor chased me down and shoved a mop in my hand. Though it was well after midnight when I returned to the barracks, some of the boys were still waiting up. They approached my bunk tentatively.

"Heard any good jokes lately?" I asked them.

"Hey, m'man," Brokedick said and put a hand on my shoulder.

"Okay, I guess it's up to me." I gestured for them to sit, and when they were all huddled around me, I began in a whisper. "A woman went to her doctor for a follow-up visit after being prescribed testosterone to treat some—how should we say—womanly problems. The drug was working great, mind you, but she was a little worried about some of the side effects. 'Doctor,' she said, 'the hormones you've been giving me have worked wonders, but I'm afraid you've given me too much. I've started growing hair in some odd places.'"

"Like where?" Brokedick asked.

"Part of the punch line," I whispered. "And so the Doctor reassured her, 'A little hair growth is a perfectly normal side effect of a male hormone. Just where exactly has this hair appeared?' 'On my testicles,' she said, 'which is another thing I need to talk to you about.'"

Yeah, well, it got laughs...

...and then an uncomfortable silence...

...then more laughs.

I CAN'T SAY I dreamt that night because I never really fell asleep. Rather my mind returned to the lurking-dark shadow places of my childhood—the monsters residing deep, angels and demons one in the same, tormenting, tormenting, death lurking, lurking. Sleep-starved and restless I paced the barracks, one end to the other—no place to spirit myself in retreat—wake up—I begged myself—wake up.

I SLIPPED OUT to the phone islands early the next morning and called a taxi. It was a long wait at the airport and my only source of human contact was with the panhandlers who would jingle their cans and expose their broken and missing teeth to prove their case. "Happy to be going home, Private?" they would jingle. "Share some happy with me?" they would grin. "Happy, happy, jingle, jingle?" One after the next they came to feed from my pockets. I was easy prey, silently floating at the bottom of an abyss where no thoughts could form and no feelings could escape, unable and unwilling to kick my way to the surface.

SIX RECENTLY GRADUATED Army Rangers sat in front of me on the first leg of my flight home. They had lost a combined weight of three hundred and forty-six pounds over the past five months and thus could no longer hold their liquor. Even still, they managed to polish off nearly a case of champagne. Along the way, one of them asked me where I was going and why. I told him where I was going but I lied about why. I didn't see the point of ruining a good party.

We touched down in Memphis at midnight and the Rangers hopped another flight. A very expensive looking lady stretched herself across the three seats to my front. One of the flight attendants, the one in charge, gave me headphones as a courtesy for gentlemen in uniform. The very thought of drowning my mind with the blare of music came as a relief, but the relief was short-lived. A moment after I had found the headphones jack, the very expensive looking lady craned over the seat and snapped, "Could you *please* turn that down! Some of us have had a bad day!"

I was glad to leave that very expensive looking lady and hop the twin-engine to Omaha. Fingers dug deep into the armrests around me as stomach-wrenching little moments of turbulence chased violent bursts of lightning. An unpredicted storm had walled us in halfway across Iowa. Babies sometimes find soothing the white noise of a vacuum cleaner or the vibrations of a car. For me it was the lightning painting grand the clouds around us, and like water finding its own level, my mind finally stilled into a lucid sort of sleep.

DOWN IN THE baggage claim at Eppley Airfield, Omaha, I watched the luggage carousel go round and round, and when it finally stopped, I wandered to the booking desk where a haggard booking agent informed me that my GI duffel bag had somehow found its way onto an International Flight to Frankfurt, Germany.

From the booking desk, I circled twice through the terminal, past the closed rental car shop, past the empty taxi stands, the bus stop, past the green zones, the yellow zones, the red zones, looking, hoping, and finally wondering how I would travel the three hours home.

It was only upon my fourth lap through the terminal that she caught my eye. They had tucked her in the shadows, behind the iron-wrought gate of a closed magazine shop. She stared at me from the top corner of the front page of the ***Sioux Falls Argus Leader***. "MISSING YANKTON WOMAN FOUND DEAD" the headline read. They had rendered her photo in black and white, the honeydew sapped from her hair and the wheat-field brown from her eyes.

I stared at her through that gate for I'm not sure how long and then was suddenly startled back to reality by a familiar voice. "I stood at the baggage claim for awhile then road the escalators topside to see if I might have missed you at the gate. I was just about to leave, thinking you'd missed your flight." Bobby Grant was the last person I expected my parents to send, but there he was, staring at my Army issue trench coat and the wrinkled Dress Blues beneath.

I slung my little knapsack over my shoulder and smelled for the first time the soiled BDUs I'd worn on Grief Hill. I had stuffed them in a garbage sack as an afterthought and stuffed the garbage sack in the outside pocket of my knapsack. I would miss Friday laundry call back at Benning and didn't like the idea of one of my summer BDUs going to mold in my wall locker.

"Where's the rest of your luggage?" Bobby asked as we started walking.

"Germany."

"I've been dying to do this for two months." Bobby grinned, rubbed the bald of my head, and then jerked back like a child given too much candy. "Your mom gave me money for gas and food. God, it's good to see you! I can't believe how good! You look good! Not sure what's open twenty-four hours around here, but I'm betting we can find a Wendy's or something."

"I think I'd just throw it up," I said.

Bobby grinned. "Car's still running!"

BOBBY'S MUSTANG WAS of the two-tone variety—spray-paint black and rust. It had vise-grips where the passenger's door handle should have been and several old quilts stuffed to fill the gaping holes worn through the front seats. "I happen to be hungry," Bobby said as we pulled into the nearest McDonald's parking lot…and as the young lady at the window bagged him his Big Mac and Fries, Bobby glanced at me and smiled, carefully turning away just enough to conceal the contents of his wallet. "I'm going to be short two buck—got some cash?"

Thirty-two cents of my change tossed in his coin caddy and the Mc-meal between his legs, Bobby pulled out and shot straight past the entrance to the Freeway. I glanced back and pointed, "I think we just missed our—"

Bobby nodded and said, "We have to take the back road home."

"Highway 81?"

"Over the river and through the woods, my brother."

CHAPTER TWO

THE STEADY PULL of Bobby's cigarette gave eerie glow to our reflections against the windshield. We would go bright as he breathed in the flame and then dim as the flame smoldered low. We would come to life, dark, red, and cast deep in the glass, and then as he brought the smoke down to the ashtray, we would vanish to the gently rolling hills surrounding us. We sped fast across the vast seas empty-dappled by the occasional distant farmyard light, racing as night yawned deeper toward morning—the road so straight and endless, the great canopy of night lit spectacular, the slow, slow dance of purple hues rising in the east, dawn blotting one star after the next.

We were traveling up Highway 81, which once staked claim as part of the Pan-American, the longest contiguous highway in the Americas. Save an incomplete portion through the rainforests of Columbia, the Pan-American Highway reached from Fairbanks, Alaska to the southern tip of Chile. Two-lane highways like 81 once had character, but with the creation of the Interstate Highway system, the Drive-Ins were ripped down, roadhouses bulldozed over, and only occasionally, like now as we passed out of Norfolk, could one still find a string of signs imparting such wisdom as...

Altho insured

A thoroughfare for small-time mules rolling from precinct to precinct, deal to deal, Highway 81 gained newfound glory in the 1960s, a loose confederation of disorganized criminals keeping steady the flow of drugs from the Mexican and Canadian borders. Highway 81 was ideal for drug trafficking, because the small towns along the way offered safe-haven and respite, local authorities incapable or unwilling to combat the scourge.

Remember, kiddo

I couldn't help staring at the speaker next to my right foot. Bobby either hadn't noticed or had learned to ignore its steady hum and the ugly little rattle of something loose inside every time we hit a bump.

They don't pay you

We were close to home—well over halfway there. Home was Yankton, a little town situated on the South Dakota and Nebraska border, tucked on the north shores of the Missouri river. Getting there wouldn't be official though until we crossed the Meridian Bridge, an old double-decker lift-span and Yankton's most famed landmark.

Yankton, jewel of the Dakotas, territorial capital and Mother City, a friendly port for Riverboat travelers and a launching point for gold-seekers, a rambling town with a checkered history, where in its time, houses of ill repute outnumbered houses of God, where in its time, dirty politics was everyday and gunfights settled more than one matter of state.

They pay your widow

Yankton had always been a fame-speckled place, beginning with Lewis and Clark who stopped here and spent time with Eh-hank-ton of the Great Sioux Nation. The Eh-hank-ton would be forced westward within half a century. Two decades after that, the infamous General George Custer would come through with plans to utterly crush the Sioux. Back then, Custer was seen as a hero and genocide as a cost-effective means of expanding the borders of Christendom.

Burma-Shave!

Wild Bill was shot in Deadwood, but his killer would be dragged four hundred miles east and hanged not far from my own backyard. Jack McCall was the fellow's name, and when they dug him up a few years later to move the local cemetery to higher ground, they found his noose still round his neck.

Yankton was above all else a river town. The Missouri, Old Muddy, was its lifeblood—violent and beautiful—ice floes in winter, floods in spring, pocked with sandbars in summer, and in autumn clogged with timber from reaches far north. A series of dams were built to harness its flow, but even still, the river slowly wins, clogging the grand reservoirs with sediment, setting its own terms for existence.

WHEN WE HIT the upper shelf of the Missouri River valley, Yankton's city lights came into view, a dim constellation of yellows ten miles deep in the valley. It was here where the air started to smell of felled cedar and haystacks damp with morning. It was here the air started smelling like home. We had ridden in silence for the past hour. Now was the time for one of us to speak.

THEY WAKE YOU up in Boot Camp by banging trashcan lids," Bobby told me as if it were a point of fact. I glanced over at him, my brow raised, and after fractional hesitation, he added, "Don't they?"

I answered with a non-committal, "We'd just spent the last week in the field," and then I glanced out into the passing wheat, "night missions—you get no sleep, so you have no need to get woken."

"You want a cigarette?" Bobby asked me. He was staring at the Zippo in my hand. "Or do you plan to keep clicking it opened and closed?"

"It was a gift," I said.

"The clicking is getting old—use it or lose it."

I hadn't noticed I had been doing it so had to answer by clicking the lighter open and clicking the lighter closed one last time. Bobby glared my way, only to find my eyes waiting stone cold. We were both tired. Our little habits had gotten on each other's nerves.

Bobby gripped the steering wheel tight and squeezed out the words: "I gotta warn you—there've been questions about why you left, questions that first came up when she first went missing."

"What kind of questions?"

He hadn't intended on having this conversation. He didn't expect me to ask anything straightforward as to the truth.

"There was a rumor going around that she ran away," he said. "You know how she was—I mean I can't say I know anybody who's completely—"

Bobby pulled back his words and as he did, the darkness of the prairie swelled darker as we traveled 81 down from the high plains.

"Anybody who's completely what?" I asked.

"Shocked," Bobby said. "The police told her Mom not to file a missing-person's report until after Homecoming." Bobby continued, but this time stared ahead as if in a trance. "She was last seen Thursday…the game was Friday night…the dance was Saturday…and then the next week kind of rolls around. It was like she was…here one minute, gone the next."

"Nobody cared," I said.

"Like I said, everybody thought she ran away." Bobby glanced at me and nearly smiled. "Blew off for the weekend, you know." Bobby shifted uncomfortably in his seat. "Your parents, they really did wanna get a hold of you." Bobby shifted in his seat again. "But when somebody turns up missing? Around here? They always come back." The road was becoming soft and Bobby's voice slowly drifted away from me.

"You said something about some party?" I managed.

"Yeah, there was one," he said, "At the Stevenson farm. Homecoming Eve. That Thursday."

"On the Nebraska side?" I asked.

"Yeah…she was last seen walking from the bonfire," Bobby said. "Nobody saw her leave with anybody…it's just like she…it's just like she vanished into the night."

"Why would she do that?"

"Trying to walk home, I guess."

My eyes went heavy, sleep washing closer.

"She lives on the north side of town," I said, unsure whether I was still speaking aloud. "The bridge to her house is three-miles…then it's another half mile across the bridge…then I don't even know how far out to the farm, five or ten miles at least, wouldn't you say?"

"Yeah," Bobby said.

"A farm out in the middle of nowhere…"

"All I know," Bobby said, "is what people have been saying."

THE HOMECOMING

"What people?"

"It's just one of the rumors."

"Rumors?"

"And if she was hit-and-run, like people have been saying, then it makes sense that she was walking."

"Alone?" one of us said (I'm not sure which.)

The smell of cedar grew strong.

"I think I have to see her."

I opened an eye to find Bobby casting an odd glance my way.

"What?"

"What?" Bobby asked back.

"I think I have to see her."

There it was again, but now I realized that I was the one speaking.

"Nobody told you?" Bobby asked.

"What?"

"It's going to be a closed casket."

My heart fell through my stomach and my mind slipped loose.

"Thing is," Bobby said, shrugged, and rolled a kink from his neck. "People are talking…and people have been asking questions."

"About me, you mean?"

My body surrendered and sank deep and soft into the car seat.

"About things that happened before you left," Bobby said. "I mean, you did write to me saying you were worried about her. Evidently, you had good reason."

"Did I?"

"You mentioned she had a secret." Bobby's voice stretched long and low beneath the groan and thrum of the Meridian Bridge, the river danced up the city's reflected light, and I felt myself quickly lifted away.

ONE PARTICULAR SCHOOL of thought, based more in theosophy than in hard science, has it that dreamers dream to light the places of shadow in their waking lives. There was a mystery needing solving, a mystery trapped in the shadows of my past, a mystery my waking mind refused to address. That's why I was carried three-months back to the roof of the Dakota.

The Dakota Theatre was built as a turn-of-the-century opera house, but when the movie craze swept across the land two decades later, the owners quickly adapted to the changing times. Nowadays, the Dakota Theatre ached from strain and fought to stay open under the pressures of a changing market. Video rental was the new thing and there were rumors of an even newer format called DVD. Gone were the days when the entire town would flock to the latest showings and crowds would stretch two blocks down and nearly to the bridge. These days, the crowds came in trickles of twos and threes, leaving minimum wagers like Tammy and me the time to lazy-make while the picture-show played. Some nights we wouldn't even have to run the popcorn machine. The theatre was just off Third, what most towns would call Main

Street and half a block up on Walnut, across from the post office and the local newspaper.

Even in its decline, historic downtown still managed to look like something out of a Norman Rockwell painting. Wal-Mart and the mall north of town sucked up most of the local business, as did the mini-plazas on Broadway, but the little niche shops managed to survive. I suppose a person really couldn't resist their homey charm, puppy dogs barking from the pet shop window, the cobbler pounding away at the heel of a shoe. The old traditions die hardest—the Boy Scouts selling Christmas trees from Rexall's parking lot, Gurney's giving penny grab sacks to the children, and in the summer, the baseball players and bikers drinking until good and drunk out in front of the old Icehouse. The Dakota, even on the verge of death, was still a window into a bigger world, a place of magic, with a hundred years of history stored up. The Dakota quite simply was a place where dreams came true.

You would reach the roof from the little ladder in the projection booth, just the soft glow of the marquee guiding you as you snuck up, and then the marquee would flicker out with the last of the crowd. In October, you'd watch in awe the branches shaking their colored raiment, a dance of swirling leaves in the fiery sunset sky. In winter, there would be a night or two when the clouds hung low enough to make a canvas. The reds, oranges, and blues of Christmas would twinkle up and hang soft in the heavy sky, a sure sign that tomorrow would bring snow. In spring, you would come up to be blasted by the winds and pounded by the rains, but soon the days would grow long toward the solstice and the air would go warm and dry. You could close your eyes on those nights and be carried off by the song of the Cicada or the sad trill of the mourning doves. You could rest your head against hers and disappear into a sky exploding with stars, the world around you fading and heaven itself bending close to hear your every prayer.

I KILLED THE magic that last night. That much I remembered. Had I stripped myself from the palate, perhaps the picture painted would have been art for the ages, but I was there in true form and ruining perfect moment after perfect moment. My watch was the problem. How little time we had left haunted my every thought. I couldn't leave the moment alone. I couldn't simply be with her. I was too busy fearing the future or dwelling on the past. Even in the dream place, I couldn't escape this. It was 2:26 A.M. and at precisely 5:00 A.M., my bus would be rolling toward the bridge. There was something else though, something that would unfold in the next few hours, a mistake I made that I spent months beating and banishing from my mind.

I was supposed to grow into the watch but never did. That was why it clicked and glided over the bones of my wrist. I rarely ever wore the thing, but time was a factor tonight, the only factor…or so I thought, and that, perhaps, was the reason she grabbed my hand and whispered warm and soft against my ear. "Stop looking at the time or I'll steal your watch from you."

Yes, she was with me—that much was certain—in my arms, her head against my chest, so maybe it wasn't true what they had been saying about some party, about some ravine...

"Are you falling asleep?" I asked her.

She didn't make a sound.

"Tammy?"

I could feel her body making a soft and gentle slide away from mine. The air had gotten sticky with warmth, so we had crawled out from beneath the quilt, the one I kept hidden in the ceiling tiles of the projection booth.

"Tamara Ann, are you sleeping?" I asked again.

Still nothing, even with me invoking her middle name.

"Cops just showed up—" I tried. "—I think we're both in big trouble."

"Good," she muttered back.

She was trying to sleep and I was trying to dream. I had been holding back for months and now I wanted to talk. It was bad timing on my part. She had a knack for making herself comfortable anywhere, anytime, and if she felt like sleeping even now, she would do just that.

I had spent my young life managing to sabotage every good thing that had come my way. It was the Lutheran in me, I suppose, the need to suffer the sin of being born. I was the type of kid who apologized for good grades, the type of kid who would stumble within ten steps of the finish line. I suppose I was brought up to believe that there was nobility in meekness and failure. I was about to do it again and I couldn't help myself. I slowly lifted my wrist and gave my watch a good hard flick.

"Stop it," she hissed.

I moved closer to her and gave my watch another grating flick.

"Not cute."

I got right over her nose with the watch and just as I was about to flick my wrist, she exploded off the blanket, threw herself atop me, and straddled my hips. "I told you to stop!" she said and then began forcibly removing the watch. "And so you will not get this back," she said in her best schoolteacher voice, "until I am good and ready to give it back." With that, she put the ill-fitting watch on her own even-smaller wrist, smiled matter-of-factly, and settled back against my chest. It was a bad moment made perfect by her.

I sidled closer and caught a hint of Coppertone still lingering on her skin. Beneath the Coppertone was jasmine and apricot. As I breathed her in, my thumb found its way across her wrist until it met with her heartbeat.

"Hey." I said.

"Hey," she whispered back.

"Don't move."

"What are you doing?" she barely breathed.

"Heartbeat."

She lay still and her heart slowed until I could barely feel it and she never once questioned why. I'm not sure how long it lasted, but finally a bird started chirping in the distance and her heart started beating fast again. She smiled and laced my fingers in hers.

"Why did you join the Army?" she asked.

All I could do was fumble some tired words.

"That's not an answer," she said. "That's what they put on the poster. What I meant is that you...aren't what I would consider Army material."

"What would you consider Army material?" I asked.

"Nobody so gentle."

The words hurt and I didn't know why.

"Hey," I said. "What did you want to tell me?"

"When?"

"Earlier."

She gave me a look of warning. "Earlier when?"

"Two weeks ago you said you wanted to tell me something important. I made a joke and you got upset. I sent you roses the next day. You sent a thank-you note." I smiled. "The note sounded formal—cold."

"It rings a bell."

"All I could think was that I would leave for the Army and not get a chance to see you again and I had never felt so helpless in all my life."

She slid up and turned away from me. "It wasn't about you, okay? It had *nothing* to do with you...and you did *nothing* at all wrong."

Suddenly, I felt even more helpless.

I would need to dream further and dream deeper. That she had a secret life away from me was no mystery, that she had a better life apart from me was something I had accepted long ago. All I could do now was nod and bleed somewhere deep inside, somewhere so deep she would never know my ache. That was how it had always been, me hoping toward some future, aching and bleeding because I knew it would never be. She had something important to tell me two weeks ago and I blew it. Such was my life and so I would stumble forward, wearing my failure like a robe of purple. "Hey," she smiled, "I have something for you, but not until you walk me home."

WE TOOK A good long shortcut across the wide-open green of the park that night, stopping to sit on the swings, burning up what little of the night we had left. She watched me take a ride down the slide. I did it standing up to show off. We lost track of time again and at exactly 4:00 A.M., just as the city had timed it, and precisely one hour before I was to get on the bus that was to take me to Fort Benning, the water kicked on and Tammy and I found ourselves quite stuck in the pit-pat pulse of the underground sprinklers. First, it spattered our legs and as we spun at each other, it ricocheted across our back. The cold of it was startling. Instinct told us to take flight. We were doused from the left, doused from the right. It was either a one hundred yard dash to go back the way we came or three hundred yards to stay our course and get her home. I grabbed Tammy's hand to pull her forward, but she didn't budge. Instead, she pulled me back hard. Pulled me straight into her arms. She pulled me tight. Tight enough so I could feel her trembling...and that's when she said, "If you want to grab me and run..."

And that was all I could remember.

There was something more, though, I was sure.

Yes, she backed away to brush a stray curl from my eye and then she pulled me close again and whispered something that would haunt me, something that had to be shattered from my memory and carried off into the winds of forever if I was to survive. Yes, she whispered something and I did nothing and there we stood in each other's arms—for I'm not sure how long—soaked by those sprinklers splashing up the twilight around us.

BOBBY SHOOK ME awake. "We're home."

CHAPTER THREE

I BLINKED AWAY the morning sun and rubbed at my baldness. This was real, here and now, and Tammy and I in those sprinklers was already slipping back into shadow, the words she said, the sound of her voice, the soft of her touch, fading, fading…

"Gotta split—some errands to run," Bobby said. "You gonna be okay?"

I nodded and reached for my knapsack, which he was already bringing up from the backseat. "What time is it?" I asked.

"Morning," he said. "You only slept for a few minutes."

He dropped the knapsack in my lap and waited.

"You sure you're okay?"

I nodded again and stepped out into the morning air.

"Everything will be cool. You'll see," he said, pulled my door shut, and rolled away.

I looked up at the little gray house on the corner. My parents and I had argued our way out of the house that last night and kept arguing all the way to the bus stop. The argument was finally cut short by the bus driver's honk. They wanted to know why I had gotten home so late and why I was so wet. I didn't want to take those last few minutes of my childhood translating the language of romance into words they could understand. I didn't want a lecture on how dangerous it was to be in the park late at night. I didn't want a lecture on how walking around in wet clothing could lead to pneumonia. I didn't want a lecture on getting my hopes up about a girl I might never see again.

My mother Grace stood in the picture window now, curtain pulled back so to glimpse me, and just as I caught her eye, she let the curtain fall.

My mother had been born in and of the hellfire of Allied bombings during World War II. She was the thirteenth of thirteen children, born into the grinding poverty of Nazi Germany's collapse. Her older brothers, just teens when captured, spent some seven years in Siberian death camps. They all managed to survive. My grandmother died suddenly when my mother was eleven, so to help support the family, my mother went to work in a milk factory. By her fifteenth birthday, she had hidden away enough for a one-way ticket to America.

My mother never talked about her childhood, but when twenty years later, her third eldest brother decided to come to America, the nightmares resurfaced. Based upon my mother's fears, I expected a monster to disembark the airplane, a monster incarnate of Nazi mind-control and the Soviet gulags. In the end, the old man who came to visit when I was six turned out to be kind, gentle, and decent. Without a common word between us, he taught me Chess on the little marble chessboard my father kept in the den. This was the first adult who ever had the time for me. Through his tutelage, I learned patience, strategy, and the elegance of reason.

We are not only shaped by our own experiences, my father once told me, but by the experiences of those who preceded us, every one of us living a winner in the game of survival of the fittest, millions upon millions of years of knowledge stored up in our DNA.

My father was a science teacher, very good at hyperbolizing to make a point. He was there too, my father, standing behind my mother as I crossed the lawn. He was the one who asked her to peek out the curtain to see how I looked. Once he was certain I was in one piece, he slid on his jacket and headed for the back door.

Those born in the wake of the American Depression were tough as the leather in their work boots, but they had one weakness—an inability to look tragedy dead in the eye. "Have him shower and change into some of his old clothes. Take him shopping," he told my mother. "Keep him busy."

I COULD TELL he had just been in the room, based upon the look on my mother's face. She was standing in the middle of the living room, unsure whether she should come to me, unsure of what she should be doing with her hands. "Are you hungry?" she asked.

I searched the living room to find the chessboard gone dusty exactly where I had last left it. The rooks had lost their parapets, and the queen had a crack down her center, super-glued together the best an eight-year-old boy could do. I could barely balance anymore and finally felt safe enough to let go. My knapsack fell to the floor. My mother came at me hard and fast, took me in her arms, held me tight. When soldiers bled on the battlefield, they did cry for their mothers—I was sure of that now.

EXCEPT FOR A few boxes stacked in the corner, my parents had left my room as it was—a few ribbons and trophies in a box on the dresser; Boy Scout merit badges pinned on a little cork post-it board in the corner; a poster of Indiana Jones atop a galloping horse, his smoking six-shooter blazing away. Everything seemed to be as it was when I left, childish and unforgivably innocent—except for something…

Something was out of place. Something was missing. I couldn't be certain what it was, but I could sense its absence the same way I could sense the missing memory of that June night. I stood their dripping in my towel. I turned a little circle and rubbed at my head in hopes that I might jar the memory loose. I turned another little circle and rubbed at my baldness again, but was still blind to it. I was beyond tired. Once I dressed, I thought to myself, and put something in my stomach, perhaps the misplaced memory of the missing thing would present itself.

Getting dressed turned out to be an unexpected challenge. The only clothing I had brought from Benning was the uniform on my back and the filthy BDUs from Grief hill.

THE HOMECOMING

I yanked the jeans up and they stopped mid-thigh. I pulled the jeans down to my knees to check the label—30 waist, 30 length. They were mine most certainly, but they felt three sizes too small. I pulled out another pair of 30x30s—same problem—and then tried on a size bigger—still far too small.

I resigned myself to putting on an old pair of sweatpants and then dug out my favorite shirt, left exactly where I had hung it nearly three months ago on my rush to make it to the bus stop on time. It still had dimples from drying on its hanger and the smell of cologne overdone. I put it on, reached the third button, and had to stop. The seams were ready to rip at the shoulder. I was frustrated and tired. "Who shrunk all my clothes?!" I shouted. "And where are all my goddamned pictures?!"

Through high school, I had kept a collage of pictures and news-clippings discreetly on the wall behind my bedroom door, but then the collage grew as I grew until filling nearly the length of the room. Now, the collage was gone.

"You didn't throw them away, I hope to God!"

I tore open the top drawer of my dresser to find my cigar box gone too. It was in the cigar box where, among other things, I kept concert tickets, movie stubs, badly written poetry, amusement-park baubles, and what was left of her sunglasses. These I had accidentally sent through a lawnmower.

I backed away, my heart racing, the air escaping me. "Where did you— Where's my—"

My mother wandered into the room oblivious to my panic. "You've outgrown that shirt," she said. "Do you want to go to JCPenney?"

I pointed at the bare wall. "My pictures?"

My mother's eyes took on a strange and bittersweet glaze and then she looked right through me. "We didn't want to upset you," she said, "so we decided that it would be best to take them down."

"Oh…"

We stood there staring at each other a confused few moments.

"I have to leave for awhile," I said.

"Where? Maybe I can take you."

CHAPTER FOUR

FUNERAL DIRECTOR RAYMOND Shay had propped himself upon a stool to do the last touches on Mr. Weidman. Mr. Weidman had been the proud grandfather of over a half a hundred Yanktonians and the illegitimate grandfather of at least a hundred more. Mr. Weidman's liver spots were blanching too purple even under the soft light of the viewing room. This required that Shay give him a thicker coat of pancake base—too much pancake, however, and Mr. Weidman would look like a grotesque. Applying makeup to the dead required far more work than laypeople could imagine, and this was how Shay wanted to keep things. In this business, what customers *did* know hurt them. A peaceful and dignified farewell to the dead—that was the trick. Within the first few hours, the blood settled black into the low cavities of the body and the cartilage began to collapse, the cells broke down and the body bloated and purged from both ends. Maintaining the illusion that what was in the casket was your loved one meant putting on one hell of a show.

All three-hundred and fifty pounds of Raymond Shay was leaning into the task of making Weidman presentable when Shay's part-time receptionist and least favorite niece Penny Shay snuck up and whispered, "There's a strange looking boy in Army clothes who wants to talk to you?"

"In regards to?"

"I'm pretty sure it's Merrill Merrill," Penny Shay whispered. "But he's bald and Merrill Merrill has curly black hair and I don't think lives here anymore. I told him about the Weidman wake, but he said he'd wait. It could actually be Merrill Merrill or maybe a cousin of his, I guess. He stinks kind of, so maybe he's homeless or something. Anyway, whoever it is, he won't leave until he talks to you about viewing Tammy…he's wearing camouflage. I don't think he's armed though and he looks too young to be in the Army. Yep, the more I think about it, the more I do think it is Merrill Merrill."

"Why don't you go see what his nametag says," Shay told Penny.

Penny left and returned. "Yep, it sure does say Merrill on it."

"And you *did* tell him about the wake?" Shay asked.

"I told him but he still won't leave."

"And you think his name is Merrill Merrill."

"Everybody just calls him Merrill, but that's the same as his dad's last name, which seems pretty weird naming you kid with your last name…you might wanna go talk to him to make sure." Penny turned to the curtains and contemplated their folds. It was then that Shay promised himself Shay's Funeral Home would not stay in the family—the gene pool just ran too shallow at certain ends.

I WASN'T PREPARED for a man of Raymond Shay's size. I always imagined undertakers as gaunt and humorless, the type of men who wouldn't come at you, but would stay in the shadows, where they could pick the blood gone to crust from their fingernails. Shay came at me so fast and big that I leapt from my seat. "Son, we usually don't honor those sorts of requests."

"I understand, sir, I'm not family."

"Not even for family in this case," Shay said. "To be perfectly honest, the body has been removed to Iowa for a second autopsy."

"Second autopsy?"

At that moment, Penny, who had been eavesdropping, let out a giggle from behind the curtain of the viewing room. More bothered by the fact I showed no reaction to the giggle than anything else perhaps, Shay gathered me up in his oversized arm and started shuffling me quickly toward the front doors. "You're on the list to be a Pallbearer, I understand?"

"I am?"

Shay pulled a notepad from his pocket, checked it, and nodded. Just then, several family sedans pulled up outside. "You look plumb exhausted, son." Shay pushed me closer to the door. "It takes great fortitude to bear a casket—you should consider it an honor you were asked."

"Did they say where they took her in Iowa?"

"You should go home and get some rest," Shay said and then swung the door open, guided me out, and barred my path back inside.

BOBBY AND I had burnt my first car, a big green 77 Impala, down to the wheels New Year's Day, 1991. We were attempting to install stereo speakers. My second car, a cherry red Chrysler Laser, purchased fourth-hand for just over a thousand dollars—a veritable fortune for a seventeen year old—had lost its second and third gears as I taught myself to handle a stick shift. This meant that to get my car from idle to appropriate driving speeds I would have to pop from first to fourth when the speedometer hit precisely seventeen miles per hour. This was the car I was driving now, left exactly where I had parked it back in June—pocket change still in the caddy, spent pop bottles strewn across its floor, and even after months sitting in the sun, the dashboard still bearing the dent worn from Tammy's heel. She would kick off her shoes and stretch out when we drove, rubbing and kneading my upholstery, her dancer's legs stretching long and perfect, wearing thin the vinyl until there was a perfect soft divot for her perfect worn foot.

I drove the back roads from Shay's in that little Laser westward out of town. I didn't know where I was going. None of it seemed real. There was no reason left. All I could do was watch the power poles come at me, glide past, and retreat into the dust. Just a hard turn of the wheel and I would plunge into a roll, flame spewing and gravel exploding around me, my last thoughts of splintering metal and shattering glass. "She walked from a party, disappeared, was found in a ditch," I said at the road coming at me. "She *went* to a party, disappeared. No, she was *taken* to a party, disappeared." I held the wheel steady, my anger focusing me. "Somebody took her to that party and she was made to walk?" My anger was forcing me to question the situation. "Can't assume the rumors are true though—make an ass out of me and out of you, so why should I even assume she left that party, why assume anything?" My heart began to race. "Why do a second autopsy? Why, unless questions remained—so questions are the key. What did he say—Iowa? Okay, so why take her body to Iowa...and why the hell am I driving the opposite way?"

I hit the brakes and brought my car hard the way I came.

BOBBY HAD BEGGED, pleaded, and finally forcibly dragged Cooper McAllister to my parents' house. His theory was that together they could split the discomfort of having to sit with the folks to wait out my return. They had come at dinner though, an opportune time for two young bachelors—German mothers could cook and when they did, they cooked for a crowd. "He's still trying to adjust to current events." My father tried to explain my absence. "He just needs some space. He'll come home when he gets hungry enough—no need to send out the search dogs just yet."

Bobby, two years my senior, had stuck with me even when it was a very unpopular thing to do. Cooper Mac, on the other hand, had only moved to town his junior year, so was unaware the ramifications of being my friend. I had been the smallest growing up and so was an easy target for bullies. I couldn't play football, but got good grades—a near lethal combination for a young man growing up in a small town.

Contrary to simple logic, it didn't help that one of the most popular girls in school was involved with me. The problem with our relationship was that it was inexplicable to the "in crowd." This point was made very clear to me four years ago when several young men who felt the need to protect Tammy's reputation beat me unconscious in the Phys. Ed. locker room. This was what got me into wrestling. I remained unpopular, but most of the beatings stopped. Bobby and Cooper Mac remained loyal though and so there they sat with my parents, waiting for me, and just as the setting sun came in through the east windows lighting golden the crystal in the curio cabinet, I came through the front door, not hungry, but out of gas.

"Where have you been?" my mother asked.

"Driving."

"For ten hours?" my father said.

"I went to Iowa for awhile, had a look around."

"Iowa, huh...find what you were looking for?" my father asked.

"No."

Cooper Mac stood to break the sudden tension. "Me and Bobby," he said, "are having some people over. Not too many, you know. Just friends."

Bobby glanced sideways and gave me a knowing look.

"Not tonight," I said. "I'm going to wait at the funeral home until they bring Tammy back."

My mother went sobbing from the room.

My father pulled off his glasses, watched her go then turned to me, doing his best to hide his anger and frustration. "Why would you feel the need to say something like that?"

"I thought you would want to know where I was going."

"Are you trying to make some kind of point?" my father said.

"No."

"Then why would you feel the need to say that to your mother?"

"Because it's the truth?" I said. "Aren't I supposed to tell the truth?"

"It'll only be a few people over tonight," Cooper Mac said.

"Maybe it's a good idea you're not alone right now," Bobby added.

"—which means you are going to go change into some fresh clothing, young man, and spend some time with your friends."

"It'll only be a few people," Bobby said.

"Just so you're not alone," Cooper added.

"You haven't seen all your friends in months. I think it's the least you could do, so go get dressed—do it, to it."

And that was that.

THERE WEREN'T JUST a few people over, as Cooper Mac had promised, but a packed house—forty teens wedged tightly in a little brick single bedroom in an alley two blocks away…and none of them mourners. It started out small enough as promised, but soon a keg was lifted through the growing crowd, and soon after that, Bobby and Cooper broke out the plastic cups and started charging admission, two bucks a party-comer.

As more revelers arrived, I found myself pushed into a corner in the kitchen. I had to wear my Dress Blues that night for lack of clothing, but this didn't bother me. What bothered me was hearing no mention of her name. I wasn't even sure the cause for celebration and had been under the impression that this get together had something to do with bonding over our loss.

Bobby had told me once that I just didn't understand the "party mindset" and I could only suppose that tonight was a case in point. Parties, in my mind, were something to be endured, much like going to church or the dentist.

My Zippo found its way into my hand and as I clicked it open and clicked it closed, I did my best to will Bobby to look my way, but Bobby was having too good of time and making too much money at the door.

My stomach churned a warning—you cannot stay here for very much longer—and suddenly somebody who looked vaguely familiar was breathing down my neck. As I looked up at him, he gestured down for my Zippo. He had a cigarette dangling from his lips and his eyes were just bloodshot slits.

"My lighter has no fluid," I told him softly. He grabbed at my lighter anyway. "My lighter has no fluid," I told him again more firmly. He stood there, balancing against my chair, processing slowly what I had told him twice. Unsatisfied, he reached for the Zippo again. This time I had no choice but to grab his wrist. "No fluid!"

The vaguely familiar fellow took on a strange, angry air. I rose and twisted his arm from my face. Three other vaguely looking fellows came at us fast, grabbed the first fellow, and dragged him into a small huddle next the refrigerator. "Fucking Merrill," the first vaguely familiar fellow spat.

"Not here," one of them said. Another offered him a light.

"Fucking Merrill," he spat again, this time losing the lit cigarette. "Thinks he's gonna come home and—" At that point, a throng of girls trampled into the kitchen, creating a wall of shrill that blocked me from hearing the rest of the conversation.

Cooper Mac was behind a makeshift bar, struggling to tap a second keg, and Bobby was tracing cartoon faces on the backs of the hands of two girls who looked about fourteen. That was when Brian Slobacek made his flourished entrance, his comely little blonde-haired girlfriend Katherine Noland in tow. Brian Slobacek had been crowned Homecoming Chief just last week, so as a gag, Brian came to the party in a Native American headdress, stolen from the High School athletics department. The headdress was what the Homecoming Chief wore at coronation, the parade, and half-time show.

Brian Slobacek's date, Katherine Noland, ran in a few of the same circles as Tammy, and as far as I knew, Tammy considered her a friend. Katherine caught my eye as Bobby Grant scribbled a smiley entrance stamp on her wrist, and for a moment, I thought she gave me a nod. This nod of hers made me reasonably certain she carried it too—the discomfort of having to hide her grief.

Brian shelled out the four bucks for the two of them and pushed his way toward the keg. That was when the oddly familiar fellow who had asked me for a light screamed out something unintelligible from somewhere beyond my view. This got Brian's attention and sent him on his heels out the door. Moments after that, somewhere beyond my view, somebody cranked the stereo two notches. The throng of girls shrilling me into the corner grew louder and then three more people squeezed their way into the kitchen. I tucked my knees as far as I could beneath my chair to make room—the smell of smoke, the smell of sweat, the smell of something rotting in the broken garbage disposal, the smell of spilt beer, the smell of bad breath—I could no longer breathe…I needed to escape.

That was precisely when a full cup of beer went tumbling upon my lap, only to be followed by a very large, very drunk girl named Misty Moore. When she struck down upon me, something small and stinging in my knee went in a direction it was not meant to go. There was a pop and a familiar pain shot up through my spine. The girl shook and heaved with drunken laughter. I gasped an agonized breath, and with a shift of my hips, sent her to the floor. Her sudden impact with the linoleum made her heave and laugh even harder.

BOBBY TRIED TO intercept me as I pushed through the crowd. The fellow who looked vaguely familiar was being dragged by his friends into the bathroom, and as he disappeared, he quite clearly and angrily shouted in my direction, "Cleaned it real good!" I couldn't stop now though. I was pushing, doing my best to create a hole. The smell was following fast upon my heels. My stomach was ready to let slip the acid that had built to critical mass.

IT OCCURRED TO me as I stood gasping in the dark and cool of the back alley—like it occurs to you just after stepping barefoot onto broken glass—that Tammy had been taken apart piece by piece by a coroner today, dissected and examined for the second time. I had seen an autopsy on TV. Now, all I could see was her face as she lay there on the coroner's cutting table.

I had made it to the Iowa border earlier today, bought a roadmap, and started going from one small town to the next, letting the Blue H signs guide me. I would ask the receptionists of the little clinics and hospitals if their county morgues were located on the premises, a question usually met with strange looks. Finally, a kindly old gentleman spraying blood from the sidewalk in front of an ER door explained to me that if a body were sent from South Dakota it would likely arrive at one of the big hospitals in Sioux City.

By the time I reached the right one, I was told by a deputy sheriff from Nebraska that the body was already out of Iowa and moving back to South Dakota, where it would be sent through the chain of custody until finally arriving back at Shay's funeral home. The deputy said this could take from three to ten hours, as there was much paperwork to change hands and many, many people involved. I wasn't sure what he meant by "many, many," but the tone of his voice made me as ill as I felt now.

Next to the three overflowing garbage cans and the tower of empty beer cases, I doubled over and heaved up nothing again, and at the back end of that second volley, I jolted upright, eyes burning, searching the darkness—the sudden sound of an angry voice bringing my gastric spasms to a halt.

It was an argument and the angry voice was hissing, "—just told me two seconds ago that the car has been cleaned, so what are you fucking worried about?!" The voice was coming from the bushes across the alley and was, as far as I could tell, attached to a very angry man.

I inched around the garbage cans to get a better look through those bushes. I squeezed between the cars parked bumper-to-bumper and side mirror-to-side mirror that filled the alley. The noise of the party masked the sound of my step against the crushed red rock. I ducked through the sharply angled swath of yellow haze wrapping around the little brick house from the nearby street lamp. I took the long way around the bushes, following the path of a man's shadow drawn long. He had a solid grip on a woman's arm and a mane of feathers extending nearly to his knees. Another step further and I could make out faces. It was Brian Slobacek with an opened palm raised at Katherine Noland.

Katherine tried to jerk away when she saw me. Brian saw the look in her eye and spun. In the darkness, my uniform gave me some semblance of authority, I suppose. We all stood there, none of us quite sure what to do next.

Katherine covered her bruised wrist with her other hand. "Merrill?"

THE HOMECOMING

Brian adjusted his headdress, took a step forward to study me, and then said with a forced smile, "We're having a private conversation."

When I didn't turn on my heels to walk away, he lost his forced smile and stuffed his hands in his pockets. "I gotta say it again, scrotum?"

"Yeah, right to my face please," I said and took two steps at him.

Bobby burst from the back door just at that moment and shouted with forced jest, "fresh air!" then pretended to see us for the first time and quickly came our way to intervene. "Hey, guys, my neighbor's probably gonna have this party busted if they see us all standing in his yard."

"We're getting ready to leave anyway," Katherine said.

Brian gave Bobby a knowing look (almost a look of warning it appeared) then put his hand around Katherine to shepherd her away.

"So you're leaving too, Merrill?" Bobby asked with an apologetic shrug. "It's just that we don't want trouble."

The music inside grew to a crescendo and people started chanting, "Chug! Chug! Chug!" A momentary silence followed and then a rebel yell, victory cheers, and the sound of bottles smashing against the walls.

"Shit!" Bobby said and hurried back inside, barely glancing back at me to say, "You don't really like parties anyway, right?"

I stood there alone in that yellow haze of the street lamp, glancing down at the beer stain covering my uniform, coming to a decision that should have been made hours ago—time to go home.

THE POLICE DID come to investigate the party at Bobby and Cooper's a few hours after I went home, and sometime in the middle of the night, my father followed the banging clatter of dumped junk drawers to my bedroom door. When he found it locked and nobody willing to answer, he put his good shoulder into it and, with a splintering of oak, busted through the jamb.

What he came in to find was his only son in underwear, back turned, music blaring from a Walkman, on hands and knees sorting through a pile of odds and ends. He lifted an earphone from my ear and said hello and then asked what I was so busy trying to find.

"I had pictures of her. Somebody took them."

"Could you turn off the music?" he said.

I shut off the Walkman but continued my search.

"What happened with Bobby and Cooper?" he asked.

I tried to hide my anger. "Throwing a party."

"A party?"

"Yeah, you know, where there's music and booze and celebration."

"Sounds like they were just trying to escape, don't you think?"

"Charging two bucks at the door?"

"Well," he said, on his never-ending quest for that silver lining. "It's probably good you did the responsible thing and came home. It probably wouldn't look good on your military record if you got in trouble for getting involved in something wrong back here."

"You don't get it, but that's okay," I said.

My father backed to the door to study the damage he'd done breaking his way into the room. "I do get it—they hurt your feelings."

"They're not here," I said, regarding my pile of junk. "They're the only photos I had of her. That's why I didn't take them to Benning. My buddies would make fun of me down there. 'If she's so incredible, why are you afraid to show us her picture?' I kept writing to her—send me some fresh pictures."

My father stepped around the three piles of junk on his way to the closet. "If you would have just taken a moment to look before dumping all this crap." He reached up to the hat rack and pulled down a shoebox, let out a weary sigh, and dropped down on the corner of my bed. "You know, when I went to Basic, I had a school-boy crush too." As he said it, his eyes searched for something long ago and far away. "Oh, yes." He smiled. "And she *was* something."

"Not Mom?"

"No, not Mom, and truth be told, a few weeks into Boot Camp, I realized I didn't mean too much to the girl." Something again shifted in his eyes. "And then came Vietnam." His voice turned to gravel. "That was a long time ago. I came home lucky and was even luckier to meet Mom." For a moment, something in my father came loose and free. I think it was fatherhood. The moment was short-lived. Embarrassed for opening up to me, he quickly stood, ran his fingers atop the lid of the shoebox, and said, "It's been a rough week for your mother, so go easy and try to get in the swing of the thing."

"Did the girl die?" I asked.

"What's that?"

"You said you had a school-boy crush. You were comparing the situations. I was just wondering if the girl died."

"No," he said, clearly stung. "No, she didn't die." He slowly lowered the shoebox onto the bed. "You have to say goodbye to her in your own way. If that means viewing her body, I understand that…I'll make some calls for you in the morning." He ran his hand across the broken doorjamb, backed from the room, and disappeared into the shadows of the hallway. I think to weep.

I OPENED THE shoebox and was overcome by Coppertone, apricot scrub, and a hint of jasmine. They had stuffed it all together, everything in the cigar box and all the photos and news clippings from the collage. The Polaroid, though, was what caught my attention first. I had forgotten about the Polaroid. It had never made it onto my wall. It was my last link to her, the nearest I could reach into the past to feel for her. It was a terrible picture and that made it all the more perfect.

She carried the camera in her tote bag and her tote bag she dragged everywhere. It was of thick cotton canvas weave with rugby stripes and rope handles. It was patched at the bottom and as lumpy as a potato sack. The zipper was broken on each end and saddle stitched with oversized baby-pins, the bag having survived dragging, stuffing, dumping, throwing, drowning, near-incineration, and a trip atop a moving car, where it remained for two of three blocks. Inside, a person could always find two pair of ballet slippers, at least three overdue library books, a Mountain Dew gone flat, four or five packs Big Red Gum, all of them opened, a pack of Marlboros, but never a lighter or matches, suntan oil and two lipsticks, her checkbook, always balanced very close to zero, package after package of Polaroid film, sunflower seeds spilled from the bag, and mirrored sunglasses pilfered from me. All together, these pieces added up to something magical. A magical bag of magical things. Yes, that is what it was…and that was what I felt just then.

It was dark and the flash from her camera played harsh against the blackness. One of her arms was around me as if to keep me from escaping frame. Her other arm was stretched to snap the photo. It was an odd, high-angled shot that made us look ghostly, our eyes red from the flash and our skin pale from the wetness, gray puddles on the asphalt growing beneath us. We had arrived from the sprinklers in the park. Dawn's light was behind us, banishing fast the deep purples from an eastern sky. "Shhh!" she giggled and blinked away the blindness made by the camera flash. We were just past the driveway of her mother's house, tucked beyond the bushes separating hers from her neighbors' yard. "I think the flash just woke up my mom."

"We gonna be in trouble?"

"Not if we don't get caught," she said, lips curling up mischievously.

We ducked deeper into the bushes, making slippery little knee-prints as we went. She pulled the Polaroid from the camera and shook it again and again, until bringing out two pair of red dots. The four red dots became red eyes and from the red eyes grew plumes of shadowy pink, our faces floating wet to the surface. She stuck the Polaroid in my shirt pocket before any more of its color could rise and there it would stay until my father would find it months later on his quest to strip my room of her memory.

"So," she said. "What's the word?"

"Goodbye?" I asked.

"Okay," she said and rose.

I stammered. "That's not what I meant—"

She dropped back down and tilted her head sideways a bit.

"Now you're making fun of me," I said.

She just smiled as if she had heard the prayer I had been praying for the past month, a prayer that had replaced every single other prayer—give me courage, help me say something wonderful, help me hold onto her… ***Courage me up, dear Jesus, I beg***…don't smile over my loss and failures, save me a moment just right…***Courage me up, dear Jesus, I beg***…

I prayed the prayer but nothing came and so the moment passed me by.

"Oh, yeah, I have something for you," she said and dug deep into her bag of magical things. "You were supposed to remind me." She wagged a finger at me and then pulled out a little gift-wrapped box.

"For me?" I said.

"You act surprised."

THE HOMECOMING

She grabbed my hand as soon as I started pulling off the blue ribbon on the little gift-wrapped box. "No!" she cried an embarrassed laugh. "You can't open it until you're over the bridge!"

The porch light flickered to life, catching our silhouettes and dragging them wide across the street. Startled, I rose to my feet, ready to run, but Tammy quickly pulled me back to my knees. "Okay…" She took a deep breath. "We have to make this fast—I have something to say to you, but you better not say anything stupid back or I'll never forgive you."

I gave her my most serious of scowls.

"Then *you* go first," she said, "if you think it's so easy."

I opened my mouth to speak but nothing came. Our bodies were wet from the sprinklers. The mud was collecting beneath our knees. The soft light of the porch cast our shadows long. The morning sun was ready to rise.

"Okay, so before you run away," she said. "I want to tell you…" I braced myself. "Never forget," she said. Her eyes went soft as she came in to kiss my left cheek. "Never forget." And softer still as she brushed past my lips to reach my right. "And never forget." She lowered my head ever so gently to kiss my forehead. "…that I will always love you."

With that, she kissed my lips with a forever sort of kiss, the type of kiss that captured up all those lost and failed moments and cast them away forever. I floated there on my mud-stained knees, not realizing Tammy had pulled back. By the time I opened my eyes, she was touching my lips with a silencing finger, and for a moment, a moment that slowed and reached for eternity, the world became right…and with that, she tossed her bag of magic over her shoulder, rose out of the bushes, and moved head-hanging home.

SCREECHING TIRES SHOOK me from my daze. I was back on my bed, shoebox in hand, smashed out of the dream and back to reality by an engine roaring very close to my bedroom window. Metal struck metal thrice and then the engine roared a spatter into reverse. I dropped to a knee and made for the window as headlights danced through my blinds and slipped from wall to wall. Tires spun. Sod splattered against the side of the house. I ducked from the north window to the west to get a look outside, but all I could see were taillights blazing into the darkness.

MOMENTS LATER, I was standing out on the front lawn in my mother's housecoat surveying the wreckage—body count, three felled garbage cans, two flattened, one with the bottom blown out, telltale tire treads ripping through the lawn. The son of two teachers, I had become accustomed to this sort of thing—nothing more than an uninspired teenaged prank.

MY FATHER WAS at the kitchen table the next morning, coffee in hand, eyes lost inside the morning paper. As I entered, he tried to conceal the paper beneath a plate of egg yoke and breadcrumbs. I still caught the headline though: "HIT-AND-RUN SUSPECTED IN HOMECOMING DEATH."

THE HOMECOMING

"Did you make those calls for me?" I asked.

"They can't show you the body," he said. "She was just there too long."

"Where?"

"In the ravine."

I offered my father a vacant stare and then walked out the door.

WHEN THE SUN set, Funeral Director Shay found me sitting out on the curb across from his funeral home. Funeral Director Shay, it must be noted, had also found me sitting in his lobby about ten hours earlier when he arrived for work, and in his parking lot just after lunch. It was that second time that he had lost his temper and forcibly removed me from the premises. Evidently, he had calmed over the course of the afternoon. "Sitting across the street won't do either," he shouted, "but you have made your point, so if a private visitation would really mean that much…" I thought I saw something sinister flash across his face, but that may have been the illusion of distance and dusk. "I'll have the casket to the church by 7:00 A.M."

CHAPTER FIVE

FIVE STORIES OF stained glass brought in glorious shafts of morning sun. The glorious shafts of morning sun shot across the haze and humidity and landed stained-glass rainbows upon a big wooden cross hanging stage right of the pulpit. I had seen the illusion many times before. As the sun would rise, those dancing rainbows would stretch and spread from the cross until bathing the nave of St. John's with so much colored light that it could almost be felt, that it could almost be touched. The pews were of fine stained oak. Rows of them stretched in three directions from two long communion rails. Beyond the communion rails were tiers of brick, three in number, leading up to a large altar cut of marble. The pipe organ in the balcony made such a noise that when it played a person could feel the sound pass through him. In the bell tower, doves would nest and, when startled by the bells ringing the morning call to worship, lift wing and take flight.

The place was alive on Sunday mornings, but when a person found himself alone in here, especially at night, a great hallow emptiness could overtake him. On certain nights, the moon would find its way in through that same stained glass, in faint blues that would play against the dancing reds of the eternity candle—the great vaulted ceiling of cedar a backdrop for an epic and eerie waltz of candle and moon.

She was thirteen, I was twelve, and we found ourselves alone in the balcony, well hidden behind the locked doors of the organ's pipe-house. We'd both grown weary of hide-and-seek so decided not to get found. We linked up near the nursery wing and took ourselves out of bounds. The light of the eternity candle flickered but there was no moon and something deep and mysterious happened inside of me when she gave me my first kiss—a miraculous, wonderful something that can only happen once and forever.

But now was now and then was then and early that morning, while the sun was still stretching its rainbow upon the cross, I found myself back in my Dress Blues sitting quietly in the twelfth pew, watching three little blue-haired ladies attending to the flowers around her casket. The rainbow bled and stretched golden, bigger and bigger as they worked, and I listened to them whisper the gossip of the day.

"So young," rattled one.

"Well, that's what happens when a girl like that—"

"I'm not one to gossip," said the third who stepped back, hands on hips, to inspect their work. "But I was told that after her father died—"

I leaned forward to listen, but she sensed me there and lowered her voice. Whatever she had to say made them gasp…and then work in silence. Finally, they finished, and I was happy to see them go, happy to feel the emptiness of the place—alone with God spreading dawn across her casket.

The time was now. Today was the day to put behind me those childish things like first kisses and hide-and-go-seek. All it would take was for me to rise and move forward, banishing with each echoing step every dream and hope I had. All it would take was the courage, the courage the boy in me always lacked...stand up, take a step, move forward child.
One step.
Two step.
Three step.
Four.
They had placed an 8X10 of Tammy on the lid of her casket. In the portrait, she was wearing a yellow dress with a hint of strawberry in the weave. Her hair swam waves down her left shoulder. Her eyes were big and full of life. I moved the frame gently to the other side and lifted the casket lid.

MY GRANDFATHER NEVER wore his dentures and always parted his hair to the left. When he grinned, his gums sucked deep into his face. This he would do to the delight of his grandkids. He was a rough-edged laborer, his skin leathered from decades in the sun. His was an open-casket funeral. The mortician had inserted his dentures and parted his hair to the right, which by all accounts made it wrong.

WHEN I OPENED the casket, I was confronted by a white drape—not a funerary veil, the diaphanous shroud they used to cover faces in the days before refrigeration and modern embalming techniques—but upholstery lining torn from its staples on the inside edge of the casket lid. The upholstery lining covered two oddly shaped objects poking up where the soft and round of her face should have been. My withering courage and piqued curiosity battled it out and my hands reached down. I had to lift the veil and see.

TO MAKE IT a stoning offense though, the mortician applied something to my grandfather's skin to give him a soft and gentle glow. The body in the casket was handsome enough, but did not look anything like Grandpa. I'm not sure if this made saying goodbye to him less difficult or more.

WHAT I FOUND when I lifted that veil were her feet resting bare and crossed at the ankles. I worked back more of the upholstery lining to uncover the rest of her legs. She was in the yellow dress with the strawberry weave.
Why would they have put her in the casket backwards though?
Her hemline had wrinkled. I smoothed it back across her knee. Her legs looked tanned far too deep and there were rows of what appeared to be tiny tire tracks spiraling up from her left shin, across her knee, and around her left thigh. They weren't tire tracks though. They were pockmarks, flesh eaten away during the early stages of decomposition. Shay did his best to fill the flesh with mortician's wax, but the wax had seeped and dried too fast leaving what looked like cracks in parched earth.

The 8X10 was on the wrong side of the casket—that was it!
On her feet were deep gashes sewn with black postmortem thread. One gash wrapped around her right big toe. It looked deep enough to have hit bone. Two more gashes ran across the arch of her left foot. Another made a lazy Z across her right heel. Gashed by what though? Glass? Thorns? The blade of a knife? I could no longer think on it—I lowered the bottom lid, trembling fear-sick, mouth gone dry, body ready to give at the knees, but somehow my other hand found its way to the other side of the casket, ready to finish what I had started…that's when I heard him gently say my name.

REVEREND FARMER HAD baptized, married, and buried nearly a thousand souls in his first few years as an ordained minister, but this for him was a first—a young man opening a closed casket and peering down at a dead girl's legs. A preacher's job demanded he be ready to see and hear just about anything at just about any time and to react with some semblance of tact. He had heard confessions involving incest, sodomy, bestiality, spousal abuse, and had read more than one suicide note involving variations on the same themes. There wasn't too much that surprised Reverend Farmer, but this was indeed a first, and the first thought that came to his mind was an ugly one—necrophilia. He quickly shook the thought away.
*The kid was strange, but not **that** strange.*

I THOUGHT MAYBE it couldn't be real," I told Reverend Farmer. We were sitting three pews back from the altar now. "I thought that maybe…the casket would be empty…that maybe all of this was some…elaborate test."
"What kind of test?" Farmer asked.
"It didn't sound stupid until I said it."
Farmer mused. "Even Jesus was tested."
"All it took was seeing her dress."
"For you to understand that it was real?"
"That it was final."
"You're angry," he said.
"I don't wanna be…I don't."
"You're asking God why this happened…why He wasn't there."
"No, that's not it at all," I said. Farmer waited for me to put the words together, the platitudes I had been taught to parrot. I opted for the truth. "I asked God why He wasn't there: He answered back, 'why weren't you?'"

SOME CAME AS family. Some came as friends. Some came to offer shoulders for those who felt the need to weep. Some came to represent. Some came because they thought there might be a story in it. Some came to ditch school. Some came because their lives were small and funerals made them feel better about themselves. Some came out of guilt. Some came proud of what they'd done. Some came, badges hidden beneath their blazers, to record faces and names. It didn't take long for the church to fill beyond capacity.

Folding chairs were lined in the aisles then placed in rows in the vestibule, and then as more and more came, the surrounding classrooms and halls were filled, the closed-circuit television system used to relay all that went on within. A few people fainted because the new air-conditioning system couldn't keep up with the body heat.

Reverend Farmer told us how Tammy was in a better place and about how joyful he was in Christ because he would get to share the Lord's love with so many new people today and that we should be joyful too. He was given $100 to perform the funeral (about a dime a head.)

We were told that as pallbearers we should do our best to show no emotion other than reverence for the dead and that when it was over, Funeral Director Shay would give us a nod, and it would be our job to lead the massive procession out the doors and onward to the cemetery.

I SAT WITH the five other pallbearers in a minivan, in silence, idling, idling, idling, at the cemetery as the back end of the funeral procession snaked its way through town. I didn't really know any of my fellow pallbearers and didn't really care to trade pleasantries. Mostly, I just stared at the back of my hands, wondering how much strength I had in them, wondering what I was capable of doing with them.

In the two other minivans were Tammy's mother, brothers, aunts, uncles, grandmas, and grandpas. As the crowd assembled, they were led to white folding chairs beneath a little tent that sat halfway up the hill.

Finally, on Shay's cue, we shouldered the casket and marched upwards. At one moment, when the grass grew slick and dangerous, I clasped hands with the pallbearer to my right.

We six pallbearers stood behind Tammy's mother and her two little brothers. One was fourteen. The other was twelve…or maybe eleven still. I wasn't sure. The boys didn't weep. This made me believe that they had been too beaten down by shock to be fully aware what was happening.

"Our Father, which Art in Heaven," Reverend Farmer prayed. "Hallowed be Thy Name." I stiffened myself against a sudden breeze. "Thy Kingdom Come." *But not just yet.* "Thy will be done on earth, as it is in Heaven." I recognized a face in the crowd. It belonged to the vaguely familiar fellow at Bobby and Cooper's party, the one who tried to take my Zippo. "Give us this Day our Daily Bread." I remembered now. His name was Eric Stukel. He was standing right across from me, his and mine the only heads not bowed, his and mine the only lips not moving in time to the prayer. He was tall and lean and swayed almost imperceptibly as if pulled by strings. "And forgive us our sins…" My jaw tightened and my fists closed. *Just trying to escape…*so they drink some booze and smoke some drugs and laugh and joke and carry on like nothing at all had happened and then he comes up and asks me for a light, tries to take my lighter to be more precise, and I don't even recognize him because I'm in my own boxed-up little place feeling sorry for myself, not worrying about how she must have suffered and how she was in that casket right in front of me, dirt piled in a heap just up the slope, ready to be dumped on her forever and ever, and the pain was so much and it was only getting worse and what would I do with my life now that she was gone and why is he just standing there with his eyes red as if he were grieving her more than me, or maybe he had smoked some drugs before coming here, just like all the rest of them—my friends—chanting in unison every last one…or mouthing the words, because they weren't sure exactly how the words went…and mostly I'm just hating myself because I was the one who wasn't there, because I played the coward, because I joined the Army, for one reason and one reason only…*just trying to escape.* "…as we forgive those who sin against us." It looked like he had a slight smile on his face, Eric Stukel. "And lead us not into temptation." My knuckles went white as I fought with everything the urge to move at him. "But deliver us from evil…" Cooper Mac and Bobby Grant were hidden somewhere in the crowd just behind Katherine Noland and Brian Slobacek. The argument had been about a car being cleaned and Bobby and Brian had shared a knowing look of warning. Brian had his arm around Katherine tight now, just like that night, that night he was going to backhand her, that night I should have come at him two more steps, that night I should have hurt him, Homecoming royalty. "For yours is the Kingdom…" Eric Stukel, opposite me, was swaying faster now "…and the Power," and a little bit faster "…and the Glory," and a little bit faster, his eyes going heavenward, a look of ecstasy crossing his face. "Forever and ever…Amen." Heads rose from the prayer. "Ashes to ashes and dust to dust…" The back of the crowd silently slipped toward their cars before the final words were said. "It is finished." *It is finished*. Let the dead bury the dead.

 FIRST, THE FAMILY had been removed quietly and quickly. A few minutes later, several girls held their own private little ceremony, one by one placing a red rose atop the casket, each moving silently into the comforting arms of boyfriends or fiancés. A few children chased and hid behind tombstones and vaults as they awaited their chatting, gossiping parents and a few older parishioners wandered the rows in search of dearly departed friends. I didn't like crowds and I was glad to see this one fade. There wouldn't be much time though. I took a step forward, but before I could reach out to her, I felt my father's firm grip upon my shoulder. "You need to sleep," he said and gently tried to pull me away.

 Bobby and Cooper Mac sat in Bobby's Mustang watching me, waiting for me at my father's request. "Why is he just standing there?" Cooper asked, more to break the silence than to get an answer.

 "Guilt," Bobby replied abruptly.

 Cooper threw Bobby a confused glance. "I was talking about Eric."

 What Cooper was seeing and not understanding was the standoff—Eric on one side of the casket, I on the other. Bobby stubbed his cigarette again and again and again and again but didn't say a word and finally Cooper Mac was forced to ask Bobby, "Why should Merrill feel guilty?"

"Why, what have you heard?" Bobby answered quickly.

BY NOW, TAMMY'S family had been deposited back at the church where the little gray-haired ladies had prepared a potluck. This would be the time for the cheapest of platitudes, words found in Hallmark greeting cards and parroted out of obligation—time heals—she's in a better place—God only takes the good ones—the Good Lord knows what He's doing—it's all part of a bigger plan—we're only given what we can handle...

FUNERAL DIRECTOR SHAY and his attendants began folding and stacking the little cushioned chairs that were used to seat the family, breezing past the casket and sending a few roses plummeting six feet under.

The air grew dead and moist, thunderheads in the distant north encroaching. Shay told me to step back so the tent could be taken down. The guy-lines were released and the tent poles were lifted from their temporary postholes. There was talk about Monday Night Football as they worked and then the four men hauled the canopy away in one giant heap.

The time had come for Bobby Grant and Cooper Mac to discuss leaving. The standoff between Eric Stukel and me could only hold their attention for so long. "Merrill doesn't fight," Bobby said. "He just walks away."

"He's changed though," Cooper said and reached for another of Bobby's cigarettes. At that point, Bobby started keeping count.

Shay lectured his custodians and then showed them how to re-roll the tent canopy to get it around the four tent poles correctly. Once this was done, they slid the whole heap into a loading van.

Two hills over, two men wearing jeans and blazers, badges hidden beneath, were snapping away with telescopic cameras.

A Chevy Berretta rolled past the Mustang and crunched to a stop and for the first time in almost two hours, the silence was broken by a double honk. Eric Stukel looked up from his daze, took a step forward, a step back, a step forward again, finally found his footing on the Astroturf dressing the ground around the casket, bent forward just inches from the casket lid, whispered something, and then placed the smallest of objects amid all the roses.

The Beretta broke the silence again, this time with a triple honk.

In the driver's seat was Noose Adarson, Eric's protector and best friend. Noose was making good on his promise to pick Eric up when the crowds finally cleared. Noose Adarson was a reasonably big follow, who started losing his hair at age fifteen. He was the type who held his eyes in a perpetual angry squint, like a gunslinger, his mouth cocked to the side, upper lip curled to expose a few teeth.

My back was turned to the Beretta, but Noose still recognized me. "You need a ride somewhere?" he shouted. Noose's voice tightened the knot already twisted in my belly. The offer sounded almost sincere.

Shay and his custodians heard the shout too, stopped stacking the folding chairs, and looked on as if spectators at a fight.

"Let's just get the fuck out," Eric hissed as he made his way toward the Beretta. A moment later, a door slammed and gravel went loose beneath spinning tires. When I was certain the car was a good distance away, I finally glanced over my shoulder. To my surprise, Bobby and Cooper had also fled the scene. I was on my own now, but I was still certain I was being watched.

"Okay, folks, we're racing a storm," Shay told his custodians.

The storm clouds were gathering quickly indeed.

As two gravediggers rolled up the hill with a backhoe, Shay whispered to me in passing, "Say your goodbyes and then step back so the men can do their work."

I nodded, stepped close, and when Shay was turned away, dug through those roses for the tiny object Stukel had placed on the casket. The long-stems drew blood, but before Shay was the wiser, I had the little object concealed in my palm. Shay glanced my way to back me off and then pressed a button.

Helped along by two thick nylon straps, the casket went slowly down. Silently, silently, downward it went, until from deep inside the grave came the gentlest of thuds, the casket bumping down against the metal of the vault.

ONE OF THE gravediggers carried a flask and took small nips as he and the other worked. They started first with the backhoe and finished with shovels, slapping down the earth to make a neat, smooth mound.

THE TINY OBJECT had left an imprint in my clutched palm and the blood that had left the capillaries was slow to return.

The tiny object was a stone, polished smooth and triangular. On one side, there were etchings, ancient like Cuneiform or Sanskrit, the kind of secret words that warned the intrepid hero of the old cliffhanger movies away.

I tucked the stone in my breast pocket right next to my Zippo, and as the sun went down, the first of the rain came, slapping heavy drops upon the smooth marble of the headstones around me. I was alone now. The town grew weary in the little river valley beneath and then quietly went to sleep.

TAMMY HAD TAKEN my Timex that summer because hours before I was to leave for the Army I kept checking the time. The watch I was wearing for the occasion of the funeral was a loaner from my father. When the rains came, the leather of its band stretched and buckled. It was probably too late to save the watchband, but I stuck it in my pocket anyway, next to my Zippo and that triangular-shaped stone Eric Stukel left on the casket.

The rains came harder and harder and the night pulled further and further along and by the time I finally wondered, and by the time I finally remembered, and by the time I finally pulled the soaked watch from my soaked jacket, it was 4:48 A.M.

Five inches of rain had fallen.

There was movement beyond the ancient pines, where the mausoleums sunk inch by decade into the tired, old earth. The tombstones that bore no name leaned hard on that south side, a century of weather rubbing them raw, little stalactites going deep where the dirt had given way to the dripping, slaked lime. Death surrounded me, dancing against the whispering splish-splash of the rain. The lightning had come and the lightning had gone. The north side of Yankton had lost power, and then the south, and then the power was restored grid by grid. The numbness in my toes had faded and the rain had become warm. The glimmer time swept over me and in that glimmer time reality had become a meaningless haze, a glaze, dreams whispered and memories lost, like fireflies impossible to catch, flashing before my eyes and quickly retreating into the shadow, into the depth. Water risen heavy from a satiated earth fell fast into sinkholes and puddles, and I, the intrepid hero, was lifted back to solve the riddle trapped in the deep and dark of my mind.

THE GREYHOUND WAS empty, save the driver and me, as it rolled over the double-decker bridge, the river roiling beneath. Mother and father watched from the riverside as it crossed, waving me one last goodbye.

The lamps lighting the bridge blinked out, one after the next, yielding to a sun just risen. In this time and in this season when day fought hard to break through the mists of morning, a sliver of a June moon bent down giant and ochre to the west and my curls hung limp and damp from the sprinklers and still, no matter how hard I rubbed them, the grass stains on my knees would not fade. I was glad I put my favorite shirt on a hanger to dry. I wished I had remembered to take the Polaroid out of the front pocket. I wished I could look at it now. Tammy would have been crawling into bed after arguing for nearly an hour with her mother. That much was certain. The fight would not resolve itself except into weariness and then she would sleep heavy and dream.

I toyed with the blue ribbon on the wet little gift-wrapped box, trying to keep the promise she forced upon me, not to open it until I crossed into Nebraska. I broke that promise though, smiling as I did, the rusting crisscross girders of the bridge humming past.

My eyes went childlike! Inside the box was a Zippo! "Fire!" I said grandly and popped the Zippo open to spark the wick.

No flame came.

A gift like this meant something—chrome-plated brass with a rough finish to keep from slipping out of the hand, a hinge spring broken in just right, and an engraving…which I couldn't make out in the darkness.

I turned on the reading light above. A tiny orb of pink splashed down. I wiped the wetness from the Zippo and made out the words: "*Fiat Lux.*"

I knew this lighter: it had been her father's.

I sparked the wick again…and again no flame came. I turned the lighter upside-down and water from the sprinklers dripped out. This put another smile on my face and for the first time in a long time my stomach settled and I was able to sit back and relax. I was ready to dream myself into afternoon now. That was when an eighteen-wheeler downshifted a howl, its headlights slicing through the tint to reveal a figure coming at me down the aisle—

Not the driver...
Now, there was no driver...
The bus was alive and driving itself...
And the figure was moving down the aisle at me...
Somebody smaller, somebody delicate, somebody graceful...
Her...
But how could that be?

A scream of anguish grew long and painful across her face in the blinding white—her eyes so vacant and her hair flaring up in a wind that rose from nowhere—her voice cried a distant heart-wrenching cry and then faded away as the eighteen-wheeler disappeared behind us. She was nearly at me and then vanished and I sat cringing at the impact that didn't come, my world gone red in the taillight glow...

I BLINKED THE waking nightmare away. A numb shiver snapped up through my spine. My eyes went to pinpoints with the reflected glare of more headlights. More headlights? Yes, they were real and slicing up the hill, fast one after another, reflecting a dance off the smooth wet surface of the tombstones. The cemetery gates had been closed at dark but still they came, one after another, a caravan approaching up the winding gravel.

Coming **my** *way...*

A caravan of cars at night, official-looking, some with sirens mounted on their tops, one after another, was rolling up through the rain, the telltale browns of the Yankton City Police, the white and blues of the Sheriff's Office, shades of red, the Nebraska Highway Patrol, all of them following an unmarked sedan with federal plates.

Definitely coming for me...

The puddled grass slid hard and fast beneath my feet as I ran a stumble up the hill. On hands and knees I tumbled, skirting around a pillar of red granite to escape the light. Ten more feet and I would be hidden, ten more feet and I would be able to catch my breath. I was confident now I could make it, but my confidence was premature. I slipped face-first in the mud, nearly opening my skull against the sharp corner of an angel's wing. The angel's wing was jutting out from an angel adorning a marker made for babies Adam and Jacob Glyn, twins born and died in February of 1982. I rolled left, only the puddled grass to conceal me now. I crawled on my stomach, their engines idling down as they closed in on me. There was something large up ahead to conceal me, but the caravan was far too near for me to raise my head and see what it was. I went blindly, inch by inch, to keep beneath the headlight beams. The sliding-wet bluegrass came out in clumps as I dug my elbows deep into the mud. Just a few more feet to refuge. Just a few more feet to salvation. One last push and all of me was hidden, hidden in the shadows of something grand atop the hill.

The cars parked, and one by one, their lights went out.

THE HOMECOMING

WHEN MY BODY went numb, so too went my sense of bladder, and only after struggling behind the grand monument atop the hill, did I feel the sudden and painful urge to relieve myself. "This would have to wait," I whispered to myself aloud, partly to be sure this was really happening, partly to gain control of my shivering lips and chattering teeth. I pulled myself around the rough-hewn granite base of the structure to get a look downhill.

Below me, about a dozen men climbed out of the squad cars, opened umbrellas, turned on flashlights, and moved across the rolling slope. I squatted up further to get a better look through the sheets of rain and this time saw Funeral Director Shay amid the pack. From a van at the back of the pack, two men in yellow slickers and carrying shotguns guided from the rear doors six men wearing bright orange jumpsuits, DOC stenciled to their back.

Two men hopped from the sedan with the federal plates. The older of the two stared up at the storm in contempt and then ran a grizzled hand through a tight crop of gray hair. His partner, far younger and less bothered by the weather, almost happy about it, tossed the older an umbrella. The older looked back up at the storm in contempt and then shoved the umbrella inside his jacket. "Well, if you're gonna be that way," the younger said to the older, "give it back."

"Lightning rod," the older man said. "Watch your step now."

The younger took two steps forward and slipped in the mud. On any other occasion, I would have laughed.

There was a smooth bronze pillar rising from the granite slab hiding me. I wrapped my arm around it to keep my balance. I let out a low gasp as my hand came across a foot. That was what nearly ghosted me out of hiding. The foot was bare and cold as stone with something hard driven into its arch, and for a moment that cold and bare foot seemed to move.

I squinted up through the rain to find a thorny-crowned Jesus bowing his head, arms outstretched upon a cross. Water streamed from his brass arms, from his brass side, from his brass legs, from his brass feet, and formed a little river that rolled over my shoulder blade and down to the small of my back. I gripped the crucified Christ tighter. The men in orange jumpsuits were pulling shovels and spades from the back of the Sheriff's truck.

The older man, the one who had tucked the umbrella in his jacket, put his hands to his hips to address the men gathered around Tammy's fresh and muddied grave. A baby-faced recruit in a raincoat too big for him shined his flashlight right in the old man's eyes. Blinded, the old man shielded his eyes and waited. Finally, another one of the officers forced the baby-faced recruit's flashlight down. "Swing the car around my way," the old man said to his younger partner, the one who fell in the mud. "Give them some headlights to work with…in fact, swing a couple of these vehicles around. Get them into a semi-circle as best we can…don't knock over any markers though…and please, no more flashlights aimed at my face."

Headlights crisscrossed through the darkness until something of semi-circle was made. One of the DOC workers asked, "You want us to start now?"

"Now would be good," the old man said.

THE MUDDY EARTH moved easily the first few feet down, but as the prison release crew got deeper into the hole, they found the walls collapsing around them. The Sheriff and two High-Pos from Nebraska got down into the thigh-deep muddy hole and helped bucket water. This eventually led to a bucket brigade. One bucket after the next sloshed up out of the hole, the entire force soon caked in black—all of them working save the old man and Funeral Director Shay. These two just stood, hands on hips, watching. Finally, one of the prisoners came upon something solid with his spade. "Mr. Shay," the old man said. "I think they've reached the vault."

Shay handed his umbrella to the old man and shimmied three hundred odd pounds worth of flesh down a ladder and into the six-foot deep hole. The prison crew climbed up to make room. There was silence and then the sound of something heavy being lifted. My grip went tight upon Christ's feet. Shay poked his head up and said, "No can do. Ground's way too saturated to raise her. If I go any further, I'll flood the whole she-bang. Flood her and it'd be like trying to raise an elephant. Better we close the grave and wait till it dries."

The old man kicked off his wingtips, pulled of his socks, and eased himself down to join Shay. There were murmurs and then the old man poked his head up and said, "Get us a body bag." Several of the men looked to each other, but none moved. "That means everybody," the old man barked and suddenly flashlights snapped on, and the crowd of officers began to move.

THE DEPARTMENT OF Corrections release workers huddled around a wet cigarette, trying to get it lit, while the men in uniform dug around in the trunks of their patrol cars. Finally, someone shouted, "Found one!"

ONE OF THE deputies unrolled the body bag with a snap. Something in me knew what was about to happen, but I couldn't put it in words that made sense. I clung to the feet nailed to that cross. I tried but couldn't look away. The casket moaned open somewhere deep in the hole and then gently, oh, so gently, the old man lifted her into the young man's arms.

Several of them helped stretch her atop the opened body bag and, at that moment, I felt my bladder go soft and the pain in my belly slip away.

"Can someone give me a positive ID?" the young one said. "Anybody?" Most of the men were looking away and would not turn to regard the body. Shay huffed and dropped to a knee, brushed a tangle of honeydew from her face and said, "It's her."

At that moment, one of the men in orange glanced at the body, spun away hard, doubled over, and heaved an early morning breakfast.

The old man pulled himself from the hole, and with the help of Shay, slid her gently into the body bag, slowly working the zipper up, and as the zipper rose across her chest, her face tilted my way…

All I remember is that so much of it was…simply gone.

THE HOMECOMING

I pushed myself from the cross and stumbled down the hill. I may have been screaming, but I remember no sound rising from my throat. I hit mud, tumbled, and then crawled. I reached the tombstone of the twins, and upon the wings of the angel, I pulled myself to my feet. I nearly made it to the semicircle of vehicles surrounding the grave. That's when my vision tunneled and the rain started a slow tilt sideways. Something sharp struck my hip, and I heard a very loud splash.

MY SLEEPING MIND raced through the blackness to find the bus screaming down highway 81. I was trying to get back to that screaming moment, that one last moment. I wanted to have her lift me up and take me into the oblivion. The sky and earth were one, a swirling mass. Feet danced across broken glass. Shrill piercing birds nipped at my flesh. They were black and wanted my eyes, but I would not blink them open. There was a whisper, a secret told, but I would not hear it. Had I heard it, things might have changed. The greatest fear to fear is fear, said the voice. The greatest hope to hope is hope and the greatest love to love is love. The shrilling birds became screaming angels, ripping and tearing at the swirling mass that became my flesh, and I had no choice but to open my eyes.

EVERYTHING SNAPPED BACK into focus—the kind of stinging focus that comes after falling flat on your back from a very high tree branch or from high atop the jungle gym. The wind shredded from my lungs, pain bringing my mind into screaming focus. The smell of earthworms came sharp into my nostrils and as quickly as everything had snapped back into focus, the world began tunneling away from me again, only this time the world seemed a dark sea splashing big with rain. "Special Agent Carriss!" the young one called out, "Somebody get some light up here next to my car!"

I was certain I was on my feet and walking, but at the same time, my legs felt stuck. Tickling, pleasant warmth flowed across my thighs and pretty beams of light danced patterns across the stone. I was certain I was on my feet and walking, but the stone and splashing world did not follow my lead and go backwards with every step. "Kid in Dress Blues," the old one said.

"Get his face out of the mud."

"Is he breathing?"

"Careful of his spine, everyone."

"Goddamn, he looks hypothermic."

THE IDLING OF an engine and the warmth of a heater were the only things I could feel when I returned from the dark and empty place. I was curled in a ball under a wool blanket. That's what my eyes told me at least. The back door was opened at my feet and the old one, Carriss they had called him, was leaning over me, yanking off my dog tags. "Gonna borrow these," he said and backed away, revealing behind him Shay and several deputies sliding a slumping muddy body bag into the back of a hearse.

"Nailed it, Ben," the younger one said somewhere beyond my line of sight. "Pallbearer."

"I think he's still half with us," the old one, Carriss, answered.

The young one leaned into the car, sniffed the air. "What's that smell?" Carriss was studying the dog tags. "Lost his bladder."

The young one waved his hand in front of my face and snapped his fingers to get a response. "Guess he'd been standing out here for about eighteen hours. Sheriff got me an address on his folks. Get him home, link up with Coroner Wong at the bridge, and off to the autopsy from there?"

Carriss answered with a grunt and the car door slammed.

LOCAL AUTHORITIES LEFT evidence flags at the 121 site if you wanted to get that mapped after lunch," the young agent said. The car was humming through the rain now, the swish-swash pulse of the windshield wipers keeping time as we went. The more I tried to eavesdrop, the more their voices drifted further and further away, my reality like the frayed ends of something thin and sheer cut loose and drifting skyward in a gentle breeze. "Prelim says they found a black synthetic on the left hip, thigh, and calf."

"Of the pants?" Carriss asked.

"Odd thing, isn't it? Possibly, we're looking at upholstery fibers?"

The young one wasn't comfortable thinking for himself just yet and it was quite clear, even from my limited perspective, that Carriss was getting annoyed. "Are we looking at fibers or are we not?" Carriss asked. "And in either case what does it tell us?"

"It tells there's a good chance she didn't die in that ditch, but I may be jumping the gun...that is if the info is accurate and the fibers are for real."

Both of them were silent for five or six wiper swipes.

"Hard to say," the young one said.

Carriss' voice was flat. "Fifty says the body was in a trunk."

CHAPTER SIX

I MUST HAVE cried out in my sleep, for my mother was bending over me, swabbing my forehead with a moist washcloth. This was how she did it when I was struck hard by night terrors as a child. She would bundle me under the comforters and draw me tightly into place to keep me from kicking and scratching. I knew *where* I was, but as to *when* this was, I hadn't a clue—last night, the previous days, the weeks and months that had passed could only creep forward bit by bit as blood shot back into my prefrontal cortex. I could see daylight coming in sharply through the north window Venetians to etch fine lines of light against the west wall. It was morning—that much was certain—and my legs felt like two freshly chopped logs.

"Dreamt I was in the Army," my voice cracked.

"Shhh, you passed out from cold they told me," my mother whispered, "Just try to go back to sleep." As she turned the moist towel on my forehead, the frayed ends of my memory came fluttering back around me and a picture began to unfold.

"The FBI," I said.

"The FBI brought you home—don't you remember?" She said it so easily, as if being brought home by the FBI were an everyday thing. "You were out there all night." As she said the words, it all came crashing down, my memory in its entirety.

"No!" I pleaded with my mother as if her name meant God.

"I know, baby, I know." She tried to hold me down. "It's okay."

The air went from my lungs and my body went deep into the mattress. "Oh, God...who's here? Who's here with us?" I tried to fight my way from my mother but lacked the strength. "They brought me home and they're still here! They brought me home and they're still here!" I shouted, my fists digging deep into the bed sheets.

"You're scaring me. You're scaring me, baby." Finally, when she could no longer hold me down, she shouted over her shoulder. "I need some help!"

The old one, Carriss, and the young one appeared atop me. "He doesn't know where he is!" my mother said.

"He's in shock," said the young one.

"Look at me! Look at me!" Carriss said and grabbed my jaw to pin my head to my pillow.

"Don't hurt him!" my mother shouted.

I kept thrashing.

"He's strong!" the young one grunted as he tried to pin my hips.

Carriss clamped his other hand around my temples. "Watch his legs!"

It was too late. My left leg was already shooting up from beneath the bedspread, my foot finding its way against the young one's head, and with a solid kick, sending him backwards to the floor.

"Look at me!" Carriss gripped my head tighter.

The young one found his way to his feet, slipped on something on the floor, and fell again, his pistol tumbling from his shoulder holster.

"Secure your firearm, Special Agent Earnstead," Carriss shouted, never removing his eyes from mine. "You're going to feel some pain now," Carriss said to me, and with his thumb, he dug into the nerve behind my left ear. Electricity seared through my neck and sent me limp and powerless into the bed. A numb silence followed and finally Carriss asked, "Everybody okay?"

The young one, Earnstead, and my mother found their way to their feet.

"My name is Special Agent Carriss," Carriss said in an almost hypnotic voice, "my partner Special Agent Earnstead and I have come to help you. You'll be able to move in a moment or two, but I would highly recommend staying in bed for the next couple hours. You'll need your strength."

The young one, Earnstead, holstered his pistol, rubbed at where I kicked him, and said to my mother, "Mind if we have a word alone, Grace?"

"Not a bad idea," Carriss said.

The three of them left the room and soon coffee was brewing. I rolled to my stomach and saw my Dress Blues in a wet pile beneath me on the floor.

One thought kept gathering despite my every effort to push it away— ***Federal agents don't come to small towns to investigate hit-and-runs.*** The more I fought it, the more the thought settled deeper, and finally it stuck.

I leapt from the covers, tried to use my legs, but tumbled off the bed. Everything below my waist was still paralyzed from the nerve strike, and there in a limp heap on the floor, I discovered myself stark naked, courtesy my mother and the FBI.

I dragged myself to my crumpled Dress Blues. My Zippo and the triangular-shaped stone were safely where I had left them. The two special agents weren't interested in me. Otherwise, they would have searched me more thoroughly. They were here for a good reason though and this good reason went far beyond simply investigating a hit-and-run. The clandestine exhumation and upcoming third autopsy told me that much.

I didn't know where I would be going or why, but I felt the need to hurry. My Dress Blues smelt of urine. The clothing in my closet didn't fit. It was a task doing it naked, but I snuck down past my mother and the two agents in the kitchen, going the long way through the living room, over the banister, and downstairs to the laundry room.

There in the laundry room I found my camouflage from Grief hill tumbling in the drier. Through the floor, I could hear my mother discuss the matter of my presence at the cemetery with Special Agents Earnstead and Carriss. My mother tried to make some excuse about me returning to the grave early in the morning to place flowers. Carriss told her that they found no flowers at the grave and Earnstead suggested that it was more than likely that

I had stayed out at the cemetery all night. Earnstead asked her why I might do that. My mother offered the men more coffee instead of answering the question. The two agents told my mother that they were on a tight schedule and then Carriss added that my behavior was perfectly normal for a boy in love. My mother suggested love was too strong a word and all three of them moved from the spot above me, out of earshot, on their way to the front door.

I made as delicate an exit as possible, grabbing my spare keys from the key rack at the back door. I opened the garage door as quietly as possible and idled into a roll down the alley. My behavior *was* perfectly normal, so I kept telling myself. Now, I needed a plan. I would have to go back to the beginning and retrace each and every last step she took. There was no time to lose and so when I was a safe distance from the house, I revved up to seventeen, hit the clutch, and slammed into fourth.

PART II

ANGER

CHAPTER SEVEN

COOPER MAC, BY the looks of it, had busied himself last night with celebration. Where I found him was on his knees, scraping a wad of gum from under the third seat, fourth row left in the Dakota Theatre's balcony. "Peach Schnapps," he told me, "doesn't taste quite as good coming back up." Cooper poured a gum-hardening solution on a wad of gum. The gum hissed as the solution did its job and a putrid smell rose. This forced Cooper backwards, hand over mouth. "Peach gum!"
"You two had a party after the funeral?" I asked.
"Just friends over...when do you have to head back?"
"Day after tomorrow," I told him. "I do have a couple questions."
"Why are you wearing camouflage?"
"Only thing I had that was clean."
"Thought maybe you were trying to impress everybody," he said and then stabbed at the gum wad with a paint scraper. "I don't know—some people have said you've copped an attitude since coming home."
"What people—all your new friends?"
"You talk to Bobby yet this morning?"
"Wouldn't wake up," I said and then bent halfway down to help him. "You have to get beneath the gum, Cooper. Peel it up. It'll only take you about two seconds."
Cooper continued stabbing. "I like doing it this way."
I dropped into the nearest seat and bent close as he continued stabbing the wad. "Who took Tammy to that Homecoming party, Cooper?"
"Why, what are you trying to do?"
"Retrace her last steps."
"You should go talk to Bobby."
The hardened gum began to break off in little powdery chunks.
"She was working that night and left for the party from here," I said.
"Probably," Cooper said, unwilling to look up. "You'd have to check the timecards to be certain."
"The timecards are gone," I said.

"Yeah, I think the police were here." Cooper continued to stab away. "Like I said, you should go talk to Bobby."

RISE AND SHINE, Bobby. It's time you and I go retrace Tammy's last steps." Bobby writhed across the shag carpet of his living room, knocking aside a stray beer cup filled with something brown and chunky.

"Go away, Merrill, I'll be sober by noon."

I straddled Bobby and opened one of his eyelids. "It is noon and you were working with her that night," I said, "so you must have an idea who picked her up and took her out to the Stevenson bonfire."

"Go away and come back after 6:00."

"Something happened to Tammy at that party to make her want to walk off into the night…if that is really what happened in the first place. I wanna poke around out at that farm—get a lay of the land."

"Out at the farm?" Bobby opened an eye. "When I'm fully sober, sure…sounds like fun, but it would really help if you got off me now."

I nodded, crawled off Bobby, found two steel trashcan lids in the alley, came back in and straddled Bobby a second time. He had fallen sound asleep again when I drew my arms way back and—

CLASH-CLASH-CLASH!

Bobby knocked me back and danced to his feet, grabbing at his ears wildly to shake away the noise. When Bobby finished the little dance, he pointed at me accusingly and shouted, "See! I told you they woke you up in Basic Training by banging trashcan lids!"

"Who took Tammy to that party, Bobby?"

"Cooper took my shift that night." Bobby grabbed a throw blanket from the couch, covered himself, and stretched out again on the floor. "You'd have to go ask him—I think he's at work now in fact."

"Bobby, Cooper Mac said you and Tammy punched out early…he made it sound like you two were together." Bobby's body went completely still beneath the blanket.

"Um, Thursday, you mean?"

"Yes, Bobby, the night Tammy disappeared from that party, Thursday, the night she disappeared. Surely, you must remember Thursday."

"Are we being sarcastic now?"

"You're right," I said and turned for the door, "your sleep is very important and I'm an utter and complete bastard for keeping you from it."

Bobby cast the blanket off him and rolled to his back. "Jesus-holy-Christ with the guilt trip! What has happened to you?!"

"She's dead, Bobby!"

"Yes! Okay, you win! I covered the first half of Cooper's shift! He covered the last half of mine! Therefore, if you go look at the timecards, you will see that I left at least a half hour before Tammy! Which means I wouldn't have the foggiest clue who picked her up! What she did with him! What she was wearing! How much booze they bought! How much weed they smoked!

If she was in a good mood or not! Whether her hair was back in a ponytail or down around her ass—"

"So you're saying you don't know who took her to the party!"

"Yes, for fuck's sake!"

"It was a simple question…my point is that you must have some clue who she was going to the party with. It's not like she kept stuff like that top secret," I said. "Homecoming is one of the biggest nights of the year. I mean, did you two spend the whole night working in silence, neither of you curious what the other was doing?"

Bobby sat up, found a half-smoked cigarette in an ashtray, and proceeded to smoke it. "You're an ass for waking me up."

"Your story about her walking from that party doesn't add up."

"Why do you care who took her to that party anyway? You were two thousand miles away. You're not going to get in trouble for anything. Why bother getting involved?"

"Involved in what, Bobby?"

"In whatever this is—Jesus!" Bobby stubbed out his cigarette. "Fucking Spanish Inquisition! That's right, you got me!" Bobby's eyes went wide. "I did come back to the theater after punching fucking out…I came to find out if Tammy wanted a ride to the bonfire, because she and I had worked for the past two fucking hours in utter and total fucking silence, but lo and behold she was already gone. It was the one-armed fucking man who fucking did it!"

"Gee, Bobby, how many fucks was that?"

Bobby stared at me a long moment. "In fact, yes, I did want somebody to go to the party with, so I did return to the theater. It turns out she was already gone. She didn't—for the record—mention who was going to take her to the party, but there was somebody who did pick her up. It was a guy, thank you, and she wouldn't say whom. You know how she liked her secrets."

"No, explain it to me, Bobby."

"It was getting late and I didn't really feel like going to a high school party alone. I'm a loser, but not a *fucking* loser, so I went home and I got drunk and it was pathetic. End of story."

"I don't remember how to get to the Stevenson farm, Bobby." I pulled my keys from my pocket and gave them a jingle. "Brush your teeth and we'll go for a ride."

THERE IS SOMETHING mythic about bridge crossings, the stuff of trolls and giants, rainbows and unicorns, the sun rising hard and fast into midday, burning off the last of a winnowing morning fog, the girders speeding past in sharp relief against the blue-green of the river beyond. Bridge crossings are to be respected, revered, for empires have been made and destroyed by them and legends born, and so we road in silence until we reached the Nebraska side. "You know that sensation of being right on the verge of sleep?"

"Waking up or falling into?" Bobby asked.

"Into."

"Sure," Bobby kicked his seat back. "Kind of like being stoned. Kind of where I am now. You can't quite think straight, so you see the world a bit different. Sometimes you catch things you'd normally miss: sometimes you miss things you'd normally catch. Trip can be good, trip can be bad."

"When the FBI drove me home this morning, I remember them talking about carpet fibers...I think on her clothing, but I'm not sure. There was something else important I was supposed to remember too, but it's hanging there in the back of my mind, just out of reach."

"You have to be in the same mental state when you heard it to remember it," Bobby said. "That's why you're not supposed to study drunk...that is unless you plan to take the test drunk."

"What?" I said.

"Exactly."

"They were talking about evidence flags in a ravine," I said. "I'm assuming they were talking about the ravine where her body was found."

"You want to go out and find the ravine now too?" Bobby said.

"Before the funeral I saw deep cuts on her feet."

"How did you see her feet?"

"I opened her casket."

Bobby wasn't sure which question to ask first. "You opened the...wait, did you just say that the FBI was in town?"

"They exhumed her body this morning."

PEOPLE HAVE GOTTEN lost on these roads," Bobby muttered. "Took one turn after another, thinking they'd find their way to asphalt eventually. Pretty soon they run out of gas, so the guy gets out and walks, thinking he'll just find his way to a nearby farm, only it's hot—and like a rat trapped in a maze with no way out, he keeps going in circles until...he just drops." Bobby whispered. "It's as if the corn were alive."

"The corn *is* alive," I said.

"People go for months without being found out here and then when it's time to harvest, some farmer stumbles along and there isn't much left to identify. That is if the bodies don't get caught in the threshers."

"Pleasant," I said. "What's your point?"

"I'm just saying this could be sort of—" Bobby tried to rephrase. "People sometimes wander off. Get lost. Die from exposure. Simple as that."

"How cold was it that night?"

"Sixty or seventy degrees."

"So we cross death from exposure off the list."

We were three gravel roads deep into Nebraska. The cornrows hugged the gravel ten feet high and stretched long shadows upon us. There were no landmarks to guide us, just the narrow stretch of gravel to our front.

"Anyway," Bobby said. "Look around. It is a possibility she got lost."

The cornrows stopped abruptly, giving way to a harvested swath of land, the rolling river valley spreading big, wide, and magnificent to our south.

"Or then again..." I spun a sharp left onto another gravel road, and once again, corn surrounded us. We traveled like this until I could see that Bobby had thoroughly lost all sense of direction. "It's just up ahead—we'll get out and walk from here," I said.

"I thought you didn't know where the farm was?"

I gave Bobby a smile, hit the brakes, popped us into reverse and whipped us into a little dirt turnabout near a fence dividing properties.

"You sure we're in the right place?" Bobby asked.

I pointed to a cottonwood shelterbelt about a quarter of a mile away. "Backside of the farm is just up ahead. I took the back route to get us here."

"Before we go any further..." Bobby grabbed his door handle. "You do know we'd be trespassing, right?"

"I'm camouflaged."

"Yeah, but I'm not," Bobby said.

"Well, it's a good thing—" I hopped from car. "—that I'm faster."

"Thanks," Bobby said and followed me through the corn.

THE GRAVEL HAD dried by midday, but the runoff from last night's storm still sat thick and black in the cornrows, dirt coming up in heavy clumps as Bobby and I snuck our way toward the shelterbelt, Bobby cursing me with each step he took.

"Almost there," I kept reassuring him as we pushed deeper.

Suddenly he stopped. "I don't see the trees anymore." He was talking about the trees of the shelterbelt. I stopped too, put a finger to my lips to silence him, and pointed at the barbed-wire fence two feet to our front.

"Snuck up on us," he said.

I pointed up to the cottonwood branches stretching over our head.

"What's the plan?" he asked.

I put finger to lip and scowled. Bobby shrugged. I pointed two fingers to my eyes, pointed down the fence-line, and walked two of my fingers across my other arm. Bobby nodded...and then gave me a confused look. I pointed back at my eyes, pointed down the fence-line, made my fingers walk again.

"I'm sorry, what are you trying to tell me?"

I pantomimed again, this time slowly whispering a blow-by-blow commentary. "Stay here and keep your eyes open. I'm going to walk the fence-line to find the best way in through the shelterbelt."

"You don't have to talk to me like I'm three."

"If I were trying to do that, I would have brought a hand-puppet."

THE PROBLEM, IT became clear, was not simply getting onto the property, but getting onto the property unnoticed, which meant crossing through a fifty-foot wide labyrinth of fallen branches, chest high in some places, all of it sitting beneath a thick, mildewed blanket of cotton droppings and cobweb, all still wet from last night's storm. One lap round the shelterbelt told me we had two choices—in through one of the dirt-paved firebreaks on the north and east sides of the property, a bit too obvious for my tastes; or a slow, painful crawl to ensure that we would enter unseen.

I returned to Bobby and told him he could wait for me in the corn, but he felt the need to follow me. I pointed out that crossing through the labyrinth of undergrowth, the fallen timber, the thick mildewed blanket of spider webs and cotton droppings may prove too dangerous without good boots. I also warned him that if there were spider webs, there would also most likely be spiders.

"Where you go," he told me, "I follow."

As we mounted the fence, I warned him again about the spiders, but still he insisted on following. He told me that he would brave it, that it was better than being in the corn.

Actually, I wanted him to follow. If he had been holding anything back from me, the pressure of crossing silently through the labyrinth, coupled with his fear of spiders, would quite possibly bring any secrets to the surface.

We had only gotten about four steps past the barbed wire, high stepping as if through hip deep snow, when Bobby hissed, "There are spiders crawling all over my legs."

I hissed back, "I warned you twice about coming!"

At that moment, I stepped right down upon a rotted branch. The rotted branch moaned ungodly and then went to pieces beneath my feet, sending me two feet deeper through the timber and cobwebs to what finally felt like earth. As the sound of branches breaking echoed up through the trees, startled sparrows took to flight. "I think you just tripped the alarm," Bobby said.

I extended a middle finger. "Shall I translate too?"

After that, we moved fast, going on our stomach as if across thin ice. Finally, we found ourselves stumbling from the branches onto fresh-cut lawn. Free to move, Bobby slapped at his legs violently. "You are such a dick. You are such a dick. I could be sleeping right now!"

I searched the trees—the sparrows had not returned to roost—I grabbed Bobby hard by the shoulder and yanked him to his knees. "We're not alone."

"How can you tell?"

"Trust me." I eased to my feet to survey the property. "Chances are they already know we're here."

It was a slight chance actually. We had come out of the shelterbelt only to be flanked by several dilapidated chicken coops on one side and a storage shed full of antique farm implements on the other. We were wedged in neatly and out of sight.

"Um...that's where the bonfire was," Bobby said, pointing to a large scorched circle of earth. I stepped out of hiding and kicked at the circumference of the scorched circle to find burnt wood, glass fragments, and rake marks. "It looks like they raked it out, doesn't it?" he added.

The farm sat on the T-intersection of two gravel roads, the bonfire placed tactically out of view of any curious passers-by. This was on the southwest corner behind the farmhouse. About thirty feet away sat a swing-set, mottled thick with rust and tipped against the west side of the house. Just around the corner from the swing-set was a back porch ready to collapse across its center. Plywood sheets had been placed as ramps across its staircase so people could safely get to and from the house. The house, by its looks, had been abandoned over a decade ago. A few of the upper windows had been knocked out and a paint job was definitely in order.

"Abandoned for about ten years would be my guess," Bobby said.

I kneeled and poked up a handful of ash from the fire pit. "Two ways on and off the property," I said, pointing to either end of the dirt roundabout. "People who came to the party would have either parked on the gravel road to the north or to the east. Either direction would be out of view of the bonfire. My guess is most of the people would have come in from the north."

"How do you figure?"

"Best lit by the back-glow of the fire—safest route to take."

"Your point being?" Bobby asked.

"Well, she has to walk one way or the other to leave the party—if that's what happened—and if the bonfire was blazing, I doubt anybody would have seen her make it too far past the firebreak."

"It's a party," Bobby said, "People are coming and going from their cars all the time. There'd also be people sitting on the fringes too—out in the dark. Who knows?" Bobby said, "I'm willing to bet somebody saw her making her way down the road…maybe even asked if she needed a ride."

I rose and dusted off my hands. "Sure like to talk to that person."

"You hadn't been around Tammy for the past three months," Bobby said and then went silent.

I turned at Bobby. "You keep making little comments like that…why?"

"She just…"

"Spit it."

"People change."

"We *are* being watched," I said.

"What do you want to do?"

"I want to get a look inside that house," I said and marched straight for the porch. "Who knows? Maybe we can flush out whoever is spying on us."

"What's supposed to be in the house?"

I jumped onto the porch. "Carpet, broken glass—who knows?"

"Dude," Bobby whispered in warning as I reached for the doorknob.

A metallic chirp echoed from beyond the east firebreak and then a voice boomed from a megaphone, "Freeze!"

I froze, arm extended.

The voice added, "Don't even think about touching that doorknob!"

I held the pose as a black 4X4 came bursting in through the east firebreak. The 4X4 spun a sharp turn and came straight at the porch. Bobby leapt down, at first ready to run and then just as ready to back against the side of the house, his hands in surrender. I kept holding my pose.

Two men in polo shirts and mirrored sunglasses hopped from the 4X4, the driver flashing his badge. "Afternoon, Mr. Grant and Mr. Merrill," the driver said, adjusted the pistol in his holster, and climbed the porch. The other one, the one with the megaphone, sidled next to Bobby.

The driver looked me up and down. "You can unfreeze now." As my arm dropped, the driver extended a handshake to me and smiled. "Merrill Merrill, Yankton Bucks one-thirty pounder, watched you nearly wrestle your way to State last year. Blew out your shoulder right before Regionals, wasn't it? Good to see you home." He kept shaking my hand. "Rich Dickson." Dickson pointed to the one with the megaphone. "My partner, Tony Harper."

"You two just out sightseeing today?" Harper asked.

"That a crime?" I asked back.

"Last night out at the cemetery and now here?" Dickson said.

"Trespassing," Harper said.

"Trespassing is such a strong word, don't you think?" I said.

"Oh, you think it's funny?" Dickson said.

"Brother," Bobby said, "just shut up and let's go home."

"Let's say hypothetically that I have an invite to be here and you came onto this property without a warrant in hand and no probable cause. Wouldn't the roles be reversed? Wouldn't I be able to place *you* under arrest?"

"Say something else, Smartass, and see where it gets you," Harper said.

"'Something else, Smartass, and see where it gets you,'" I answered.

"Jesus, Merrill," Dickson said, losing his smile, "just make haste and let us dot our T's in peace before we do have to run you downtown."

I hitched my belt, pretending I had a pistol too, looked down at Bobby, smiled, and then quickly turned to press my face up against the glass of the back window and to touch the doorknob again and again. My impertinence was answered with a nice hard shove to get me moving along.

We tried to go out the way we entered, but Dickson pointed us eastward out the firebreak. They watched us go, and when I was certain we were thoroughly out of the effective range of their pistols, I shouted back to the two detectives, "See you tonight."

CHAPTER EIGHT

WE WERE OFF gravel now and nearing the bridge, driving fast with the windows down, and it had been eating away at him for the past five miles. "I told you it was a stupid idea from the start. Why did you want to look at the carpet and glass in that farmhouse anyway?"

"Something I remember the FBI saying." I could feel the lack of sleep stretching my nerves thin—the more I tried to weave my thoughts logical, the more they unraveled. "Something about fibers found on her body—that the ravine wasn't really where she died."

"Why did you have to get so cocky with those two cops anyway?"

"Wanted to see what they'd do...what did I have to lose?"

"You could have gotten arrested."

"So?"

"Or worse."

"So?"

"Well," Bobby kicked back in his seat. "No use looking for the ravine now. You're on their radar."

"They don't have jurisdiction in Nebraska."

Bobby sat up. "Those two cops? You think that matters to them?"

"Surveillance on that farm?" I rubbed my eyes, adjusted my visor, and eased the car back into the proper driving lane. "Two cops sitting and watching that place? Something happened out there...and why not use Nebraska cops for surveillance? You pull surveillance on territory you know. You stay on your own turf...something fishy about Dickson and Harper."

"When was the last time you slept?" Bobby asked.

"Hour or two this morning maybe...why?"

"Because you're about to run us into that oncoming pickup."

I swerved hard to get us back to our side of the road. The pickup's horn blared. I let off the gas and the car slammed from fifth into first, bringing us to a near-lurching halt.

"You want me to drive?" Bobby asked.

I looked to the odometer. "Nearly eight miles, just to the bridge...so we throw out the theory that Tammy tried to walk home from that farm...so the last place we know where she was alive is on that farm."

"Maybe she wasn't trying to walk *home*," Bobby said.

"Somewhere other than home?" I said.

"It is a possibility."

I considered this for the next two miles.

"Okay," I said. "She walks from the party. In the middle of the night. Alone. In the middle of nowhere...but where would she be going? Nothing out there but corn...you said so yourself."

"There may have been more than one party going on in the area. She may have decided to walk to the lake...it isn't that far...or maybe to the river. Maybe she had a bit too much to drink and just wanted to walk it off. Do a few laps on the gravel road you know. Slip off to pee or puke."

We were nearing the bridge. "Let's find out who else has farms in the area," I said. "We need gas and a detailed relief map. I want to chart any and all possible routes she might have walked."

WE PULLED INTO the Pump-n-Stuff Convenience Store, which sat just off the north end of the bridge, about two blocks down from the theater. There I purchased a Nebraska County Roadmap. It was the most detailed I could find, but I would have to make guesses on many terrain features and service roads, based on the course of nearby rivers and streams.

"The ravine could be just about anywhere," Bobby said as we walked out. "All we know is that it's somewhere in Cedar County. That's hundreds of square miles to cover."

I lurched to a stop at a newspaper vending machine. A headline had caught my eye. At that same moment, Cooper Mac came walking down from the Dakota, arms spread wide. "Road Trip?"

As I dug spare change from my change caddy for one of those newspapers, Cooper Mac and Bobby disappeared into the convenience store to make their beer purchase. While they were at it, the clerk heard them talking about what had just taken place at the Stevenson farm. By the time we were rolling back over the bridge, a phone call was being made.

The little conspiracy was rather simple—the lady behind the counter had sold booze to dozens of kids who went to the party Homecoming Eve. She wasn't the only person, however, who was doing this that night. It was common practice in the town of Yankton that the legal drinking age would be ignored after tourist season. Business was business and a paying customer was a paying customer. The local authorities would look the other way as long as noise complaints remained nil and the youngsters stayed relatively out of trouble. Liquor was big business in Yankton and no overzealous state prosecutors or angry parents threatening lawsuits were going to stop a practice that had been going on for decades.

The lady who overheard Bobby and Cooper Mac made a phone call to her boss. Her boss made phone calls to his fellow businessmen. Those businessmen had already been hammering out options with their lawyers. These lawyers had already been putting pressure on certain badges to see that this hit-and-run case (or whatever it was) be steered in a certain direction, namely away from them...and so with one phone call from a crack-dealing booze-selling gas-station attendant, I suddenly became Yankton's newest complication and efforts were quickly set in motion to have me stopped.

FULL TANK OF gas, roadmap, and newspapers in hand, we were back in Nebraska, rolling to find that link between the Stevenson farm and the ravine where she was found. The newspaper, it turned out, was a lucky break. "CLUES SOUGHT IN TAMMY HAAS DEATH" read the headline and beneath it stretched a page-wide photo revealing a handful of investigators lifting a white sheet heavy with human remains over a guardrail of twined steel. The ravine was deep, only tops of trees poking up in the frame. "Spruce and cottons," I said, "halfway up out of the river valley maybe…on hardtop road and close to the Stevenson farm."

"That still could be just about anywhere," Bobby, now driving, said.

I studied the photo more closely. The foliage of the trees was lit well by a sun hanging either mid-afternoon or mid-morning. "We're looking at a road running north-south…as to what side of the road the ravine is on, east or west, I would have to know what time of day they—" The lack of shadow caught my eye. "—there are trees in the background of this photo, trees coming up from the ravine, but there isn't a single shadow in the foreground. That means this side of the road is tree-lined, the side behind the cameraman isn't."

"You know," Cooper Mac said, cracking open a beer in back, "the dam isn't too far from the Stevenson farm. I'd even say within walking distance. The road going across the dam gets a person back to the South Dakota just as easily as the bridge. A lot of people use that road as their drunk-route home…and if I'm not mistaken, the dam has payphones."

"The dam's in walking distance of the farm, you think?" I said.

Cooper leaned forward. "I'm just saying it's a possibility she walked from the party to the dam. Maybe she was meeting someone there. Maybe she wanted to call home for a ride from there. I don't know. Maybe she was meeting somebody there to bring them to the farm, so they wouldn't get lost on the gravel. This would put her on a hardtop road, right? At some point, this hardtop road would have to travel northward down toward the river, right?"

"There aren't any payphones at the dam," I said.

"Pretty sure there are," Cooper said.

"Pretty sure there aren't," I said.

"Sounds like a bet to me," Bobby said. "So, the stakes: if we're right, you give this up and come home? If we're wrong, we follow anywhere you want to take us…no questions asked."

Agreed, they had me sidetracked toward the dam.

I ADMIT IT wasn't the wisest bet I'd ever taken in my life. The little single payphone sat at the edge of a small parking lot midway down the little scenic byway. The byway, the payphone, the little picnic area not far downstream, the chalkstone bluffs that rose about a hundred feet above the river's edge—there was more than one gaping hole ripped from the picture I had of this place. The one thing I did remember though was the lone cottonwood tree, where from its branches a bald eagle, steadfast over the years, watched down on me even now. Just beyond the cottonwood was a Y-intersection. A right turn on that Y-intersection led down a low road to the power-generating plant dug into the bluffs at the southern end of Gavin's Point Dam. A left turn led up through the bluffs and wrapped around to the topside of the dam. Following this road would take you the length of Lewis and Clark Lake and back into South Dakota (the so-called drunk route.)

Bobby and Cooper Mac watched, beers in hand, from inside the car as I examined the payphone. "The cord's gone," I shouted over my shoulder.

Bobby leaned out the window and shouted back, "Gone how?"

I tossed the phone's receiver to Bobby and stepped aside the phone box to show them that the cord had been ripped clean from both ends. "Nobody made any phone calls from here."

"Yeah," Bobby said, "But that is, in fact, a payphone."

I adjusted my headgear. "We're not going home."

"What's that?" Cooper Mac shouted.

"It's too convenient," I shouted.

"What is?" Cooper shouted.

"That the phone cord has been ripped out," I shouted.

"You've seen one too many movies!"

There were hundreds of thousands of gallons of water exploding down the spillway of Gavin's Point Dam—that's why we were doing all the shouting—that along with the humming of electricity from the power transformers lining the chalkstone bluffs.

Perhaps, Bobby was right—perhaps, I had seen one too many movies. I stuck my finger in the coin return to check for stray change. "Okay, you win," I said on my way back to the car. "Let's fly."

"Reason prevails!" Bobby exclaimed.

I came to a stop, felt the soft of my fingertip, the one that had been inside the coin return.

"Jesus, what now?!" Bobby shouted.

I turned back and poked my finger into the coin return again. This time though I gave the phone box a good, hard slap. This brought a small cloud of white powder down from the hidden places inside the phone. I stepped aside and showed Bobby and Cooper the phone box again. "Dusted for fingerprints!"

"We're almost out of beer," Cooper Mac shouted.

"You were right, Cooper!" I shouted. "It could have happened here. We're on the right path."

The thought of it made me ill, and for a moment, I nearly considered accepting the terms of the bet. All this stalling was only creating doubt. I needed forward momentum. I decided to move before Bobby and Cooper Mac could protest. The high road off the Y and around the transformers was poorly lit and led nowhere for pedestrians. "Path of least resistance…if her feet were already cut up at this point, she'd keep walking downhill."

I started walking the service road down toward the power plant.

Bobby popped the car into neutral to roll after me.
"You could always just tell him what happened," Cooper Mac said.
Bobby hit the brakes. "I don't know what happened, Cooper!"
Cooper put up his hands in defense. "But, you *were* at the bonfire."
"No, I wasn't," Bobby said. "And let's put a period on that right now...unless, that is, you'd like to get yourself involved in this too."
Cooper rose up in his seat. "Which way did Merrill go?"
A knock on Cooper's window startled the beer out of both of their hands. I had backtracked and circled the car to square up a loose end. "Look on the map to see if there's any road or landmark designated 121."
"What do you mean?" Cooper Mac asked.
"Something I remember the FBI saying."
Cooper opened the map and I continued forward.
"Think he heard any of that conversation?" Bobby said.
Cooper shrugged, because at this point, Cooper didn't really care.

THERE WAS A little parking lot at the bottom of the service road leading down to the power plant. At the edge of the parking lot was a scenic overlook. There had been coin-operated telescopes at this overlook at one point but for safety reasons, the railing had to be raised chest high. This made the telescopes obsolete and so they were removed. If people lifted themselves and bent out over that chest-high railing, they could see straight down the concrete wall to the water churning out from the power plant seven stories below. Here walleye congregated in massive schools, unable to migrate back to spawning grounds further upstream. Here fishermen would drop line and pluck their limit—the only trick, dragging their catch up the retaining wall.

Bobby and Cooper parked in the shade of the chalkstone bluffs, while I made my way down to the two old fishermen struggling to bring in a rope. "Have the police been out here?" I shouted.

The two fishermen were identical twins and, as far as I could tell by their dialect, Sioux by adoption, Nordic by birth. "You wanna give two old men a hand?" The only difference between the two was that one had a small eight ball for a glass eye and the other wore his hair in a ponytail.

I came in and got a grip on the rope, so the one with the ponytail could make a half hitch. "Have the police been out here?" I asked again.

"Police! Sheriff. FBI not twenty minutes ago."

"They give any particular reason?" I asked.

"Particular reason was that we called them."

I was too busy struggling to keep my grip to know which of them said that. I was beginning to breathe hard and the rope was beginning to burn against my palms. "What do you have at the end of this rope?" I grunted.

"Catch of the day," the one hitching the rope, the one with ponytail said.

I swung my body around to get leverage, now taking on the full weight of the load. Behind me were the fishermen's poles, a tackle box, and a cooler full of bait. The contraption I was pulling up was a large mesh steel net used to keep their catch alive. Inside the net were at least a dozen very angry fish, weighing in at over one hundred and fifty pounds all together.

"Don't jerk the rope so much," the one with the eight ball warned.

"Doing my best," I grunted.

"You're going to snap the—"

Suddenly, there was a loud snap and I went forward into the rail, the rope singing over my head. By the time I got to my feet, the two old men were leaning over the rail, staring down at the water below. From up between the schools of fish snaked the broken rope, at the end of the broken rope bobbed the net, and inside the net came a churning, thrashing heap of white bellies.

"Oops," the one with the ponytail said.

"Told you we needed stronger rope," said the one with the eight ball.

"Told you we didn't need so many fish."

The thrashing heap fought against itself to stay afloat, but the current proved too strong. The net went down, the rope snaking after it.

"Ninety-three years and every now and again you do get to see something new," said Ponytail.

"Told you we needed stronger rope," said Eight Ball.

"Told you we didn't need so many fish." The two were already going back to their fishing poles. "We'll have to cut 'em and gut 'em here then."

"Told you we needed a bigger cooler."

"Told you this was a bad spot to fish."

"Now that's something on which we both agreed."

The two had forgotten that I was there. "You said you called the Sheriff about something?" I asked gently.

"He wants to know about the night of the hit-and-run up on 121."

"Took the Sheriff a week to finally take notice."

"And when he did take notice, they all came full force."

"121?" I asked.

"Just up the road a quarter mile…County 121…takes you to Crofton."

"Frog," said Ponytail to Eight Ball.

"Frog?"

"Cooler."

"Ah, frog!" said Eight Ball enlightened. "Looks to be only one left."

FROM OUT OF the cooler came the last bullfrog, and as the bullfrog came from the ice, bullfrog thought, *ah, warm hands, ah, warm sun.* Bullfrog was happy now. *Ah, I can move my legs again, ah, I can feel my toes again, ah, I can trill!* Bullfrog trilled loud and listened for an answer. No answer came. This did not dishearten bullfrog though. *I can hear the water and I can hear the buzz of the flies, and, oh yes, I can lick my lips and stretch my legs. I have not a single care in the world.* Unfortunately, at that moment, a fillet knife was unsheathed and off went bullfrog's legs at the hips. Bullfrog was not sure what was happening at first, but was quite certain he was falling, falling, falling. Bullfrog tried to kick to slow himself but nothing happened.

Bullfrog opened his eyelids, and his other eyelids, and saw water coming at him fast. It was churning ugly water and something was beneath…but what? Bullfrog braced for impact. Something rose from the water to greet him…but what? Bullfrog flicked his tongue to find out, but it was too late…into the waiting mouth of the walleye he went. Bullfrog wondered what the moral of this story was, but only for a moment, for Walleye gulped and Bullfrog wondered no more.

BULLFROG'S LEGS KEPT kicking, however, and kicking, and kicking as Ponytail and Eight Ball strung each onto their respective hooks. "County 121 was a works project me and my brother helped build back in the late 40s. Spent months blasting through the chalkstone, but once we wove it on up out of the valley it was easy goings and a straight shot from there…hot though."

"You said you called the police the night the girl was hit-and-run?"

"We called them sure enough," Ponytail continued where his brother left off. "Called their answering machine to be more precise…gets past midnight around here, the Sheriff goes home. It was all said and done, though, what we saw down here, so we didn't think the need to wake him, didn't think it justified as an emergency, so we satisfied ourselves with the message…"

"Just today it seems like they all take notice," Eight Ball said.

I looked up the service road to the payphone and then beyond it to the cottons shading what looked to be a golf course tucked neatly in the adjacent valley. There had to be a connection—the farmhouse, County 121, the torn-out phone receiver. "You called the police the night my, uh…the, uh, night of the hit-and-run up on 121?"

Ponytail glanced sidelong at me. "We was just across the water there, bait-hunting for bullfrogs." Both of them pointed across to the levee that separated the power-plant channel from the spillway channel. Along the banks of the levee were warning buoys and large signs that said, "DANGEROUS WATERS–NO TRESPASSING." The currents were vicious here and there was no way to get to the levee by foot. It would take a small boat with a strong motor to make the journey, but there would be no safe place to moor.

"How'd you get over there?" I asked.

"We could tell you," both said at once, "but then we'd have to—"

At that, I started walking off, but then they both began to tell me what happened down here the night in question, and why in their opinion they thought the authorities were only getting interested now.

"It may be nothing," Ponytail offered when their story was complete.

"What did you get yourself into?" I said to her as if she were here.

"You loved her," Eight Ball said.

"What?"

"We can see that in your eye," Ponytail said. "You're a young man trying to follow a ghost who doesn't want to be followed."

"I don't believe in ghosts," I told them.

THE HOMECOMING

"It doesn't matter what *you* believe. What matters is what *is*," Eight Ball told me. "At times a man looks into the darkness and all he finds is his self."

"You're scaring him now, brother," Ponytail said.

"He should be scared," Eight Ball said. "The fact is we saw what we saw. Take it for what it is. Like anything in life—believe us or don't. Either way it'll probably come out the same."

A tug on Ponytail's line caught the brothers' full attention and I decided to skulk away. It was when I got halfway across the parking lot that Ponytail shouted, "The FBI told us you'd be coming."

I turned. "What did they tell you to do?"

"Nothing, just told us you'd be coming."

I KNOCKED ON my passenger's window, interrupting a heated conversation between Bobby and Cooper. They both went silent, and then Bobby opened the door and pulled the seat forward, gesturing for me to hop in back. I pushed the seat into place and stared out over the car's roof and across the parking lot. "Those two fishermen saw a guy threatening a girl down here the night Tammy disappeared."

Cooper Mac followed my gaze to the two brothers, looked back at me, and smirked, "Those two old Indians, you mean?"

"The way they tell it," I said, "is that the guy and girl came walking down from the trees, just beyond Calumet bluff." I pointed across the highway beyond the Y-intersection. "They were arguing, the guy gesturing pretty wildly. As they come closer, the argument gets more heated. From the looks of it, she's trying to get away from him. Only once she reaches the overlook, she's got nowhere left to go. The guy starts getting violent, he grabs her…hoists her off her feet, dangles her over the rail."

"Why would he do that?" Bobby said.

"Threatening to drop her over the side," I said.

"Wouldn't that kill her?" Cooper Mac asked.

"I think that was the point," I said.

"And you just happen to think this was Tammy?" Bobby said.

"Why?" I said. "You think they made the whole story up?"

"You never considered that?" Cooper Mac asked.

"I showed them a picture of Tammy and they were pretty sure it wasn't her, so no, I'm not saying that it was Tammy at all." I stared up into the trees where the couple supposedly first emerged. There was a golf course not far up the slope, nine holes tucked in the valley. "They said the girl was short, shorter than me, shorter than Tammy even, and that she had long blonde hair. It was almost an hour after midnight they said."

"You just said it yourself," Bobby shouted. "It wasn't Tammy!"

"The two old men were across the channel," I said, "over on the levee, when they saw it happen—hundred meters away would be my guess. They couldn't hear much from that distance, just one thing he kept shouting."

"What one thing?" Cooper asked.

"'Keep your mouth shut or they'll kill you."

"Who are *they*?" Cooper Mac said.

"I don't know."

"And then he drops her?" Bobby asked.

"No, then she starts screaming bloody murder, he pulls her back up, wraps his arm around her as if nothing happened, and they walk back up the road and disappear somewhere near the fifth green." I pointed up the road to show them where I was talking about. "County 121, that's the road we're after. It runs pretty much north to south along the backside of the golf course."

"I'm not following," Cooper Mac said.

"Somebody saw something and was threatened," I said.

"That sounds pretty vague to me," Bobby said.

"Tammy being dead isn't though," I said. "That's why we have to get to the ravine before it gets dark. The FBI was out here. They know we've been following them...which probably means they know about what happened with those two cops at the farm...which probably means we're on the right track."

Bobby gave Cooper Mac a look and then Cooper Mac cleared his throat and leaned toward me. "We've been talking, Bobby and me. We know you have your own way of 'dealing,' but you gotta ask yourself—do you really think Tammy would want you doing what you're doing right now?"

"What am I doing exactly?"

"Chasing her ghost."

"Or do you think," Bobby said, "that maybe she'd want you spending what little time you have of your vacation with your friends, remembering the good times, doing what you have to do to let her go."

"You gotta let her go, man," Cooper Mac said.

"You do, brother," Bobby said, "It's what she would have wanted." Bobby pulled the seat forward to herd me into the back of my car.

I leaned against the roof, for I'm not sure how long, staring at the two old fishermen, thinking about what they had said to me—that no matter what I did the ending would be the same. Bobby saw this journey of mine as a vacation. Cooper saw it as a road trip. Me? I didn't have a name for it. All I knew is that I wanted Tammy back. I stared up through the trees, trying to retrace the path the blonde and her would-be killer might have taken.

"All she ever did was bring you pain," Bobby mumbled.

I bent down into the window. "What?"

"Be realistic," Bobby said. "You know it's the truth."

I stared up through those trees some more.

"I should have been here," I said. "I should have never left."

"It wouldn't have made a difference anyway," Bobby said.

I was looking for a path up through the trees, the easiest way to the top. Cooper whispered to Bobby. "Grab me a beer."

Next came the hiss of two beer cans opening. That's when it was decided. I cocked my shoulders, adjusted my headgear, and started walking.

CHAPTER NINE

I WAS PASSING somewhere between the ninth and first greens on my way up the valley when a golfer teed a slice into a small stand of spruce. The golfer shouted, "Hey, Soldier, you just foozled my shot!" Only moments after that, did it occur to me that I had just walked away from my own car, leaving it in the hands of two friends who had spent the afternoon working their way sixteen beers deep into a case.

THEY WERE WAITING for me when I crested the fifth hole. I didn't even notice them until I crossed through the sand trap and found myself standing on the edge of County 121—Bobby and Cooper Mac sitting roadside atop the hood of my car, smoking and joking, unaware yet of my presence.

It's always an odd thing to trudge a hill and then look back to see how far you've come. The golf course rolled a stretched S down through the valley, disappearing and reappearing through scrub trees and hedgerows as it went. Nestled deep in the bluffs at the bottom of the valley was the dam, the narrow channel of the river spitting from its little mouth. Across the dam's miles-long back, the lake hung long and distant in the haze, gold shimmering firelight reflecting off its face as far as the eye could see, sailboats made small by distance crisscrossing lazy and slow through the glittering afternoon.

Bobby and Cooper Mac finally noticed me standing on the shoulder of the road. I turned and Bobby pointed and swept his hand long to the south to show me where the road twisted beyond the trees and out of sight. In that one sweeping gesture he was saying this was where it happened, this was how it happened, this was why it happened—live with it.

I pulled my newspaper from my cargo pocket to compare, and he was indeed right—this *was* where it happened. Across the road was the guardrail with its three strands of thick-twined steel, and beyond it, the thick-crowned autumn-gilt foliage of treetops poking up from the ravine.

This was the place, but instinct no longer served, not the way it had at the farmhouse. I felt nothing now—no sense of doom or tragedy, no echo of her suffering to shout at my senses, not one aftershock, just the near silence of a gentle breeze and an old road scattered with fallen leaves. Perhaps, my mind had been flooded by too much in the past twenty-four hours. I needed a good hard jolt to shake me from this daze, a good solid kick in the proverbial ass.

I paced the shoulder of the road, my eyes on the rough and savage of the ravine across. "The golf course, Cooper and Bobby, does it have a clubhouse that stays open at night?" I yelled.

"Out here in the boondocks? Doubt anything would be open past five. Besides the clubhouse is over a mile down the road," Cooper Mac shouted and pointed back over his shoulder. "We passed it on our way up."

"We're off the beaten path," Bobby said. "What did you expect?"

"Not for her to be walking out here," I answered back with teeth.

"Have your look and let's go," Cooper Mac shouted.

I paced, building up the nerve to cross, and when I did, I felt nothing but a self-absorbed sense of curiosity. I wanted to understand at all costs. I wanted to prove myself right to them. I wanted it to be about me and I hated myself for it. Weather and erosion had taken its toll on the shoulder adjacent to the ravine. The guardrail had been moved inward inch by inch until finally it sat right atop the yellow line. Even now, the guardrail was ready to give way, ready to take large chunks of asphalt with it. Crossing from the golf course was like crossing into a different world, from wealth to poverty, from nurture to blight. What I was doing wasn't safe. Even standing knees against the guardrail, I was still in the path of oncoming traffic. One gentle nudge was all it would take to send me tumbling down a slope of crumbled earth and thickets, a slope that disappeared into darkness, shadow, and seeming infinite depth. This indeed would be the perfect place for a hit-and-run. A driver could so much as graze a pedestrian and be none the wiser. The curve was sharp and blind. It was perfect…too perfect.

I had walked too fast up the slope of the golf course and had stopped too suddenly—my head was getting light and my anger was turning towards Bobby and Cooper Mac. I had to maintain discipline, had to control my temper. I needed forward momentum and they were getting in my way. "She wouldn't be walking on this side of the road!" I shouted.

"Tammy?" Cooper Mac asked.

"There's no place to walk over here," I said. "Come look!"

"We trust you," Bobby shouted.

I pointed up and down the road. "The curves are blind and there's no shoulder. You'd have to be stupid to walk over here. Not when there's twenty feet of shoulder on your side of the road and the golf course beyond." I stepped out onto the road. "It doesn't make sense." I listened for approaching traffic. "Just watch and see."

"Watch and see what?" Cooper Mac shouted.

Somewhere south beyond the trees, an eighteen wheel rumbled. "You can hear it coming and have plenty of time to get out of dodge!" I shouted.

"Watch yourself!" Bobby shouted back.

Beyond the trees, the truck downshifted to make the push up the slope.

"I can't see it yet, but I can *feel* it coming!" I shouted.

Bobby and Cooper hopped of the hood of my car. "We get it—would you just back off!" Bobby shouted.

"You're gonna get yourself killed!" Cooper Mac added.

I stretched my arms wide and opened myself to the oncoming truck.

"He's not going to see you in time to swerve!"

I closed my eyes and stepped back against the guardrail. The eighteen-wheeler exploded into view, leaning hard into the curve to pull itself through. If it caught me, it would drag me the length of the guardrail and spit me up in chunks upon the road. I would only feel it for an instant though—a surge of pain and the sudden sensation of being lifted and spun. I have to admit I liked not knowing…and so its shadow was upon me.

I WAS SEVEN and had just gotten my first bike—a hand-me-down that I fell in love with at first sight. I never had training wheels and pretty much was self-taught, rolling through the alley, riding sidesaddle until working up the courage to throw my leg over the seat. Then came the day of reckoning, the day I decided I would brave out onto 19th Street.

I pushed up the gentle slope of the alley with all my might, zinging past the poplars and the mulberry bushes that gave shade that hot July morning. One last push and I would be speeding onto the concrete, where the big kids played. That was when it hit me—a '76 Mustang doing fifty in a twenty-five mph zone. My front tire folded in half and I was thrown over the hood of that car. The driver sped on and I dusted myself off. I wandered home more frightened than in pain and then tried to hide my bike behind the woodpile.

That night, I was grounded for a month for riding on the street.

BOBBY AND COOPER Mac watched in horror as the eighteen-wheeler screamed past, unsure for those few split seconds where or in how many pieces I would reappear. The startled truck driver yanked hard on his horn, but it was too late—he had already crested the hill and was disappearing around the next curve, leaving me still leaning hard against that guardrail, pelted with rubber and asphalt kicked up in his wake.

"You stupid fuck!" Bobby yelled.

"See what I mean?" I shouted back. "There's no logical reason whatsoever anybody would be walking on this side of the road. They'd be run down by the first car that came along."

"Amen and case closed," Cooper Mac said.

I mounted the third rung of the guardrail and squinted down into the long shadows. The boughs swayed gently and then a tapestry of greens, reds, and browns exploded into view as a gust of wind swung the leaves like sails into the late day sun. I mounted the second rung of the guardrail and stared down into the ravine. The moisture from last night's rain sat in small pools, the remnants of an ancient streambed. I pulled myself up to the third rung. Perhaps, it was the sun playing trickster, but those little pools suddenly went dry and dissolved into mosquito swarms hanging low like roiling fog.

I could feel the ravine breathe and beckon.

"Neither of you saw her leave work?" I shouted back.

Cooper Mac's eyes darted to Bobby.

"And neither of you has any clue who took her to that party?"

Bobby pulled a cigarette from his pocket.

"And neither of you has any clue who was even at that party?"
"Dude." Bobby lit the cigarette. "Everyone was at that party."
"I wasn't. You weren't. Cooper Mac wasn't."
"Point taken."
And so I threw a leg over the rail and started down.

I DIDN'T KNOW just how much the slope had crumbled beneath the asphalt until I threw my second leg over the guardrail. I tried to go hand over hand downward in search of solid ground, using the three rungs of guardrail as a hand ladder, but the slope was quick with damp sand and my bottom half was suddenly caught in an avalanche. I had no choice but to let go and hope for the best.

The broken road shot past, the loose earth turned solid against the wall of the ravine, and I went backwards head over feet, tumbling through a tangle of thickets, barbs clawing at me, branches snapping against my weight.

Pain shot around my skull as I slammed into the stump of a tree. This slowed me enough to let me catch a stray branch and turn myself. Dirt and sand hissed down around me. The branch I held to was thin, oily, long, and my hand was traveling too tightly down its length. When I finally tried to let go, the branch ricocheted up and away, taking a two-inch crescent of flesh from the soft spot between my left thumb and forefinger.

Day spun to dusk then all spun black.

I was at the bottom of the ravine, facedown in mud. I rolled and stared up at the little patches of dancing blue sky coming in through the trees. My spine felt in one piece and no bones were poking from the flesh. A welt was forming just above my right temple, but I wasn't dizzy. My left hand was my only concern. I would need it back at Benning. I squeezed at my wrist to stem the flow of blood and sucked at the flesh to see how deep the gash went.

The wound was ugly but not deep. This was my lucky day, I would survive, and so I began to laugh…but it was a laugh lacking mirth, a laugh of misery, a laugh of rage. This was the bed somebody had made for Tammy, a bed where she lay hidden from the world for six days.

I pushed myself up slowly, taking in the ravine floor as I went, careful not to upset the swarms of mosquitoes that hung in small clouds two feet above the water. The heat that had settled was the kind that had a stench to it, the kind that crawled across the skin, the kind that got into the pores, the kind so thick a person couldn't tell the difference between mud, sweat, and blood.

A fresh blanket of leaves covered the ravine floor, greens, reds, and browns camouflaging any evidence the police may have left behind…

Night was coming fast.

"There would be police tape…and markers pointing to where they found evidence…they would be prepared for the elements, they would raise the markers high enough off the ground to keep them from getting covered." I was speaking aloud to myself. For some reason, it made me feel not so alone. "They would use something bright, reflective. That way they could take wide photos of the crime scene and plot their map…but where would they take those wide shots? Where-o-where indeed?"

I had to get above the situation.

I worked my way back up the slope, testing branches for handholds and rocks for footing, crab-crawling my way up, wedging myself against the trunk of a small cedar rooted deep into the slope.

At that instant, a strong gust whipped down the length of the ravine, leaves scattered, and the cloud of mosquitoes lifted and spread. The mosquitoes found me and nipped, but it was a small price to pay, for once that top layer was removed, the matted and decomposing layer beneath was revealed, and up from that layer rose every glimmering piece of trash dumped or blown from the road—beer bottles, newspaper, a milk jug, a rotted shoe, a twisted nine iron, a fluttering yellow scrap of tape…

Bingo.

I slid back down into the ravine, snagging and uprooting the sapling to which the yellow tape was attached. I unfurled the tape and stretched it find the words…

—OLICE DO NOT—

It was the remnants of Crime-Scene Barrier Tape. Whoever was commanding the perimeter had come through to remove the crime-scene tape quickly, leaving an oblong polygonal border of ripped knots about fifty meters across and thirty meters wide. I had points of reference now and from those points of reference, evidence flags began emerging from the underbrush.

The first evidence flag sat four feet from a felled cottonwood. As I knelt for it, slapping away the gathering mosquitoes, the air hissed as a small object lost orbit and came splashing down through the tree branches right above me. Before I could raise an arm to protect my head—the small object dropped past my nose and buried itself in the mud. I dug for it, and predictably enough, found a shot misfired—a golf ball sent slicing past the sixth hole and over the road. I pocketed the golf ball and returned to the evidence flag. It read:

09/24/92		16:42
	PRADA, 6½, LT.	
N.H.P.		Cleared

The N.H.P. meant Nebraska Highway Patrol, I could only assume. Prada meant nothing to me. The rest was date and time stamping.

I crawled along the ravine floor, kicking aside leaves, my search taking me to the other side of the felled cottonwood tree.

09/24/92	16:49.
PRADA, 6½, RT. - HEEL BROKEN	
S.D.C.I.D.	Cleared - R.W.

"Prada is a brand name," I said aloud. "She was wearing high heels." I crawled faster, kicking aside leaves, racing the sun.

09/24/92	16:16
WOMAN'S RUGBY TOTE BAG-ZIPPER BROKEN **APPROX 25 LBS.-CONTENTS INTACT**	
Y.P.D.	— Contents custody Y.P.D

I suddenly felt dizzy. I rose and looked up at the guardrail looming forty feet above. I turned a circle, looked at the blood going thick in the palm of my hand. "Not possible though…Tammy hated high heels." I made my way back to the bottom of the slope and searched up through the thickets. I turned and scanned the ravine floor again. I would need a flashlight soon.

"If she were wearing high heels," I continued the monologue, "she would have taken them off along the way—that would explain the cuts on her feet…and if she'd tumbled through those thickets barefoot," I looked at my bloody hand again, "like I tumbled through them barehanded…"

Back and forth, I walked, looking for signs of footprints, for something, for anything—and then, right under my nose, right where I had stepped at least a dozen times, right at the edge of the slope, it appeared:

09/24/92	17:02
MEN'S TIMEX - WRIST BAND BROKEN	
C.C.S.D	Dusted and Cleared - wristband pin not recovered.

There was more though, far more. My eyes had fallen upon it, but my mind wasn't ready to make the leap. My stomach churned. I didn't want to look down. I wanted to climb the slope and go home. I was standing right where the wind couldn't reach, right where the leaves backed away, right at that sweet spot at the bottom of the slope. I gagged at the smell of decomposition—perhaps just a memory culled up from early childhood—my

THE HOMECOMING

first time turning over a rotting log maybe, or finding a dead squirrel in the road, gasping at its slithering maggot-ridden underbelly.

The smell was so real I could no longer deny it.

I was right atop it.

I had no choice but to look down.

THEY USED LIME-green reflective spray paint to outline her body. Most of the outline had faded with the rain, but what remained (when the fading light caught it just right) played like soft shadow against the creases of a bed just abandoned. Her left arm was outstretched near her face, her right arm tucked beneath her chin. She came to rest on her stomach, her left leg bent at the knee, as if cradled around another's hip.

This was the bed someone had made for her.

I backed away and stumbled across the ravine bottom until finding myself gripping the low branches of the bent cedar. There I purged the blood I'd swallowed from my hand, and there, through the stinging tears, the last piece to the puzzle, the piece my intuitive mind had been seeking, came into focus right at my heels.

ATOP THE HOOD of my Laser, Bobby and Cooper Mac, down to their last three cigarettes and long out of beer, whispered the rumor going round about the little boy with the bag of golf balls.

The little boy with the bag of golf balls would walk two miles from his grandpa's farm every Wednesday at the crack of dawn. He would make his way down 121, careful to walk the wide shoulder where the road weaved toward the river, careful to cross when he absolutely knew it was safe, careful to listen, because that was the only way a person could really tell, careful to crawl down the gentle slope, and not where the asphalt fell loose or the thickets grew thick.

The Club House gave him a half dollar per Top Flight, and sometimes a whole dollar for Pinnacles or Pro V. The white balls were the easiest to find, the wash of his flashlight bouncing quite nicely off their dimpled face. The green and yellow ones were harder, but if he were really looking, sometimes these would reveal themselves too. Once after a very windy weekend, the little boy with the bag of balls earned sixty-seven dollars. (Grandpa told him some of the money would have to go into his college fund.) Rumor was, early last Wednesday morning, the little boy tried to shake Tammy awake.

BOBBY AND COOPER Mac weren't prepared to see me crawling over the guardrail, my face pale and smeared with dried blood. It wasn't until I'd staggered halfway across the road that they finally came to my aid. They didn't touch me, not just yet, but circled and followed as I slowly raised my arm and offered Bobby the evidence flag.

THE HOMECOMING

09/24/92		16:12
	WOMAN'S JEANS	
Y.S.D.		Clear

"What does it mean?" Bobby asked.

Free of the evidence flag, I continued across the road and onto the golf course, dropping to my knees at the edge of the sand trap. The glimmer light was growing deep orange across the lake.

"Where did you find the flag?" Cooper asked as the two approached.

Cooper and Bobby knew where I had found the flag and knew why I had carried it up. They also knew why the color had run from my face and why I couldn't speak, but they had to ask and they had to have an answer.

"It wasn't near the body," I said. "They were taken off her and thrown against a tree." I looked up at Cooper Mac. "It wasn't a hit-and-run. She was raped and murdered in that ravine."

There was a silence.

"Cops sometimes plant false evidence to get rid of bad leads," Cooper Mac finally said. "They had to have known that people would be out here poking around. What other reason would they have to leave evidence flags just lying around for anybody to find?"

"It's how they map a crime scene and deal with chain of custody," I said. "The evidence flags were left behind for the FBI, who joined the case late."

"You said the FBI knew you were out here. Do you actually think," Cooper said, "that they would just sprinkle a trail of crumbs for you."

"Merrill, you need to have someone look at your hand," Bobby said. "I think we should take you into town now. Don't you think, Cooper?"

"Yeah, that sounds like a good idea."

"I'm going to watch the sunset now," I told them.

AND SO THEY stood guard over me as I watched the world go to night.

SHE WOULD LET me dream aloud as I sat next to her. How small we were when we gazed up, one star after another blinking down though the inky forever, my mind yearning heavenward, my heart yearning toward hers! I would tell her of all I wanted to do, the impossible dreams I would dream. She would just smile and tuck her head softly against mine, never saying a word, never sharing her own dreams…

But she had them.

I know that she had them.

I THINK IT'S time," Bobby said.

THE HOMECOMING

I dusted the sand from my hands and backward glanced. The glow of the dam in the distance, big and bright, cast soft on Bobby and Cooper's faces. They were tired, had been patient, and now it was time to go.

"You're right, Cooper—they wouldn't leave a trail of crumbs," I said. "They screwed up. She wouldn't go to a party on a farm in high heels."

"What?" Bobby asked.

"High heels were found not far from her body, one of them was broken," I said. "You're right—they did plant false leads." I got up and walked back toward the road. "The only pair of heels she owned was her work shoes. She hated them. Took them off every chance she could...so why would she be in high heels at a party on a farm?"

"She came to the party straight from the Dakota," Bobby said. "Maybe she forgot to bring her party shoes with her when she punched out."

I looked down and up the road. "It's as good of place as any."

"What is?" Cooper said gently.

"Right here," I answered.

"This place is as good as any for what?" Bobby asked.

I looked up and down the road again and then I turned at them. "You take a girl to a party. You get to talking, and as you get to talking, you talk her into driving off somewhere private 'just to talk.' She goes with you. You find a nice secluded place to park." I looked up and down the road again and then wagged a finger. "But not too secluded, mind you—that would make her too suspicious. Next to a golf course is good though. You can get out and walk, take off your shoes, go barefoot on the grass...especially if your feet have been hurting from wearing heels all night. She finally asks you what was so important that you had to leave the party and that's when you make your move. Only she wasn't expecting this move to be made, so she fights you and she fights you hard, harder than you expected, but you keep pushing, and things get rough, and you just can't stop..."

"What about the girl at the dam?" Cooper Mac said. "The one the fishermen said was a blonde?"

"She saw something," Bobby offered. "That makes it a group event."

"Tammy runs. Tries to make it across the road...*they're* chasing her, not *he*. Tammy is with a blonde and at least two other guys...possibly. Okay, I need to backtrack and rethink all this." I gazed up at the stars, drank in the lake, breathed in the fields. "The Stevenson farm," I pointed straight over the ravine and through the cornfields beyond it. "Lies a half mile that way."

"You're sure?" Bobby said.

I didn't answer—I just started walking.

THE HOMECOMING

CHAPTER TEN

IT WAS NEARLY October, Indian summer along the Missouri River bottom, which meant that unseasonably warm days were chased by abruptly cold nights, thus as soon as I had disappeared over the guardrail of the ravine, Bobby and Cooper quickly retreated to the warmth of my car.

Wafer thin ice, sparkling crystalline in the twilight, had formed atop the little pools of mud in the ancient streambed. The freeze was unnatural. It was colder down here than up above. It was as if the air were fighting to hold its warmth here and sucking what heat it could from what life still lingered upon the branches and ground. The foliage that still hung upon the trees went a slow and gentle white against a sliver of moon, giving the illusion of something beautiful taking shape where only resided death.

Upon the gentle slope that brought me out the far side of the ravine sat the remnants of an ancient wagon trail. Where the tree line ended, a switchback of barbed wire weaved up into the corn. This switchback was meant as a thoroughfare to divided pastures for grazing cattle, two of which, a yearling and her mother, stood chewing their cud.

I kept count, letting my hand glide over each cornstalk as I went.

After six hundred and twenty-two cornrows, I took a hard right and began descending ever so gently until emerging upon gravel one hundred and thirty-eight cornrows later.

I had been here, I was certain, but at night, the world looks different, sounds grow louder, shadows and shapes grow sharp, and color bleeds to gray. I had missed my target by half a field. I was on the correct road, but the shadowy contour of the Stevenson shelterbelt sat a quarter-mile southwest.

I broke into a double-time, rounded into the corn, and was quickly back into the cottons, feeling my way over the spidery underbrush, toe-first going, doing my best at stealth beneath a cloudless, moonlit sky.

I came out on the other side confronted by flashlights bouncing through the darkness just ahead. I backed behind the chicken coops and got my bearings—the flashlights were coming from inside the farmhouse. There were at least a half a dozen people inside and flashlights meant that whatever was going on in there was being done covertly. I ducked out from the chicken coops and tucked myself against the west end of the house, masking my shadow with the shadow of the overturned swing-set.

I glanced up at the window in search of the bounce of the flashlights. Had they heard or seen me cross they would have either killed their light or aimed out into the darkness to track my movement.

There was the bounce still.

They had propped a loading ramp from the back door to the bed of a black 4X4. The loading ramp sat just a few inches above the dilapidated porch, and just to the other side was the 4X4 driven earlier today by Detectives Dickson and Harper. I knew with whom I was dealing.

I searched the back of the 4X4. Turned on its side was an old loveseat, the upholstery scorched by cigarette burns. Wedged next to the loveseat were two rolls of shag carpeting, one mildewed through to its bottom.

From the back foyer came the bounce of the flashlights, followed by heavy footsteps and men grunting beneath the weight of a load. Not enough time to make it back to the shelterbelt, I ducked between the broken porch and loading ramp. The screen door ached open and the ramp sunk against my chest, four men above me hauling a couch.

As they slid the couch onto the truck bed, one of the men hopped off the ramp, and for the briefest instant, his eyes met mine.

OUT ON COUNTY 121, across from the ravine, Bobby and Cooper Mac had just dug up $8.32 in change from the floor of my car and had made the decision to return to town for more beer and gas.

The night took an abrupt turn, however, when a Nebraska Highway Patrol vehicle pulled alongside them. The patrolman shined his spotlight, got on his loudspeaker, and asked, "Which one of you is Bobby Grant?"

Bobby shielded his eyes from the light and Cooper Mac pointed.

"FBI would like to ask you a few questions," the patrolman said, "get in front of me and I'll follow you back to the bridge."

HAD I WAITED a moment longer beneath the loading ramp, the man who had jumped off and met me eye to eye would have not written me off as a figment of his imagination. He swung his flashlight into the narrow space where he thought he'd seen the glimmer of eyes staring him back, but discovered nothing save unpopulated air. My roll under of the broken porch steps and scramble beneath the idling truck went smoothly and silently until I discovered the sleeping dog chained to the front bumper—a Doberman, trained to attack at the first smell of blood.

The Doberman woke before I could react and had her jaws around my wrist. Something metal near the radiator spun at my head as I tried to roll to my belly and twist away. She fought to keep hold, but something hot went up against her spine. She let out a frightened yelp and my arm was free. The frightened yelp gave warning to the men above me. The snapping jaws came at my throat again. I tried to kick back the way I came, but the dog stretched herself atop me. I twisted and pressed myself against the passenger's wheel to gain leverage—barely room to breathe—and forced my legs around the dog's torso. She was nearly at my throat and I let her get closer, close enough for me to lock my ankles and squeeze the air from her chest. The more the dog thrashed, the tighter I was able to lock in my scissor grip. Still, her jaws were close to my throat, so I clamped them shut with my good hand and took her throat with my other. The fight was perfectly fair until I discovered her choke collar. She knew what was to come and tried backing away. I yanked hard and her puppy eyes bulged, and within moments, she was dead still in my arms.

I slowly and silently unhooked my ankles and pulled her close to check her windpipe. The carotid arteries were still pumping blood to the brain and nothing was crushed. The only sound I could hear now was the idling engine and the dog rasping low, sleepy breaths.

The men atop the truck bed were standing dead still, listening for one of us to emerge from beneath the truck.

One short sprint to the cottonwoods and I would be a ghost, but in those twenty paces, all one of them would have to do is draw his sidearm and fire—and likewise I would be a ghost. I had two options, neither a thrill—stay beneath the truck, let them catch me, suffer unknown consequences, or make a run for it and risk taking a bullet.

I rolled myself free of the 4X4 and ran.

What I wasn't expecting was some fancy driving. By the time I had gotten halfway to the cottonwoods, Dickson and Harper's 4X4 was spinning a wide circle to cut me off, its floodlights blazing me down.

Cut off from the cottons, I darted around the east side of the house. I veered, ducked through the overturned swing-set, the other 4X4 behind me now, and cut a tight path to the front of the house. They would have me pinned once we all rounded the corners—there was no escaping that. I had no choice but to skid to a stop and vanish.

WHEN THE HIGHWAY patrolman had run my plates, he had assumed Cooper Mac was yours truly, and so let Bobby and Cooper pass to get on the bridge. As he did, he radioed across that Marc Merrill and Bobby Grant were on their way.

AT ONCE, THE two trucks came around the corners of the house and slammed their brakes. The game of hide-and-seek should have ended right there, but the drivers had blinded each other with their lights.

There was an old maple, its low branch scarred from the rope of a tire swing. This old maple with the scarred branch reached over the front eaves of the farmhouse. I didn't like the idea of being trapped like a raccoon, men with guns and flashlights beneath me, but I only planned on keeping the high ground long enough to build up speed.

"There he goes, there he goes!" One of them shouted as I bounded from the roof of the house to the roof of the 4X4, to the lawn, to the firebreak, and out onto the gravel road. Flashlights swung my way, but before they could reach me, I vanished with a sidelong dive into the corn.

A SOUTH DAKOTA Highway Patrol vehicle was waiting for Bobby Grant and Cooper Mac on the north side of the bridge.

DICKSON AND HARPER'S 4X4 plowed a path along the fence line until getting ahead of me, while the other 4X4 stuck to the gravel. Going blindly through the corn, I followed the natural terrain of the valley, moving at a full sprint toward low ground. I hoped that I would either make it the long way back to the ravine, or that I would stumble upon another stand of trees. In the trees, the men in the trucks would be forced to dismount and take to foot.

As I moved further into the valley, the corn became riper, and riper corn meant fields ready for harvest. The 4X4 to my left had gotten ahead of me, so when I stumbled onto the first of several plowed rows I was able to retreat back into the corn. The drivers didn't make that mistake twice, and as the chase progressed, as I leapt one fence after another, I soon found myself trapped. Intersecting power lines not far ahead pointed to gravel roads in my path, and the building of a gentle breeze, to the plowed fields beyond.

When the men knew they had me boxed up and ready to be delivered, they hopped from the trucks, armed themselves, and formed a wagon-wheel skirmish line to flush me onto gravel. There was nothing more I could do but crouch and wait for one of them to make a mistake.

BOBBY WAS LED past dispatch, through a processing area, and past the black-and-white security monitors. These monitors were attached to cameras that watched down upon the pacing, sleeping, shouting, singing, shitting, masturbating miscreants serving out terms in the county jail. It was purely for shock value that the local police brought him through this way instead of taking him straight through the back door to Interrogation.

The room was small and blue, lit only by an open-faced fluorescent. Here, Bobby remained until Special Agents Carriss and Earnstead were fully certain his bladder had stretched beyond capacity.

I CROUCHED NOT twenty feet from Dickson and watched as he swung his arm over his head and threw it forward to signal his men into the corn. They took tentative steps at first, their feet clumping heavy with mud until they figured out how best to step.

I backed and backed, trying to maintain distance, waiting for the perfect moment to break through their ranks, that moment when one of them stumbled or turned their gaze. The game continued until I found myself within three rows of being pushed onto gravel. The perfect moment wasn't coming on its own, so I picked up the hardest dirt clod I could find, one held together by roots and gravel, a cornstalk poking through its center. I tested the clod in my hand. It had the weight and feel of a German potato-masher grenade.

I meant to miss the man, to send the potato-masher over his head and slapping into the corn behind him. Instead, I hit him right between the eyes—not hard enough to drop him cold, just hard enough to make him mad.

There was a moment of confusion that followed and then the unmistakable sound of rounds being chambered in pump-action shotguns.

I slid forward a cornrow and...

"BOOM!" went a shotgun!
Slice went steel shot over my head…
Down came corn fronds like confetti around me…
And from everywhere thirteen pheasants took to foot and flight…

The birds made so much noise that I was able to leap up and crash through the skirmish line. Weapons swung to follow me, but I was a ghost moving at full sprint, not slowing a step until finally leaping the barbed wire that switched back and forth along the path of the old wagon trail leading down to the ravine. The two cows were gone, but the headlights weren't, the 4X4s plowing through the fields brighter and brighter my way.

Moments later, I was back on County 121 and as I caught my breath, fear turned to anger and flight to fight, and so I paced back and forth the double yellow lines, waiting for Dickson and Harper to come.

Come they did, but only as far as the barbed wire beyond the ravine. They shone their floodlights through the treetops until finding me on the road, beckoning them to come. They drove the fence looking for easy access around, but finally their floodlights went out.

A few moments later, there were indistinct shouts and engines roaring. I watched with a smile as spinning fountains of mud rose over the treetops some fifty feet high. They had buried their trucks and were only making matters worse. I listened as they revved and revved and cursed and cursed and then I grew bored. After that, I spent an hour walking up and down the road in search of my missing friends and the car I had entrusted to them.

Finally, I resigned myself to a twelve-mile hike home.

CHAPTER ELEVEN

A SCENE

SPECIAL AGENT CARRISS: So, in the initial statement you made to the police you said that you left work at least a half an hour before Tammy. What you failed to mention was your return.
BOBBY: I didn't take her to that party.
SPECIAL AGENT EARNSTEAD: Bobby, think about it. If ten different people say that they see you arriving at the party with Tammy, and one person — that being you — says this didn't happen, who do you think we're going to believe?
BOBBY: Ten people said they saw me and Tammy come to the party together?
SPECIAL AGENT CARRISS: Give or take.
BOBBY: What ten people?
SPECIAL AGENT CARRISS: We have names.
BOBBY: Ten people saw us arrive at the party?
SPECIAL AGENT EARNSTEAD: You're denying this?
BOBBY: No, I'm... No, I just want to know, before I say anything else, what ten people we're talking about here... I mean, not one person said they saw Tammy come with... Come with somebody else?
SPECIAL AGENT CARRISS: Bobby, we don't believe you were the primary agent involved in her death, but we do think you were involved.
SPECIAL AGENT EARNSTEAD: We have reason to believe people have been coerced into making false statements. People have been threatened... If you happen to be one of these people who have been threatened, you need to let us know.

(A magnificently long pause.)

BOBBY: I punched out a half an hour before Tammy.
SPECIAL AGENT CARRISS: Yes, we went over that.
SPECIAL AGENT EARNSTEAD: And have the timecards to verify.
BOBBY: I went home and took a shower... And, uh, then came back and picked her up to go to the party...

(Carriss scribbles a note.)

SPECIAL AGENT EARNSTEAD: You're sure, Bobby?
BOBBY: Yes.

SPECIAL AGENT CARRISS: You arrive at the party when?
BOBBY: About 10:00… A little bit later than the crowd. That's why I… why I didn't understand how, uh, how ten people could have seen us arrive.
SPECIAL AGENT EARNSTEAD: How do you figure?
BOBBY: You can't see the gravel road from the backyard of the farmhouse, not at night, not with the bonfire burning, or with the noise…

(Bobby scratches at a spider bite.)

BOBBY (CONT'D): That shelterbelt is pretty thick.
SPECIAL AGENT CARRISS: *(mumbles)* Bobby showers.
SPECIAL AGENT EARNSTEAD: *(mumbles)* Tammy doesn't.
BOBBY: What?
SPECIAL AGENT CARRISS: Nothing, no, it's probably nothing. It's just odd that you would take the time to shower before going out to a party on a farm, what with the smell of smoke that gets into your clothing and taking into account that she didn't shower herself… It's just odd.
BOBBY: I'm hygienic.
SPECIAL AGENT EARNSTEAD: What was she wearing that night, Bobby? Did she leave the Dakota in her work clothes? Did she change when you came to get her? Did she change clothes on the drive over?
BOBBY: She changed in my car.
SPECIAL AGENT CARRISS: So, she was pretty comfortable in front of you?
BOBBY: Huh?
SPECIAL AGENT CARRISS: To get naked in front of you.
SPECIAL AGENT EARNSTEAD: It suggests intimacy.
BOBBY: Or that she didn't see me as a threat… She didn't get naked though. She was able to get her jeans on under her skirt. She'd kick her legs up on my windshield, smudge my windshield, and with one big yank, she'd be dressed.
SPECIAL AGENT EARNSTEAD: Smudge? With her footprint?
BOBBY: You're trying to say this was some kind of a date. Some kind of a date that went bad. If that's the case, I'll take my public defender right now.
SPECIAL AGENT CARRISS: Relax, Bobby.
SPECIAL AGENT EARNSTEAD: What kind of shoes was she wearing, Bobby?
BOBBY: High heels. Her work shoes. Prada.
SPECIAL AGENT CARRISS: Strange thing.
BOBBY: *(suddenly confident)* Going to a party in high heels? Not if she forgot her loafers… Not if she's in such a rush that she thinks she's packed them, but really left them on the steps leading up to the projection booth.
SPECIAL AGENT CARRISS: So it *wasn't* a date for you?

BOBBY: I never said that either.
SPECIAL AGENT EARNSTEAD: She did carry an awfully big bag that night, which makes us believe she had plans to stay out… maybe to sleep at your place?
BOBBY: She always carried that bag, ask anybody.
SPECIAL AGENT CARRISS: She in a ponytail that night?
BOBBY: Her hair? I don't remember.
SPECIAL AGENT CARRISS: Really?

(Another grand pause as Bobby considers his fate.)

BOBBY: I stranded her, is that what those people told you?
SPECIAL AGENT EARNSTEAD: I don't know. You tell us.
BOBBY: Yes… Jesus, I felt stupid when she didn't see it my way. I'd been *(sinks into his chair)* I'd been planning the night all week. Jesus Christ, she was the one who invited me, and when I discovered it *wasn't* a date in her eyes…
SPECIAL AGENT CARRISS: You got mad?
BOBBY: I got embarrassed! Jesus, I didn't think she would have any problems getting a ride home that night. My God, she was the most popular girl I knew. Any guy would have cut off their pinkie to get the chance to… be with her.
SPECIAL AGENT CARRISS: *(rips a fresh piece of paper from his notebook)* Okay then, Bobby, what we're going to need is a list. A list of everybody you can remember who was at that party. If you could group them into who was hanging out with whom, this would be very helpful to us. Think carefully, because we do compare these lists. Once you have that done, we'll find you a ride home.

THE HOMECOMING

CHAPTER TWELVE

AND SO AS Bobby set about recalling all the names of the people at the party, reconsidering some of the names and scratching them from the list for fear of reprisal, adding a few other names to settle old scores, Agents Carriss and Earnstead retreated down the hall to brew up a fresh pot of coffee.

"Bobby Grant has told a fib or two in his life," Earnstead said.

"Uh-huh?" Carriss said.

"We need to get him on the polygraph."

"Uh-huh," Carriss said.

"So you think we should hold him overnight?" Earnstead asked.

"No," Carriss said, "I think we should cut him loose, let him go home, give him a taste of freedom, let him sleep on it, and then we sweep down hard, offer the polygraph as a way out. It's late anyway...and you need sleep."

THE PHOTOCOPY OF the notebook came to Special Agent Earnstead anonymously that night, left at the front desk of the Super 8 out on Highway 50. The original notebook had been misplaced, if you could call it that, as it passed through the chain of custody. However, certain honest members of the local law-enforcement community had long ago learned to safeguard against such loss by routing certain bits of pertinent evidence through the library copy-machine before final processing. The 164 pages of laser copy that came to Earnstead were stuffed inside an unmarked manila envelope.

Earnstead had dealt with this before so knew no amount of forensic or investigative work would ever indicate how the notebook arrived or who had sent it. Whoever had gone through the trouble would leave no trace.

Earnstead tossed the photocopied notebook, all 164 pages of it, on the nightstand, kicked off his shoes, and threw himself down on the bed in hopes of catching a good three hours of eyes tightly shut. If all went as planned, he'd have the chance to give his wife a call in the morning, shower, coffee up, and be ready to hit it before his partner borrowed the key from the front desk and invited himself into the room. It was Earnstead's belief that Carriss had gone the past year and a half of their partnership entirely without sleep.

Earnstead stared at the ceiling. They had been awake for the past three days and the painkillers he had been taking for a back injury were making the Spackle swim. Finally, the manila envelope and its contents got the best of him. Whoever sent it knew what he or she or they were doing. They had photocopied the cover of the notebook along with the inside leaf, and done so in color so to ensure as little decay of forensic information as possible.

There was nothing on the photocopied cover, save a few marijuana-leaf tracings and the word MIND chiseled over with ballpoint again and again. On the page photocopied from the inside cover, was a doodle of a skateboarder extending an oversized middle finger, oversized cigarette dangling from his oversized lips, skateboard and half-pipe ramp floating beneath him.

Earnstead immediately had two conflicting theories about the artist. His first theory was that the young man (and he was certain it was a young man) came from a family environment overly lenient and lacking in affection, possibly a broken home. His second theory was that the young man was raised in a highly repressive home, one also lacking in affection but dominated by a hyper-religious father who ruled with an iron fist, a biblical literalist, a spanker who enjoyed it. These were the two cases he knew best—years of abuse erupting in violence unfocused, unpredictable, and on a grand scale.

Earnstead yearned to be home with his wife and dreaded turning to the next page. Careful reading, Earnstead warned himself, as he rubbed his tired eyes. This was his job and time was a factor. He turned to the first page:

> They say I have to do this fucking journal for the stupid fucking family therapist at the fucking hospital and I have to write two fucking pages a day and it can be anything I want, anything at all, so I'm just going to write fuck, fuck

The print was neat and the theme continued relentlessly for six pages. On page seven, a new theme emerged—"everything has to die." From that page forward, Earnstead learned a bit about the author of the notebook and his family situation—eldest child of four, two parents at home, the father being the biological parent of only the youngest three. "Black-sheep syndrome?"

The author remained cryptic and did not share his name.

By page thirteen, Earnstead's eyes went heavy and the words blurred into bleeding-black mush. The Super 8 had put a wonderfully comfortable chair in the corner and the lamp above it warmed a glow that melted

Earnstead and sent one page after another spilling to the floor. A funny thing happened though in those melting moments when sleep cradled up against Earnstead and time softened its desperate ticking. That everyday mind of his shut down, and the deeper, darker mind, the one that resided in the shadows, the one able to look past the words, words, words, slipped free of its bonds and began to play. It was shadow-mind now looking at the squiggle of the S and the slashing dot of the baby j.

It was shadow-mind playing upon the page, dancing, prancing over 'n under the words, dangling from modifiers, splitting its way infinitively, voweling syllables in ways that have never been voweled before. One page after another, on and on it went, quicker than the blinking eye. The shadow-mind played faster and faster, flipping, flipping, flipping, flipping…and then on page forty-two shadow-mind came across Ms. T.

Ms. T always found herself crossed bigger at the top, not with a slash but with a crooked little crinkle that rose high with a splash of dash…or, perhaps, a dash of splash. The words, words, words that came after Ms. T and before Ms. T and around Ms. T always seemed much more…much more…much more…much more **something**. Shadow-mind couldn't wrap himself around why Ms. T didn't play like all the rest, and so halfway down page fifty-six, shadow-mind shook Earnstead awake. Earnstead gathered himself to his feet, gathered up the pages, and moved fast with his highlighter pen.

That was where Carriss found him two hours later.

Earnstead raised the pages at his partner, a sparkle in his eye. "Locals **have been** holding out on us, Special Agent Carriss!" Earnstead handed the pages to Carriss. "I highlighted a few portions you might find interesting."

Carriss put on his reading glasses and flipped until he found:

I admit I play with T's mind…
T makes love to me forever…
I wait for T in my bed…
If this is love,
I'll take it on my face!

THE HOMECOMING

Carriss dropped onto Earnstead's chair and turned a few pages deeper:

> Someone special sent me here to change her.
> We made love forever.
> She is the greatest to me.
> I have no girl, no car, but I have pot.
> I treated her like shit.
> I would give my life just to hold her.
> I am taking her to L.A. with me
> Even if I have to kill her.
> Kill Tammy,
> Yeah I thought about it.

Carriss pulled off his glasses. "The locals held this back from us?" Earnstead gave Carriss a shrug—he was ink-giddy from too much face-time with the pages. "We know who the author is?" Carriss asked.

"Eric Stukel, I'm thinking, though he doesn't say outright. It matches the facts thus far though," Earnstead said. "His name has come up. And look, look, look." Earnstead took the pages from Carriss and flipped to the end. "Somebody took the time to lift an impression off the back."

"Last few pages were torn out?" Carriss asked.

It was an old trick involving the smearing of graphite to lift impressions left behind from the indentation of pencil or pen. It was an old trick, but at times old tricks worked, and this time the message was unmistakably clear…

> I WANT TO
> FUCK T'S COLD
> BODY ON A
> COLD SLAB!

"Okay," Carriss said. "Let's go mark our territory."

I DIDN'T THINK about much of anything that last half a block home. It was Wednesday, I was certain, and on Thursday, I would be flying back to Fort Benning. I had no choice about this—the government owned me—but there were questions yet unanswered and I did have the time. All I needed to do was stay awake. I walked into the house and made straight for the sink, where I ran my wounded hand under cold water until it was numb enough for the iodine. I did a little dance through the house to shake away the pain of the iodine. This dance led me finally to the refrigerator where I found a note:

> **Breakfast**
> **Haas residence.**
> **8:00 A.M.**
> **Go in uniform.**
> **Dad.**

The clock read 8:45 A.M.
Shit.
My shoes were neatly spit-shined and sitting dress-right-dress beneath my uniform, which somehow got freshly dry-cleaned. My brass was polished and my medals re-pinned. There were also a few pairs of new jeans and shirts, several sizes larger, sitting on my bed—parents sure do okay sometimes.
By 9:00 A.M., I was dressed and ready to make a late and apologetic entrance. Unfortunately, my friends had misplaced my car, forcing me to trudge the great wide open of Memorial Park.
I did my best to feel nothing as I walked.
Fifteen minutes later, I was there.

YES, IT IS his notebook!" Detective Dickson shouted at Carriss and Earnstead. "But he has an alibi! Little sister hears Eric come home at 10:00 P.M. Tammy Haas doesn't even show up at the Stevenson party till a quarter after that. If we bring Stukel in based upon that notebook, and he's backed up by that alibi, we'll be fucked right back to square one!"
"You deliberately withheld evidence from the FBI!" Carriss shouted.
"It's our case, old man!"
Carriss stepped right up in Dickson's face. "Your case?"
"Gentlemen!" Earnstead squeezed between the two.
"What!" Dickson and Carriss said at once.
"Does the Stukel family have money?"
"What does that have to do with anything?" Dickson said.
"I'm just thinking that if we nudge," Earnstead said, "the Stukel's will go for a polygraph to take some heat off the family."
Dickson backed away from Carriss. "Yeah, they have money."
"And are lawyered to the teeth—I'll tell you that for nothing," Police Chief Fuller said, entering the room. "And the lawyers are coming at us hard."

They were supposed to be meeting in the conference room for the 0915 interdepartmental briefing, but things escalated in another direction when Carriss slammed down the photocopied notebook right under Dickson's nose.

"We need a paper trail," Carriss said. "P.Y.A. in every damn direction as far as the FBI is concerned. We need to know what's being put on record in Nebraska, what's being put on record here in South Dakota. We need ducks in a row and marching lockstep."

"PEE-WHY-what?" Harper whispered to Dickson.

"Protect Your Ass," Dickson whispered back.

The swelling had gone down, but Harper still had a nice gash between the eyes, four stitches worth, courtesy of a potato-masher badly aimed.

"We need a search warrant for the Stukel property, the kid's car if he has one would be nice," Earnstead said. "All of this kept low-key if we could."

"Warrant's on its way to the Circuit Judge, South Dakota side." Chief Fuller said. "The judge wants to look over the kid's alibi before signing off."

"Judge goes our way," Dickson said, "we'll have his car by noon...and be in his house by 3:00 P.M. I'm guessing it's the break we need."

REVEREND FARMER WAS right there to answer, when I finally knocked on Tammy's front door at 0920. Farmer had been spending a lot of time with Tammy's mom since her husband died and perhaps this was what had been creating the rift between mother and daughter. "Merrill." Farmer pulled me through the door. "You just missed breakfast."

I couldn't help noticing the new sign over the front door as we entered:

ANGELS WATCH OVER THIS HOUSE

I couldn't say those angels were doing much of a job.

The message my father had taped to the refrigerator was oblique enough that I entered the situation with no clue as to what to expect...besides a missed breakfast, but this is what I gleaned from the seating arrangement—a vote was taken to send the recent Homecoming royalty, Brain Slobacek, and girlfriend Katherine Noland, to the house as representatives of their class. They arrived bearing a spray of flowers that the student council had purchased from a fund-drive the afternoon prior. They only planned to stay as long as courtesy dictated before skipping home to get high and have sex in Brian's sauna (a habit Brian developed to burn off weight during wrestling season.) Tammy's two aunts were there too and two of Tammy's friends who had gone off to college this fall. Tammy's brothers were notably absent, back in school trying desperately to make up a week's worth of homework.

Reverend Farmer had taken a seat on the piano bench on the south side of the room. This raised him a few inches above the rest of us and thus created, for all practical purposes, a pulpit. He had the Holy Bible opened and bookmarked in several places, along with about ten pages of handwritten notes, and when I had arrived, he was just getting on a roll.

I declined a breakfast plate, but did accept coffee, and when the coffee arrived, it came with a slice of angel food cake. I took the last seat available, on the left hand corner of the couch, next to two shoeboxes of cards, probably five-hundred in number, most of which had yet to be opened. I kept a close eye on my bandage, watching carefully the blood slowly seeping up through the gauze. The last thing I wanted to do was make an awkward situation worse by dripping on the living room carpet.

Once we were settled again, Reverend Farmer dropped upon his piano-bench pulpit to continue where he had left off. "What we were discussing, Merrill, was dealing with the uncomfortable emotions we might experience over the next few days with all that has happened. For example, if you feel the need to talk about what has happened, you can express those feelings in a letter. If you're dealing with issues of anger or hurt, you can stop those thoughts right where you are with some prayerful reflection, asking yourself, 'do I have the right to these emotions?'" Farmer smiled. "The wonderful part is that when you have Jesus, you don't have to bother anybody else with these problems—you just take it to the Lord in prayer. You see, it is *your* sin that brought death into the world, so before you go on blaming or complaining, you must remember it's *your* fault. You were the one who nailed Jesus to that Cross, but Jesus loves you, so you must be obedient and careful in questioning those in authority, you must not concern yourselves with answers, because Jesus *is* the answer. The curse of original sin is yours and mine. Hit-and-runs happen all the time and have been happening since that day Eve ate the—"

"Um," I interrupted.

Heads turned my way.

"This may not be the right time for it." I choose my words carefully. "I've been out on County 121—out to the ravine—and I'm not really so sure it was a hit-and-run after all. I mean none of this makes sense just yet and none of this even seems real—"

Dishes clattered somewhere in the kitchen. Little did I know that Tammy's mom had vanished from the room, and now the sink was running full blast—the sound meant to muffle her weeping. Reverend Farmer bristled. One of the aunts hurried into the kitchen. Katherine Noland glanced to the front door. The rest of them just glared at me. Brian shook his head and smiled a twinkle of delight. "Nice one, Merrill, really nice."

As fortune had it though, the bandage held, not one drop spilt.

MY FATHER AND I shared words beginning with: "I just had a very uncomfortable phone conversation with Reverend Farmer."

What came next: "I'm not in the mood for a lecture."

That, for the record, was the first time in my life I had ever turned my back on my father and walked away. This stumped him, but only for an instant, and soon he was chasing me down the hallway. "Are you brain-dead," he said, "or do you just not care?"

"Bit of both, I suppose."

"You spend Night One out in the cemetery and Night Two out in that damned ravine," he said. "I'm bewildered and your mother is traumatized to cotton-picking hell. What sort of sick fantasy are you trying to play out?"

"Yeah, that's it, Dad—I'm sick and living out a fantasy."

"You're an adult—your actions are your choice, but—"

"Gee, thanks, Dad—"

"But when you inflict yourself on others, we run into problems."

"I'm an affliction now?"

"You're twisting my words."

I raised my bandaged hand. "I have to go put something on this."

"A friend of yours—" He followed me to the bathroom. "—Detective Dickson stopped by school this morning."

"Dickson!" I spun. "He was one of the cops at that farm who—"

"Think about Mom. Think about me. We have to live and work in this town. We have reputations to consider. Think about the Haas family, what they're going through. Think about that uniform you pledged your life to. Think about your role in the church. You need to set a Christian example."

"Oh, really…'But God will smash the heads of his enemies, crushing the skulls of those who love their guilty ways. The Lord says, "I will bring my enemies down from Bashan; I will bring them up from the depths of the sea. You, my people, will wash your feet in their blood, and even your dogs will get their share!"' so says Psalms 68," I answered.

"You're taking that from the Old Testament!" he shouted.

"'All scripture is inspired by God and is useful for teaching, for refutation, for correction, and for training in righteousness,' 2 Timothy 3:16."

"Conversation over," Dad said and marched away.

I HAD TWELVE hours before my flight to Benning, the last three spent on the road. That gave me, if my math was correct, nine hours to make some sort of peace with Yankton. That meant answers. Answers, as it turned out, were getting harder and harder to come by. My parents wouldn't help me. My friends wanted nothing more than to un-sober themselves. The local police had crossed state lines to remove evidence from a farmhouse, and when they found me lurking about, armed themselves and chased me through a cornfield. I couldn't continue this quest alone. I needed an Ace or two.

THE FIRST THING I learned about the FBI was that they didn't let you come to them on your own terms, thus I burned two-and-a-half more hours waiting in that little blue interrogation room downtown.

While I waited, I occupied my mind with a rewrite of the past summer, what might have happened had I not joined the Army. It was an exercise in futility, a mind-game ending only in self-flagellation, yet still I hit the replay button and returned to the scene in the park, to the sprinklers coming to life right on cue, to the words whispered, to a choice born not of courage, but fear.

"Looks like you have a thing or two on your mind," Earnstead said as he entered. "Sorry for the wait." Earnstead sat and gave me a genuine smile.

"Please don't tell me it was a hit-and-run," I said. "I'm not stupid."

"Ah," Earnstead said and then dug in his pocket for a pen. "We are glad you came down tonight, because we did want to talk to you about your relationship with Tammy." Earnstead dug into his other pockets and then stood and turned a circle to search the floor.

I handed him my pen.

"Thank you." Earnstead tested the pen by making ovals in the margin of his notepad. "Or if you like, we could start off," he said, "by you telling me why you think Tammy wasn't hit-and-run."

"You want a list?"

"Sure."

"Multiple autopsies, my friends keeping secrets from me, the FBI called in to investigate, an exhumation in the middle of the night, two fishermen seeing a girl threatened at the dam, talk of fibers found on the body, her body half-clothed, South Dakota police out of their jurisdiction, busy removing evidence from a farmhouse…"

"What were you doing out at the Stevenson farm anyway?"

"Getting shot at."

Carriss walked into the room right then and said, "You got shot at?"

Earnstead leaned back in his chair and shared a look with Carriss. "The thing is," Earnstead said, "Dick Dickson and Tony Harper claim they saw you and Bobby Grant tampering with evidence flags out on 121. According to them, they tried to shoo you away and you ran, eventually trespassing on nearby farmland. They fired a warning shot, but you kept running. They didn't get too excited, knowing you'd eventually turn up. They also said you were out at the Stevenson farm earlier that morning snooping around."

"Ah," I said.

"Tampering with evidence in a criminal investigation is serious business, Merrill," Earnstead said, "that could get a person in serious-hot water."

"That's why I thought I might mention Dickson and Harper," I said.

"All of this must be very difficult for you," Carriss said. "Hell, I remember going through Basic Training myself. We both do. Hard enough losing all connection with the real world, but then to lose somebody you care about? To have that be the way you come home?" Carriss took pause. "I'm not speaking out of line when I suggest that you cared for Tammy, am I?"

"It's a terrible thing. Terrible thing," Earnstead said. "Couldn't imagine anything worse. I'm just impressed at how you've handled it so far."

"Hundred-percent soldier," Carriss said. "Through and through."

They both sat back and waited for me to react.

"Could one of you just please talk to me?" I pleaded. "Nobody will talk to me. My God, I don't know if she was stabbed, shot, beaten to death. And the only thing that's holding me together right now—"

"You have questions," Carriss said.

"I don't wanna know, but I *have to* know. And I don't know if that makes any sense to you, but I'm in Hell right now and—"

"Her neck was broken," Carriss said.

The gash on my left hand slowly opened and began to bleed.

"You need a drink?" Earnstead dug in his pocket for change. "A cola?"

I rubbed my bandage flat, shook my head.

"You came to tell us Tammy wasn't hit-and-run, thank you," Carriss said. "Now you have to ask yourself if you actually think the FBI would be on the case if we didn't already know that. You have to ask yourself if the FBI would even bother if there weren't questions about how this investigation has been handled by the local police thus far."

"I thought I heard you tell my mother it was a matter of jurisdiction," I said. "Tammy being from South Dakota, her body winding up in Nebraska."

"Well," Carriss tried for a smile. "That's one of the reasons."

"I didn't think it was possible to do more than one autopsy."

Earnstead looked to Carriss.

"It kind of isn't…but we needed to attempt a rape kit," Carriss said.

"Rape?" I said and felt my body go light and mind go distant.

"You're sure you don't need a drink of water?" Earnstead said.

"You asked me about my relationship with Tammy. I don't understand."

"What we try to do when we analyze cases like this is get insight into the victim," Carriss said. "We're looking for anything really—history of problems in the family, troubles at school, troubles at home, the way the victim dressed even, any sudden changes in their appearance, dating habits, or in the case of rape, prior history of promiscuity, sexual assault—"

"Sexual assault?" I said.

Carriss and Earnstead glanced to each other.

"Your friend Bobby did mention the possibility," Earnstead said, "that Tammy had been raped in the past. If there's any truth to this, we'd really like to know."

"Bobby told you that Tammy had been raped?"

"She wouldn't have kept this from you?" Carriss asked.

"You've, uh, you've talked to Bobby Grant? He isn't a suspect, is he?"

"Relax, we just got to town," Carriss said. "We know very little about Yankton…so we conduct interviews with friends and family."

"Hundreds of them." Earnstead was half reminding Carriss.

"And time is a factor," Carriss said. "So forgive us if we cut to the—"

"Tammy was never raped."

"Just asking if it was a possibility," Earnstead said.

"And being that we're trying to exhaust all possibilities," Carriss said, "what we'd really like to talk to you about is Tammy's dating habits."

"Meaning what?" I asked.
"Was she the promiscuous type?"
I rose. "I need that drink of water now."

CARRISS AND EARNSTEAD placed a wager. Earnstead was convinced I was going to walk right past the water fountain and out the front doors. Carriss assumed I just needed a minute to breathe. At stake: twenty dollars.

HE WAS JUST standing over it, entranced by the lulling spurt of water rising up from its spout, stopping and dancing in midair before spiraling down onto the silvery drain tray. The silvery drain tray reflected up his face, distorting it like a funhouse mirror, and this enthralled him. He had his palm across the water-fountain's button and just couldn't let go. He just stared at the water arcing up and splashing down, and at his shadowy reflection glimmering beneath. Here was where the water crested its peak on its short journey away from the river, and from here, it would return down through the sewage back from where it came. He liked the waste of it and he liked the feel of the sedatives he had stolen from his mother's vanity, the sedatives stolen to make their questions easier.

There he stood as I rounded the corner in search of my drink—Eric Stukel. This was three times now our paths had crossed—the first time was at the party. I was squeezed into the corner of the kitchen as he loomed to ask for a light. I didn't recognize him then. The second time was at the cemetery, across from me, swaying in the breeze, a standoff one might call it. Now, here he was, staring at the water splashing down. An ugly crunch—his temple would meet the sharp edge of the spout, the weight of both our bodies driving him down, his skull folding inward, a walnut-sized chunk of the temporal lobe scooped and grinded aside, blood and brain fluid oozing down the drain, his body slumping, dangling from the water fountain, hooked and twitching.

It was a thought...a thought driven by nothing perhaps...or had he done something to harm Tammy in the past?

Why else this hate?

Eric smiled a shrug at me, backed away, rounded a corner, and before I could move to action, he was gone.

ERIC! ERIC STUKEL! Two years ago!" I burst in and slapped the triangular-shaped stone on the table. "Maybe not so long ago even!"

Earnstead was on his feet pacing. Carriss was leaned back, open palm stretched out behind him. Without a word, twenty dollars was exchanged.

"You know Eric then?" Carriss said.

"No," I corrected myself. "Yes." I corrected myself again. "In passing."

"Have a seat," Earnstead said.

I did as ordered.

"So," Carriss said. "Something happened two years ago."

"Maybe not so long ago even." I closed my eyes and fought to frame it right. "A girlfriend introduces Eric to Tammy at some party, and they..."

"You were jealous?" Carriss said.

"She wasn't speaking to me at the time," I said. "It was just after her dad died. She, uh...I don't know how to explain it. She needed space and time and...who was I? A big nobody. I didn't have friends, wasn't popular..."

"You had feelings for her," Carriss said, "and you were jealous."

I rubbed my bandage flat. "It was a bit more complicated than that."

"How so?" Earnstead asked.

"I don't know...it just was. Eric and Tammy were together awhile...then one day Eric spooked her. So she came to me. And I got mad. I wanted to hurt him. Hurt him *bad* you gotta understand."

"Spooked her," Carriss said and circled the words in his notebook.

"How'd he spook her?" Earnstead said.

"I don't know. She wouldn't say. I guess she just wanted to make it all go away and my getting mad wasn't helping."

"So this 'spooking her' was something rather serious?" Carriss said. "Something, by the way you make it sound, that brought her to you in a panic, something he said, did...maybe even wrote?"

"I don't know...Eric was like any other rich kid, spoiled, a bit possessive maybe, so who knows. I don't know, maybe it was nothing," I said.

"No signs of injury? Anything like that?" Carriss said.

"What do you mean by injuries?" I said.

Carriss shut his notebook. "When do you go back to Benning?"

I blinked.

"No, I'm not going back now."

"Not sure desertion would be in your best interest," Carriss said.

"Ten years in Leavenworth," Earnstead added.

"So?"

Earnstead picked up the little stone Stukel left on the casket. "Merrill, do you have any clue why Eric would have left this on Tammy's casket?"

"No."

"Merrill." Carriss treaded carefully. "Does the possibility of Tammy and Eric dating again make sense to you? Like after you left for the Army?"

"You must have been in some sort of communication with her these past few months—letters, phone calls," Earnstead said. "Did she say anything that might have clued you in about any changes, emotional or otherwise, that she might have been going through?"

"I talked to her Mom the Sunday before she went missing."

"Merrill." Carriss pulled of his glasses. "Tammy wasn't living at home anymore. She and her mother had a falling out this past summer. Tammy was living with her aunt."

"Living with her aunt?"

"After moving out from some friends of hers," Earnstead added.

"She was bouncing around from place to place…you didn't have any idea any of this was happening?" Carriss asked.

"I tried to call her every Sunday. That's when they let us use the phones. Five minutes. I always tried to dial her number first…she was never home."

"Merrill," Carriss said, "If you're going to help us figure this thing out, we're going to need to cut to the chase about a lot of things that went on in Tammy's life—no more patronizing, no more minimizing."

"Time being a vital factor," Earnstead added.

"Yes, we do think a crime was committed here, but we have to be sure we're right," Carriss said, "and that means people have to start being direct with us, with no worry of sparing feelings or hurting reputations. Do you understand what I'm trying to tell you?"

As Carriss kept talking, I felt something deep in my mind burying itself deeper. I don't remember what happened after that, the memory of me leaving the police station and trying to walk home gone save but for a foggy recollection of stopping at Bobby and Cooper Mac's along the way.

FROM HIS RECOUNT, Cooper Mac went wide-eyed when he saw me standing in his door. He took me in and made me drink something very strong, and then poured whatever was in the same bottle on my wounded hand before going at the puss and ooze with a razor blade. He told me it would leave a bad scar then went to wash his hands. When he came back into the room, he could not—for the life of us—find his spent and bloodied razor.

AT DETECTING LIES, Caroline Kern had become better than the machine she had been using for the past decade—the catch in the breath, the slight strain in the voice, the eyes dilating ever so slightly. A person's past was a bundle of secrets shouldered through life, most of the time carried unnoticed. Under the right circumstances though, when the right questions were asked, and asked in the right order, the seams came apart and the lies came tumbling. "There's a common misconception that polygraph machines detect lies—they don't," Caroline Kern tells overly ambitious prosecutors. "All they detect is miniscule changes in stress levels. It is the trained examiner who interprets these miniscule changes and determines truth."

Caroline Kern was good at detecting lies. In fact, she was so good that it cost her three husbands—a pornographer, a cheat, and a thief.

On the night I came through, Caroline Kern was waiting outside the door of the little blue interrogation room to give Special Agents Carriss and Earnstead the news about Bobby Grant, who was being held just down the hall. Carriss was attracted to the woman. He liked the bags under her eyes and the extra pounds that came from eating out of vending machines. Kern reminded Carriss of his wife (or rather, how his wife might have turned out, given another twenty years.)

Caroline Kern had an hour's drive to the Iowa border and an hour's drive home from there. "I'm cutting out, gentlemen, unless the FBI is willing to put me up for the night?"

Carriss winked. "Finest room at the Super 8."

Kern liked Carriss too. He reminded her of her father.

"Bobby Grant," she told the two, "I'm pretty sure didn't kill your victim." She saw a tension lift on Carriss' face. "But I won't go all the way with that. Was he complicit somehow in her death? He saw something and is holding back...sorry, I can't tell you anything more...and he was my last," Kern said and started for the doors. "You want me to tell the locals to cut him loose on my way out."

"And tell him we'll be in touch."

I DO REMEMBER something from that evening—or maybe it was simply what they call a confabulation, imagination as the thread to stitch rips in the memory. It was moments after Carriss and Earnstead had cut me loose. The attractive older woman was standing outside the interrogation room door. She smiled, loosened her hair from a bun, and then looked right into me—just for an instant—like a scientist examining a dissected specimen.

After that, I must have turned a wrong corner because I couldn't find my way out of the building. It came like a dream and went like a dream and there were no signs of exit. That was the problem. Just door after door until I came upon the one big door. It didn't look like *the* answer, but it did look like *an* answer. There were voices beyond the big door. "Over eighty people at that party," one of them hissed.

I opened the door to find a long conference room of mahogany and black leather, lawyers and detectives sitting across from one another, a cheese and meat tray between them, and at the head of the table Eric Stukel, back turned to me, his mother seated behind him, her manicured fingers gently running through his hair. "If you offer immunity, we'd be willing—" the man at the right hand of Eric Stukel said. That was when Detective Tony Harper stepped out from the shadows, a bandage in the shape of an X on his forehead. He flashed his teeth and then swung the big door straight back in my face.

IN THE HALLWAY outside their rooms out at the Super 8, Carriss and Earnstead did their best to tie up today's loose ends. If things went well, they would be off the case and out of town by the weekend. "The rape kit," Carriss asked, "how much time?"

"Quantico is saying ten months, if lucky."

"Then that won't do any good to help us ease an exit out."

"The locals are going to bury this case," Earnstead said. "They're going to kill it before it opens wide and swallows Yankton up."

"Two fishermen say they see a guy threatening to kill a girl at the dam?" Carriss lowered his voice as a security guard passed. "Let's leak it was Tammy with Eric...see who takes the bait."

"And if it wasn't Eric and Tammy at the dam?"
"Oh, I'm pretty sure it wasn't," Carriss smiled.

IT HAD BEEN Carriss' experience that a single rumor could make or break a case in a small town. Rumors were virulent little creatures that spread through school hallways, over cups of coffee at the local coffee shop, and most contagiously through church kitchens. Indiscriminate in their destruction, the more foul, the more farfetched, the more perfect and swift they traveled, sometimes mutating, sometimes combining, ever evolving…

The manufacture and unleashing of a mind virus was risky business.

There was a lounge inside the Super 8, not a nice place, but it saw its share of traffic. It would do just fine. The rumor would be simple: a young man named Eric Stukel took Tammy Haas out on a date. On that date, they drove to Gavin's Point Dam. There, he threatened to kill her. Two old fishermen watched, but were across the water so unable to stop the event unfolding. Six days later her body would be found in a nearby ravine.

Carriss guessed it would take the rumor twenty-four hours to make its way through town, taking into account the dozen other rumors it had to compete with, far more virulent, about the night in question.

Carriss wandered into the lounge just before closing, plopped down at the bar next to several regulars, and upon his second vodka rocks, asked offhandedly, "Have you heard anything about those two fishermen seeing the guy threatening to kill the girl?" Heads turned, a few gathered around him, and so the unleashing began.

THE IDEA HADN'T even occurred until I found the razor tucked in my boot. Its blade was caked black with dried blood but still had the sharpness to penetrate deep into the arteries with one swift stroke. I remember the steam and the water bringing my veins to the surface.

I remember testing the blade's sharpness on the hairs of my arms.

The bathtub would go red, so red that I would disappear beneath the bloody surface as my pulse slowed and slowed…

That's all I wanted—to disappear.

There was a knock at the door.

I pulled back just before the razor penetrated the flesh.

It was my father's knock and he would keep knocking, and once he realized nobody was going to answer, he would break down the door, find me too weak to fight him, and staunch my bleeding before I had even lost a pint.

"It's unlocked," I said and poked the razor into a nearby bar of soap.

My father pulled the bath curtain shut to hide my nakedness. The toilet squeaked on its hinges as he sat and then, as he had done thousands of times before, he let out a weary sigh. "I called Reverend Farmer, I called your recruiter, I called Senator Daschle's office…" He went silent for a good while. "This will take time and distance…a lot of distance."

"I'm not going back to Benning."

"You have no choice...the Army is not the Boy Scouts."

"Yes, I'm aware."

"Discipline, that's what we're talking about here, structure—these are the things you need. Give it a shot." He let out another weary sigh. "Nothing's going to happen with the case for a good long while. It takes a long time for evidence to be processed. DNA, fingerprints, soil samples—this is the work of criminologists, not nineteen-year-old boys. I know you want to help. I know you have given the FBI your statement and that's good. Now it's time to let these men do their job. I'm sorry this is happening to you." He rose. "But now it's your time, your time to choose a path and stay strong with it."

The door opened, the door closed, and that easily he was gone.

The razor was in the soap and the soap was floating gently between my knees. He was right. I had a choice to make. This was a grand moment, a moment that called for action, and so I gave the soap a push, and the soap capsized and floated gently toward the drain, carrying the razor with.

Death would bare its teeth surely and soon enough...but not tonight.

BOBBY WOKE JUST after 3:00 A.M., his bladder sore from the hours spent in the little blue interrogation room. He sat on the toilet, trying to push through the pain, all the while entertaining thoughts of suing the police for cruel and unusual punishment, and just as he was about to release, light bounced off the back wall and stretched long across the floor. The light was reflecting in from the kitchen refrigerator as its door swung open, which was strange considering Cooper Mac was soundly snoring in the top bunk of their bedroom. There was the clanking of bottles—somebody was indeed inside. The refrigerator swung shut and the light shrunk to darkness. Bobby armed himself with the plunger and crept into the living room. "Hello?"

There was somebody sitting on the couch looking up at him, but it was far too dark to make out a face...and then from the kitchen, the sound of one bottle, then two bottles, then three hissing open. Something went tap, tap, tap against the coffee table and with that tapping Bobby suddenly could smell freshly smoked marijuana. "Who's there?"

The living room light flickered to life, a large fellow making his way out from the kitchen, three beers in hand. The little fellow on the couch didn't bother turning to regard Bobby as he spoke. "I thought we'd let you sleep. It's always better to wake on your own, naturally, from a medicinal standpoint that is...better on your nerves, better for your immune system." The little fellow was tapping out marijuana residue from a pipestone chillum and collecting it on creased forensic bindle paper. "Some tasty skunk—I thank you for swinging through Omaha to pick it up."

The large fellow forced one of the freshly opened bottles into Bobby's hand and then positioned himself in the corner, just within arm's reach of Bobby. Dusty Fist was his name, eighteen and full of piss, with a constipated grin that never left his face. This was the grin of a person who liked kicking dogs, who liked snapping the necks of kittens, but with Dusty, it went further.

THE HOMECOMING

Dusty kicked dogs not to hear them yelp, but to hear their ribs crack one by one…and with the kittens, he would twist and twist until their heads came clean off. The little one, the one on the couch, was Don the Itch. Don was only twenty, but was already making nearly six figures a year piping drugs across the bridge. Most people confused him for an albino, his blond hair nearly white, his skin pale from lack of sun. He wore red-tinted glasses and shirts buttoned up to the neck. The relationship between the big one, Dusty Fist, and the little one, Don the Itch, was this: Dusty Fist punctuated with brute force every sentence Don the Itch spoke—the theme invariably the same, money owed—that was except on this occasion.

"I didn't tell them anything," Bobby said. "I went with what you told me to say—that I took her to the party, that I stranded her."

"Relax, Bobby," Don the Itch began removing beer bottles from the coffee table. "Drink your beer," he said.

"They put me on a polygraph machine and even then I didn't—"

"The question is why you agreed to a polygraph," Don the Itch said.

At this point, back in the bedroom, Cooper Mac had stopped stirring and was listening through the cracked bedroom door.

"It's not like they gave me much of a—"

Don shifted sideways upon the couch to make room. "I'll warn you now that it'll only hurt more if you don't relax."

Bobby tried to shield his face as he went over the couch, but impact against the coffee table was still fierce. It was all happening too fast—all two hundred and twenty pounds of Dusty Fist upon Bobby without a breath wasted or drop of beer spilt. The ashes from the ashtray went up in a little mushroom cloud as the ashtray flipped and spun to the floor. Dusty's knee went deep into the small of Bobby's back, his right arm popped and twisted out of the socket. Don the Itch was right—he should have relaxed.

"This has been our second conversation now, Bobby," Don the Itch said, "Don't make us come back for a third."

It took several seconds for Bobby to feel that Dusty had released his arm. The back door opened and the back door closed. Bobby listened. There was no sound of an engine turning over or of screeching tires. There was nothing, just the drip of the faucet from the kitchen sink.

ONLY WHEN BOBBY was good and soused—which involved three hours of power drinking—did Cooper Mac use a 2X4, rope, and cinder block to put Bobby's dislocated shoulder back into place.

CHAPTER THIRTEEN

THE DUFFEL BAG that disappeared on my flight into Omaha arrived via United Parcel Service currier just as Bobby and I were pulling from my parents' driveway en route to Omaha for my flight back to Fort Benning.

Sleet marked a quick end to Indian summer, and Bobby's heater groaned the loss on our way down Highway 81. We drove in spurts, jumping out every few minutes to scrape ice from the windshield, and once we got a rhythm down, we traveled in silence, listening through heavy static to radio newscasters charting the progress of the storm. They told us it would roll southeasterly, just missing Omaha.

My flight would not be delayed.

Bobby pushed the little Mustang as fast as his worn tires could hold to the road and as we neared the western limits of Omaha, robin's egg slivers of blue quickly broke through the gray.

My flight would not be delayed.

Bobby shut off the radio, and just as I was about to relax into a sleep, he began to speak. "I've found out two things." His voice was tense. "Dusty Fist and Brain Slobacek were selling drugs at the Stevenson party—"

"Brian Slobacek?" I glanced over. "The Homecoming Chief?"

Bobby winced and pinched his shoulder to his ear as we rolled through a curve. "There's also a rumor," he said, "about a fight breaking out at the dam. I guess those two old guys you talked to did see what they said they saw."

"What's wrong with your shoulder?" I asked.

"What I'm trying to tell you," he took a long drag from a cigarette, "is that their supplier is yoked."

"Brian and Dusty Fist's you mean?"

Smoke from his breath swirled against the windshield. "So yoked that they will make life painful for anybody who asks too many questions."

"Tammy is dead, Bobby. I'll ask whatever goddamn questions I please."

"I know you will," he said. "That's not what I'm saying."

Bobby turned the defrost blowers to high.

"You think this whole thing involves drug running?" I asked.

"I think that drugs are involved."

Just then, something began taking shape against the glass of the windshield, something emerging from the retreating condensation, helped along by the smoke of Bobby's breath, a ghost and portent materializing.

"Pull over," I said.

Bobby saw my eyes fixed forward.

"What?" he said.

I hit the dome light and leaned in close, my trembling fingers reaching, but refusing to touch. "Her footprint."

"Her what?" Bobby said.

"Her footprint."

Bobby slowed the car to the side of the road and saw for himself her footprint left upon the glass—a ghost conjured into existence by cold and freeze, by heat and thaw, by the driving through and the passing of a storm. "I meant to tell you that I was picking Tammy up for work," Bobby whispered.

"From her aunt's?"

"I meant to tell you that part too—that she was kicked out."

Something ugly and painful rose up inside me—rage that did not want to be controlled, that did not want to be quenched—rage at myself, rage at the world—rage that tasted of blood—blood that made me spit the words: "She was *raped*...and you *knew!*"

"You understand why she never told you?" he said. "How bad you would handle it if you ever found out?"

"Who?"

"A guy," he said. "An older guy. I don't remember. It was years ago."

"Think hard."

"She said something about it once. She didn't know what to do. It started out normal, she told me. It was the first time she had gone out on a real date. She was so young that she had to sneak out to do it—eighth grade, maybe ninth. I guess she was more afraid of getting caught sneaking back into the house than anything else, and then he said he'd tell everybody if she didn't keep going along with it, if she didn't keep coming over whenever he told her. She said it would be her word against his, that it would just be easier if—"

"Enough," I said.

"What?"

"Enough."

I stared at the fading footprint and beyond it the parting clouds.

"What do you want me to do?" Bobby asked.

"Finish what we've started."

My flight would not be delayed.

CARRISS AND EARNSTEAD insisted Eric Stukel call his lawyer before saying anything more, but Eric was determined to get this matter straightened up here and now. Eric had tracked the two agents down at the Super 8 and when neither answered their doors, Eric talked the desk manager into opening one of their rooms for him (Earnstead's as it happened) so he might sit and wait. Eric had the ability of talking people into things. Carriss had logged thirty-nine years in the Bureau, had seen just about everything, but having a person of interest invite himself into an agent's motel room was a definite first. The two agents were speechless. There Eric was, sitting on the edge of Earnstead's bed, mouth breathing and glassy eyed as he watched TV.

Eric explained to the two agents that he had been sleepless ever since hearing the rumor going around about his presence at the dam. "I ran into Tammy at the Stevenson bonfire," he explained his version of events.

Carriss stopped Eric straightaway. "So what about your sister saying you came home at 10:00 P.M.? How could that be true if Tammy didn't even show up at the party until…how late was it Special Agent Earnstead?"

"After 10:00 P.M."

"Yeah, my sister had the nights screwed up…she thought it was the night before I came home alone. The night *before* was the night I came home at 10:00 P.M. That's when she heard me coming down the steps at 10:00."

"So you were at the party at the same time as Tammy?" Earnstead said. "And you two had some sort of conversation?"

Eric stared at the TV. "We made up from a fight."

"You two had a fight?" Carriss said and switched the TV off.

"Yeah, she had come over the night before."

"I guess you're sister failed to mention that part too," Carriss said.

"Well, my sister thought I came home the night before, but I didn't come home alone that night either. It was the next night, the night of the party, that me and Tammy made up—Tammy decided she would drive me back to my house." Eric smiled. "I guess it was pretty much back to normal from there. We went down to my bedroom and listened to some music—"

"Eric, you're saying that you took Tammy home the night she disappeared, you're saying you were the last one with her?" Earnstead said.

"I'm saying that it wasn't me and her at the dam."

"Eric," Carriss stopped him. "I'm going to advise you to say no more until we call your lawyers."

"I don't need my lawyers," Eric said. "I didn't do anything wrong."

"Eric, for the record," Earnstead said, "I'm advising you of your Miranda rights. You have the right to remain silent and the right to an attorney. If you can't afford an attorney, the Courts will give you one. Do you understand what I'm saying to you?"

"Of course I do," Eric said. "Does that mean I'm under arrest?"

"Not exactly," Earnstead said, "we just need you to know your rights."

"Once again," Carriss said. "Call your lawyer."

"I told you I don't need a lawyer. I didn't do anything wrong."

Carriss looked to Earnstead. Earnstead shrugged.

"Have it your way." Carriss said.

Eric continued. "And then once I put on the music, she and I—"

"Start from the beginning," Earnstead told him.

"I ran into Tammy at the party and we made up from a fight."

"This fight happened the night before the party?" Carriss asked.

"Yes."

"And you were fighting about what?" Earnstead said.

"We were trying to get back together."

"So you went to the party alone and arrived before she did?"

Stukel looked back and forth at the two agents.

"I didn't like the fact she was seeing other guys. She didn't like the fact that I didn't like the fact she was seeing other guys. She said that I was too possessive. I was with her that night—and the night before…I guess I should have been more honest with the police—I know it looks bad." Eric stared at the blank television screen. "I guess it doesn't look good that we had a fight."

"So, tell us again why you came to us," Carriss said.

"If she was raped," Eric said. "They'd find my DNA."

"So you two made up at the party and you two went back to your place and had consensual sex?" Carriss said. "What time would you say that was?"

"A bit after midnight," Eric said, "or maybe a bit before, I'm not sure. Like I told you, I was too stoned to even drive and I don't even own a watch."

"Was Tammy wearing a watch, Eric?" Earnstead asked.

"Yes."

"Whose watch was it, Eric?" Carriss asked.

"Other guys were jealous of us, but she never took any of them seriously," Eric said. "Anyway, I wasn't paying attention to the time, that's why I say it was around midnight when we got home."

"And after you put on the music?" Carriss asked.

"We made love for awhile. I smoked some more pot. When she finally said she had to go home, I offered her a ride. She didn't take my offer though," Eric smiled wearily. "She walked home…walked to her aunt's, I mean…I don't know…I really don't. I just know that she left…for all I know, she walked to Bobby Grant's place."

"You think she may have walked to Bobby's?" Earnstead said.

Eric went silent.

"Eric," Carriss said, "If Tammy walked from your house to Bobby's, how did her body wind up ten miles away, in a ravine, in Nebraska, within a half mile of the Stevenson farm?"

Eric thought about it a long moment and then finally came up with the only answer he could. "I'll take a polygraph if you want."

THE COFFEE WAS being poured by the flight attendant, the airplane jiggled back and forth, the entire pot, cup with it, went upside-down onto my lap. "You do have something to change into?" The flight attendant tilted her head and gave me a polished smile. "Don't you?" It was a fitting end to the journey and so from my Sunday best back into camouflage I went.

What I didn't know was how much this would upset the Military Police who were patrolling the airport back in Georgia. One of them was in plain clothes and walked up discreetly as I was waiting for my baggage. Flipping out his badge, he told me to follow. As we walked, he radioed for backup. Moments later, three MPs with nightsticks came running our way.

"Scum-fucking little turd thinks he can come into my goddamned mother-fucking airport wearing his goddamned mother-fucking BDUs?" shouted the liaison officer as I stood in his little office. "I should rip the green right off him and take a pound of flesh with it!" The liaison officer was yelling at Drill Sergeant Eccles over the phone to make the point that I needed learn military regulations regarding proper dress when traveling.

I changed back into my coffee-stained Dress Blues in the backseat of the MPs squad car as we rolled back to barracks. I walked into Eccles office and came to Parade Rest. "Nice to see you back in uniform," he said. "Dismissed." End of story.

BACK IN THE stark white barracks, I stared down the row of bunks—one bald head after the next poking from olive-drab wool, marching orders to sleep soundly and in military fashion until properly woken.

This was all that was left for me…

I had a good reason for coming back, something I needed to do, but as I stared down the dim-lit barracks, drained and on the verge of collapse, the reason made little sense. I simply knew I didn't have the courage to do it. I was a baby. The word vengeance sounded silly coming from my lips. I didn't know who killed her. I probably never would. Put in a room alone with her killer, I doubt I would even be able to stand up and challenge him with words. I was cursed with what some called niceness. It was really cowardice though and that's why Tammy was dead. I might as well have watched it happen. I was worthless. A worm. Nobody.

I needed air.

I went out the backdoor and down the fire escape. I made it around the corner and had the payphone islands in view. What I failed to notice was the glow of the cigarette as I crossed through the Company Assembly Area.

"Where do you think you're going, Private?" Eccles puffed from the shadows.

"Just needed air, Drill Sergeant," I said.

"Always drag a packed duffel bag with you when you go out for air?"

I reached to get the duffel bag off my back.

"Leave it," Eccles said, stepping from the shadows, "and cinch it tight."

"I suppose there's fresh air in the barracks too." I grinned and took two steps back the way I came.

What came next came suddenly, my feet soundly rooted on terra firma one moment, my face against the concrete the next. I could smell the smoke on his breath as he bent in close. He was holding his smoldering cigarette next to my eye. "Push yourself up on your hands, Private," he said. I strained against the seventy pounds of my duffel bag, but finally my arms locked out.

Eccles took a long drag from the cigarette, squatted back on his heels. "An orphaned or widowed slave, back when that was the way of the world, was whipped by his master after suffering his loss." Eccles stubbed out the cigarette on the concrete. "This lashing," he said, "was meant by Master to keep the bereaved orphan or spouse from running away. It was a way of reminding the slave who was in charge, a way of reminding the slave that the days would go on business-as." Eccles lit another smoke. "No, it isn't fair, Private, but it is the way it's gotta be." Eccles rose and disappeared from view. "You'll stay there in the front-leaning rest, Private."

The wound on my left hand had reopened in the fall and was now spreading wide against the grain of the concrete. I did my best to grind my palm deeper into the cement to slow the bleeding. As each moment bled into the next, the pain slid from body part to body part, first through my shoulders, next into my elbows, into my wrists for a time, and across my lower back. Sweat went heavy against my Dress Blues and sometime after the night artillery fire faded, a puddle of sweat began to spread beneath me. By the time the Rangers jogged past, the puddle of sweat had swollen ten feet in every direction. Morning crept closer, and when I had no more sweat to give, the puddle came back upon itself, slowly but surely, bleaching little white rings one after the next as it shrunk. With the clatter of first call, I felt myself go dizzy. There were commands shouted and then the company marched out for physical training, and when the company returned, they found me unconscious and rolled to my side, dried vomit spattered across my pale cheek, my duffel bag still cinched tightly to my back. Later that day I was pumped full of saline IV. By nightfall, I was back doing K.P.

AFTER THAT DAY, Eccles didn't have too much to say to me. I had fallen out of his good graces. My graduation certificate told me I met every requirement of Advanced Infantry Training and my orders stated that I was to be shipped straightaway to Army Parachute School.

THE GEORGIA DIRT spreads grand swaths of reds eight hundred feet below and the wind hisses a roar through the cargo bay as you hook up—the green light comes on—and you shuffle to the door. One fateful step gets you into the blast of the turbines, lifts you away from the airplane, sends you into the spinning fury of freefall. The ride is short. Within four seconds, silk explodes from your pack and a jolt called opening shock rights you. You watch the C130 disappear up and away, and for a few glorious moments, you sail a quick-majestic ride to the ground.

That's the rush you were promised, the power and the glory, to drop like a god from the sky. But like any high, it comes and leaves you too quickly—so you pain yourself up to feel those few precious moments of rush again, and once it's over, the emptiness comes, this time carving deeper.

You don't know normal anymore.

You tell yourself not thinking about her will help.

Every muscle aches for her. Every stray thought escapes back to her. The world moves forward and cannot take the time to care. You never mention her name because that would betray a weakness and bring the hungry dogs. You simply do what you are told. The days ache slowly forward and sleep becomes your only retreat. You get that sleep when you can—an hour here, an hour there. You learn to sleep standing up, you learn to sleep as you march, you learn to sleep in the back of trucks, in airplanes, in helicopters, in the rain, in the cold, in the heat. Sometimes, you cannot tell the difference between sleep and awake.

They call you a patriot, All American, a paratrooper, hero—but these words mean nothing. Rumors of war keep those around you on edge, but you feel only numb. The training gets fiercer and sometimes goes bloody, and like smelted steel pounded one too many times, many of your brothers-in-arms break. Your secret pain burrows deeper and the word *home* becomes a dream-myth, a place trapped in a past that never truly existed.

You wait for news, but news rarely comes and when it does it comes in erratic and meaningless spurts, sideshow oddities—an end-time preacher rolling into town, claiming to see what no others can, and for a price, revealing the secrets of the Almighty. The good preacher calls down angels to battle demons, shakes convulsions, calls on the Lord to rescue the town from its sinful ways. The good preacher conducts secret exorcisms at the ravine, at the farmhouse, at the cemetery. He does so with credulous children entrusted to him by even more credulous parents. When he is exposed as a fraud, he is run out of town. A psychic gets hired by the police, speaks of watery and wooded places where secrets are hidden (and for a price) puts on the same sort of show. The ghost hunters follow on her heels—bottom feeders all.

That was the way of the world while I was silenced and tucked away. I did my best to fight the good fight, to soldier on and count the days. I did my best, but soon confusion had overshadowed my soul, and by September of the next year, the nightmares and the waking had become one...

WORD CAME TO me that a small band of Tammy's girlfriends came home from college that next summer and started asking questions. These girls accused the wrong people. This brought threats against their lives. The local police thought this all very amusing, their belief being that if those meddlesome girls were dumb enough to go stirring up hornets nests, they deserved to get stung.

Mostly though, things had settled down. Most of the people who truly cared about Tammy had fled out of fear and in their place came those who just didn't care. This was how small towns survived—limping along, festering, hiding the injured limb for fear of the stinging medicine and the bitter pill.

North Carolina nights, so silent and serene, could make a soldier weep.

ON THE SECOND anniversary of Tammy's death, I sat inside a C130 moving toward combat on some small tropic nation taken over by a band of para-militant thugs. We were told that upon the blood-soaked ground of that little impoverished island we soldiers would sow the seeds of liberty and peace. We shook hands with our brothers, took photos of each other, and promised to meet at our rallying points upon the ground, and then we sat silently, waiting, waiting...

It was September 18, 1994, three hours before our landing, when a deal was brokered with the thugs, thus putting a deposed president back in power. The mighty fist of the United States was pulled back, the thugs shown mercy, and we returned home. There were parades and a vice president on crutches told us we were heroes, but still there was that emptiness. It was back to business as usual, that was the way of the world. A few days later though, as I bent to pick up a pinecone, as I rolled it in my hand, I felt something held delicate deep inside my soul shatter in two. In that unparticular moment of that unparticular day, the last shreds of hope fell away, and upon the shattered nothing of my soul, the coldness took root. It was then and there that I remembered why I had returned to finish my training.

It was simple and singular and I was ready now.

"Avenge her," Soldier said.

Upon that altar, I nurtured unadulterated hate for an enemy without a face. The world had gone mad long ago and finally I was catching up. A vague picture-show began playing in mind—the future—my future—dark and beautiful—I would find out who did this to her and I would make them pay.

THE HOMECOMING

PART III

BARGAINING

CHAPTER FOURTEEN

CHRISTMAS HAD FALLEN upon the sleepy little hamlet of Yankton when the eighteen-wheeler carrying Christmas toys pulled over that double-decked bridge and the wayward soldier stepped out into a snowy winter morning. Randy Edison who had picked me up on the road gave me a wave and rolled north. Randy, a veteran himself, had found me drunk and ready to be thrown from a roadhouse somewhere in Tennessee (or possibly Kentucky) and for the sake of conversation and a sense of brotherly duty loaded up my bike and drove me the rest of the way home. His plan was to travel hammer-down through the night up into North Dakota to be there Christmas morning when his three little girls woke.

We hadn't stopped since Kansas City, so I wasn't prepared for the suddenness of the cold. Little could I do to fend it off but park my bike, hoist my bag upon my shoulder, and walk with purpose. That would be the mission. No more distractions. Stay ahead of the cold, stay ahead of the game, let nothing stand in my way. Splitting my soul had been a tactical decision— there was the boy I once was, the one who suffered silent the screaming ache, and there was Soldier, cold, calculated, capable of anything, no love, no pain, just the mission at hand. When the child needed him, he would rise from the deepest parts, the Empty and the Nothing, the place where God retreats when Creation seeks His face.

Carolers from the Baptist League were busy singing a slightly off-key rendition of *O Holy Night*, on the corner of Third and Walnut. One shook a can full of change as I tried to pass. Their sign said something about monies going to purchase material to make the costumes for next year's Christmas Pageant. Baptists can persuade mercilessly and so when I passed Bashful Jim, the town indigent, a half block later, I found myself with nothing in my wallet to offer him except a few brochures about everlasting damnation, the end times, and the evil of freethinking.

Bashful Jim appeared cold digging through the dumpster tucked in that alley, blowing on his hands with all his might each time he dropped a salvaged can in his shopping cart. It wasn't pity, as I was in short supply, and he wasn't the type to ask. In fact, he didn't even notice me staring at him. Having a healthy pair of hands seemed critical to his line of work, so I tossed him my gloves. Bashful Jim put the gloves on quickly, gave me something of a salute, and then went about his business.

The plan was to stop in the Dakota, another half-block up the street. I'm not sure why—maybe to warm myself, maybe to make a phone call home, maybe to simply to take a crack at the nostalgia, to drink up a few fond memories that might spur me hopeful. I couldn't remember much, but I did remember that she would sneak up behind me and cover my eyes, whisper into my ear, "Guess who," but only when I was terribly busy or attempting to concentrate terribly hard, or when I was worried, or staring off into space, tackling a stray thought about future dreams impossible. She would cover my eyes, blind me to my worry, and make whatever secret pain I carried lift away.

I tried to remember more, but as I reached the doors of the Dakota, it caught my eye. I'm not certain how long I stood there staring at it, but the medals on my uniform had gone to frost and pinched cold little pinpricks against my chest. The Dakota had been closed for business since summer, but someone was still good enough to keep it in the window, yellowed at the edges, with her photo in black and white at the bottom:

10,000-DOLLAR REWARD
FOR INFORMATION INVOLVING
THE DEATH OF TAMMY HAAS

The air had gotten cold and as the Baptists had begun *Joy to the World.* Her face seemed strange in black and white. Her eyes were lost in the grain. She was so young, or maybe I had gotten older. I stared and I stared and I stared and then I heard Soldier whisper, "Enough."

On our way through the wide-open white of Memorial Park, Soldier and I found another reward poster, faded worse than the first, pinned to a bulletin board near the baseball diamonds. Scrawled ugly across this one was:

LET IT GO!

Soldier ripped down that poster and whispered again, "Enough."

ATOP THE OVERTURNED picnic tables beneath the picnic shelters at the edge of the park sat two figures. The two figures were watching me make my way through the snow. It was when I had gotten past the elephant slide and the beetle-go-round that one of them came to his feet to give me a harder stare. The fellow who rose turned to say something to his compatriot and just as I was about to veer away he beckoned me with a wave. Neither of them were wearing coats, the Baptists had taken all my cash, and Bashful Jim had my gloves. Even in my pockets, my hands were stinging from cold. I wasn't ready to reward sheer stupidity by unburdening myself with the rest of my clothing: there were warmer places to be for free and they were making the choice to be cold. In the dead-cold stillness that had settled with dusk, I could smell a faint hint of marijuana hanging around them both. I pretended not to see them and kept steady my gentle path away. This prompted the one who was standing to say, "Merrill! That *is* you! It's me, Eric, Eric Stukel."

I turned sharply and moved his way, one eye upon the one behind Eric, the one perched atop the overturned picnic tables. Noose Adarson was his name and he was watching me closely too. He was Eric's protector.

Eric looked my uniform up and down—the red beret, the jump boots, the duffel bag cinched as tightly as it would go—the way Eccles had taught me to wear it. "You're home," he said and stared through me vacantly.

"You were dating her?" I said.

Eric shrugged as if he weren't quite ready to commit to this. "I miss her," he said. The pain in his voice stung me. He was grieving the grief openly that I had learned to bury deep. He had a lightness of being in his grief. The pain came upon him and then washed right through, effortlessly and without shame. This made him free and I hated him for it—he was the better man.

Eric glanced backwards again, "You remember Noose?"

Noose gave me a half a nod, never losing his squint.

I cinched my duffel bag tighter.

"It sucks, I guess," Eric said, "for all of us."

"I guess it does," I said, thinking too little and already walking on.

THE CHRISTMAS LIGHTS were strung under the eaves outside, but that was just a façade. The holly and ivy, the nativity set by Gorham, the baked snowmen cookies covered in lacquer, the ones we made in second grade, the fresh-cut spruce bedecked with hand-knit snowflakes, a trumpeting angel atop, and present after present neatly wrapped in shiny reds, whites, and blues beneath—a great and mirthless void where all this should have been.

MY MOTHER WAS busy setting table service for two. A bottle of wine or two between them, between her mostly—it would be a quiet, bittersweet affair, but they would make the most of it. They would give themselves that much. That was the plan, at least, until the doorbell rang. There was a foot of snow on the ground. It was Christmas Eve. Nobody should have been out ringing doorbells. She was so surprised by the broken silence that she nearly dropped the plate in her hand. She had grown quite attune to omens over the past few years, or so she thought, and this, a doorbell ringing in the dead of winter, long after dark, could only mean one thing—trouble.

She checked her hair in the foyer mirror, but was still so frazzled that she had forgotten to set the plate still in her hand, and when she answered the door, the plate dropped, bounced twice on the carpet, and shattered one fine line ever-so-slowly, ever-so-perfectly dividing it in half.

"Can I come in?" I asked.

She didn't know what to do at first, her hands trembling, her face going flush as she tried to fight tears bound up for far too long. It was then that instinct took over and she did what any mother would do. She grabbed me by the shoulders and captured me in a desperate embrace, and I felt something I thought I could never feel again…

Home.

CHAPTER FIFTEEN

AS I SHOWERED, she hurried to pull from storage what Christmas baubles she could find. The homey Christmas Service, red porcelain white-specked and hand-painted with Christmas trees, would do quite nicely for dinner. The wine could be opened right away. This was a time of celebration—nerves needed to be calmed.

MY FATHER FOLDED his hands for the dinner prayer and my mother took her third long swallow from her third glass of wine. "Let us pray," my father said, and so he prayed, and so we broke bread.
Finally, I asked, "Can I stay the night?"
My father sighed. "No, you have to sleep out in the snow."
"I just didn't want to…I wanted to make sure that I wasn't—"
"Of course you can stay here!" he snapped. "You're our son!"
The rest of the night was spent in silence.

THE SILENCE LASTED another two days.

MY FATHER HAD a way of starting conversations while leaving one place in haste toward another. This would ensure that answers you gave him would be unburdened with explanatory information. "You've found yourself an apartment?" he asked me as he pulled up his parka on his way out.
"I put a little money away." I said.
He was already out the back door before I could finish, but then he poked his head back inside. "Well, you need to think along the lines of college or finding a job. You can't just sit around here."
He was right. I had become too comfortable in his home. The two days I'd spent recovering from my cross-country trek had been unearned.

I THREW ON my boots and chased my father out into the night, pounding on his windshield as he was backing his truck into the street. He cracked the window. "I'm late."
"For?"
"Late."
"Every single day it's been like a cancer eating me away…you told me it would get better if I gave it time and space. That was a lie to get rid of me, and it has ripped me apart. You want me to lie down and die—get a job, go to school, humdrum my way through life as if nothing happened!"
"You don't think we've tried," my father said. "Your mother has written letters to the editor. She's helped with the prayer chain. They held a special church service last year on the anniversary—do you know how hard that was

to put together when nobody wanted to see it happen? She sits up every night worrying for you, praying for you, and then you come home with this chip on your shoulder, acting like the world owes you something—"

"She's drinking again," I said.

He went silent and the truck nearly idled dead. "It would make your mother very uncomfortable—" He gave the truck some gas. "—to know we were having this conversation." He threw the truck into reverse and before I could blink, the red of his taillights streaked up the street and out of sight.

MY MOTHER FOUND me packing my duffel bag and sensed exactly what had just happened between my father and me.

"Please don't," she said.

"It ends."

"And you think you're the one to be—"

"I didn't ask for this!" I shouted. "And I do thank you for all your help!"

She backed from my room and looked to the ceiling. "God wouldn't have let this happen if there weren't a good reason for it. People die and it may seem to make no sense to us, but we don't have the right to question—"

I cinched the duffel bag so hard I nearly ripped the shoulder strap.

She tried to grab me as I made my way down the hall. "God doesn't give us any more than we can handle—"

I turned at her. "Says who?"

My mother trembled to contain something impressive and when she could hold it no more she cried out, "Death threats in the middle of the night!"

"From whom?"

"It's not like they left their name and number," she said. She had gotten older in so little time. They had taken the strength from her. "We would hang posters," she said, "and they would tear them down. We would question the police. They would tell us, 'you don't want to know, you're not going to bring her back anyway.' Don't you get it?" she cried. "We've tried. We've pleaded...Now all we can do is pray!"

"No, no, no...now is the time those who did this plead." I opened the front door to a snowy gray night. "Now is the time those who did this pray."

CHAPTER SIXTEEN

A PLACE WHERE misery smiles—that's what I was looking for and that's what I found. The walls were of cinder block. Swollen from the winter freeze, mortar in the joints mostly crumbled to chalk, and where the water came in, mildew crawled. The place above was once an egg-processing factory, so I was told. The smell of sulfur that lifted when the draft drew down through the cold-air returns came mostly just before morning. The floor of poured-thin concrete had layers of ancient paint, flaking and thick with lead. In the center of the room, jutting up two inches was a small drain that seemed to serve no purpose. The only light came from a naked eighty-watt hanging bulb above that drain. The only sound came from an antique little icebox with fiberglass insulation poking from its door. At times, it sounded as if there were a baby inside crying as if woken by a bad dream. There were no windows and just one door with double bolt and chain, and so it would come to pass, that in this little apartment of mine there would be only one direction to come under attack and only one direction to retreat.

The bed in the corner was Army surplus. From what I could gather from the smell, something small had crawled in through a tear in its seam, tried to nest, found itself trapped, inadvertently making a grave for itself. The E-Z chair had duct-tape covering its armrests and behind it was the mirror, large as I had requested, taken from an aerobics studio shut down in the late 80s. When I pulled the E-Z chair away from the wall to point it toward the door, I found the mirror's bottom left corner shattered. I could only assume this happened upon delivery. This at least would explain the shards of glass kicked beneath the bottom step of the outer stairwell, shards of glass I quickly retrieved to duct-tape and fashion a bathroom mirror.

Actually, it wasn't what most would consider a bathroom, just a shower and sink surrounded on three sides by a 2X4 frame, paneling scrap from the dump stapled up as walls. A hastily fashioned door hung badly on the three-sided frame, catching against the bare floor and scraping to a sudden stop as it got halfway opened.

A family of five lived here before me, paying two-hundred a month for rent, but with food bills and medical expenses, wages earned from the four jobs between the two parents wasn't enough to survive. The family was evicted and forcibly relocated to a homeless shelter out of state…out of sight…out of mind…God bless America.

I dumped everything in my duffel bag onto the Army surplus bed with the decomposing rodent inside. Army duffel bags, it must be noted, are impressive things when packed correctly, much like magic hats. In fact, they were designed in such a way as to allow a soldier to step inside them and stuff and stuff and stuff with both feet and all his weight, and so it came to pass that everything I owned, save the clothes on my back and my motorcycle, was now spilling in heaps onto my new bed. Much of it was battle dress—chocolate-chip desert, concrete jungle, winter snow, smoky branch, tiger stripe, midnight blue, urban tiger, and one charcoal chemical protective suit of the woodland green variety (just in case.) These uniforms were stuffed around a motorcycle helmet, a German paratrooper's knife, a Maglight modified to fit on the conversational end of an M16, knee pads to save what was left of my withered knees, bottle of Brasso, shoe polish, and boots for every season—jump boots, winter boots, jungle boots, combat boots, desert boots, and inside those boots, my lock pick set, camouflage paint, smoke grenades, a bit of ordinance, some shotgun shells, a weapons-cleaning kit, and a locked-and-loaded Turkish model .380, a highly concealable small-caliber pistol that I won in a game of Batak. Also in the bag: two panels of silk blown from the backside of a parachute during a jump that ended high in the trees. I kept these two panels of silk wrapped tightly around an ammunition drum converted into a lock box. This kept the sharp corners of the ammo drum from poking into my back as I walked. I kept inside the lockbox my Zippo, DD-form marching orders, the few ribbons I hadn't given away, and newspaper clippings. Many of the clippings had gone yellow with time, but that was okay. Sorting them by date was just a matter of color-coding them from dark to light.

I also had a fifth of Jack in that bag in desperate need of drinking.

I spread the news-clippings on the floor, sorting them by color, and then took a good long pull from the bottle. When the bottle was half-gone, when I was half-gone, when the edges of my world blurred to wonderful spinning grays, the smell of sulfur came thick through the cold-air returns. It was an unholy and unnatural smell and so I kept drinking a spin downward until the smell went away...until there was the empty and the nothing, the place where the Everlasting resides when humanity seeks his face. If I were lucky enough tonight, I would crawl into my rotting little bunk and roll up in my two panels of parachute silk before hypothermia ambushed me. In the morning, I would vomit, fill my stomach with water from the sink, and then vomit again—that was the plan, but then sometime that night as I floated in the empty and nothing something crawled up through the drain in the floor, wrestled me down, and carried me silently into the fury of a fever-dream.

In that fever-dream, someone anguished an agonized cry from a darkness far beneath. I knew the voice and so followed her through the pit towards a lake of black fire. She was amid the billions writhing, those who in life were unable to believe their way up the narrow path. I reached to free her from the fires, but they, the castaway masses, also stretched arms toward me. They thought I was God and pled for my infinite mercy. Their hands were too many and so she became lost, swallowed down, screaming for God, drowning in unquenchable flame, flesh ripped and torn, clawing and clawing, so much pain, so much agony, dying the forever death, begging for God in a sea of fiery sorrow. I plunged down after her, but they were all pulled deeper too.

This was their punishment, their cries for mercy only compounding their pain. I followed her deeper toward the unknowable center, souls around me rent apart under the strain of immeasurable and unknowable holy wrath. Here, the finite were condemned to infinity, flame and void together as one, an impure thought or two punished billions and billions of times over, forever and ever. As I went deeper after her, from high above came music down through a firmament, a celestial window to entertain the Few and the Elect, grinning believers celebrating all the suffering, and the song they sang was:

Praise Him, Praise Him,
All ye little children.
God is Love, God is Love...

There was a stone amid a casket and a ravine with thickets and cuts on her feet sewn thick with black thread. There were questions unanswered and faceless enemies. "Finder of lost loves, you must go back," a voice cried out from everywhere, "and when you go back, God will turn his face." The voice shook me and the lonely darkness embraced me and through space and time I traveled, the exploding cosmos letting me ride upon its wake, massive flickering fire-lights forming in a creation far more amazing, far more incredible, far more awe-sweeping than anything ever written or dreamed. This was the beginning and I was speeding through an expanding space, shooting through time towards a tiny ball of wetness on some unnamed spiral arm stretching from some insignificant little spiral galaxy amid a tiny cluster of galaxies. Everything seemed so small and far away at first, but then came at me bigger and bigger, faster and faster. The tiny little ball of wetness spun around a tiny little ball of fire, little creepy-crawlies crawling across it, evolving into men and beyond...amazingly beyond...in a blink of an eye, I had gone too far, two billion years too far into the future...and from beneath the clouds I heard a voice whisper, "yet it moves." In that instant, time spun backwards in a blink and I found myself home, lying on a cold floor next to a drain that went nowhere. God appeared before me in that little basement apartment and He was big and I was small and He said, "Bear fruit."

I said, "I am out of season, but take my branches, my roots."

God grew angry and cursed me and I withered, but as I withered, I saw that it was not really God standing over me but my Kindergarten Sunday School teacher who was telling me that I must turn my cheek. I was a child now and dared to ask, "What if he keeps hitting me and will not stop?"

"You must let him keep hitting."

"What if he hurts somebody else, somebody I love?"

"You must let him persist and love him even more."

"And what if he—"

Sunday School Teacher grabbed my arm and dragged me to the closet, where she struck my hands bloody with a ruler. "This will teach you to ask questions," she raged. Bleeding and afraid, I fell to my knees and she locked the door. That was when the floor gave beneath me and revealed stars moving faster and faster around me. I was floating, dreaming, escaping...and finally I was thrust up from the fever-dream some six days later.

My mind was alive again. The dream had woken something deep and now I was unfettered by the chains that had been sinking me. The old superstitions and the magical thinking were gone. There was only the world of here and now—a world free of unfulfilled blessings and unfounded curses, free of all the childish delusions of grey bearded saints looking down from the clouds. I was no longer a slave to my fear.

My mission was singular and it started with answers...

BUT FIRST I needed a drink. During that fever-dream of six days, those newspaper clippings that were my only link to the case had gone wet with condensation. It was reconstructive work of the most delicate kind, involving surgical scissors from my first-aid kit and electrical tape from my ammo box. I would start from the beginning, and piece by piece, arrange the facts, peeling each clipping off the floor as best I could, using tracing paper to reconstruct words imprinted on the paint flakes where the newspaper had utterly dissolved. The big cracked mirror would make a better canvas than the floor, and so right in its center the first news clipping went.

"OFFICIALS TIGHT-LIPPED ABOUT CASE." The bottom corner of this one was curled and lost, but I remembered its contents...no news.

"DEATH DID NOT OCCUR IN DITCH" had managed to stay dry. The wounds on her body, the terrain, and the nature of the crime scene made death by hit-and-run impossible according to the coroners—the news story said nothing more. This one went right next to the first.

"MEDICAL EXAMINER: 'NECK INJURY CAUSE OF DEATH.'" Blunt force and defense wounds—hyperflexion of the neck, the killing blow.

I began scribbling down questions at a fevered pitch: why not throw the body in the river, where it would be lost or where, at the least, trace evidence would be washed away? Why not bury the body? Why not find a more remote location? Why not take the time to do it right? Were you rushed or did you want the body to found? Why not steal the money in her purse?

I was doing my best to get into the mind of the killer, but only found myself washed up in my own anger and drunkenness.

"DEATH NOT CONNECTED TO OMAHA MURDER." A young black girl had been raped repeatedly and then skinned alive by white supremacists a few days before Tammy was killed. The little girl's skinned body was shoved into an oil barrel and left for dead. (It turns out that the two murderers were on death row until human rights activists had them freed on a technicality.) This news story was meant to calm nerves right after Tammy's murder, to assure the local population that these two deaths were in no way related, that this wasn't a serial case.

This clipping went beneath a banner headline reading: "POLICE OFFER REWARD IN HAAS INVESTIGATION." The date on this clipping was some five months after Tammy's death.

"VEHICLE IMPOUNDED: BODY RUMORED IN TRUNK." The date on this clipping was just over six months after her death.

"HAAS LAST SEEN WALKING HOME." By whom, the article would not say, but this article came nearly seven months later.

"FRIENDS CALL HER CHEERFUL PERSON." What friends? The same ones at the party who saw her walking home? Eight months.

"FAMILY STILL WAITING FOR ANSWERS."

We make ourselves another drink and scrawl down a nine.

"REWARD POSTERS AVAILABLE – $10,000 OFFERED."

A whore's ransom and an insult—ten months.

"MOTHER WANTS TO FORGIVE."

Eleven.

"ONE YEAR LATER—STILL NO ANSWERS."

Two years later, still no answers...

"FRIENDS HOLD PRAYER SERVICE."

Words, words, words—filling up the mirror...

"NEWSPAPER RECEIVES THREATENING CALLS."

Only one more patch where I could see my reflection...

"RUMORS SURFACE AS CASE STALLS."

I smiled blood as that last little puddle of mirror disappeared—
"Rumors..."

CHAPTER SEVENTEEN

RUMOR AFTER RUMOR, most of them ugly, most you don't want to hear." Cooper Mac had gotten broad in the shoulder and heavy in the waist. His eyes were tired from late hours of work. He went from looking very young to very old virtually over night. "Why can't you just let it go? That was—how long now—over two years ago?"

"Humor me," I said.

"Humor you?" Cooper laughed. "I don't think so." A few months ago, Cooper went from customer to bartender at the Eighth Street Pub, a back-alley joint and lone vestige of the railroad glory days. It was New Year's Eve, but this little out-of-the-way pub was empty save me bellied up on a corner stool and Cooper Mac serving.

"You worked with Tammy that night," I reminded Cooper.

"Yes, I'm aware," he said and then gestured for me to down the concoction he'd mixed, the house special he called it, whiskey, a stout, and an unlabeled bottle, which when poured with the others instantly stripped the drink of carbonation and created three wonderful churning layers of color—a Lava Lamp he called it. "You ever think about talking to the police," he said.

"The police won't talk to me."

"You could talk to Tammy's mom."

"If I talked to Tammy's mom, I'd just—" I pressed the heel of my hand to my temple to squeeze away a coming migraine. "These things need to be handled delicately. I have to be careful to whom I speak. Tactical decisions need to be made. You have to be careful about who you hurt, who gets involved…coming to you, trusting you was tough enough."

Cooper stubbed his cigarette in the ashtray. "You could talk to your minister." He then dumped the contents of the ashtray immediately in the garbage, as was his habit, and lit another. "You could try to get some, you know, emotional help is what I'm saying."

"I don't need a support group," I said. "I don't need therapy. I don't need a prayer circle! Or whatever else you're about to suggest." The slow throb of the migraine swelled round my skull, seeping through the cracks like ice through concrete. "I just need my friend to talk to me."

"You want to hear rumors?" Cooper asked me.

"Yes," I said. "I want to hear rumors."

"Okay, rough sex, things got out of hand."

I downed the chaser Cooper slid my way.

"There's also the car surfing theory. Everybody panicked…or some of those guys were out on the gravel making cookies, slid into the ditch, and hit her…or how about this one—she was peeing out the window of a car and fell out, or was peeing at the guardrail and was clipped, or out the window of that farmhouse and she slipped…or was accidentally pushed. That's the one most people have accepted—just a stupid, drunken accident."

"Peeing?" I said. "Tell me you're not that stupid please."

Cooper turned his back on me to run some water down the sink. "You've been looking for somebody to blame for two years now…just let it go."

"What if it happens again, this time to somebody *you* love?"

"You want my theory?" Cooper turned back at me hard and leaned in close. "Do you want to know what I believe happened that night?

"Yes, Cooper, I'd like that very much, thank you."

"Two guys get in a fight over Tammy. She tries to break it up. A punch is thrown and she's in the crossfire—she lands on something hard. A log. A rock. Something. I don't know what. The thing is, everybody sees it happen, and everybody sees that she's not getting up. The two guys who were fighting get drafted to dump the body. They find the nearest ravine. They pull her pants off to make it look like some stranger came along and grabbed her. Nobody is really at fault, just a stupid accident."

"What two guys?"

"What?"

"What two guys were fighting over her?"

"You should go home, Merrill. It's New Year's and you've killed all my business." Cooper dug for a ring of keys. "I want to shut down and go home myself. Listen, you're a model citizen, a Boy Scout. What would you do anyway if you knew? What would you do if her killer walked in here right now and said it to your face?" Cooper smiled. "Do you know what you'd do? You'd do nothing! Why? Because you have integrity."

I slammed my glass against the bar. "I wrote you asking for help!"

"I work two jobs, brother. I have a life to live"

"I asked you to find out who took her to that party. I asked you—"

"God, Merrill, don't you get it, I have a wife and baby now! I want to, but I can't get involved in this!" Cooper grabbed the glass from me and dropped it in the sink.

"If it was your wife, your child?"

Cooper spun, glass raised to strike me down. "Don't ever fucking talk about my family like that again! It's not the same—not at all!"

"Did I bring a jacket?" I asked.

Cooper dug under the bar and pulled up my jacket. "I married the woman I loved…and she loves me back. The difference between you and Tammy and me and her, it ain't the same…it ain't even close."

"Well," I said. "You have a happy New Year, Cooper Mac."

"Jesus fucking Christ," he shouted. "You act like you're some kind of hero. You ain't no hero! You had a crush on this girl and she died. That's all. You meant *nothing* to her! Nothing at all! You were the punch line to a joke…and now you can't get over it…and now you act like it's this big deal or something. But people die, that's life."

I pushed and the door slammed open into the howling wind.

"I'm happy things worked out for you, Cooper."

"You talk to Bobby yet?"

"I've tried." I turned and managed a smile. "He's dodging me."

"I promised him," Cooper said, "two years ago, I'd keep a secret."

BOBBY'S LITTLE BRICK party house had become a depot for the dispossessed. The way it worked was that the right people, the ones trustworthy enough not to snitch, could slip their way into the back bedroom to kick whatever trip they so chose, all of it hassle free and only for a small price, the only other big no-no—making mention of troubling events from the past. They called this infraction stepping on another person's buzz. If you were involved, you were to keep your mouth shut. If you were curious—same.

This very night Bobby was throwing a New Year's Party to welcome in 1995. He expected more guests to float through, snorting, swallowing, or smoking whatever tripped their kick, but the bitter cold kept many away. Still, there was a small crowd and one of the two kegs Bobby had purchased from Cooper Mac this past weekend had just gone dry. To make more dance space in the living room, Bobby decided to deposit the dead keg out in the snow.

A push and kick of the back door and Bobby was out from the smoky stench, able to take in a sobering gulp of fiery-cold winter air. He would have to remember to tape a note atop the keg to keep the garbage men from taking it, but that could wait until tomorrow. Things were good in Bobby's world tonight, a mellow embracing of a new year…that was until a good hard blow to the small of his back sent him spinning over the keg and tumbling into the three garbage cans with the steel lids good for banging.

I had gone shoulder first into him harder than I had intended, thinking the snow would slow me in those last few steps, softening impact. The snow, however, gave way to ice, and my body became like a bullet unstoppable, and upon impact Bobby and I were thrust forward by inertia, the keg spinning beneath us and across the drive until coming to a clanging rest against Bobby's old Mustang, the three garbage cans dropping like bowling pins.

Bobby wheezed the wind from his belly and threw up his hands to protect his face, but I wasn't going for his face—I was going for his throat. "Thirty seconds you're unconscious, two minutes you're dead." He didn't recognize the voice.

"Can't breathe!" he cried.

As my grip grew tighter, his vision blurred worse. Soldier was guiding me now. "Clock's ticking for you to tell me none of it's true," I said.

"Merrill?" he wheezed.

"Tick-tock goes the clock!"

"Jesus, what the fuck! Not true—whatever you think—not true!"

His vision tunneled and body surrendered, his eyes pleading mercy.

"Her footprint was on your windshield and I didn't get it! You left work together! She changed pants in your car! She put her foot up against the glass to pull up her jeans! That's how the footprint got there! That's how you knew she was wearing high heels! Because she had forgotten her other shoes when you two left!"

"Her footprint! But that doesn't mean—"

Bobby felt the world go soft as I ratcheted tighter my hand on his throat.

"—can't breathe—"

"I'm not choking you!" I whispered. "I'm pinching off the blood supply to your brain."

"—can't breathe—"

"You got into a fight over Tammy—with somebody, some other guy. I want to know who that guy was—that's the only chance you have right now—she tried to step in and break it up. One of you swung, she fell, hit something hard, broke her neck. I want to know which one of you did it—that's the only chance you've got."

There was confusion in Bobby's eyes and then a sudden surge of adrenaline. He kicked and writhed and we both came off our feet, spinning across the ice until he had me lifted and pinned atop the hood of his car. Desperation gave him strength but not control and so as he bashed at my wrist to remove my hand from his throat, he lost his footing, and we both slid a tangled dance off the hood of the car, across the ice, up and over the empty keg again, until finally hitting the ground exactly where we had begun.

"Thirty seconds unconscious, two minutes dead."

"Okay! I took her to the party!" Bobby shouted. "But I didn't do it!"

"That's not what Cooper Mac thinks."

"That Judas! That fucking Judas!"

"Not helping your situation here, Bob!"

"You're so fucking naïve!"

I slapped the spit from Bobby's lips.

"You think she gave two shits about you, Merrill?!"

I slapped Bobby again, this time drawing blood. "You tell me what happened that night, Bobby. You tell me everything!"

Bobby smiled. "I stranded her, I don't fucking know! I left her at the party and I went home!"

"Bullshit!"

"Bullshit?"

I reared back, my fist clenched.

"They impounded a car!" Bobby was mad now and wanted me to hit him. "Think about it, do the math, you fucking idiot! They impounded a car!"

"And what?" I said.

"And my car's here!"

I lowered my fist. "Her body in the trunk and your car is here."

"My car's here…and it can't be in two places at once."

"You're still not telling me everything. I can see that in your eyes."

Bobby rolled away and spit the blood from his mouth. Through the window of his little brick house, six blushing faces had watched it all take place. It was his ego that had taken the brunt of my attack. "I have a party to get back to," Bobby said and shoved me away. I rose to my feet and offered him my hand. He slapped it away.

"That's it then, huh?" I said.

"You're so fucking naïve," he said.

I dusted the snow from my shoulders and disappeared back into the shadows, back into the brisk fiery-cold of that New Year's night.

RETIRED SPECIAL AGENT Carriss had decided not to take refuge in warmer climate, even though several lucrative job offers awaited him there. Instead, Carriss decided he would stay where his last case had stalled. He had found a little trailer house on the outskirts of town. It wasn't much, but was functional and served his needs. He spent his mornings trolling the local coffee shops, mostly listening, always carrying with him the old case files, always picking through the past in search of something missed. He would spend the afternoons at the local library or the Court of Records, sifting through family histories, compiling something along the lines of an anthology of local lore. It was his belief that in small towns everything was connected somehow, no matter how far back you looked. He traced land rights to the first settlers, the ones who had taken the land from Strike-the-Ree and his tribe of Eh-hank-ton in the 1850s, and then dug even further back to Lewis and Clark, and before that, to the French fur trappers. He made mental maps of how land moved from hand to hand, shady dealings in the Mother City, an unsolved old murder or two every generation or so. In the evening, he would stop by the local liquor store, grab a bag of chips and a six-pack, or sometimes a twelve, go home, and settle back in front of the TV to drink himself to sleep.

It was New Year's and retired Special Agent Carriss was deep inside a dream about a case forty years old—an ugly and personal case—when sudden knocking yanked him to his feet. His former partner Special Agent Earnstead was on the other side of the door and had been there a good two minutes, getting cold and worried, ready to smash down the door with a kick.

Carriss wanted to shave and press a shirt, but Earnstead told him not to bother. It was parka season—wrinkles were expected. Besides, it was 3:00 A.M., Earnstead had driven two hundred miles, and Coroner Wong, as it happened, was braving an even longer drive to bring them the results. It would be very informal and done in secret.

Quantico had snipped the last bit of red tape from the Tammy Haas rape kit in one big end-of-year house-cleaning push. Coroner Wong was going to give Carriss and Earnstead twenty-four hours to do what they could with the results before sending the file through the proper chain of custody, which in the end meant the local police.

Carriss threw on his parka, disappeared somewhere beneath the fluff and fur of its hood, and with a slam of his thin little trailer house door, followed Earnstead into the brisk new air of a brand new year.

THE HOMECOMING

TOO OFTEN THE obvious buries itself right out in the miry open and so you stare at a thing hours on end, never really seeing what needs to be seen. I had sifted through those news clippings hundreds and hundreds of times, but it took a nudge from a friend to see that—"VEHICLE IMPOUNDED—BODY RUMORED IN TRUNK"—meant that the police had been sitting upon a major piece of evidence for over two years.

I pulled the news clipping down from the big cracked mirror.

So simple—just find out whose car they impounded.

If not the killer's, somebody close to the killer.

I zipped the news clipping in the lining of my winter battle dress, changed the battery in my Maglight, and made sure I was carrying the color filters I needed to dampen its glow. My Zippo was filled with fluid and the flint was in perfect working order.

I holstered my freshly loaded pistol, slid my paratrooper knife into my ankle sheath, grabbed my lock-pick set, and then searched for my gloves…and searched…and searched…and decided that I would have to go without—it was now 3:30 A.M. and I would be a racing to beat morning.

BECAUSE IT ROSE up out of a snowdrift, the fence into the impound lot turned out not much to negotiate. Instead of climbing, all I had to do was lift a leg, take a step, and hope that the snow inside the fence was just as hard-packed as the snow outside. The three strands of barbed wire at the top poked gently across my inner thigh as I made the crossing, leaving the slightest of scratches, the kind of scratches a soldier wants, the kind that bring just enough pain to remind him of the delicacy it would take to complete his mission.

They had packed the cars and trucks bumper to bumper making just enough room for a patrol car to navigate a narrow path from the front gate to the back. Some of the compact cars were completely buried, only their antennas poking through. I had made the simple assumption that I would merely have to navigate the fence and bust into some cars until finding the right one, but I had been away too long. I had underestimated the wind-driven snow of South Dakota—its ability to amass, to become rock-hard strata with each melt and freeze. What confronted me inside that fence was a mighty fortress of hard-packed snow as solid as the Detroit steel beneath.

Three hours until daylight—two-dozen automobiles buried, give or take—I would pick the locks in search of owner's registration, credit card receipts, proof of insurance, anything that would point me toward her killer.

I had never broken into anything without explicit orders.

My hands were going numb.

Process of elimination—I knew I was looking for a car with a trunk. There were three trucks, one jeep, two hatchbacks, and an El Camino in the lot. None of these had trunks, thus none of these needed to be searched. That meant roughly half a dozen vehicles eliminated from my list and somewhere in the neighborhood of eighteen vehicles to go.

My hands were on fire.

THE HOMECOMING

I searched the snowy fortress looking for the easiest way to penetrate. I had to think. I had to think my way around the digging. I needed to simplify the process, find the best way inside—at most, I would be able to reach and search four cars by morning. By morning, somebody would take notice and the game would be up...I had to make those four cars count...

For two years, the car had been impounded, which meant...

...the car had to have been made before September 1992.

1994s and 1995s—eliminate those from the list.

That was as far as my mind would reach to solve this problem.

Sobriety was still an hour or two away.

Dig now—think later.

A shovel would have been nice.

There was no turning back and so I heaved and kicked up snow and ice to get my way through the strata. There was a half-ton piece of evidence just waiting beneath the drifts—a few hours of pain and I would have all the answers I needed.

Two layers deep, the snow broke and lifted in sharp icy sheets...

So close...

...and that's when the long fracture formed beneath my knees...

...between the length of the two cars flanking me it ran...

...and like a trapdoor swinging open...

...the two great slabs gave way...

...and down I went...

I fell at least five feet and landed on my side, the two great slabs smashing down in chunks atop and around me. Some sort of air pocket must have formed deep in the drift, from day after day of melt and freeze, the deepest snow melting and the water running off beneath the cars, creating expanding air pockets beneath bridges of ice and snow...

I rose, hip screaming, and peered through the slick, thin layers of ice coating the two cars on my left and right.

The first was a two-door Toyota, mid-80s. I drew my knife and chipped at the ice to get to the door handle. I pulled out my lock-pick kit, but to my chagrin, moisture had bled deep into the locking mechanism, making the door impenetrable with such delicate tools. The temptation was to find a brick and smash the glass. Destroying evidence, however, didn't seem wise.

Sometimes the simplest solutions are often the best.

In this case, that meant giving the door handle a tug...and sure enough, the door gave with an aching, icy groan. Evidently, around here impounded cars went unlocked.

I poked my head into the Toyota and got one look at the driver's seat. Buckshot had ripped through the headrest. An oblong mushroom of blood-turned-black stained the ceiling right behind it. The shotgun went into the mouth. The brains came out of the back of the head—death by suicide. It wasn't the first time I had seen this. It was how several of my comrades in arms decided to leave the world.

I turned to the Bonneville next to the Toyota. It looked as if it had been rolled several times in a wreck, abandoned on the side of the road, and finally gutted for parts. The rust was at least a decade ago. I tried the door, only to be confronted by a blast of unnaturally warm air and the smell of propane. I scanned the darkness with my Maglight. Strewn across the belly of the car were dishware, foam insulation, and heaps of crumpled newspaper. Sitting neatly in the opened glove box was a tiny Coleman stove—its heating elements still red-hot. This was somebody's home, he or she had heard my grand entrance down through the chimney, got scared, and took flight…

"But how could that be?" I whispered. "No exit but this one."

I unzipped my coat to let in the heat. There was a neatly rolled sleeping bag in the corner, a battery-operated television propped in the rear window, and gloves…gloves that looked like mine on the backseat. I crawled to the back to get at them and sure enough—M.C.M. was inked in the lining.

It occurred to me as my hands began to warm inside my gloves that I couldn't be sure I was in the right impound lot. For all I knew, the car I was after could have been in Nebraska. Jurisdictionally speaking, this would make far more sense. Along those lines, perhaps, the Feds might have towed the car off to some regional crime lab. It was no good, none of it. I had gotten myself so cold that it hurt to warm up.

If I turned back now it would be over. If I turned back now, I would give up and in—another year would slip past, my courage and my conviction lost.

It hurt to think.

I had just found my gloves in the car of a homeless person who had somehow vanished…but he couldn't have gotten far.

I switched off my Maglight, stilled myself, and listened.

A slight draft was coming up from behind the back seat.

I switched on my Maglight and very carefully lifted the blankets that were being used as seat-covers. Beneath the blankets was plywood and beyond the plywood, the torn guts of the seat, and beyond the torn guts of the seat, a secret passageway. The secret passageway led through to the trunk, where, beneath a layer of Styrofoam insulation, a hula-girl mud-flap trapdoor was screwed into the floor.

I drew my pistol and gently lifted the hula-girl mud-flap.

"A tunnel…"

Headfirst, I went, pistol and flashlight aimed into the blackness. Straight out from beneath the Bonneville's trunk, into a snow tunnel that led through a break in the impound-lot fence, through more snowdrifts, and into the twilight twenty feet beyond.

I followed the tunnel until coming across a side-tunnel. This side-tunnel led to arteries that passed row by row between the cars. Things were looking up. Old receipts in the glove boxes, insurance paperwork hidden in the visor, empty prescription bottles wedged under the seats—I was into my fifth car and moving fast, sobering up and beating the coming dawn. If all else failed, I would exhaust the possibility that this impound lot was the one.

It wasn't until car number nine that I hit a wrinkle—quite literally a wrinkle—canvas frozen thick with ice, canvas shrunk by cold, canvas covering snuggly the car beneath.

"Geronimo," I whispered because through the ice I could make out the faint shadow of words. I went gentle with my knife to shave the ice away to get closer to the words, faded stencil barely visible in the frozen fabric—

> PROPERTY OF THE
> UNITED STATES
> FEDERAL BUREAU OF
> INVESTIGATION

The art of infiltration was much like the art of chess—measure your every step, think far enough ahead so that no novice could ever see you coming, and always, always, always have an exit strategy. There was too much snow heaped atop the car to remove the tarp. I would have to burrow beneath the fabric, pressing myself along the side of the car to get to the driver's door. Every move had to be precise or I would lose the few inches of crawl space I needed to force open the door.

The plan was wonderful and executed quite flawlessly. Unfortunately, I had overlooked one minor detail—a locked car door.

So there I found myself, tucked snuggly against the side of the car, every breath a battle against the pressing squeeze of the shrunken fabric of the frozen car cover.

I was tempted to draw my knife and slice my way out.

My lock-pick kit was thoroughly out of reach inside my jacket. Not that it mattered—the lock of the door was frozen solid. My Maglight was between my teeth, my lips frozen around it. Still, I was able to crane my neck and bounce a little halo of red light through the window. There was nothing distinct about what I saw inside the car—just shadow residing atop shadow, the darkness barely broken by the glimmering orb of red. I did discover something unexpected though—a control panel for a moon roof.

It would take some patient slithering, but I was certain that I could force my way inside through the top. It was no easy task, pressing myself beneath two feet of hard-packed snow, the ice going soft and wet beneath me, sending me slithering down the windshield again and again.

I was tempted to use my forehead against the glass.

Finally, I was curled atop the moon roof, feeling along its seams for the latches. In subzero temperatures, springs and hinges made of steel alloy contract and go brittle. This meant that with the application of the right kind of pressure the springs could pop, allowing hinges and hasps to fall loose.

Finally, with a bit of patience and some forcing of my disposition, I got the moon roof open, but in the process of getting the moon roof open, I dropped my Maglight down into the car. As it hit bottom, its light bounced back up at me once, toppled sideways, rolled, flickered, and went dead.

I was staring down into what could just as well have been a bottomless pit. I had no choice but to go headfirst blind, one hand firmly planted on the roof, the other feeling through the blackness.

My left hand missed it, but my right shoulder found the top of the driver's seat. I twisted myself to get my left arm around the headrest. With what leverage I could muster at this awkward angle, I pulled and twisted to get my legs through the roof. Where I expected to slide down into the passenger's seat, I slid down upon nothing. Sliding down upon nothing threw me into a very short and uncontrolled inverted freefall. This was followed by sudden impact against something rigidly, pointedly, and inarguably metal.

I was once again lying on my back, head beneath the dashboard, spine twisted beyond decency, one leg wrapped over the steering column, the other...I'm not quite sure where, because I could not feel anything below my hips. The jabbing sensation between my two shoulder blades was caused by what I could only assume was my pistol fallen from my holster.

I fought the urge to roll to my stomach, instinct often not serving the beast. I stilled myself to get my bearing. The sharp, cold pinching between my shoulder blades grew fierce and as sensation came back to my legs, I could feel my pistol safely holstered against my thigh. I was atop something else, something sharp enough to penetrate my jacket, my skin—something sharp enough to burrow into my muscle.

A gentle arching of the spine and a shifting of my weight—a gentle exhalation and the tear of fabric—relief coming in spasms—a gasp of pain as the skin pinched slowly away from the metal object—and with the gushing of blood, I was free.

I felt around for my flashlight, gave it a shake, felt something inside shatter. I dug for my Zippo, clicked it open, clicked it closed, clicked it open again and gave it a snap to bring up the flame.

A juicy warm flicker of orange revealed that the passenger's seat had been removed, leaving only the sharp metal runners beneath, the sharp end of one icing over with my blood.

I was inside a Chevy Beretta according to the insignia on the glove box.

"Who owns a Beretta?"

I squatted up to scan the dashboard and upon first fleeting look nearly missed it—the AC vent covers were gone and the vents were taped over with a clear adhesive.

"The passenger's seat, the vent covers—collected as evidence. Latent prints and trace fluids lifted from hard to reach places—because the car was had been cleaned...why else would the FBI take the frigging vents?"

My breath froze crystals against the windshield. It was becoming harder to focus. I had to remember to scrape my blood from that seat runner.

At that party, the first night I was home, the night before the funeral, I heard it said twice—"the car was cleaned real good." Who was at that party though? Bobby, Cooper Mac, of course, and the Homecoming Chief and his girlfriend too, having an argument in the bushes...and, shit, Stukel, Eric

Stukel...he asked me for my lighter. No, in fact, he tried to take my lighter...and he was standing out in the cold in the park only a few days ago and standing at her grave after the funeral...at the water fountain of the police station the night before I left...and in the conference room, cutting a deal.

My glove was beginning to smolder against the heat of my Zippo.

My mind was going soft. Stukel had left some sort of carved rock on her casket—I gave the rock to the FBI, and at the funeral, Noose Adarson pulled up in Eric's Beretta...and the very car I was in right now was a Beretta and on the passenger's window there were controls to the side-view mirror, and those controls to the side-view mirror were broken, and trailing away from the controls was a deep scuffmark, and that deep scuffmark was taped over with a clear tape...clear tape to retain the scuff...a brown scuff...and I was slipping...the brown scuff was forensic evidence, preserved beneath what they called forensic lifting tape...how the hell could a person leave a scuff at that angle unless they were on their back, stretched awkwardly across the seat? Why the hell would a person be stretched awkwardly on their back?

"A struggle?"

I smoothed my hand over the dashboard hoping to divine more...my hands were so cold...and had just come upon another piece of forensic lifting tape. This piece of forensic lifting tape was covering another scuffmark...but there was more...somebody had used an abrasive cleanser to try to buff out the scuff...it was so obvious, so obvious...but only if my mind would work faster, connect the dots, beat the day...too cold, too much bleeding, too much fear, too much pain...

"Focus, Merrill!" I shouted and watched the steam from my breath puff across the glass of the windshield...where it revealed... revealed...revealed... the arc of the scuffmark moving upward from dashboard to windshield...and there on the windshield was a little crack in the glass.

"She was kicking to get free?" the steam swirled from my breath.

On her back, struggling...trying to get out the driver's side door?

"Stukel..."

I couldn't hold out much longer—don't forget that name—Eric Stukel. My sweat had dried too fast...had dried to ice...had to breathe to calm myself, disorientation meant death...had to focus...had to breathe!

A strange sound gathered around me, like water beneath racing ice. I exhaled another steady breath and listened, and as I listened I saw it coming, the fog stretching across the windshield and swirling away once more to reveal the source of the strange sound—a tiny fracture etching an arc across the glass, a slow smile forming from the tiny crack, the sound growing to a shrill pitch beneath the stomping weight of the extreme cold.

"Not good..."

The blood was turning to ice on the back of my jacket—not much time until daylight now. Purple light was gathering against and piercing through the canvas. Time to go. Enough evidence already compromised.

"Hate the cold!"

THE HOMECOMING

Use that hate. Search the trunk. Check the plate number to confirm my suspicion...because that's all it was right now—a suspicion.

Imagine yourself into a sobering warmth and keep moving. Remember how she would warm me when we would sit on the roof, beneath the thick blanket I kept hidden in the tiles. Remember the stars shining down as our eyes stretched toward Heaven. Remember the furtive glances, her shape beneath the blanket. Remember how I would pull the blanket tighter to bring those curves a bit closer to the surface. Remember how she would slap my hand away and giggle. Remember how sometimes it would feel so real on the waking. Remember how I would dream her with me, how she would fade on the waking over the years that passed, how I would feel so soulless. All I would have to do is go still and die...make a bed for myself and bleed my way into her arms...and first call would be in the morning, and Eccles would wake us up and we would road march until blisters hardened on our feet and then get in the airplane and jump and sail and float and dream...

No!

Stay awake!

Or better yet remember...

Give myself fully to the cold, unzip my jacket, remove my hood, loosen my boots, swim darker and deeper. Give in because it feels so good to be carried. Lift myself downward into the darkness where the bleeding stops and where day breaks, where all is...all is...all is...

CORONER BETTY WONG had just turned up the heat and braved to toss down her coat on the cold of the cutting table when Earnstead and Carriss arrived. Earnstead smiled big through the hood of his parka, the kind of smile smiled after a nightlong drive. "Tell us it's going to be a happy New Year, Betty," he said and tossed his coat atop hers.

"Coffee?" Betty Wong asked.

"Sure." Earnstead said.

"Not if you want some, but if you brought any." The way she said it made Carriss laugh so hard he doubled over in pain. Coroner Betty Wong wasn't Asian, but she had been married to one for thirty years and thirty years ago had decided (against her parents' wishes) to take his name. She was good at her job—her husband was the best, a groundbreaker in forensic science.

"I'll buy the coffee." Carriss was still laughing. "But first those labs."

From her attaché case, Wong pulled a FED-EX package stamped and sealed with an FBI tamper warning. "Gentlemen?" she said in a way that warned them that she was about to break protocol and the law.

"There is one nice thing about being retired." Carriss took the FED-EX from Wong and quickly ripped it open. "Job security." A ream of lab results spilled from the package and for the next twenty minutes Coroner Wong read in silence, pacing for the first five minutes, sitting atop the cutting table the next ten, and pacing again the last five. Finally, Wong slid the lab results back into the FED-EX and smiled a smile that gave away nothing. "Where's your wife tonight, Special Agent Earnstead?"

"Abandoned her to a party when you called," Earnstead said.

Wong went to a file cabinet and began to pull up files.

"If this pregnant pause has something to do with the building up of suspense," Carriss whispered, "remember that I'm not getting any younger."

"The urine on the underwear?" Wong found the file she was seeking. "You were right about it coming from a different source than the urine on the back of the jeans—which is strange, considering that within the timeframe of the night in question there should have been cross-contamination."

"Which one of us was right about this?" Earnstead asked.

Wong pointed at Carriss. "Sure enough, the urine on the jeans matches the urine on the passenger's seat...the urine on the underwear? I still can't be sure considering the timeframe. We *can be* sure neither matches the victim."

"So what are you saying?" Earnstead said. "She gets into the car and sits in the passenger's seat where someone has urinated? The urine doesn't pass through the jeans to the underwear? How is that possible?"

"The urine on the underwear had to have gotten there well before the urine on the jeans...with time enough to dry..." Carriss said.

"Not necessarily," Wong said.

"How so?" Carriss asked.

"The urine on the underwear could have come *after*," Wong said.

"After she was dead?" Earnstead said.

"...which shouldn't be possible," Carriss said.

They were all surrounding the cutting table, all staring down at it, all secretly wishing the body were here, that they could go back two years and process the victim, be the first on the case rather than the last.

"The urine on the jeans *does* place her in his car," Carriss said.

"We have DNA?" Earnstead asked.

"DNA wouldn't have told us a thing we didn't already know," Wong said. "You have to understand, two years ago the technology wasn't there to do DNA polymerase chain reaction, to work with trace samples."

"So no DNA?" Earnstead said.

"Two sources of urine." Carriss was hung up on the notion. "The urine on the pants comes from the seat of the car. The urine on the underwear had to have gotten there after the pants came off. We're dealing with two separate events...we're dealing with Bobby Grant and Eric Stukel—"

"You're saying Eric and Bobby were acting together?" Earnstead asked.

"No," Carriss said. "I'm saying they were acting in opposition."

Wong laughed and then went silent...silent as if she had just been struck. "Rapists don't reach climax generally," she said. "They urinate—an act representative of the male orgasm."

"According to Stukel, she drove them home...back to South Dakota," Carriss said. "They have consensual sex and then she dresses and goes."

"She walks to Bobby's from Stukel's. The urine has dried. Bobby rapes her. Kills her...takes her across the bridge, dumps her body near the party spot," Earnstead rubbed at his chin. "It's thin, but a strong possibility."

"Not if we trust the polygraphs," Carriss said.

"You have the two sources switched," Wong said. "The urine on the underwear matches Stukel's blood and secretor type, not Bobby Grant's."

"Bobby's urine on the seat of Stukel's car then?" Earnstead said.

Wong hurried to her file cabinet.

"So," Carriss said. "Our victim and Stukel are leaving the party together. She gets into his car and gets wet with urine. Where does the urine come from? Bobby most likely...Stukel says he took her home, incriminating himself in the process...but first, there's some sort of struggle in the car."

"Is it possible that it was Bobby in the car and not Stukel?" Earnstead said. "Is it possible that the three of them were in there together? That a fight broke out? That they dump the body together and concoct alibis?"

"Second source did come later," Wong said, coming back to them with a stack of case files. "We find no signs of vaginal or anal trauma, no bleeding, but we do find trace amounts of sperm, the sperm Stukel admits to."

"Consensual sex in the car?" Earnstead said. "At the party?"

"We have trace evidence we don't know what to do with," Carriss said.

"I do have a theory," Wong said, "actually, it's my husband's, but I've reserved judgment until Quantico got back to me with these results. I had hoped to nail the case shut with this, but I'm not sure anymore. It's out there and thin," she said. "But I think we can give the theory some muscle."

"You don't think Stukel ever took her home?" Earnstead asked.

"You have to think like a woman," Wong said.

"How so?" Earnstead asked.

"No woman would accept a ride in a urine-soaked car."

"She sat down and got up fast, that's why it never penetrated the jeans," Carriss said. "Shit...he's trying to account for the evidence—the trace sperm, the urine on the underwear—by saying he took her home."

"Exactly, exactly, exactly," Wong said.

"Why not just stick with the story she walked away from the party?" Earnstead said. "It was simple and it was working."

"It's not an allegation of murder he fears," Wong said.

Carriss let out a sigh. "It's what he does next."

THERE WAS A big smiling crack, gaping, ready to swallow me up—glass, the kind ready to shatter, all around me, fine lines etched finer, splintering, splintering, again and again. I tried to let out a scream. "It's going to eat me!" but the only sound I heard was a shrill hiss. The blood had spread and gone to ice against my jacket, the loss and freeze coupled to nudge me deeper into hypothermia. The hiss rose to a deafening pitch. The glass shattered and swept me up, shattered through me, and I shattered back. I shattered back because I was angry, shattered myself back to consciousness. I raged, raged up out of the black warm pit, raged up with everything I had, raged myself up from death's womb and was reborn.

I took inventory of my situation. I had passed out kneeling between the two runners of the missing passenger's seat. A crack in the windshield smiled back at me and beyond the glass was canvas. Cold air whipped down through the cracked moon roof. I was in Eric Stukel's car. His car was inside the impound lot. Outside, there were voices and lights, the kind of lights that swung round and round, red and blue, red and blue. I wiped at the ice pasted to my eyelashes. I listened. It was Bashful Jim and two young local cops having it out. From the sounds of it, the two young patrolmen had had a long, rough New Year's Eve, and did not want to be enduring the subzero weather. "It was a big fellow, six-four, six-five." Bashful Jim stammered. "Comes in and chases me through the tunnels, knocks all the walls to holy hell."

"Well, what do you want us to do about it, Jim?" One of the patrolmen said. "We can't charge a person for doing damage to snow."

They were close.

"He's still in there!" Bashful Jim shouted. "Armed to the teeth."

I lowered myself to the floor of the car, bit off my left glove, and breathed through its lining to mask the steam from my breath.

"Well, if there is anybody in there," the other patrolman said, "the man's probably cold and dead by now."

I drove my thigh, where my pistol was concealed, into one of the seat runners to give myself a sobering jolt of pain.

"Somebody did jump the fence it looks," one of the patrolmen said.

Bashful Jim shouted, "He's still in there I tell you!"

"You're sure it wasn't a buddy from the VFW coming to visit?"

"My buddies from VFW come in the through the front gate!"

"Yeah, we have to get a new lock on that," one of the patrolmen said.

I couldn't do anything about the damaged windshield, but the blood and prints I left behind would have to be wiped down. The car had already been processed, the evidence already collected. I just had to make the car clean to the naked eye. The biggest task ahead of me would be squeezing out through the canvas without tearing it to shreds. This time I would avoid the moon roof and go out through the driver's door.

First things first though—stay low and don't get caught.

I studied the space around me, opening my intuitive eye, feeling my way through the car with my mind. This was where it happened, I was certain…and so the images began closing upon me, shaky and blurred at first, but then clearer, details coming into sharper relief, color washing upon the white haze of my mind, detail adding upon detail, arms and legs flailing then finding purpose, scuffing and scratching, twisting to find the door handle. She had struggled to escape, but only made it so far. Bobby had stranded her and so she needed a ride. She got in with Stukel because they had history—that's all it was—a convenient choice. She had forgotten that he had frightened her once and now she knew she had made a mistake. She went for the passenger's door first, but in the confined space, he was able pin her arms. She had dancer's legs though, nimble and strong. She kicked and kneed to twist around him, using the dashboard as leverage. She fought and did her best to survive...and so the images gathered clearer...

"THE STOMACH CONTENT was the first thing that struck me as off," Coroner Wong said as she sorted through the stack of crime-scene photos.

"She purged after rigor mortis," Earnstead said, "There was nothing in the stomach contents out of the ordinary."

"Not off as in content, but as in geography and timeframe."

"Geography?" Carriss leaned in close.

Wong slid Earnstead and Carriss a crime-scene photo—an extreme close-up—Tammy's sunken, decomposing cheek matted with fallen leaves, her lips dried and curled back, exposing the white of her teeth. Carriss drew in a long steady breath and fought the sickness of a coming hangover. The skin of her cheek had turned a color just short of black, her nose had collapsed upon itself, maggots hatched and ready to break the surface, ready to come up through the bloated-green film that had replaced her big brown eyes. Carriss hated seeing the eyes. The eyes brought back the forty-year-old nightmares. She had died, eyes wide open, struggling, suffering, and he admired her for it, and at the same time, felt a strange sense of pity. He didn't want to refer to her as the victim: he wanted to refer to her by name. Being away from the job so long had made him soft. Her body was facedown, but her head was cocked sideways—a spattering of fly-infested something oozing off her extended tongue and onto the ground. "What you're seeing is spaghetti." Wong told them, "Eaten at Pizza Hut sometime between 6:00 and 6:30 P.M., according to receipts and witnesses, which puts her death right around midnight." Wong pulled out a magnifying lens and held it over the photo. "The point is she still has enough content to purge...she does so after rigor, about forty hours later."

Earnstead and Carriss bent closer.

"Somebody wiped her lips and cheeks," they both said at once.

"I thought it was sloppy collection by the locals at first," Wong said.

Carriss looked closer. "It couldn't have been wiped that late in the game: otherwise, we'd see discoloration of the cheek due to the stomach acid."

"Bingo," Wong said.

"Somebody wiped her lips right after she purged?" Earnstead said.

"Bingo."

"Somebody was down in that ravine two days later," Carriss said.

There was a long silence. Carriss and Earnstead felt slapped in the face. All the evidence they needed was right in front of them the whole time.

"We're burning time," Earnstead said.

"We have to dig," Carriss said...and so they each took a stack of case files. The coffee would have to wait.

It would be another half hour before anyone spoke.

THE HOMECOMING

"I think we need to get fresh heads," Wong said. "I want to cross off the list what we thought we knew and work with what we do know for sure. I want to eliminate every other possible scenario before we get any further."

"No pitting on the clothing. Pitting would indicate being dragged across gravel, no marks from the asphalt, no impact wounds that would indicate collision with a moving car," Carriss said quickly. "Hit-and-run is out."

"Just some yellow reflective paint on the heels, not only telling us that she wasn't hit-and-run, but that her body was dragged into the ravine from the edge of the road. A few cockleburs on the hem of the jeans too," Earnstead said. "This gave us point of entry into the ravine."

"Next they carry her underarm and logroll her down the slope," Carriss said. "We know this from the cuts on her feet, and the debris found in her hair and on her clothing. All of it consistent with the terrain of the ravine."

"We also know that they tossed the shoes down into the ravine from the guardrail. Tossed the overnight bag down the hill too." Earnstead added. "The trajectory patterns we can trust I think."

"Not a penny taken from the bag—no robbery."

"No attempt to try to hide the body—"

"Don't forget the trunk," Wong said.

"Right," Earnstead said. "Hair and fibers from the victim found in the trunk. Fibers from the trunk found on the victim…and he's seen the next day trying to clean his car."

"Shit," Carriss said. "He was protecting her. Spending all the time he could with her. Shooing the animals away. That's why we see no signs of scavenging. He wipes the vomit from her lips, cares for her…keeps vigil."

"The two sources of urine," Earnstead said. "The proximity of the farmhouse to the ravine and time of death—she died at or near the farm and was moved to the ravine in his trunk. They got rid of her fast—his partners in crime helping him…unaccounted time, next few days he returns to the body."

"He couldn't resist," Carriss said.

"This is all just theoretical so far though," Earnstead said.

Wong spread out a series of crime-scene photos. "Look closely and tell me what's missing from any one of these photos."

The two men stared long at the photo.

"Her pants," Earnstead said.

"Shit is the word…if there were cuts on her feet," Carriss said. "There should be cuts on her legs too. Her pants were still on when she was thrown into the ravine. They had to have been. Shit, it's the only possible way."

"Shit," Earnstead said and then looked up at Carriss and Wong.

"Exactly," Wong said.

THE SMEAR OF a flashlight against the canvas cut through the shadows. I should have stayed alert, waited for that distinctive slam of the car doors, the distinctive slam that cops make when they hop in and out. I had made my way to the driver's side door. I was easing it open, following the path she had taken to escape. I was easing the door open when the light washed in on me from the other side. They had followed Bashful Jim through the snow, knocking the tunnel down as they went, and now they were atop me. I eased the door shut and held my breath. One of their handhelds gave off a metallic chirp. A dispatcher's voice chimed out indistinct words.

"How would he have gotten beneath, Jim?" One of the officers whispered. "The canvas looks to be frozen to the car as tight as a drum."

"Slithered under like a snake," Bashful Jim whispered back.

There was a silence and stillness and then very slowly the brown smear of flashlight spread wide across the canvas and flickered away. There was movement of feet through the snow and then the distinctive sound of car doors slamming. The engine roared from its gentle idling, the snow crunched under the tires, the impound gate swung shut, and finally, I let out the breath that I had been holding for I'm not sure how long.

Morning was growing bigger across the white and the cold, the southern sun fighting through the darkness. "Jim?" I whispered through the canvas. "Jim? It's me—the one who gave you the gloves."

There was no response.

"Jim, I'm going to come out and we'll talk about this," I whispered.

Still nothing.

I didn't have time for this—the cops could easily return, grown curious after some thought and with backup. Now was the time to make my escape.

CARRISS, EARNSTEAD, AND Wong were sliding into their parkas. "Manslaughter 3 in Nebraska, Murder 2 if we're lucky," Earnstead said. "New D.A. is political. He'll feel the pulse, do what's politically expedient."

"Statute of limitations?" Carriss asked.

"Three years on Man 3," Earnstead said. "Clock is ticking."

"I'll give you an hour lead before I pass them the FED-EX," Wong said.

Carriss gave Earnstead a slap on the back. "Alright, you wake up the D.A. I'll slip downtown, rattle some chains, see how the locals proceed."

Earnstead couldn't get over it. "Goddamn, they so much as told us they were out there in that ravine. That Saturday before she was even reported missing, Noose Adarson tells us he and Stukel were out on that road, out on 121. They practically place themselves at the scene, saying they were just out looking for her."

"They knew somebody on the golf course might have seen the car. They had to account their presence." Carriss opened the door for the three. "Hey, circumstantial if admissible."

"Back in business, old friend," Earnstead said.

"Thank you," Carriss said. "Thank you for bringing me in."

TIME IS THE worst thing. With its passage, doubts turn traitor, reason becomes clouded, and purpose goes blind. The righteous man rubs on the salve of due process and chokes on the pacifier of what he believes to be religious conviction. His boiling blood grows thin until he finds himself smiling graciously at his enemies, holding court with his killers, offering them phony gestures of forgiveness and, in his darkest hour, obeisance.

She was my soul.

I went silent.

My rage sat dormant two years too long.

A good hard push against the driver's door stretched the canvas just enough to offer me a crawlspace to freedom. My toes had gone numb, but I was making progress.

Scraping my legs out through the narrow space of the cracked door sent white-hot pain up my spine. Still, I pushed, curling my toes and wedging my feet into the ice, pressing my heels to burrow for leverage.

There was a sound like somebody thwacking his finger against the surface of a drum. It came from all sides, rose to a crescendo, and then suddenly the door stopped moving and, as if ten men were on the other side pushing back at me, the door closed on my hips. The canvas had stretched to its limit and now was returning to original form.

The saphenous vein in my left leg and the femoral artery of my right pinched tight. One leg swelled, the other went dry, and all I could do was fight not to scream. I pressed back against the car door with all my strength. I fought to get my hand beneath me, to get at my knife tucked neatly at my ankle—one little prick of its point to split the canvas wide.

I struggled and writhed, but in the end only wedged my legs tighter beneath the door. I had two options: pull myself back into the car or fight my way to freedom. As I rocked back and forth, the snow atop the car began a slow slide, big chunks splitting and smashing down around me. The canvas breathed and then grew tight, breathed and then grew tight, breathed again...and that was when I laid into it with all my might.

I was making progress. My hips first, and I'd let the canvas tighten. My stomach next, and I'd let the canvas tighten. My chest next and I was down to my shoulders, and like a breach baby, with one final contraction and one big push, my head would pop free beneath the door. The canvas began a slow slit up one of its seams and the winds of freedom cut cold against my legs.

That's when I heard the war cry. There was no time to think. The canvas breathed and his body came crashing hard against the door. It was Bashful Jim, making a running tackle to get the door shut. Everything snapped black for a second. I went deaf in one ear. For an instant it felt as if my stomach was going to explode...and then there was nothing, just the sound of Bashful Jim rising, panting, kicking at something, stomping upon my belly perhaps...and then there was nothing again, just footsteps through snow, the sound of barbed wire shaking with a leap, more footsteps, and one last war cry in the distance.

Whatever had just happened was not good.

I did my best to assess the situation. My neck was neatly tucked in the door hinge, that much was certain. My toes wouldn't move. I couldn't feel my legs. The ice wasn't cold anymore. My breath escaped me, but no air returned.

It seemed fitting, almost funny, but not funny enough for me to resign myself to it. The blood from the puncture wound between my shoulder blades had seeped through my jacket and was now staining the snow. I saw only triplicate through my left eye, and through my right eye, I could see nothing but a big brown pulsating splotch two inches to my front.

My cheek was pressed up against something soft in the door. I strained my left eye to see, and as I did, the big brown blotch went away. I was now staring sidelong at forensic tape that was covering the missing tweeter speaker in the driver's door. Something happened down here in the hinge.

My vision tunneled…

Maybe it was only my imagination, all of it. Maybe she hadn't been pulled into the hinge of the door, deep in the darkness of that September night, upon the side of some gravel road, in the crabgrass under a half moon, where nobody else could see. Maybe she hadn't been pinned down, couldn't free herself. Maybe she hadn't bled…maybe she hadn't died.

If I just stayed here and went to sleep, maybe it would all go away…and so as I resigned myself to death, little did I know that Soldier was quietly working, fingers moving with steady purpose, searching the underbelly of the car for a leverage point, a place to lift. Fragments of a little picture-show began to play upon the patchwork fabric of my imagination, diced and spliced together as if by a madman.

Scream and somebody will come.

Scream loud.

Scream over the noise of the music and the blazing fire, scream over their laughter and jeers, fight your way to freedom, claw your way into the corn and run.

But first you must scream!

She reached the driver's door handle, and when the door opened, she could smell the fresh-cut hay. She clawed at the crabgrass to pull herself to her feet, but he was faster and his reach longer. He snatched her back by her ponytail, and with all his might, brought her down into the doorframe.

He pins her to the ground.

He straddles her.

They goad him to go further.

Scream!!!

Too late—a knee into the belly—her wind knocked out…

Struggle!!!

Cheering him on!

Don't show fear—don't give him that.

Oh, God, send somebody to rescue her as he punches again and again. They laugh. They think it's funny. She tries to throw up a hand to protect her face. O, rescuing Angels defend and protect her! He smashes her neck in the hinge of the door. She tastes the blood draining down her throat…so alone now and he's just too strong. She can't struggle anymore. She doesn't want to

struggle anymore. He leans back and grabs onto the door. He rages joyously…he wonders how it would feel on her neck if the door would close.
SCREAM!!!
He leans back and heaves…
There is the sound of bone twisting against bone…
He feels the warmness in his groin and the soothing in his head and he smiles at her. She has gone lifeless. Her eyes move yet her body has gone soft. She is like a warm plaything now. Her leg twitches, but only for a moment and the moment passes. He sits next to her and stares out into the corn. "It's over now, isn't it?" he asks her, but she doesn't respond.

Her eyes plead to God, to him, to anybody, and then her eyes go soft.

"You shouldn't have tried to run," he says with a smile because he knows God would agree. Now, he'll be the last one with her and knowing this brings him more warmth in his head and in his groin. He is happy for the first time, content, for in that one sweet raging moment they had found forever…

AS THE LITTLE picture-show ended, Soldier found a solid grip upon the front axle and with that axle firmly in hand, he found the fury, and lifted that car off its wheels. He screamed the rage of two years as every muscle strained and through his rage and through his fury, he found himself up on two feet.

AND SO ALL that fury and all that rage needed quenching. It was a march up Douglas Avenue past the merry twinkling lights of Christmas—greens, blues, and reds left burning by New Year's revelers stumbling home. It was up Douglas, pistol in hand, over the Marne and across the tracks, up Observatory Hill—the sun cracking blue the bitter pink sky of a brand new year. It was one more block. It was the second house on the left—two cold, undecorated stories of hard-fired brick.

GO SLOWLY, SOLDIER, and recon your point of entrance. Ease open the mailbox. Find it stuffed with Christmas catalogues at least a half-week old. Slide past the two giant pines bearing the weight of winter in their massive, ancient boughs. Careful though! Hidden behind those trees are motion sensors. They were just installed last week. Don't be too careful though! Don't come to a dead stop! Just go easy and stay beneath the long icicles dangling from the eaves. These will help blind you to their electronic eyes. Round the house north and come to the three doublewide garage doors. You'll get five chances at the security code before the alarm sounds. Slide beneath the opening garage door and punch the button on the other side before anyone can hear a sound. Stay in the shadows and listen.

NOT A CREATURE stirring? Not even a mouse?

YOU'RE INSIDE NOW—don't play games, don't get sloppy. Take the gloves off and let the heat come back to your hands—you'll need them. Easy with your pistol! Don't let it go smacking to the floor. Wait for the steel to warm, wait for the blood to return to your fingers. Make your way through the door leading to the kitchen. Ten words, that's all you have to say.

Ten words, best served with a whisper.

Ten words and he would know the gravity of what he had done.

Ten words and all of it would be over…

Ten words.

If he's sleeping, nudge him awake. Make sure he's fully sober and staring us straight in the eye. Let him plead all he wants...

You have only ten words to say.

You've been rehearsing them from the start.

Ten words whispered to seal his fate.

THE KITCHEN LACKED the usual smells—pine-scented cleaner, berry-scented plug-ins, Arm-n-Hammer gone crusty in the refrigerator's bottom drawer, the lingering stench that rises from the garbage disposal when the sink sits dry too long.

In the living room sat brand new furniture still covered in its shipping plastic. There was a faux Christmas tree in the dining room, twelve-feet high, its lights set on a timer.

I moved through the narrow hallway that flanked the staircase and found an antique rotary phone sitting atop a little hutch. Scribbled on a notepad next to the phone was a list of flight numbers out of Sioux City. I called the airline. Evidently, the Stukel family had taken a last-minute trip to the Bahamas. "Why would restaurateurs go on a vacation at the busiest time of the year?" I asked under my breath.

The airline operator heard me and said, "Maybe to get away?"

"That would make sense," I said and then hung up.

The question running through my thawing mind was would those same restaurateurs take their twenty-one-year-old stay-at-home son with them?

I liked the idea of being in the house alone with him.

I prayed that he was still here.

I moved back through the living room, stopping at the mantle. A family photo showed a teenaged Eric Stukel standing behind his mother and father and flanked by his two baby brothers and little sister.

I didn't like the fact that they all looked so happy.

I prayed again that he was here.

The knocking that came through the walls sent me spinning. I dropped the safety on my pistol and aimed into the darkness of the kitchen. For an instant, I thought I saw the long shadow of a figure passing from the dining room up the stairs. Two more knocks and rushing air followed. I backed along the balustrade, taking aim up through the balusters. I spun again. The sound was coming up through the hollows of the basement—just the furnace blazing to life. I tread gently to mask my step as I climbed. The person who had ghosted a shot up the stairs did it perfectly, did it with complete silence and speed. He was smart. He had heard the furnace kicking in and made his move. If he wanted to kill me, I would already be dead.

I sidestepped up, turning and training my pistol through the balcony railing. These old houses were built for big families and big families meant many small rooms, some of them interconnected by double closets and balconies. I was chasing a ghost up into a labyrinth. A good enemy sets the terms of engagement, sets the tempo of the fight, draws the attacking force in for the kill. I was at a definite disadvantage.

I reached the second to last step and stopped. There was no movement, no signs of doors opening or closing, no creaking of the floorboards. I had only one option—retreat and let him come to me. I gently backed down the staircase and moved toward the kitchen.

The kitchen had two exits: one to the garage, the way I had entered; the other attached to an entryway, which led into the basement one direction and out into the backyard the other.

Cold air and the odor of cheap incense met me as the door swung open. A potentially deadly moment passed as my eyes adjusted to the light of morning coming in from the window looking out on the backyard.

The furnace suddenly fired down with three loud thumps. I spun, weapon aimed into the darkness of the basement stairwell. I had made myself the perfect target atop the steps, silhouetted wonderfully by a risen sun. I took the staircase fast, weapon trained into the darkness, bounding down three steps at a time. I hit the bottom and kept moving. I moved so fast and moved so hard that I passed three doors and smacked directly into a back wall.

"Dead end," I whispered as I came to my feet.

A glowing red splotch rose up from my cargo pockets. I dug at the red splotch and out came my Maglight, perfectly restored.

I swung the Maglight through the darkness and found myself face to face with a very large marijuana leaf. The marijuana leaf was of the felt variety. It was a poster hanging on the bedroom door.

X marks the spot.

I didn't bother listening at the door. Instead, I made my entrance full force, bounding over the bed and across to the far corner of the room, sweeping my pistol and Maglight through the darkness as I went.

Nobody home…

There was a lava lamp on a nearby nightstand, bubbling up blobs of red against orange. Display racks of compact disks lined one wall and three beanbags sat in the corner. Between the three beanbags was a filthy rag. Beneath the rag was an ashtray. Within the ashtray were several roaches. These roaches were the kind people smoked. The bed was unmade and atop it was a hamper of neatly folded clothes.

As I neared the walk-in closet, I was stopped cold. It was there on his dresser, taped down heavy, thick with yellowed layers of scotch and postal tape. I could barely make her out in the photo, but I knew. The photo had been taken nearly where I was standing. She must have been about seventeen. She was sitting on his bed, nothing but joy on her face. She looked so at home. She was in her jean jacket, faded and hugging tight. Her bag of magic was next to her. She was leaning forward, eyes beckoning and fingers spread wide across the bed sheets. All I could do was sit down and weep. This was what they had tried to tell me all along, that I was merely a footnote in her life.

A preacher had told me once, when I was about ten, that in the eyes of God I was worthless and corrupt, that deep down I had no goodness in me. I was told that this was why I would someday have to die. I had spent much time lately thinking about God, and now I sat there, thinking about God again, not fully aware that my pistol had risen from my lap, barely feeling that it was now pressed firmly beneath my chin...and right as the hammer was about to fall, I heard the sound of footsteps, and so I cocked my head and listened.

The footsteps were coming closer, coming my way, and so curiosity got the best of me. I eased my finger off the trigger, lowered the hammer gently, and backed into a deep shadows residing just beyond the light of the egress.

There I took aim at the bedroom door.

THE MAN IN the parka looked right through me, his body betraying neither surprise, nor fear, nor caution. He crept from the bedroom door to the bed and then kneeled to have a look beneath. He didn't turn the light on and moved as if trained for darkness. He felt the spot on the bed where I had just been sitting. He felt my lingering warmth. He turned a circle, hands on his hips, and then he stopped cold. He stared past the egress and into the shadows beyond, and as he moved closer, I moved too, circling until I had him.

"Shit," he said, right as he stepped into the window light.

"Behind you, Special Agent Carriss," I said.

The man in the parka turned slowly. "I'm going to take two steps," he said and then backed into shadow.

I lifted my arms in surrender. "Would you believe I was house-sitting?"

"I was down at the police station, picking up some files, when I heard the APB go out: white male, five-six, five-seven, medium build, dressed in white, should be considered armed and dangerous."

I smiled.

"What do you think is going to happen," he said, "if Tammy's case goes to trial and a jury finds out you broke in here...or the impound lot for that matter? What do you think will happen to both of us if the locals would come busting in here right now?"

I shrugged.

"Don't play stupid. It doesn't suit you," he said.

I took a step forward. "Collecting files for what?"

"I'd step back," he warned.

I took another step forward and that's when I heard the distinctive sound of a button unsnapping and metal sliding against leather beneath his coat.

I took another step forward and Carriss' .38 Special was in my belly.

"You could always let me walk," I said.

"Where to—the Bahamas?"

"If I have to."

"You're so sure Eric's the one?" he said.

"What are you going to do? Shoot me?" I said. "I could disarm you...and quickly too." I felt the rage come and did my best to hold it back. "But I don't see a search warrant in your hand, which means...you're breaking and entering just like me." I laughed. "And I was afraid I was going to get arrested tonight." I pushed his pistol aside with my pinkie, scooted around him, and walked for the door. What I could not fathom was just how fast the old man was. I didn't even have that split-second to brace. I was only able to let out a little whimper as I fell. Without a word, without a sound, he had come down on me, the butt end of his pistol smashing against the base of my spine. The last thing I could recall was the sudden and cold embrace of a carpet and a knee grinding deep into my neck.

CHAPTER EIGHTEEN

THE LITTLE PICTURE-show played further—she had been at a party, she became the party. She tried to escape the car. He slammed the door shut and she was struck dead. They squeezed her body into the trunk and they drove down the gravel road in search of a ravine to deposit what was left of her. When they opened the trunk again, they could see the color leaving her skin. It was easier for the others now, because she didn't look so real. One of them stood lookout for approaching cars, while the other two dragged her across the road and tossed her over the guardrail. Her body didn't make it all the way, so they had to climb down the slope and give it another good hard kick to roll her through the thickets.

He had yanked her shoes off in anger after the struggle, because she nearly caught him in the eye with her heel, and so they had to go back to the party for them, searching the ditch next to the gravel road with a flashlight. By the time they rolled back to the ravine, they had forgotten where they had dumped her. An argument ensued and nearly went to blows, but passions stirred led to a jarring of their memories. Quickly atop the situation, they started having fun. It was like a game, the rules being not to get caught. They decided it best to toss her belongings into the ravine with her. They took aim from way up at the guardrail. The trick was to miss the tree branches. The challenge was to see how close they could land the objects next to her body. The shoes they threw like boomerangs. Her overnight bag they spun like a hammer and let fly. They laughed when, upon impact, it did not break.

My head swam.

The little picture-show dissolved to blackness. I was moving. I was on my side moving. I was on my side moving and my hands were pinned behind my back. I was on my side moving and my hands were pinned behind my back by something…by something metal…by handcuffs. I was in the back of a car. The car was moving and I was on my side, on my side because that was where he had placed me—that much I remembered.

We took a corner hard and my mind sloshed painfully in the bucket that was my skull. We iced a bounce over a curb and my eyes popped open. The blowers were running to keep the windows from steaming. The ceiling of the car was stained from water damage.

"I need to sit up so my head doesn't explode," I said.

"Nothing's stopping you."

As I sat up, I tried to hide my wince with a smile, but the ruse was up when I was forced to blink and shake and groan away the dizzy stars exploding two feet to my front. Carriss was staring at me through the rearview mirror. We were in his station wagon, driving south towards downtown.

"Feels like we've done this before," I said.

"Your CO claims you were a good soldier—"

"A *great* soldier."

"—when you wanted to be. He also said you were a decent human being—when you saw fit. But, he also said that when you get a wild hair up your ass." Carriss glanced back. "You don't flinch. That sound about right?"

There were file boxes stacked on the floor of the backseat, giving me nowhere to go with my legs. These file boxes, as it happened, had some videotapes inside. These tapes were labeled. The one label I could make out had Tammy's last name written on it and hyphenated after her last name were the words: ***Grand Jury***.

"Collecting up some old case files?"

Carriss didn't bother answering.

"Where you taking me?" I asked.

Again, Carriss didn't answer.

"Special Agent Carriss, this *could be* construed as kidnapping."

"I should be taking you to the emergency room to have that hole in your back looked after, but that would mean more explaining to do than I think either of us wants right now. So," he glanced back, "if you promise not to interfere in my business, I'll take you home."

I bent forward and started wiggling my handcuffs under my ankles. "Let me show you a trick I learned in POW survival training."

"Trick had nothing to do with self-preservation, I'm gathering."

"You have to listen to my shoulder as I do it," I said and then gave my arm a hard snap.

"Really smart," he said.

I grinned and then quickly snatched my handcuffed wrists up from beneath my feet. "Ta-Da!" I proudly displayed my hands, still cuffed, but now in front of me. Unimpressed, Carriss tapped his brakes and knocked me back in my seat.

CARRISS MADE GOOD on his promise and brought me back to the little apartment beneath the abandoned factory that stunk like sulfur. In the little alcove at the bottom of the staircase leading to my door, he removed my handcuffs and began lecturing me on the subject of my future. "You have no clue what's going on or what you're getting yourself into," he said. "You need to rearrange how you are living your life. You're not a soldier anymore. This isn't a war."

"Can I have my pistol back now?" I asked.

"I'll keep it safe for you."

I CHAINED MY door behind me and waited until I was sure Carriss had gone. I did this propped up against the door because my balance was only coming in spurts. A welt the shape of the blunt end of his pistol was inching up right behind my left ear. Only when I heard the roar of his engine did I yank to loosen my pant cuffs from my boots. A shake of the leg and a one-legged hop brought a VHS tape to the floor.

It occurred to me just then, as I looked around my apartment, that I didn't have a TV or VCR. My mother and father had the equipment I needed, but bringing them into this situation seemed unwise. My list of trusted friends was short, and being that it was New Year's morning, there weren't many places open for business that would sell me TVs and VCRs. In fact, I could only think of one. I loathed the thought of it, but these were desperate times...

SO THERE I was standing in the electronics section of Wal-Mart, searching for the feed source to the display model TVs and VCRs. I needed sound, but didn't want the conspicuity of thirteen screens playing out the tape that I had stolen. I needed to do a little rewiring. The assistant electronics manager, a balding lady with one curly long hair under her chin, gave me an odd look as I worked, but in the end said nothing. When I pulled the tape from its sleeve, I discovered the inside label, which read: ***Archive Footage Compiled for Preparation in Sept. 1993 Grand Jury – YANKTON, SD.***

"Grand Jury hearing over a year ago?" I whispered.

What appeared upon the screen when I popped the tape in was the little blue interrogation room under the single fluorescent. The image only lasted an instant and then the screen went blue as the tape started rewinding. I cued the tape up in review mode and watched the compilation of interrogations play out in reverse, familiar faces speed talking invertedly, gesturing in wild frenetic bursts, lifting up from their chairs as if possessed and walking backwards out of the room.

The woman with the chin hair circled the CD racks to get a closer look at what I was trying to do. She glanced up once at the security cameras and then pointed my way and then finally brushed past with a look in her eye that said, "Not by the hair of my chinny-chin-chin."

I moved to the next television as if comparing features. Her phone rang and she hobbled around the corner. As she disappeared, I quickly hit play on the VCR to find a fellow named Dan Stevenson sitting in front of Carriss and Earnstead in the blue interrogation room.

There was nothing particularly striking about Dan Stevenson. In fact, he was so un-striking that he looked like the perfect boy to bring home to Mom and Dad—a regular bore. Dan Stevenson was the one who threw the Stevenson bonfire at the Stevenson farm, and with hand to heart, he was at this moment on the tape assuring the two special agents that he would never encourage illegal activities on his father's property.

"Minors drinking alcohol isn't illegal?" Carriss asked.

"Nothing *really* illegal," Dan Stevenson corrected himself and then took on the authority of a wealthy child accustomed to getting his way. "It's kind of an unwritten rule that we just keep it in Nebraska and don't bring it back over the bridge...that we all get home in one piece."

"But you all ***didn't*** get home in one piece," Earnstead said.

"What do you mean?" Dan Stevenson said.

"Tammy died," Carriss said.

"Yeah, sure, but...you know what I mean," Dan Stevenson said.

"No, we don't," Earnstead said.

"Some people are kind of..." Don tried to rephrase. "If a bum on the street gets shot, nobody gets too excited. If the president gets shot, we lower the flags...you see what I mean."

"Oh, you're saying Tammy doesn't count?" Carriss said. "But if she had a trust fund or maybe had a membership to the country club..."

"I'm saying it's not really surprising that a girl like that—"

"Like what?" Carriss said.

"She was outgoing, everybody got along with her, and she wasn't afraid to get along with *anybody*...if she was walking along and a stranger pulled up and offered her a ride, sure, she'd hop in with him."

"Oh, like a prostitute, you mean?" Carriss said.

"What time did the party end, Dan?" Earnstead jumped in.

"Eleven—it was a school night."

"Interestingly, we have a couple people saying that they were out on the farm until after midnight," Earnstead said.

"I guess I couldn't actually say how long the party lasted, only how long it was *supposed to* last," Dan said. "I had to take my girlfriend home."

The tape cut off for a few seconds and then suddenly a tape recorder appeared atop the table between the three.

Earnstead hit play on the tape recorder.

"Dan and I stayed nearly till morning," the girl on the tape recorder said. Earnstead fast-forwarded the cassette then hit play. "No, the scream freaked me out," the girl said and Dan's face turned pale, "It must have been 12:30 and came from somewhere on the gravel road. I told Dan to go investigate, but he laughed and said that somebody was probably just playing a prank..."

At that point, Earnstead stopped the tape recorder, because the look of betrayal and fear was apparent enough on Dan Stevenson's face. Just as Dan was about to make some sort of plea, however, the VHS tape cut to snow.

I hit the seek button and what appeared next was Katherine Noland walking through the door. I didn't like how they had sliced and diced the hundreds of hours of interrogation footage together. I could only suppose that they only had so much time in front of the grand jury to weave some sort of narrative. In the first interrogation, time and place were established, along with the mention of a woman's scream. Now came Katherine Noland, who was dating Homecoming Chief Brian Slobacek. Those two were the pair in the bushes at Bobby's apartment the night before the funeral and the pair at Tammy's house two mornings after, delivering the spray of flowers.

"You went to the party with some girlfriends," Earnstead asked Katherine Noland, "while Brian came with a fellow named Dusty Fist?"

I backed up the tape.

THE HOMECOMING

"You went to the party with some girlfriends," Earnstead said, "while Brian came with a fellow named Dusty Fist?"

The folding table slid as Katherine crossed right leg over left. "Brian and I were trying to get back together," she said. "We sat in my car and talked…that's where we were most of the party."

"Did you?" Carriss asked.

"Did I what?"

"Get back together with Brian?" Earnstead said.

"Yes."

"You don't sound happy about that," Earnstead said.

"I'm not happy about being *here*."

Earnstead smiled. "Neither are we."

"You didn't go home with Brian that night though," Carriss said.

"What?"

Carriss said it slower. "You didn't go home with Brian that night."

"No, I didn't—I had to take my friends home."

"In your car?" Earnstead said.

"Yes."

"And Dusty drove home alone too?" Earnstead asked.

"What?"

"And Dusty drove home alone too?" Earnstead repeated.

"No, he drove home with Brian."

"How would you know he did if you weren't there?" Carriss asked.

"Look, all I know is I spent some time with Brian at the party. As we were sitting there, we saw Tammy and Eric leave…saw them drive off."

"Why do you mention that?" Carriss asked.

"Well, isn't that where you're going with these questions?"

"Brian ever hit you?" Carriss asked. "Talk abusively?"

"We argue, yes."

"You ever see Eric hit Tammy?" Earnstead asked.

"They were getting along great that night," Katherine said quickly. "At least that's how it looked from where I was sitting."

"In your car with Brian?" Earnstead said.

Carriss leaned back deep in his chair.

"You and Brian ever get…"

As he said it and before she could answer, the tape scribbled out and fuzzed to white. I backed up the tape and played it again.

"You and Brian ever get out to the…"

I backed up the tape, went to full volume, and did my best to listen through the interference.

"You and Brian ever get out to the dam?"

From the snow, Brian Slobacek suddenly leapt upon screen. Unlike his girlfriend Katherine, Brian hadn't come by himself. The first had faced her interrogators alone: the second, holding the hand of his mother. A fascinating thing occurred during this interview and was not lost on Carriss and

Earnstead: before Brian would answer a question, he'd look to his mother for approval. This kept happening until finally Brian's mother accidentally leapt in and answered a question for Brian. "We can't stop you from being here, Ma'am," Earnstead told her. "But you can't answer his questions for him."

Brian told the agents that he spent much of the weekend with Katherine driving around Nebraska looking for Tammy.

"Why would you be out looking for Tammy all weekend," Earnstead asked Brian, "when she wasn't reported missing until Sunday?"

"See, the whole thing was," Brian explained, "Tammy had stood Eric up Friday night. They had gotten back together the night before. That's why they went home together. They were going to be doing the whole homecoming thing that weekend for his birthday."

"But why look in Nebraska, if she was last with Eric in South Dakota?"

"I don't know," Brian said. "It was, uh, Katherine's idea."

"Did Eric help you look for Tammy?" Earnstead asked.

"No...just me and Katherine and some of her girlfriends."

"Strange," Carriss said.

Earnstead gave Carriss a glance. Carriss gave Earnstead a nod. Earnstead came in hard and fast at Brian. "We understand panic. Who expects to stumble upon a dead body when you show back up at a party? You don't know what's happened to the girl, but everybody is telling you something has to be done. You're the Homecoming king, you have to be a hero to them, they voted for you. You owe it to them."

I felt somebody breathing behind me, so turned the TV off and spun. "Are you just here to watch your home videos?" the chin-hair lady asked.

"I have to see if my video tapes work on this model," I answered and stepped in her path to keep her from taking my tape. "I've had some Wal-Mart brand VCRs eat up my old tapes. I could shop elsewhere...but if I'd do that, I'd have to write letters to your manager and your manager's manager and so on up the chain, explaining why Wal-Mart will get no more of my business."

A phone rang giving Chin-hair an exit out of the conversation.

I turned on the TV and found Dusty Fist sitting where Brian had just been. Dusty Fist was the one that dislocated Bobby's shoulder under the direction of Don the Itch, the one Bobby claimed was selling drugs with Brian Slobacek at the Stevenson farm. The odd thing about the Dusty Fist interrogation was that Brian's mother had never left her seat. At one point, she was sitting with Brian, the next she was sitting with Dusty.

"—that doesn't explain how you got your thumbprint in her shoe," Earnstead said to Dusty.

"I'll explain it again," Dusty said. "Tammy couldn't walk in high heels. She fell flat on her face. I helped her up, picked up her shoe."

Carriss leaned in close. "Dusty, we know you, Brian, and Eric Stukel ran halfway across the state the day the body was found."

Dusty glanced to Brian's mother for permission and then said, "We were just getting away to cool off a bit, drink some beers and do some grilling."

"But you weren't even friends with Eric Stukel before the night of the Stevenson bonfire—you even said so yourself!" Earnstead shouted.

"Maybe I have a benevolent penchant for people in dire need!"

"Maybe you have a what?"

Brian's mother interrupted. "Brian had my permission to go with the other boys on that road trip. They were dealing with a lot of emotions at the time. It doesn't mean they were trying to run from the authorities."

"No, I think they left town in search of a safe place to get their stories straight," Carriss said, "and Stukel's attorney had to go track them down."

The tape scrambled for an odd instant and then Noose Adarson appeared with his mother. "Who would be stupid enough to get rid of a body like that anyway?" Noose Adarson's mother hissed, "Just tossing it in a ravine?"

"What would you have done?" Carriss asked her.

"Tossed it in the river," she said.

"The mothers, the families," I whispered. "They all know."

It was then that I felt the barrel of my pistol poking me in the back. "Pop the tape out and we'll walk out of here nice and quiet, have a nice long chat over a cup of coffee."

I DON'T CONDONE knocking weapons out of the hands of FBI agents (even if they do happen to be retired.) However, if or when you ever do, your next course of action should be a simple one—run.

WAL-MART WAS POSITIONED on the northwest part of town. My apartment was on the southeast. I had run the entire length at full sprint, at first to make distance from Carriss then to stave off the cold. I leapt over three fences, was chased by one dog, tripped twice on ice, and finally stumbled into my apartment, chained my door, and doubled over to catch my breath.

I didn't even know I had a phone until I heard its ancient metallic ring. The search proceeded and on the fifth ring, I found it connected by six inches of naked wire to a wall socket. I answered and the lady on the other end was already talking: "Shopping at Wal-Mart may not be the safest thing to do anymore, Merrill."

I wasn't willing to play any cagey little games, so I told the lady, "I'm not really willing to play any cagey little games, lady."

"Don't hang up, Marc," she said.

She knew my given name.

"Who is this?"

"I can't tell you that."

"You saw me at Wal-Mart?"

"You have to stop now," she whispered, "Tammy wouldn't want you getting hurt."

"Tammy," I said. "What is this?"

"I came back to the party after taking home my girlfriends," she said quickly. "Maybe if she had come with me too, maybe she'd...still be...by the time I showed, there was nothing I could do."

The picture-show played.

"You saw her die."

"She was just lying there. She looked almost peaceful by then."

"On the gravel road?" I said.

"How would you know that?"

"Next to his driver's side door?"

Her voice went flat. "They were all standing over her when I showed up. They were standing there in the ditch, at his trunk...and I didn't know what was happening, so I just came driving up. They were like deer in my headlights and then...and then my...and then, uh, one of them knew it was me...and jumped out into the road and waved me down."

"Who? Who was standing over her?" I said.

"After it was over, they had Eric call Tammy's mom pretending to look for Tammy...We had to go back to town to get our stories straight. They knew who to threaten, who to buy. I thought it would be over quick, that somebody would come out and tell what really happened, but nobody did. The three of them, they put her body in his trunk. But I don't know...I don't know which one of them did it. I screamed when I realized what happened. They grabbed me and told me it was an accident...to keep that much straight. I caught them in my headlights when I was driving up. I knew something was wrong and I should have just kept driving, but they knew, they knew it was me and there was nothing I could do but stop and...help them."

"What three?"

"I have to hang up now."

"You were the girl." It suddenly dawned on me. "You were the girl at the dam, the one who was threatened—the blonde."

"Somebody *saw* that?"

"You have to come forward. I know people, people with the FBI."

"If they even knew I was talking to you, they'd kill me."

"Not if I protect you, they won't."

"You can't protect me...they watch," she said with frightening absoluteness. "They know you're back in town now. They'll..." There was a noise in the background. "They'll kill you, Merrill." She spoke quickly. "They will. They won't even think twice about it. You don't mean anything to them. They know they can get away with it, just like they got away with her."

"No, please." I pleaded to keep her on the line. "Tammy was raped and murdered at that party. You say she was your friend, but you're acting like you can just—"

"Raped?" she said. "Why would you say that?"

"They found her body with her pants off," I said. "They did a rape kit."

"I was there, Merrill—her pants were never off."

THE HOMECOMING

A sudden feeling of sickness washed over me. My right hand went over my left, over the spot where an old scar lingered. A dial tone droned steadily. A recording told me to hang up. The picture-show played, horrible and macabre. I didn't want to believe it could be true but couldn't think any other way around it. Now, I just needed somebody to tell me I was right.

CARRISS WAS NEITHER surprised nor pleased to find me banging on his mobile home door. When he answered, I pushed my way immediately inside, barely taking time to catch glimpse of the amassment of file boxes littering his kitchen and living room. I shoved the ugly little scar on my left hand in Carriss' face. "I got this when I crawled into that ravine. Cuts on her feet! But no cuts on the rest of her legs. Her pants weren't off! They weren't off until after they dumped her body!"

Carriss pushed me toward the door. "Not now, Merrill."

I pushed back. "If she was killed during a rape at that party, they wouldn't have taken the time to put her pants back on. They would've been moving too fast to take the trouble. Eighty people at that party. Somebody would have come along, right?"

"She was attacked. She was killed. The killer's friends did come along." Carriss kicked open the door. "We're working to prove that."

I forced the door back at him. "Cold case, yes?! Everybody wants it to go away, yes?! 'Well, shuckee-fuck, Mildred, when kids go out and party, these things are bound to happen!'"

Carriss didn't like my shouting or my sarcasm and stepped nose to nose to make it known. "You could have been useful to us," he said. "We could have used you to gather evidence. You could have pressed certain buttons. Problem is you're as subtle as a six-car collision, and that makes you dangerous, and that's why you find yourself more and more alone. Our prime suspect was obsessed with Tammy, and in a jealous rage, he killed her, be satisfied we'll be able to prove that in Court."

"Prove what?!" I yelled. "With what?!"

"We have the evidence."

"I have a witness who says she was killed in the ditch, not on the gravel! In the ditch! Where, when you park a car, the *passenger's* door would be, not the driver's?!"

"What witness?"

"I don't have a name."

"You have a witness but don't know his name?" Carriss asked.

"*Her* name...a rape takes time!" I shouted. "There would have been screams, a struggle. Somebody would have heard something. Somebody would have come along to stop it."

"A true believer in humanity, huh?"

"Her pants weren't off! She wasn't raped and murdered!!! Her pants weren't off when they put her in Stukel's trunk! If she was doing something at that party like car-surfing or if she fell from—"

"Oh, you wanna blame her now, huh?" Carriss shoved me back and then dropped into a chair to gather his breath. "My God, did you even watch that tape? There was a scream, not Tammy's, but a scream no less…shit, Merrill, think about it. Car parked backwards. His door in the ditch. Someone comes along. And then what? They get caught in the headlights putting the body in the trunk, because, yes, the car is pointed backwards. Your witness—you said it was a she, right?—screams. They silence her. A short drive to the ravine, a short drive to the dam…and once again, you *are* right—no cuts on her legs."

"Bullshit!!!" I screamed. "Don't you bullshit me!"

Carriss went gentle. "You already *have* thought about it, haven't you? That's why you came here tonight. It's your disbelief that's getting in your way, and you're here now hoping I'll tell you it isn't true?" Carriss pulled in a low steady breath and then coughed a laugh. "Hell, I understand that alright—it's not even gonna come out in trial—far too incredible for any God-fearing jury to believe says the District Attorney." Carriss rose and I backed away. "It's not what he did, Merrill: it's what can be proved in a Court of Law…"

"Don't you say that to me! Jesus Christ, don't you say that!"

"Yeah, you accept it now, don't you?" Carriss said.

A wind, hot and searing, swept through me. "Murdered and then raped?"

"That's right. Murdered *and then* raped."

"No, she wasn't," I pleaded. "Don't you say that to me!"

"That's why you came here tonight. That's what you needed to hear. That's why you can't interfere."

"Who?"

Carriss slumped in his chair, closed his eyes, let go of his breath. "You know I can't tell you that. We have witnesses ready to testify to the perpetrator's post-offense and pre-offense behavior. We have hearsay he confessed to the crime. We found relaxants in his system after his Polygraph. He tried, but he didn't beat the machine. Look around the room—boxes of circumstantial evidence ready to go to the DA." Carriss looked around the room himself and then a look of absolute calm crossed his face. He tried to stand, winced, tried to sit again, but only made it halfway down. "Pills above the sink," were his last words, and as I turned for the sink, I heard the thud.

THAT LOOK OF calm was his heart stopping, and the thud, the table toppling beneath him on his journey dead-standing to the floor.

CHAPTER NINETEEN

THERE ARE CERTAIN words in the English language rarely used, Latin rooted and only found in medical dictionaries or criminology handbooks. Take this word for example:

> necrophilia (něk'rə-fĭl'ē-ə) n. an irresistible attraction to dead bodies; morbid fondness for being in the presence of dead bodies; the impulse to have sexual contact, or the act of such contact, with a dead body, usually of males with female corpses (see also: necrophile, necrophiliac).

I, myself, had only heard the word in passing before that night and could never possibly have fully fathomed its implications.

Insanity is not the cause of necrophilia, in that the necrophile has no moralistic confusion between right and wrong. A necrophile has full control of his faculties. In fact, most necrophiles are quite intelligent and clearheaded about their actions. Ted Bundy was a necrophile and, as psychologist Erich Fromm argued, so was Adolph Hitler.

The necrophile tends to be an anal personality type, fastidious but at the same time unusually fascinated with their own fecal matter. The necrophile is physically aroused by the smell of early-stage decomposition, the same smell that attracts detrivores and scavengers like coyotes and wild dogs.

Overly pampered as a child by overbearing mothers, the necrophile tends to be unable to break his motherly bonds as an adult. The necrophile lusts for the same power and control he had when as a baby, he cried for his mother's nipple and she came. When the necrophile discovers, in early adolescence, that he can't control others by such ham-handed means, he seeks other means of control, often through fantasy and roll playing with dolls or other inanimate objects. It has been found that many necrophiles have a childhood history of torturing and killing neighborhood pets. In adulthood, the necrophile craves non-rejecting partners so much so that he can be driven to violence.

Most notably, necrophiles love the psychological power that the death of their victim-partner provides them. Like the hoarding scavenger, the necrophile will secret the victim away, thereby indulging in his fetish as long as physically possible.

Indulging in his fetish, the necrophile believes, hurts nobody. The necrophile justifies his actions by blaming the victim, or in a similar manner, by claiming divine right, divine retribution. There is no cure for necrophilia, and if there were one, it would be atypical for the necrophile to seek such treatment. Necrophiles have no wish to change their ways.

THE NEXT MORNING found me standing outside Carriss' ICU room. It took his heart about a minute to get going again, but to me it seemed like longer. In situations like that, I suppose it always does. Once he was breathing again, I found his phone and called the ambulance. The Paramedics let me ride along to the ER and now, after a long night, I found myself clicking my Zippo in time to his respirator. "There's really no point in you standing at his door, Merrill," Earnstead said as he made his way back from Admitting. "You really should go home and get some rest."

"Does he have family I can call?"

"No...no, he doesn't." Earnstead was in the uncomfortable position of not knowing how much Carriss had told me before his heart stopped beating. "I will call *you* if anything changes—if we, uh, make progress with the DA."

I nodded, too tired for a goodbye, and made for the doors.

"Special Agent Carriss did tell you about the little hold-up we've been having with the judge?" Earnstead asked.

I stopped, turned, gave away nothing.

"There are powerful people," he said, "interfering in this thing, but rest assured, we *will* remedy the situation."

I nodded again and hit the down button on the elevators.

"It's a game of hurry up and wait," he called after me. "We have to be patient, very patient with this thing."

"Justice delayed is justice denied," I said and stepped through the opening elevator doors.

AS THE WATER ran over the wound scabbed black on my back, I went weak in the knees with guilty pleasure, the skin going loose and gentle around the flesh as puss oozed an opening for the blood to flow, the mist from the shower playing tricks with the newly exposed nerves. The blood went thin and down my back, wrapped around my left leg, crawled thinner over my toes, and quietly slid down the drain. The scar that would form would join many, inside and out, chunks of flesh taken, nerves severed—searing hot moments leaving their mark across the flesh, across the bone, across the sinew, the stomach, the liver, the mind, the heart, stealing your idealism, your innocence, your compassion—no pain, just the emptiness—but sometimes the emptiness is a good thing if it helps you get along. I don't know how long I stood under the shower in that little hole of an apartment. I know the water had long since gotten cold, but this was also a good thing—what little I felt needed to go numb.

Rape of the dead...

I had nothing left to vomit but doubled over anyway, purging the emptiness again and again, sucking up and gorging on the shower water gone cold and then falling into a fetal ball and letting the water rise from my stomach—purgation to clean me inside out.

They snipped the chain lock on the front door and moved through the darkness with military precision. The smell of sulfur, strongest this time of day, masked any scent they may have been carrying. It was only when they reached the rickety outer walls of my shower room that the cold draft from my opened door finally reached me.

I left the water running and eased my way through the shower curtain. I needed to arm and shield myself fast. They would blast down the bathroom door to catch me naked. I searched around me for anything—my towel to wrap around my forearm, to defend against their blows, that would be a start. Their shadows played across the ceiling. Three of them were out there just beyond the thin wood paneling, maybe six. My half-cocked plan was to plow through them and make it to the steps leading up from my apartment. There I would gain the advantage of high ground. There I would make my naked-wet stand, holding them back as I moved up the steps.

The problem with living a threadbare existence is that you only have threads to protect yourself in the event of something like this…but, as fortune would have it, I did have the broken corner of an aerobics mirror, the piece that had been serving as a looking glass for my shaving needs. I didn't plan on doing anything clever like using it to see around corners or beneath the door. No, this was going to be raw, ugly, dangerous—the only chance I had.

I smashed the mirror against my knee to give myself two long shards and then swung at the nightlight bulb serving to light the bathroom. As a shower of sparks and glass burst and brought blackness, all of them came in at once, but not through the door as expected. Instead, they smashed through the walls, knocking the panels in with baseball bats, tire irons, a sledgehammer, and angry feet. The whole structure creaked sideways thirty degrees. I scrambled back through the shower curtain to stand my ground, but slipped on my bar of soap, and went headfirst against the hot water knob. My head swam and vision blurred, but one of those long shards of mirror bit deep enough in my hand for me to keep hold. The intruders brought the shower curtain around me. Time fractured and played in bursts then came back full force as one of them drove his thumb into the wound between my shoulder blades. I answered by driving that shard of mirror straight into his shin. He howled and I recalled sprinklers. I wasn't sure why I was recalling sprinklers and wasn't sure where I was. Part of me felt like I was back in the park, being held in the dancing light of morning. Perhaps, it was the play of water against the plastic curtain surrounding me. Something solid came down upon my shoulder bringing pain monumental. Kicks and blows overwhelmed me and then all smashed to black. Somebody told the others that the whole place needed to be cleaned up real good—I think it was a woman speaking, but I couldn't be sure. After that, I was dragged along by the wrists through the cold.

On the verge of death, they say your life passes before your eyes.

Mostly, I saw her.

THE HOMECOMING

PART IV

DEPRESSION

CHAPTER TWENTY

MY FATHER HAD taken a seat in the corner and was staring out the third story window at the little icebergs making gentle way down the river when I woke. It was night and the bridge was lit a hypnotic glow. I came out of it slowly, for what seemed like days. Finally, I gathered the strength to swallow, and again what seemed like days passed. Finally, I found the strength to turn my head on my pillow. When I did, my father said, "Easy, your shoulder."

That's when the first wave of pain came.

There was a control button in my hand and my thumb went to it on impulse. A hiss of warmth went through my veins and the pain melted away. My father went fuzzy and, for what seemed like days, I went back to sleep.

IT WAS HIS heavy snoring that woke me on I'm not sure what day. All I really could be sure of was that the sun was pouring hot across the bottom left corner of my bed. My father was curled uncomfortably on a chair, and when the nurse entered, he jolted up as if woken from a bad dream. They gave me juice in small doses to keep me from vomiting. They told me that the morphine could do that. When my mouth was wetted enough to speak, I asked for a mirror. It would be three days before they'd grant my wish.

"They didn't find anything in your apartment indicating a struggle," my father said. "It looks like the walls of that little shower fell in on you and you slipped face-first into the faucet."

"The chain on the door?" I asked.

"Intact."

I laughed.

"It's not particularly funny," he said. "You were drunk."

"How did I get from my apartment to the hospital?"

"You checked yourself into the ER," he said.
"Was I wearing clothing?"
"You were in a blanket."
"One of mine?"
My father didn't answer.
"Where's Mom?"
My father didn't answer.
"How long have I been here?"
My father didn't answer, but just stared long and hard out the window, until finally saying, "They'll make an arrest, they've promised me that much."
"An arrest? You just said it was drunken fall."
"Not what happened to you," he said. "Her."
My heart raced. I hit the button for the morphine.
"That means you can stop all this," he said. "The games you were playing on New Year's Eve, attacking your best friend at his party, breaking and entering, making threats—"
"They'll arrest him when?"
"September…so they can keep gathering evidence."
"September?"
"Right before the statute of limitations runs out."
"There is no statute of limitations on murder," I said.
"No…Manslaughter 3, involuntary…That's what they can prove."
"Involuntary? That's like saying it was an accident."
"You just can't accept anything good anymore, can you?" he said.
"It's good that she's dead?" I asked.
"Son, we don't even recognize you. You've become dangerous to yourself and others. You don't come to church. You don't have a…"
While my father lectured, I kept pressing the button and soon the morphine washed me up and away from the conversation.

I WOULD HAVE to stay in the hospital another night. When I was discharged, my parents were waiting. They took me home, promising I would only have to stay until my broken leg and separated shoulder healed.

It turns out that caged animals forget their better instincts and, when well fed, become complacent. I put on fifteen pounds and for a time even watched soap operas. I went to church again and volunteered for the Boy Scouts. I learned to fake my way through life and hated myself for trying to conform, for caring what people thought of me. The bones healed but the muscles atrophied—especially the heart—and soon it became difficult to stand up straight. Then one day I remembered the little apartment that smelled of sulfur and determined that to it I would have to return.

ON THE DAY the pain medication ran out, I switched back to drink. Anything to keep the edges soft of a shattered life and the emptiness filled of a broken soul. For a time, the booze does blunt the shards and fills the empty space, but it does so by carving you out. You become stupefied, weak, and comfortable with the way things are.

Late that spring, I sat with Tammy's mother for a time, the basic premise being that we would catch up on old times. It was something I suppose we should have done much sooner, and if I had been a better man, we would have. A mother's grief is something I would not dare to contemplate or understand. We can only see the world through our own eyes and feel the pain thrust down upon us in our own way.

Tammy's mother spoke gently about getting to a place where she could forgive, never mentioning how she had to leave this whispering little town just to do her grocery shopping. She didn't say too much about her worry for her boys, how they had lost many of their friends, how she had lost many of her friends. She didn't tell me she was haunted by the nightmare of losing them too. She circled around the fact that they were unable to talk about their late father and murdered sister. Not that it mattered—those who counseled around these parts didn't encourage such talk.

Before I left, she did ask me if I would be at the trial. I said yes, but in reality, I had become far too jaded to believe that a trial would ever take place.

I DIDN'T VISIT Carriss in the assisted-living home until June. The heart attack was only the beginning of a series of mild strokes and coronary episodes that would leave him mostly confined to a bed. Being mostly of salt and action, this did not please him and often times he begged for death. He didn't recognize me the first time I came to visit. He was nearly blind, but when he took my hand and felt my scars, he smiled and knew. After those first few awkward meetings, a time of finding common ground, the two of us came to be an excellent fit.

IN THE PASSING months, I found myself dreaming again. Hope, I came to learn, had the power to endure, but the price of its enduring power was heartache. I found myself retreating to an idealized past, a fairytale childhood that never was. All that was right about her was resurrected in the shadows of a would-be poet's dreams. She had too generous a spirit to fight back. Perhaps, this was her greatest flaw. She carried a secret pain she rarely revealed, but when she did, the stars and moon stopped and bent to listen.

September rolled around.

There were the football games and another Homecoming.

I took some classes at the local University and began to train for the day of reckoning. I pushed my body past every limitation, my fury focused like a laser, my pain driving me home.

The day did come.

On the anniversary of Tammy's death Eric Stukel was arraigned in Cedar County, Nebraska on the charges of Manslaughter in the Third Degree. This news was kept from me until he was out on bond and ferried away by his parents to a drug treatment center.

There was a collective sigh of relief in Yankton. The few reward posters that remained intact came down. Mostly, people were happy that the trial would take place across the river, where the whole thing would become someone else's problem.

There are those who say patience is a virtue, but in actuality, it is something that gets thrust upon us, an affliction we must endure, when we have no other option. A trial date was set for September of the next year, the bond for his promised return set at five thousand dollars.

CHAPTER TWENTY-ONE

I DON'T REMEMBER too much about the next year. I suppose I just couldn't see beyond the impending trial, all my hope stored up and held tight as the days bled slowly forward. Would the decision of those twelve strangers on that jury bring me some sense of peace? If the jury ruled that Stukel was the one, he would face five to ten years in prison or a fine of twenty-thousand dollars—a pittance. The matter-nothing world of everyday danced on around me carefree, and my hate and my grief and my rage grew. Finally, came September and with it the trial and when I slipped into the back of the courtroom, late from a flat tire, Coroner Wong had long since taken the stand.

There was still some argument among authorities over where Tammy actually was murdered (the buck passed from one county to the next.) The county line between Knox and Cedar sat only a few hundred yards from the ravine, and the Stevenson farm was not far from there. The dam and surrounding waters fell under the jurisdiction of the federal government but was patrolled jointly by the Cedar County Sheriff, Yankton County Sheriff, the Corps of Engineers, and the South Dakota State Game, Fish, and Parks. As well, some still argued that Tammy was murdered in Yankton and transported back across the bridge into Nebraska, this based on Eric's story about taking her home. In the end jurisdiction fell to Cedar County, just opposite Yankton County right across the river. Clearly within in its borders were the ravine and Stevenson farm. The choice seemed correct to me.

The Cedar County seat was Hartington, Nebraska, population 1580, roughly a tenth the size of Yankton. Hartington popped up as a rail town in 1880s, which meant that its primary function was to serve as a refueling and water stop for passing trains. Besides nine-man football and 4H, not much happened in Hartington these days.

It didn't take much for family and friends of the accused to fill the defense side of the little courtroom gallery on the second floor of the courthouse. The unusually large crowd brought the ambient temperature somewhere into the nineties by midday, the two ceiling fans that served as air conditioning straining above the small, sweating crowd.

Tammy's mother sat alone behind the prosecution table, a small Bible held near her heart. A young female reporter for the local newspaper sat two empty rows back. I took my seat in the fifth and final row and searched the faces on the other side. There was Eric Stukel next to his lawyers, his look overhauled from druggie burnout skateboarder to junior high school hall monitor. Stukel's mother and father were right behind the defense table, Mrs. Stukel positioned carefully to keep eye contact with as many jurors as possible, one of them in particular, a woman her age, who seemed to be passing her knowing looks. The rest of the faces on that side of the house were vaguely familiar, relatives perhaps. Absent from the proceedings were Noose Adarson, Dusty Fist, and Brian Slobacek.

"As the cock crows, Peter…"

So the saying goes.

Coroner Wong was being questioned by Nebraska Assistant Attorney General Gabriel Attebaum, a tenderfoot out of Lincoln, a reserved and quiet man, perfect for the sensibilities of a small town. This case he was told by his associates and mentors was career suicide, but he had taken it anyway, and from the start, had fought uphill to get it to see the light of day, compromised and mishandled evidence thrown out left and right along the way.

No photos of Tammy would be allowed in the courtroom, Judge Horn ruled, and any autopsy and crime-scene photos presented would be limited to the essentials. It was his honor's belief that a good jury acted without emotion and such pictures of the victim would only evoke sympathy. Stukel's prior history with Tammy wouldn't be admitted either because under strict interpretation of the law, Manslaughter 3 didn't involve premeditation. The events of that night, according to the law, existed in and of themselves. No amount of legal wrangling, nor the facts at hand could change that.

Most of this was an obvious victory for Mr. Michael Stevens, Eric Stukel's lead attorney. Stevens had age and experience on his side. His strategy was to paint Tammy as an unsympathetic victim, the rules that protected the accused doing little to protect the victim. According to Stevens, Tammy's death was the result of a self-inflicted accident, mysterious in nature. She lived a reckless lifestyle and was out by herself doing something she shouldn't have been doing. According to Stevens, Stukel became the unfortunate target of a four-year witch-hunt as he was the last to be with her.

Coroner Wong did her best to make the hard data of the autopsy findings soft enough for the jury to understand, while still abiding by the procedural guidelines of the Court. "The second autopsy," she explained, "this is where the medical examiner was able to make use of an x-ray to help determine cause of death—revealed a tear to the soft tissue of the first and second vertebrae of the neck, right at the base of the skull. This damage to the spine resulted in full paralysis. Full paralysis brought on cessation of the diaphragm. In other words, the lungs could not take in air and the victim slowly died from asphyxiation. It took approximately two minutes for her to be rendered unconscious and six to eight minutes before her heart finally ceased."

"As for time of death?" Attebaum asked.

"Around midnight on September 17th or 18th," she said. "I based this upon the stomach contents. As you already pointed out, the first two medical examiners placed the time of death later, based largely upon spurious sightings of the victim and statements made by the accused. This was a rush to judgment, necessary to process the body and move it on to better facilities. I based my findings largely upon the time of the victim's last meal. Simply, it takes six hours for a person to pass food through the stomach. You look at stomach content and evaluate how far digestion has gone. If the victim, for example, has stomach content four hours digested and last ate at 6:00, you place the time of death roughly at 10:00. In this case, we knew the victim last ate just after 6:00 P.M. and that her meal was nearly digested. This puts her death right around midnight, with room for error of about twenty minutes."

As Wong took a sip of water, Stukel glanced back at me then whispered something to his attorney. Stevens considered whatever Stukel had whispered, glanced back at me too, and then rose. "Your honor, quick sidebar, please."

Jury decisions often teeter upon the rulings made in sidebar. Lawyers on both sides cast manipulative little spells called motions—these motions help to tip the scales of justice one way or the other. An unseen battle ensues between defense and prosecution, one spell cast against the next—evidence ruled prejudicial, witnesses ruled unreliable, testimony ruled invalid. Sometimes these rulings are fair, sometimes they are not.

"The kid was in Basic Training at the time, halfway across the country on the night in question," Atteabum whispered at Judge Horn. "The only reason Mr. Stevens wants to subpoena him is to get him out of the courtroom, to keep the jury from seeing his face."

"He was a friend of Ms. Haas," Stevens said. "I may want to call him."

Atteabum sighed. "You've done this to about forty of her friends. You're trying to load the gallery with a sympathetic audience."

"You think I'm trying to keep her friends and family out of the courtroom to shift sympathy toward my client?" Stevens said. "That's a serious accusation. I hope you can back it up."

"Mike, you haven't an inch to stand on for keeping that kid—"

"I won't fight you if you want to bring in his testimony," Stevens said. "You subpoena him yourself if you like. I won't fight you."

"His testimony is hearsay," Atteabum said.

"Like I said, I won't fight you."

I KNEW SOLDIERING, a bit of home medicine, advanced theories of physics and evolution, the Boy Scout motto, the Bible, but I was quite clueless when it came to judicial process, so when the bailiff told me I had to leave the courtroom because I had just been put on the witness list for the prosecution, I told the bailiff that this was a public trial and that I wasn't leaving. He quietly explained to me what a subpoena was and that I didn't have a choice in the matter. When I rose for the doors, Eric Stukel glanced back at me and gave me the slightest of grins. This grin was the last thing I could recall before waking up on my floor in the middle of the night with a raging hangover.

IN THE MEANTIME, Coroner Wong didn't have too much more to say about Tammy's murder. Atteabum instructed her to keep things simple, to paint in broad strokes. She did her best, but painting in broad strokes led to major problems. Keeping it simple meant that it would be impossible for her to pinpoint the precise location of death and the weapon used to kill Tammy. She did discuss the hairs found in Eric's trunk and the fibers from Eric's trunk found on Tammy's body. She also described livor mortis and decomposition and argued how these major post-mortem events strongly suggested that Tammy died away from the ravine. She discussed serology and crime-scene procedure, and the false notion that smoking guns exist in every case. Even as simple as she kept her testimony, much of what she said passed straight over half the juror's heads. An afternoon recess was called and several more fans were brought into the stuffy gallery.

WHEN THE JURORS returned they were reintroduced to Coroner Wong. This was where Mike Stevens was able, for the first time, to demonstrate his gift for cross-examination. "Good afternoon, Ms. Wong," Stevens said.

"Dr. Wong," Wong answered.

"You, uh, you say the death occurred at close to midnight—but you're not really sure on what day?"

"Because," she said. "The 17th becomes the 18th at midnight."

"Ah, I see...but the, uh, the other two coroners, the ones who were involved in the case from day one, said that the death occurred when?"

"2:00 A.M. on September 18," she answered. "This disagreement over two hours resolved itself with the introduction of more facts. I'm sure if you call them to the stand they would agree with my assessment."

"Can forensic scientists make mistakes?" Stevens asked.

"Of course."

"And in your field guesswork is done?"

"Absolutely."

Attebaum sifted through his files, unsure where Stevens was taking this.

"Care to explain, Dr. Wong?"

"Yes, I would—it's called the scientific method."

"So you're saying all scientists make mistakes, that this is part of the process?" Stevens was taking a gamble but had a good feeling that Coroner Wong would walk into the trap.

"Am I saying all scientists make mistakes?" Wong said. "Good scientists admit when we're wrong—we take nothing on faith. We interpret facts and come up with theories based on those facts."

"Would you admit you made mistakes in handling this case?"

"I mistook some of the evidence at the outset as did my colleagues. With the introduction of more facts, we came up with better theories."

"What about these so-called defense wounds?" Stevens said. "There is a chance that these could have been accidental?"

"The wounds we found on the hands and arm were consistent with a person shielding their face from blows by a fist or other blunt object."

"But, you're not sure which? You can't even say with one-hundred percent certainty these were defense wounds. Like you said, you scientists don't act on faith, but simply come up with the best theories you can, right?"

Wong shifted in her seat.

"It's a simple question," Stevens said.

Wong shifted in her seat again.
"Yes."
"Nothing further."

A FELLOW WAS pulled from active duty to get on the stand the next morning. Four years ago, he was working the graveyard shift at the 24-hour slop-joint Stukel's parents owned, a place called the Fryin' Pan. Two nights after Tammy disappeared, Eric wandered into the restaurant and found a booth. "Eric looked like a zombie," he said. "He was drunk or stoned or both and wouldn't look up at me. I asked him what he wanted. He didn't answer. I asked if everything was okay and he mumbled, 'I think I killed a girl.'"

"What did you do?" Attebaum asked.

"Well, I didn't take him seriously, but I knew he was messed up, so I went and got one of his friends who was in back washing dishes."

It never came out in trial, but the dishwasher was Noose Adarson.

ARE YOU SURE he said, 'I think I killed a girl'?" Stevens asked.
"Yes."
"Didn't you at one point say he said, 'I'm *thinking* of killing a girl'?"
"I don't recall saying that."
"Didn't the police put a wire on you? Send you over to the Stukel house a few weeks later to see if he would repeat himself?"
"Yes."
"Did he?"
"No."
"Nothing further."

SPECIAL AGENT EARNSTEAD tracked me down the next day. I believe Carriss sent him after hearing news of my removal from the courtroom. Earnstead invited me for coffee. I said no at first, but decided in the end that I could use the company. I found him at Ma and Pa's grill, sitting in the corner of the booth, eyes on the door. He started in on me even before I had the chance to sit. "If we can nail Stukel, we can go after the others."

"On what?" I said.

"On witness tampering, obstruction of justice, maybe even drug charges." Earnstead leaned in close. "But first things first. Man 3 has got to stick. Attebaum has to do his job without interference."

"Is that why he subpoenaed me?"

"That was a mistake in my opinion."

"The proof you have against Stukel," I said. "What he did to her in that ravine, won't come out in trial—far too incredible for any God-fearing jury to believe! Man 3 is not what happened and simply saying that her body was in his trunk does not prove the case…not with the others involved."

"That's why we have to go after Stukel singularly." Earnstead said. "Conspiracy is hard to prove. That's why people conspire in the first place."

"None of you actually believe it was Man 3, do you?"

"No, of course not...you remember that talisman, the one he put on her casket, that little triangular-shaped stone?" Earnstead leaned back. "Meant to draw sexual power from the dead. He built a shrine to her in his bedroom. We have witnesses that will testify to that."

"A shrine?"

"A funerary shrine—built the weekend she first went missing...or maybe even before. Textbook. All of it, everything he did—*what he is*—it all adds up. Now, his friends are running scared. If we can convict Stukel, we can—"

"Dusty Fist, Noose Adarson, Brian Slobacek—known them since grade school. They are a lot of things—one thing they are not is scared."

"You've heard Eric's alibi, saying her took her all the way back to Yankton, that she left his house and just somehow her body winds up in that ravine, ten miles away, spitting distance from that party. Why?" Earnstead asked, "Why would he say he took her home and had sex with her? Because he had to account for the blood, the urine, the semen! He's told too many lies. He's going to get up on the stand and he's going to slip."

"He's had four years to slip, four years to prepare," I said.

"I know you feel helpless right now, and I understand all that rage you got pent up—these guys celebrated while she was lying in that ravine. Make no mistake—we want these remorseless sons-of-bitches just as bad as you."

"I doubt it," I said. "You don't have a case...against any of them."

"Give due process a fair shake," Earnstead said. "Those are good people in that jury box. They'll see through to the truth."

"What about Eric's sister?" I asked.

"What about Eric's sister?"

"The rumor is she's given him an alibi."

"But it's shifted with the winds from the start."

"You need one of his friends to testify against him."

"It isn't like we haven't tried. We've offered money, immunity, anonymity, witness protection—"

Earnstead stopped mid-laundry list and looked up to find me gone.

I HEARD EARNSTEAD shouting for me moments later. Though it was still September, the downtown businesses were holding their Oktoberfest Krazy Sale. "I read every letter you sent Tammy from boot camp!" Earnstead shouted through the crowd. I spun and came back at Earnstead, nearly knocking him back into a display of dancing cola cans. "I'm sorry you feel violated," he said, "but from what I read in those letters you have a strong sense of right and wrong. I know you wouldn't be stupid enough to go beating people into confessions. It's called witness tampering and it does not fly."

"No worries," I smiled, "subtlety's my strength."

CHAPTER TWENTY-TWO

I WAS TOLD the trial would last not much more than a week. This meant that I would have to work fast.

DURING CERTAIN MISSIONS, soldiers must learn to disassociate, to go into a sort of hypnosis. This state of disassociation makes certain deeds that were impossible under normal circumstances possible.

ANOTHER MAJOR OBSTACLE to overcome was constant surveillance of the bad guys by the local police.

I SUITED UP and got into character.

IT WASN'T QUITE a look of surprise on his face when he found me staring at him through his rearview mirror that morning. He knew he had seen movement in the pile of leaves in the back of the truck. He was nearly tempted to dump has gas can over the pile and drop a match. Instead, he hopped into the truck and went for the .357 under the seat. He didn't mean to grin, but he knew it was going to be that easy.

"Bang!" I said, as he pulled the trigger.

He gave the revolver a confused look then aimed the pistol between my eyes and again pulled the trigger. I couldn't bear the thought of him making it all the way around the cylinder without any comprehension of what I had done, so I extended my palm through the back window to reveal the six bullets I'd removed from his weapon.

Dusty Fist was so strong that when he grabbed my wrist with both his arms and cranked down, I felt the cartilage popping in my shoulder. All I could really do right then was twist my other arm in and force my thumb into his eye. That was enough for him to loosen his grip and enough for me to get my hand down around his throat. "Thirty seconds you're unconscious—"

Dusty leaned hard into my grip and clenched into a grin as he tried to get his chin down to bite my wrist. "You're a grown man," I hissed, "you've had that constipated grin on your face since the second grade—life isn't that goddamned funny."

"Let my neck go!" he said with frightening indifference.

"I don't know which one of you did it or if it was a group effort—"

"That was four years ago, you sick fucker!"

"They found your fingerprint inside her shoe, Dusty!"

"Fuck you!"

His face was going deep red as he pushed harder into my hand.

"Con-fess-your-sins-to-Att-e-baum." I smashed his head against the back window to punctuate each syllable. "And once on the stand, tell the world what happened that night."

"And if I don't?"

"I know how to get rid of bodies too."

A RIVETED JURY watched Assistant Attorney General Attebaum read from Eric Stukel's journal. The original copy that went missing early on in the case turned up in the evidence room of the Yankton City Police Station after the threat of a Federal shakedown. The journal was nearly thrown out because Man 3 does not allow for premeditation, but Attebaum made the case that Stukel's writings proved "a manifest depravity of mind and disregard of human life," and so the judge allowed it and told him to proceed cautiously.

"'I admit I control her,'" Attebaum read, "'But, I know that someone special sent me to change her. I admit I play with her mind. I'll take her to LA with me, even if I have to kill her. Kill Tammy? Yeah, I thought about it.'"

NOOSE ADARSON HAD threatened to kill his wife, but that was not what had him behind bars that weekend. He had two unpaid traffic citations. He owed the taxpayers of Yankton County money.

The visiting room wasn't really much of a room at all, just a little beige cubby with two doors and a glass partition down the middle. One door led from the cellblock, the other from an admitting area. On either side of the glass were handsets jacked into a closed phone line.

When he finally arrived, Noose had the look of a man woken from a deep sleep. He knew why I had come and wasted no time in saying, "I wasn't there that night."

I put a hand to my ear and gestured for him to pick up his handset.

He lifted the phone and repeated: "I wasn't there that night."

"However," I told him, "Eric did take you out to that ravine for show-and-tell two days later. It was the proof of it you wanted and it was the proof of it he gave you. It was a Saturday, late afternoon, when the bugs were at their thickest. He got to know that ravine and you followed him the long way around. When you finally got there, you found yourself impressed with what he'd done. However, being impressed wasn't good enough for you. You wanted more. So, you watched as he took things further—"

Noose hung up. I gestured at his phone. He answered.

"And further—"

He hung up again and I gestured for him to pick up.

"If you don't cut a deal today with the DA," I said, "someday very soon you and I will find ourselves together on that side of the glass."

THE JURY SPENT late Monday morning staring at the back of Eric Stukel's car as Assistant Attorney General Attebaum showed how it was possible to get a girl who stood five-foot-four and weighed just over one hundred pounds into a compact trunk. The smiling crack in the windshield was attributed to the weather, as was some rust damage to the moon roof.

ERIC HAD BEEN on top of things the morning after the Stevenson bonfire. Sobriety kicked him square in the face and he was out the door from Noose Adarson's and off to make a showing at school. School was released early for the big Homecoming parade, and when the parade ended, Eric purchased three rolls of quarters to go to work on the interior of his car. Several witnesses observed Eric at the car wash. One had the courage to testify. Evidently, Eric's car cleaning technique was quite a sight—every door opened including the trunk, super-soaker hose inside the car, spraying away.

I HAD GROWN a ponytail, but Brian Slobacek's was longer. I owned a motorcycle, but Brian's was bigger. If you looked at the two of us from about twenty meters away, those would be the only discernable physical differences. People liked Brian though, enough to make him Homecoming Chief, enough to offer him easy jobs for good pay, enough to let him stroll through life on the backs of others. Most things went right for Brian—most things but one. At about the time of the South Dakota Grand Jury proceedings, Brian took some good advice and disappeared from town. That was almost three years ago. Now, with the trial well under way and a guarantee of not guilty, he felt it safe to return. For the first time in a long time, he felt unconquerable.

Motorcycles that were very big and very fast tended to have one design flaw. They could not take tight corners. That was okay for Brian though—he liked taking his bike out on the open road. The most amusing game he played was putting girlfriends on the back and driving at bone-shattering speeds—especially if they said no.

My motorcycle, on the other hand, was small, old, and inherited third hand from an Army buddy. On the open road, my little bike fought to balance against even the lightest of prairie winds. It also leaked fuel and got far too hot at speeds above fifty. There was one advantage to little bikes: they were quick out of the gate and took corners tight, perfect for back-alley driving.

NOBODY WORE HELMETS around here, so Brian was sure he was getting teased into a street race by an old high school friend with a sense of humor. The fool in the helmet teased him around corners and pushed close, nearly locking spokes once or twice. Finally, the joke went too far and Brian found himself smashed over the curb as he rounded the corner up the steep hill at Eighth and Mulberry. "I could have gotten killed!" he screamed at the fool in the helmet, as the fool in the helmet slowed to make sure Brain survived the crash.

As Brian hopped back on his bike, the fool in the helmet shot over the railroad tracks, across a short field and down a walking bridge. Once across, the fool looked back to make sure Brian would follow. The chase took them past Webster School and around a tight corner that led into an alley.

THE HOMECOMING

What Brian didn't expect when he lumbered a wide turn around the corner was the fool in the helmet at the far end of the alley, facing him, like a knight clad black and ready to joust.

Brian roared his engine and spit gravel as he raced forward. The fool in the helmet took his time, however, and eased gently from first to second and then from second to third. By the time Brian had gotten to full speed, he realized the fool in the helmet wasn't planning on veering or slowing down. Brian swerved at the overgrown raspberry bushes. The fool in the helmet stayed his course, reaching out as he passed to count coup. Brian got the joke now and understood why the fool in the helmet had waited so long before coming at him. Hidden behind the raspberry bushes was a loading dock, dozens of 2X8 planks jutting neck high off its lip.

Brian slammed his brakes hard. It was the perfect save, back tire spinning up against the loading docks, the 2X8s inches from taking his head. When the dust settled, Brian was pinned, the fool locking up with him front tire to front tire. "What the fuck's your problem!" Brian shouted.

"I know you were there that night," the fool in the helmet said.

"What night? What the fuck are you talking about?!"

The fool in the helmet unscrewed his gas cap and lit the Zippo. "Do you know what it feels like to fear for your life?" They were so close Brian could make out the Zippo's inscription—*Fiat Lux.*

"What are you doing—you'll blow us both to Hell!"

"You didn't protect her—you only worried about yourself."

"Who the fuck are you talking about?! Who the fuck *are* you?!"

"You threatened to kill her if she ever spoke," the fool said.

"That was four fucking years ago!" Brian shouted.

"You dragged her to the dam and you made her silent with fear. You dangled her until she was sure you would drop her." The fool in the helmet teased the flaming Zippo through the rising gasoline fumes. "You liked her fear. You liked the control of it. She was paralyzed. She would do anything for you now." The burning Zippo went lower toward the gas cap.

"What do you want me to do about it now? The police, the lawyers—we tried to cut a deal—none of them would hear us out!"

A siren chirped a patrol car's slow approach. Brian grinned, but quickly lost that grin when he realized the fool in the helmet did not intend to quash the Zippo's flame. "You were taking orders, your strings were pulled," the fool in the helmet said. "I want to know by whom."

The leather of the fool's glove caught fire.

"You're crazy," Brian said.

"Yeah."

The patrol car slowed through the school zone a block away.

"Put out the flame and I'll tell you!"

"Tell me and I'll put out the flame."

Brian could feel the fool in the helmet smiling.

"I can't do that!" Brian cried.

THE HOMECOMING

"Have you ever had burnt flesh scraped from your bones?"

"Just put it out please," Brian pleaded.

"Some pain you can escape, but not the pain of a third-degree burn. No drug in the world can save you from it. Even when you're unconscious you feel it piercing your very soul."

A hollow swelling sound rose up from the gas tank.

"Don the Itch!" Brian Slobacek shouted.

"Thank you," the fool in the helmet said and blew out his glove.

Brian could only sit atop his bike and shake. By the time the patrol car rolled up to the loading dock, the fool in the helmet had already gotten three blocks away.

SEVERAL ANGRY LETTERS crossed the editor's desk at the local newspaper. Front-page coverage of the Stukel trial, according to several concerned citizens, was making Yankton look like a very ugly place.

DON THE ITCH never really considered himself a drug dealer. He didn't haunt some street corner in the ghetto. He had never even fired anything but a BB-gun, and that was just to take out the neighborhood cats and dogs when he was a kid. He didn't flash gang-signs or bounce down the street low-rider style. He dealt with friends, and friends of friends (and sometimes friends of friends of friends.) One of the perks was that he got all the sex he wanted, had friends willing to watch his back, and because he kept things small and simple, he maintained a flight pattern just underneath the radar of state and federal law enforcement. Strangely enough, with this trial so oddly timed, business had actually started to boom. He guessed it made enough sense— that's how it usually was when anything big happened around here. Major events brought about a major need for recreational substances. Lately though, traffic had picked up so much that he barely found time to get to the local tit joint for a squeeze and blow. What drove him crazy was that when he did find time, he was constantly interrupted.

Puffing the magic dragon was still good enough entertainment for the high-school crowd, but for the blue-collar man it was Billy-Whiz, Methamphetamines, Crystal, Ice, Speed, (or Nazi-YaBa if you could get it in pill form.) Don the Itch wasn't a user himself, because frankly he got so sick of YaBa-Nazis rambling on about nothing for hours on end. This was sometimes the price of business. Crank-heads and YaBa-Nazis were good customers. They weren't always on the best behavior, but they always came back for more. This was where Don the Itch found himself—cornered in the tit-bar shitter by an old high-school chum turned YaBa-Nazi.

The YaBa-Nazi was twenty-minutes into his conspiracy theory about CIA operatives putting mind-controlling drugs onto those little stickers that go on bananas. The stickers only worked on little kids, according to the YaBa-Nazi, because little kids always stuck those stickers on their noses (which was the only part of the body where the drugs could be activated) and that was why the whole school lunch system was set up in the first place, as a means of mind-control...and the story went on and on, with racial overtones and second comings of Christ, until the YaBa-Nazi suddenly broke from his two-hundred mile-per-hour rant and shouted, "This is a private conversation!"

Don the Itch glanced over his shoulder to find a reasonably familiar face. Don the Itch had actually punched this face before, back in grade school.

"Knock his ass out!" Don the Itch shouted at the YaBa-Nazi and ducked away from me. The YaBa-Nazi swung and grazed my nose. I backed away just enough for him to overextend his thrust and when he came out of the swing, he found me lifting him by the back of his belt. He couldn't have weighed more than one hundred and twenty pounds, but his belt was so ratty, it ripped in two, and he went splattering to the floor.

The YaBa-Nazi tried to rise to his knees, but I was quick to slip what was left of the belt around his neck and cinch it like a dog collar...and like a dog on a collar, the YaBa-Nazi was led out the door.

I locked the bathroom door behind me and turned to find Don the Itch bolting himself in the last of the toilet stalls.

I decided I would wash my hands before things went any further.

Don the Itch was nearly ready to slip out through a little window high above the stall when he heard a gentle scratching against the stall door. "I don't even like Stukel, fucker!" he shouted.

I answered by stepping back and giving the toilet stall a little kick. The bolt went more easily than I anticipated and the door slammed open and closed again, and for an instant Don the Itch was revealed hugged up around a moldy plumbing pipe, one leg kicked up into a window far too small for the rest of his body.

"You're a dead man!" he shouted down at me.

I pushed the stall open again, looked up, and said, "You'll never fit."

"You touch me and you're dead!"

"You know, I used to blame myself for Tammy's death." I gave Don a push upwards to free his leg and then hoisted him down on my shoulders. "But now?" I said, planting him on terra firma. "Now, I blame you."

"I have drugs," he said. "I have money."

"That'd be a start." I slid up against him and went slowly, as if I had all the time in the world, lifting from his coat pocket a hefty bag full of pot. "Did you know she took a blow so hard to the stomach that her small intestine tore open against her spine?" I dropped the bag of pot in the toilet. "But what concern would that be to you, correct?" I dug deeper into his jacket and pulled out a bag of small pink rock—the Crystal Meth. "I'll tell you why you should be concerned." I emptied the rock into the toilet. "Your boys Dusty and Brian were involved in Tammy's death. They were taking their orders from you, tell me I'm right." Don didn't answer so I took him by the chin and nodded his head. "'Yes, Specialist Merrill, they *were* taking orders from me.'"

"So fucking what if they were?!" Don shouted.

"You're dumber than you look," I said and took Don by the throat. "You told them to discard her body." I slammed his head against the moldy pipe. "You told them it was the right thing to do." I smashed his head into the wall.

"Can't breathe!" Don shouted.

"The money," I said. "The rest!"

"In my fucking boot," Don hissed.

"Bend over," I said.

Don the Itch didn't immediately comply, so I lifted his left leg to remove his boot. Out from the boot and into the toilet went a chillum, two poppers, rolling paper, and a stamp book with a little picture of an alien on the cover.

"I'm not finding any money," I told him.

"Other leg," he said, pulled off his other boot, and handed it over.

I tipped the boot and heaps of money fell out into the toilet. "Don, you've been doing well for yourself! There must be over two grand in there!"

"Flush it and we're both dead!"

"That's right," I said and flushed the toilet.

When it didn't all go down in one slosh, I gave the toilet a second flush. This gave Don an opening to rise and throw a wild punch. The punch caught me square on my left brow. The cut that opened would have been distraction enough for Don to make his escape, but when he ran, he slipped.

"Listen to what I have to say," I said, squatting over him, bleeding on him. "And once I've said it, we're going to take a walk."

MY HEAD HURT as if chunks of hair had been pulled out at the root—only those roots felt as if they had been connected to bits of my brain and those bits of brain had been squeezed and drained out of me like little sponges dipped in gall. The more I tried to think about it, the less I could fathom what was happening to me. I could not understand why my world would go from sudden day to sudden night. I did not understand how I would go from lying in bed on the verge of sleep to sitting outside of my apartment on my little motorcycle, contemplating those extra thirty miles on the odometer. One moment I would be getting dressed, the rage would come, and suddenly I would be in the shower, bleeding, letting my shoulder go loose in the heat.

ASSISTANT ATTORNEY GENERAL Attebaum looked surprised enough to see Don the Itch getting dragged into his office at that late an hour. He had been staring so long at his case files he could think of nothing better to say than, "What the hell?" which he phrased more as a statement of bewilderment than an inquiry of fact. Don the Itch needed a pinch on the neck to make him talk. "Brain Slobacek and Dusty Fist found Eric sitting in the ditch next to Tammy's body." He went silent. I pinched. He winced. "They just thought she was passed out at first. They called me and asked me what to do. I didn't know. I thought it was a joke. I told them if it was for real they should just dump the fucking body quick and get back to town to make up an alibi." More silence. Another pinch. "We roughed up some people, me and Dusty, a couple of her friends who went around asking too many questions—fucking bitches!" I pinched Don's neck one last time for good measure.

Attebaum sat back considering. "Okay, you can go now," he said.

Don the Itch grinned, gave my shoulder a good hard slap, and made way backwards out the door. When Assistant Attorney General Attebaum was sure Don the Itch was well out of earshot, he rose from his desk and pointed an accusing finger. "Witness tampering, that's what I could charge you with!"

"Charge *me* with witness tampering?"

"I'm going to speak slowly, so you can read my lips," Attebaum said. "There is no cover up. In the eyes of the law, Eric Stukel acted alone."

"That's not the truth!"

"If you throw factors at the jury like other potential suspects—Brian, Don, Noose, Dusty—you've created reasonable doubt. Reasonable doubt is the only excuse that jury needs to acquit and they *are* looking for a reason. Eric acted alone. I don't like it either, but that's the way it has to be."

"So you lie to get the desired result…you whittle away at the truth until it fits in a neat little box…that makes you no different, no better."

Attebaum was stung. "Yeah, it may seem that way. Look, I appreciate what you tried to do, but you're not a soldier anymore and this isn't war."

Suddenly, there was a third person in the room.

"There a problem, Mr. Attebaum?"

It was Detective Dickson.

"This young man could use an escort out of the building," Attebaum said and then dug back into his files as if nothing between us had just taken place.

FINDING YOURSELF WALKING through a courthouse in the middle of the night with an ethically challenged police officer thirty miles out of his jurisdiction tends to make you nervous, especially when you, yourself, have no clue how you traversed those thirty miles. If the clocks on the wall were correct, I had lost four hours from my life, gained a nasty gash on my temple, and smelled of cheap cigarettes, booze, and strippers.

It was only the low glow of the running lights guiding us to the front doors and the heavy echo of our feet against the marble when Detective Dickson began to speak to me as a father would to his child. "You don't seem to understand," he said. "There are people in this town that would do anything to protect themselves from exposure—big fish who just want to see Eric disappear." He stopped and smiled at the thought. "A swift and silent guilty verdict would do that."

"You sanitized that farmhouse. You destroyed evidence in the middle of the night," I hissed. "You did it to make sure that that farm wasn't connected to her death. Why, I asked myself, would you want to do that? Why, I asked, would you want to put your career at stake? Do you know what I did? I dug. It seems there is family connection—some of that farmland will become yours?"

Dickson slowed to a stop.

"Unless, of course, the D.E.A. would take that property under the drug seizure laws now on the books," I said.

"These people," Dickson smiled as if he hadn't heard a word, "would hurt your family, your friends—they'd go so far as to hurt your friend's little baby even—"

Dickson found himself against the wall, my fingers at his throat.

"These people," Dickson kept smiling, "want to see Eric go away quietly. A confession on the stand would make that possible."

I eased my grip.

"Eric takes the stand in his own defense Monday," Dickson said. "He needs proper motivation...do you take my meaning?"

My hand went slack. Dickson loosened his tie, winced as the blood returned to his skull, and then punched me full force in the gut. "You have a job to do—go do it," he said.

I rose from my knees.

"It happens tonight," I said. "Tell your people to stay out of my way."

"Done."

CHAPTER TWENTY-THREE

ERIC STUKEL ENJOYED Indian summer. Life was as easy as shaking the leaves off the outdoor hot-tub cover and popping in for a late-night dip. Across the alley and through the fence was Crane-Youngworth Field, the place where the hometown football games were played. From the perfect vantage point of his tub, he would watch the cheerleaders rehearse their halftime routines through the chain-links of the back-alley fence. The girls would gather up in the dim light behind the end-zone stands and there they would kick their legs high, not knowing anybody was watching, and sometimes they would touch each other, not knowing that anybody was watching. They would laugh and sometimes he would laugh with them, but they would never hear him and that is what he liked best. It was the control of being invisible and it made him feel like a god.

He would smoke and smoke and watch them and the band would play and he would smoke some more as the bubbles came up around him, hot tiny bubbles hissing, and there would be cheers and sometimes he would imagine the crowds would be cheering for him. He could never see the football game itself, for those bleachers were in the way, but this was another thing he liked. There was the noise of the tackles, and the whistles blown, and he could imagine it instead, and he liked imagining. He imagined himself a giant, an invisible god, moving the football players to and fro like pieces on a little green game board, smashing and bashing them together, feeling the relief, reveling in their pain, as he smoked and smoked more and more.

They were jealous of him—those crowds—he knew it.

He would sometimes imagine himself coming down in the shape of an ancient god to have his way with those dancing, prancing, touching, feeling, giggling, pyramid-making girls. They were putting on a great show tonight and it wasn't even Homecoming yet—life was good indeed!

All the boys wanted her, but he made sure that wasn't possible. He was the last to be with her. He was truly a god and she would forever be his.

EITHER THE AIR was growing cooler faster tonight or the hot tub was getting hotter than usual. The steam was rising and Eric's lighter had gone slick with steam. When he tried to grab it to smoke some more, it slid off the side of the tub and splashed down upon his thigh. He recovered it in an instant, but no matter how much he blew, the flint would take an hour to dry.

It was like that sometimes—these little inconveniences—but he would wait it out in the tub until the cheerleaders had taken to the field. When that was done, when his private performance was over, he would retreat to the silence and cool of his basement, where he had plenty of dry lighters and bags more to smoke. There were those sharp edges from the trial, of course, but this was his blunting time, the softening of night upon day, the dreaming of himself away, the dreaming of himself to her, warmer and warmer, darker and darker…

They all wanted to take her away from him.

The cheerleaders danced and pranced their way onto the field and Eric smiled at them, but no matter how much he blew on his flint, it would not dry, and he knew it would take an hour, and he really needed to smoke, and that's when the sound of metal gliding over flint high above him made him blink.

The band played a fanfare and the flickering glow of the flame drew Eric's eyes away from the twelve disappearing cheerleaders. He couldn't make out the face, but could see the figure standing on the lip of the tub, just beyond the flickering blue of the tub's underwater lights. "As you die, Eric, you too will be looking into the eyes of hate."

Eric recognized the voice at once and spun to make his escape. He was too slow though. The Zippo went shut and Soldier dropped down from out of the darkness. Water sloshed up, over Eric, and across the back deck. The steam cleared. The water settled and Eric had to turn back. He had to see.

Through the hissing wetness, a flash of movement came up from the water and then came eyes, just eyes, and in those eyes, Eric caught his first glimpse of Hell. He tried to cry out for help but found himself being lifted by the throat. "Sooner or later," Soldier said, "the hate catches up to you."

"Merrill, wait!"

"I'm done waiting!"

Soldier's legs found Eric's and they both went underwater, heat meeting air with a grand belching puff, the soft blue lights of the hot tub flickering, flickering, and with a kick of a jungle boot, finally going dead. Soldier held Eric under for I'm not sure how long, but not long enough to kill, only to make him suffer. When Eric began sucking in water, Soldier raised him up to let him steal a few breaths of precious air.

The cheerleaders ran laughing and giggling off the field, the halftime horns blared, and Eric knew nobody was going to save him. He swam backwards and clawed at his searing lungs. He slapped at his eyes to blink away the chlorine. He grabbed his wrist and felt to make sure it wasn't broken. He had swung a punch underwater, missed, and hit the side of the tub.

Eric just didn't think any of this was fair and said so and that is why he found himself suddenly free. He sucked in a few more stinging breaths, waited for something more, but nothing happened—just a voice from the darkness. "She was my soul…and you *took* her from me!" The voice seemed to be coming from everywhere, from nowhere. "You take the stand in your own defense tomorrow? Admit your part in her death and beg forgiveness."

Bass drums thundered as the players took the field and when the lights beneath the hot tub finally flickered back to life, Eric Stukel found himself alone, and for those few precious moments of the second chance he had been granted, he wondered if it was all a dream.

THE HOMECOMING

THEY PLACED TWO at his parents' house from that night forward. Two more escorted the family across the river and the thirty miles southeast into Nebraska. When they arrived at the courthouse, there were two more at the door and two more roving the lower hallways. It was a taskforce built with only one thing in mind—to keep Eric Stukel from harm.

Combined, President McKinley, rolling through town on a whistle-stop tour, and President Teddy Roosevelt, doing the same a few months later, didn't have such a well-heeled security contingent. Of course, McKinley was assassinated—two in the chest—and not much later Roosevelt took one point blank from a .32. He was bleeding and in pain, but got up anyway and delivered a speech that started: "It takes more than that to kill a Bull Moose!"

I couldn't hear too much of Attorney Mike Stevens' opening statement, so had to gather the pieces from second-hand accounts.

"A lot of evidence has been presented against my client," Stevens said. "We admit that much, but key facts still remain undressed: where Ms. Haas died, how Ms. Haas died, why Ms. Haas died. I tell you this, friends, those are questions you needn't answer. Your job as members of this jury is to determine reasonable doubt, no less, no more. There has been some grand speculation by the prosecution about a hair or two and some carpet fibers, but I'm going to show you how easily this evidence can be explained away, and once I do that I am going to show you how easily it is for an overzealous young prosecutor and a pressured law-enforcement agency to target a young man and his family…even when that young man has had a solid alibi from day one." There was movement in the jury box, a gasp from one juror. "Witch trials were supposed to have ended four-hundred years ago. Young people go out and make bad choices and sometimes those choices cost them, and that is a tragic fact of life…but a greater tragedy is to point finger at an innocent young man, to strip him of his dignity, to strip him of the best years of his life! Eric Stukel is a good kid, who comes from a well-respected family. He has been an easy target, harassed for years by the police, treated like an outcast. Members of the jury, I am going to show you how and why the facts don't add up, and we're going to talk a great deal about reasonable doubt and what that means, and in the end, you are going to have to make a very important choice. I thank you and look forward to getting to know you better."

BY LUNCH, ERIC Stukel was on the stand…

WE CAME TO my place after the party at the Stevenson farm, around about midnight…we drove straight there, so I don't know who would have seen us along the way," Eric told the jury. "When we got home, I lit some candles, like we always did, and we talked awhile, laughed…then made love for awhile." Eric stared off into space. "I don't know how long."

"You feel guilty about letting her walk home that night, don't you?" Stevens prompted. "You brought her home from the party and you wanted her to stay all night. You thought that was the safest thing to do, but she insisted on walking home and you let her. I mean, how could you stop her? And if you hadn't, she may still be alive and that makes you feel guilty?" Mike Stevens moved in close on his client. "Guilty enough to blame yourself for what happened to Tammy? Enough to even tell a few people you thought you might have killed a girl?"

"Yes." Eric looked to the jury. "I felt that way at the time. I suppose I wasn't thinking straight. She was having some problems with her family. I thought she might have left town without telling me. I thought she might have run away. I suppose that made me mad, because I always thought if she ran away..." Eric stared at his hands a long moment then said in a small voice, "I thought she'd run away with me." One of the jurors, the one that kept getting the knowing looks from Eric's mother, wiped a tear from her eye.

"This isn't the first time you suspected there might have been other men involved with her," Stevens said. "But you loved her in spite of that..."

"Objection, leading."

"Sustained."

"Let me rephrase that," Stevens said. "You and Tammy were the typical odd couple—she was outgoing, the life of the party; you were shy, reserved, a bit of an introvert."

"I wish she could have been faithful to me."

"Do you think that this fact might have led to her going back out to that party at the Stevenson's farm?" Stevens said. "Do you think she might have gone out there with another guy? With the wrong guy?"

"I don't know—"

I HAD TO get up and get away from those doors. I needed to go downstairs and pace the halls. Back and forth, up and down the stairwell, thrusting myself toward the exit home, drawn back to the courtroom doors, like a pendulum swinging madly and unable to stop. Could she have gone back out to that party? Was there any truth to what he was saying in there?

IT WAS HIS time now and he was reigning victorious over that courtroom, but wasn't that how it had always been. The everyday people always sided with the victor. Eric would be their hero—whether they believed him a killer or not. They would side with him because he had the wealth, the power, the control.

THE DOORS WERE shut upon me and I was swinging back and forth, a fool caught between Heaven and Hell. Could anything he be saying be true? As I slipped out the courthouse late that afternoon, taking the long way around to avoid the crowds, I passed a television reporter rehearsing her sound-byte for the ten o'clock news. "An audible murmur from the jury," the reporter said, "as the victim's history with several other men was brought to light by the defense." I went home that night and got very drunk.

THE HOMECOMING

I WAS QUITE near the bottom end of that bottle when I found myself beneath my bed dialing that old rotary phone. I didn't know who I was calling or why. I just let my fingers move on instinct and finally heard a familiar series of clicks and a voice on the other end of the line. "Charlie Company, this line may not be secure."

"Eccles?" I said.

"This is First Sergeant Eccles, who is this?"

"They're going to get away with it and I don't know what to do about that," I said. "Maybe just lie here beneath my bed for the time being."

"Soldier, I suggest you sleep it off," Eccles said and moved to hang up.

"My friends, my family!" I shouted into the phone. "Nothing would make them happier than it all going away...but for that to happen, I would have to go away too!"

"Soldier..."

"I have to tell you a story," I said. "Just so you know what kind of soldier I've become...Do you like stories, Drill Sergeant Eccles?"

"You were one of my recruits?"

"You remember how you said a slave would get beaten by his master after experiencing loss? You said this was to keep the slave from running."

"Merrill?" Eccles whispered.

"I think I did something very bad." I stared up at the mold running across the bottom side of my bunk. "At least I found out something bad, which—which—which, as it were—makes me feel very bad."

"You're very drunk, Merrill, I suggest you sleep it off."

"Once upon a time there was a very battered old federal agent who lived in a trailer on the edge of a little dead-end town. I don't know why he cared, because nobody else did, but he stuck around upon his retirement. Maybe it was all he had left—this one last unsolved case. Or maybe the little dead-end town just grew on him...like mold on bread...or on the back of a bed."

"You need to hang up and dial the police if you've committed—"

"Relax." I tightened the phone cord around my wrist to keep the phone at my ear. "I didn't kill anybody or anything like that...yet. Well, maybe I did kill him and he just hasn't figured it out—tough old bastard—what with the heart attack and now the little strokes he's been having. His mind's still there, but he's bedridden, and for men of action, men like us, being bedridden is just as good as being dead...but he is the only friend I've got, and really the only one who ever listens."

"A captive audience?"

"You're still funny." I laughed. "I broke into his apartment in search of my pistol and stumbled upon some stray case files. I should not have gotten curious. I should have gone straight for the pistol. That's why I went there—to recover the pistol he'd taken from me...but temptation got the best of me."

"So you've tangled yourself up in something that you—"

"I found the pistol eventually—mission accomplished, thank you—but only after reading those files." The mold beneath the bed seemed to be

THE HOMECOMING

spreading before my very eyes. "I should have known. I should have seen it coming three clicks away. She never said it in so many words...or maybe she did. I guess if you don't want to hear something, you won't, until you're ready for it...but, Drill Sergeant, I don't think I was ready for it, even now, even after all of this, and after all you've trained me to do. And I think something has finally and utterly broken inside of me that can't be fixed."

"I can't help you if you don't—"

"Clearly, I should have seen it," I said. "It hasn't come out in trial and I don't think it will—I think it was leverage used on both sides—but if it does come out, they'll crucify her, the good folks on that jury."

"Crucify who?"

I drew a finger over the trigger assembly of my pistol. "People judge others around here too harshly," I said, "but only if the ones they are judging are the weaker. Do you understand that?"

"I haven't understood a word you've said," Eccles told me.

"The strong," I said. "The strong get away with it."

"That's how it is everywhere," Eccles said. "Now, listen to me—"

"It was the perfect motive for murder and they couldn't use it against him. Not around here, they couldn't. People judge. People hate...and they call that hatred love. Well, I've had just about enough of that kind of love."

"This is about the girl who died?"

"I should've known—she practically whispered it in my ear when I left."

"That was over four years ago, Merrill."

"Oh," I said, as if this had never occurred to me.

"Son, do you need some help, is there somebody I can call?"

"And the secret she never told me?" I said. "She was pregnant."

THE HOMECOMING

CHAPTER TWENTY-FOUR

SHE DIDN'T LOOK like the awkward little girl of fourteen who first told the story. She was almost a woman, eighteen now. She was Eric's little sister and she took the stand the next morning. "You heard your big brother and Tammy making love from your bedroom?" Mike Stevens asked Sarah.

"That's right," she spoke softly, so softly that the jury had to lean forward to hear, so softly that the county decided they would use the discretionary fund to put a microphone in the witness box for next time. "His bedroom was right next to mine," she said. "I had just gotten to sleep a little after midnight and I'm a pretty light sleeper."

"You went to bed...and what happened next?" Stevens said.

"Well, I went to the bathroom at 12:36 A.M. I know because I remember looking at my alarm clock," Sarah said, "and Tammy startled me. She was just standing there in Eric's black bathrobe. I think we both startled each other. She said hello and we talked while she dressed."

"She didn't dress in Eric's room?" Stevens asked.

"No, she had her bag and she was freshening up in the bathroom. We hadn't talked for awhile, so we were catching up."

"And you just went back to bed after that?" Stevens asked.

"No, she...I mean Tammy...she told me she was going to walk home because it was such a nice night, and then after that I finally went to bed."

"And you never saw Tammy again?"

Sarah nodded then pulled out a tissue to wipe the tear that had been working up in her left eye.

"No further questions."

The courtroom was dead still when Attebaum rose. "Do we need to take a short recess, Ms. Stukel?"

Sarah shook her head and tucked away the tissue.

"You say at 12:36 A.M. you looked at your alarm clock?" Attebaum said. "That's some memory."

Sarah shrugged. "Some things just stick in your mind."

"But this isn't the statement you initially made to the police, is it? In fact, your memory of events has changed somewhat as the years have passed."

"Objection."

"Grounds?" Judge Horn asked.

"Immaterial in that it is of no consequence to any issue in the case?"

"Overruled...move with caution, Mr. Attebaum."

"So," Attebaum continued. "First, you weren't home the night Tammy died—this is according to the statement you made to the police while Tammy was still missing—making it impossible for you to have seen or heard her at

12:36 A.M.—according to your own statement." Attebaum took a slow drink of water, slow enough so that the schoolteacher, the minister, and two farmers in the jury box could lean back and ponder the contradiction. "A few days later, once Tammy's body was found," Attebaum continued, "you told the police that, in fact, you did hear Eric return home that night, but it was earlier, at about 10:00 P.M., and he was all by himself?"

Stevens rose. "Objection, compound questions!"

"Sustained," Judge Horn said.

"No, I'll answer," Sarah said. "I thought he was alone those first times."

"Because you never really did see Tammy in that bathroom?"

"I had remembered the nights wrong because of the way Eric always comes down the steps, gliding his hands along the walls. I didn't go out and look or anything to see if anybody was with him and I wasn't looking at the clock then, but I knew he had come home a little before midnight."

"Before you went to bed?" Attebaum asked.

"Yes, and like I said, I wasn't looking at the clock."

"But you *were* looking at the clock and he *wasn't* alone according to your third interview with the police?" Attebaum said. "Wait, wait, wait, let me get this straight—upon first questioning, you told the police you didn't remember Eric being home that night; on second questioning, after Tammy's body was found, you say Eric came home alone at 10:00 P.M.; and then when the police followed up months later, after you knew the police had impounded Eric's car, after you knew they had searched his room, after you knew he was the prime suspect, you decided to tell them about a detailed conversation you had with Tammy right before she walks home—at 12:36 A.M.?"

"Well," Sarah said, "I think sometimes a person's memory gets better as time passes."

One of the elderly ladies in the jury box nodded approvingly.

"If Eric was at home with you while Tammy was walking off into the night, that means that Eric couldn't possibly have killed Tammy, doesn't it?" Attebaum said.

"That's right," Sarah answered.

"You love your brother, don't you, Sarah?" Attebaum asked.

"Of course, I do."

"And you don't want to see him go to jail, do you?"

"Of course not."

"And you really want to believe that Tammy Haas was in your house Homecoming Eve, don't you, at 12:36 A.M.?"

Sarah turned and looked straight at the jury. "But she was…"

ATTEBAUM REQUESTED TO bring Coroner Wong forward as a rebuttal witness to reestablish time of death at midnight. The Defense and Prosecution stipulated and came to an agreement that they would let the record show that only one coroner out of three placed the time of death at or around midnight.

SISTER BACKS UP ALIBI AT TRIAL" was the next day's headline.

I BELIEVED SPECIAL Agent Earnstead when he told me there would be justice. I believed him because I needed to believe him.

HER HAIR IN his trunk, fibers from his trunk on her body." Assistant Attorney General Attebaum closed. "Urine and blood matching Eric Stukel's found on her undergarments. Her pants removed from the body. Her body found at the bottom of a ravine. Her hands and arm covered with defense wounds, her face battered and bruised, her neck broken. 'Kill Tammy? Yeah, I thought about it.' Eric at the carwash. Eric at his parents' restaurant: 'I think I killed a girl.' Only Eric can tell you what happened to Tammy that night, because only Eric knows. Eric didn't love Tammy. He was obsessed with her and in a fit of rage, killed her. That's where all the evidence points. He stuffed her body in his trunk, and like a piece of garbage, dumped her body in a ravine. Eric Stukel is guilty of Manslaughter in the Third Degree and today justice must be served. I thank you and the Prosecution rests."

MOST OFTEN, HOPE strings you along and drags you into the emptiness, all the while making you feeble and blind to the world you could be living in now. You dream, you pray, you patiently wait your way too close to the sun and the wings of hope melt beneath you. The cruel truth is that there was no point in her murder, nothing good has come from it, and nothing ever will.

LIFE IS FULL of mysteries," Attorney Mike Stevens began his closing statement, "that is tragic, but why turn one tragedy into two? What good is going to come from ruining a young man's life? A sense of satisfaction? What ever happened to forgiveness?" Tears of rage rolled down Mike Stevens' cheeks. "Ladies and gentlemen of the jury, if you cannot say without one-hundred percent certainty why Ms. Haas died, how Ms. Haas died, when Ms. Haas died, where Ms. Haas died, you *cannot*, I repeat, *cannot* convict! The Letter of the Law!" Stevens pounded his podium. "Not the intent! That's what this trial is all about, that's what you need to go into that jury room remembering." Stevens circled to the jury. "Nothing you can do in that jury room will bring Ms. Haas back." Stevens looked over at Tammy's mother. "We pray Tammy's in a better place. That's all we can do. She made choices in her life—some of them not the best." Stevens gathered his notes. "But ruining a young man's life, a young man who loved her, is not what Tammy would have wanted. Members of the jury, Eric's life is in your hands. I thank you," he said, "and God bless you as you make this very difficult decision."

CHAPTER TWENTY-FIVE

YOU PRAY EVEN if you believe in nothing—you pray because there's nothing more you can do. Twelve strangers battle behind closed doors and must come to a decision. You pace and you pace until you are too tired to pace and then you rise to your feet after the sitting has driven you mad. You pace and you pace and you pace and then a bailiff comes out a small door near the courtroom and tells the lingering crowd, "Nothing yet folks, the jury's gonna call it quits for tonight." He does this with a smile, while zipping his coat, one foot already out the door.

You watch Tammy's family exit out the north doors. You watch Stukel's family exit out the south. You stand there alone, watching them comfort one another, awkwardly at times, and at other times with such amazing grace, and you end up wondering how you have gotten yourself so alone. You decide it best not to ask these questions. You decide it best just to go home and drink yourself to sleep. That's when an old friend emerges from the shadows. "Do you know why she got in the car with him?" the old friend says. "Do you know why she chose him instead of you?"

"Bobby?"

"You're a nice guy," Bobby said, "and nice guys finish last."

"What are you doing here?"

"I saw her get into his car that night," Bobby said, "I wasn't sure at first. It was so dark. So I snuck in closer—and sure enough—it was her."

"You never left the party?"

"I was so mad at her. She was with him, you see, and that's not how it was supposed to work out." Booby teetered forward so he could whisper in my ear. "She was compelled—do you understand what I mean by the word compelled? She was compelled to him—she couldn't help herself."

"You didn't strand her—you stayed."

"I got them both back!" Bobby extended his arms, grinned, and then clutched his hands together. "You think I feel good about it?" he said.

I grabbed him. "What did you do, Bobby?"

"His window was open—that's what caught my eye. I was on my way to my car and I walked past his car and I saw that his window was opened." Bobby began laughing. "And when nobody was looking, I pissed in it. Pissed all over his car seats. Fuck it, I thought and warm and splendid it came!" Bobby did a little shuffle and then went dead still. "You see, Mr. Merrill, I asked her to go to the party with me and she said no…just one night is all I wanted and she said no." Tears suddenly streamed down Bobby's face.

"I don't understand," I said. "You didn't even take her to the party?"

"You're not too quick," Bobby said.

"So explain it to me."

THE HOMECOMING

"They made me tell everybody that I took her to the party to throw everybody off Eric's trail. I mean how stupid was I to go to that party, knowing that she would be there with him." Bobby teetered close to whisper. "Do you know what I did after I pissed in his car? I waited in the corn...waited for them to come...to see their reaction as they got into the car...I had marked my territory and both of them were going to be wet with me...and you know what?" Bobby smiled. "Right around midnight...almost as the bells struck twelve...sure enough, they got in the car."

"The second source of urine," I said. "It came from you."

"It was amazing how slow they were to react. It was like in the cartoon, where the coyote doesn't know he's going to fall, so he just hangs in the air. I see Eric shifting and scooting around in his seat and then I see Tammy doing the same thing, both of them wondering how the seats got wet. I hear her start laughing, because she smells it and has figured out what happened—you remember how her laugh was—and so out in the corn, I start laughing too."

"Eric got mad though, didn't he?" I said.

"He might have yelled something first—I'm not sure. All I know is he grabbed her and smashed her face against the dashboard. She was in shock at first...stunned. She had her hair in a ponytail that night, so he got a good hard grip. His stereo was turned up and there was the party just beyond the trees, so I couldn't make out any of the words...I tried to make out the words...but couldn't bring myself closer."

"What words?"

"She was pleading for him to stop...and when he wouldn't—"

"She tried to fight back," I said. "She tried to get out of the car."

"She struggles for his door and in the struggle they get themselves turned around. I wanted to tell myself they were just playing...and I see her legs kick up in the air, like an acrobat, and I see her crawl out his door and just when I'm about to go running up to see if she needs help, he crawls out of the car after her. She tumbles into the ditch and nearly makes it away. The weird fucker had parked backwards, so I couldn't see it all," Bobby said and then stared off into space a long moment. "He hit her again and again and then I heard him slam his door. I couldn't see exactly everything from where I was, but I knew. I knew right then what had happened. Because the dome light never shut off. The door closed, you see, but the dome light never shut off."

A janitor came gliding past with mop and bucket.

"Brian and Dusty came along," Bobby whispered, "and as they loaded up the body, Brian's girlfriend arrives too. She catches them in her headlights as they're doing it, because—like I said—his car is parked backwards."

"That was the scream people heard...hers, not Tammy's," I said.

"She starts screaming, yes, and they get scared that somebody from the party will hear her and come running to see what has happened, so Dusty calls up Don the Itch on his car phone and Brian tries to calm Katherine down and I'm still hiding in the corn." Bobby spoke faster and faster, building to a fevered pitch. "And Eric's just standing there smiling, like the whole thing is some glorious joke. Once they get her in the trunk, they start going from car to car to see who was still at the party and that's when I tried to run. They caught me in the corn though. They told me to go home—that I didn't see anything—that they'd take care of it, all I had to do was tell nobody." Bobby smiled and then twitched as if startled. "You were right about the guy and girl at the dam and what happened at the ravine. You were right about everything—every step of the way." Bobby started laughing again, but this time it was a laugh of catharsis, and then his laughter turned to sobs, and he stood there trembling, trying to catch his breath. "It was just supposed to be a practical joke. It was just supposed to be a practical joke. A few dribbles on his car seat. I didn't think he'd get so mad. I didn't think he'd get so mad. And I wanted to stop him from hurting her, and I wanted to tell, but they would have hurt me."

"You were scared," I said as sympathetically as possible.

Bobby shoved me into the wall. "Fuck you too, I was scared!"

"It's too late now though, isn't it? Now you're stuck with the fear." Bobby slowly processed what I had just said. "The trial is over—you can't come forward now. Now you have to live with it," I said.

Bobby shoved me again and then ran…ran nearly through the glass doors leading westward…ran out to a waiting car…screamed a rebel yell…and roared away. The janitor mopped his way back down the hall, gave me a nod…and I just stood there for I'm not sure how long…and then there was nothing left for me to do but go home and prepare.

MY BAG WAS packed atop my rotting little bed in my basement apartment. I spent the night cleaning the place as best I could for the next tenants, pulling down the news-clippings that covered the big cracked mirror, piece by piece, and folding them neatly away, watching as I did the rebirth of my reflection. Those four years had chipped away at me, but it wasn't so bad what I saw. I folded those news-clippings and tucked them away, and when there was nothing more I could do, I sat on that bed, pistol in hand for I'm not sure how long, and then decided it was time to see an old friend.

My old friend was pale. Maybe this is how he always looked and it was simply the first time I had noticed. There was a blue to his lips and the white of his eyes had gone deep yellow. They had him sitting up in bed, aided by a strap, to keep the fluids from swelling around his heart.

Our chessboard was back in its box. Somebody, a nurse probably, put it away, ruining a match that had lasted us a year. I had taken more of his pieces, but he always remained at a strategic advantage. I took the board out, shook the pieces onto his bed, and started arranging them, hoping this would rouse him. He didn't open his eyes, but right when I was about to get the last piece set, he grabbed my hand and said, "Don't bother, Merrill."

"You say where, Special Agent, and I'll move the pieces for you."

"You'll cheat," he answered, "which isn't very nice to do to a poor old blind man." His voice had so little strength left.

"If I cheat, you'll catch me."

"I *was* with the FBI," he said.

I set the last piece. "I'm thinking one of us could have the other in five moves...maybe four if I'm able to distract you."

"Just sit, Merrill...relax."

I did and he didn't let go of my hand. He was battling for breath, he was battling to rouse himself from the morphine that was keeping him just above the pain, he was battling for the strength to clear his mind, to speak, and when he was finally ready, he said, "Anything you want to know...just ask."

"Am I right for holding onto this?"

The question surprised him, but only for a moment. "Not long after Tammy..." he breathed long and slow... "Not long after Tammy, Eric started dating a girl. He got rough with her. Scared her. One night she ran."

"Didn't she press charges?"

Carriss rolled his blind eyes.

There was a picture on Carriss' nightstand. It was taken upon his graduation from Quantico. I had seen it many times but had never asked. He was with a young lady and a baby, a girl, I think. He looked very happy and so did they. "They were yours?" I asked him.

Carriss smiled. "A long time ago...could I have it?"

I handed him the photo and he held it until he didn't have the strength anymore. "Sometimes all you remember is the pain," he said. "But I guess that's okay too...it kept me in the fight for a good long time...used it to do good I hope." Carriss smiled. "I was wondering when you were going to find your way into my trailer. Took you nearly two years. What else did you find?"

"Oh, God." My mouth was so dry. Every bone in my body ached. "She was going to have a baby?"

"Oh, kiddo, yes...yes, she was. But she..." Carriss went silent.

"But she what?"

"There were complications."

"Complications?"

Carriss swallowed hard and then ached in a big breath, and for a moment, I thought it was going to be the end for him, but then his hand grew strong and he squeezed at my wrist until I felt the blood tingle away from my fingers and thumb. He exhaled slow and long, and as he did, his grip slowly loosened, his eyes opened, and for a moment, his voice came back strong and clear. "She terminated the pregnancy a month before you left for the Army."

"Terminated..."

"Nobody was ever supposed to know." he said, "Eric found out somehow. That's what we think at least. That's our best guess."

"Motive," I said.

"I don't think he thought it out that far," Carriss said. "I think he was full of rage and one night he struck."

"Not motive for him: motive for *me*."

"I know you want to let loose all that rage pent up," Carriss whispered.

"I faced them. Talked big. Thought I could make a difference."

"You got your pistol back too," Carriss added.

"I left it at home." I managed a smile. "Not because I thought it was the right thing to do...but because I'm so scared."

Carriss tried to laugh. "Sucks having a conscience, huh?"

"Don't give me too much credit," I said.

"Don't sell yourself too short." There was a beep and the sound of drugs delivered through his IV, the morphine coming to wash him up from the pain.

"She was beyond me," I said. "She let me share time with her though."

"That's good," Carriss murmured.

"I never really fit in or found my place unless I was with her. She always made me feel so...needed. I had a pretty miserable childhood and loving her gave me the hope to endure, and I thought maybe that when I was older, stronger...I guess it didn't matter if she loved me back or not. You dream and hope in spite of the facts at hand. Oh God, I hate who I am...I hate myself so much...if I could just disappear, just stop existing..."

"That's good," he murmured again.

"All I wanted to do was be near her," I said. "They had this Bible School at our church for the little kids and we older kids would help out. We must have been fifteen. The kids would go out and play kickball on this baseball diamond. I use the term loosely though because it was really just an overgrown field full of gravel and broken glass where we threw down four ice-cream lids as bases. We were in the kitchen on our break, me and Tammy, and one of the little kids comes in hurt. He must have been five. I don't remember his name. Tammy would though. He comes in and has a scraped knee. It was superficial, but for a kid that age, Purple Heart material. She takes him up in her arms and I find a bandage and we clean his wound...and the way she smoothed on the bandage, with so much love and so much care...she took his pain away and if God exists, he existed in that moment, and right then and there I knew she was the one..."

"That's good," Carriss murmured.

"I asked her to marry me that night and she said yes and so we drove and drove, trying to reach Vegas. We didn't get too far because it got too late." I smiled. "Curfew, you know...she was such a daddy's girl," I said. "She called me from the hospital the night her dad died. She sounded so alone. She had lost somebody she loved, and she was suffering...and what did I do? If I could...just go back...fix it...fix it all...instead of doing ***nothing***..."

The hospital was so silent. There was golden light slanting in through the window. It was coming off the brick of an adjacent wing. I stared at it and stared at it, and thought that maybe if I could stare at it long enough, if I could empty my mind into it long enough, I could soften the pain.

"You said there were complications?" I asked.

Carriss squeezed his eyes shut and tried to fight through the morphine. "Eric came along when Tammy was at her most vulnerable. When she felt very alone. Very troubled."

"Did he ever hurt her?"

"Abuse, you mean?" Carriss said. "He can't hurt her anymore. That's where he loses and that's why you don't have to fear her suffering anymore."
"How far do you go to right a wrong?"
"You didn't kill Tammy, Marc."
"But I didn't save her either."
"With all the evidence—" Carriss winced and coughed heavy the fluids filling his lung. "With all the evidence the jury has, it won't be your responsibility to right the wrong. He'll go away and by the time he's out—" Carriss coughed and coughed and finally a nurse came. I thought she'd come to see in on him, but all she did was poke her head through the door to say, "Mr. Earnstead called. The verdict is going to be read an hour from now."
"People like Eric get away with what they do," I said, "Because people like me do nothing to stop them...but I can stop him from doing it again."
"And then what?"
"And then nothing."
"We all wish we could play God, turn back time, right all wrongs...but make no mistake: you served with honor, you held on. You think you ran away. You didn't! To *kill* is nothing! The hate just spreads further. Expose them! Find a way. If you want justice, make it your mission to tell her story...to tell yours...people will care if you give them the...if you...give them..." He tried to finish what he was saying, but couldn't, and within the hour, alone in that little room, my friend Special Agent Ben Carriss died.

HOMECOMING BANNERS WERE hung in the store windows and parade floats were being stripped of their paper-mache facades at the parade-route end. It was a hard push through traffic, but I finally rolled over the bridge and slid hammer-down toward the courthouse.

There was standing room only when I arrived. Tammy's friends and family had been allowed back inside once the subpoenas were lifted. Not many of them recognized or remembered me and that was good. Across the aisle, my enemies had arrived too, Eric's happy accomplices—Dusty Fist who had helped cast her body into ravine; Brian Slobacek, Homecoming Chief, who had dangled his girlfriend over the dam to ensure her silence; Don the Itch, string-puller and candyman, making the threats, having the connections; and finally Noose Adarson, Eric's shadow-man and protector, even now watching me out of the corner of his eye.

Judge Horn entered from his chambers, black-robed and with a face of stone. Everybody in the courtroom went silent in anticipation. "I'd just like to say," he said. "How much of a pleasure it has been working with the Defense and Prosecution on this case." As Horn kept talking, I searched the room for the armed guards to take Eric Stukel away. "I would also like to admonish everyone here that there will be no outbursts once the verdict is read."

Horn sat and the jury made their way to the jury box.
"Anything from the Prosecution or the Defense?" Horn asked.
"No, your honor."

THE HOMECOMING

"Has the jury reached its verdict?"

Eric Stukel dropped his head against the defense table and went limp. Mike Stevens put a fatherly hand to his back and began gently rubbing. In the jury box, the retired Catholic school teacher rose and put on a pair of bifocals to read, "Yes, your honor, in the case of the State of Nebraska versus Eric D. Stukel on the charges of Manslaughter in the Third Degree—"

TO ANSWER ONE question, Eric's sister Sarah Stukel admitted years later that she had lied for her brother under oath and that his alibi was phony.

SEVERAL OF THE jurors were weeping now. "We the Jury find the defendant—"

Dear God, if you exist, please...

"—Not Guilty."

CHAPTER TWENTY-SIX

THE COURTROOM SHOOK with victory cheers. Eric Stukel threw his hands to Heaven in a sweet Amen! They had done it! Hugs and backslaps all around and somebody in the back—a middle-aged gentleman I had never seen before—got up and did a constipated little dance. There was silence over on our side of the courtroom. It was their grins maybe, the sound of joyous celebration perhaps.

I backed out the big oak doors and the next thing I knew I was halfway up the steps leading to the courtroom, pinned by at least five very strong men, some carrying guns, one of them Cooper Mac. He had come to watch over me...to protect me from myself.

Was this temporary insanity? Had I done it? Had I gotten him? If I had, I felt no relief, no catharsis, no liberation. My mind was a blank and the more I tried to remember the less I felt. There were men holding me, but I could not feel the sweet ache that should have lingered in my palm after emptying my pistol. And where was my pistol? I never brought it in the first place.

Suddenly, I felt an incredible sinking feeling. Eric Stukel and his bunch were coming out of the courtroom, laughing. "Another day, Merrill," one of the men holding me whispered, "Another day."

ON HIS WAY out of the courthouse, defense attorney Mike Stevens was rushed by reporters. "You must be a happy man today!" shouted one of them.

"Happy?" Stevens trembled with anger. "My client and his family have lost four years of their lives, four year they'll never get back!"

"And what about Tammy Haas?" another reporter asked.

"You'll have to excuse me now!"

I BLACKED OUT again and the next thing I remembered was being back in the courtroom, alone, watching the light come in from the upper windows, the sunset growing long as it died in the west. Finally, all went to shadow and silence, and for a moment I thought I had written myself out of existence. The lights flickered on above me and a janitor pulled his mop bucket through the heavy oak doors. The janitor rung out his mop and as he did quietly whispered that he had work to do, that it was time for me to leave.

WHEN DELIBERATIONS BEGAN the straw vote was eleven in favor of guilt. The juror who had been exchanging looks with Eric Stukel's mother was a plant. After that first vote was taken, she told her fellow jurors that there was no way Eric Stukel would ever be going to prison, that she could outwait them all. In the end, there were jobs, wives, husbands, children, grandchildren, and everyday lives waiting the eleven others. "It was so long ago," some of them said as they folded. "It isn't our problem anyway."

THERE WAS THIS one time—we must have been sixteen—it was June, when the days were warm, but the nights still got cool. It was the second night of the camping trip, and by midnight, the firewood ran out. We had made the fire big, burned it long, and when the night grew deep, we tossed in our sitting logs as a last resort. As a gentle breeze picked up across the lake, one by one, the other kids began retreating to their tents. In childhood, you wait for perfect moments like these, and when they happen, you really aren't sure what you're supposed to do. It was just the two of us now, and after more than one moment of uncomfortable silence, we both said at once, "I'll stay up until the fire goes dead."

Little by little, the embers gave less and less heat and so to stay warm we moved closer and closer. When it hurt to sit, we folded a leaky air mattress in half and curled it beneath us—sliding and squeaking it around us until it buoyed us together just right. We found a blanket, her head found my shoulder, her hands found mine. "Just to keep warm," she whispered.

As the night shortened toward day, the earth gave up its warmth, and too soon, the dampness of morning came to play against the heat of our sunburned legs. Each time one of us would move against the other, the other would inevitably whisper, "Ouch." This was the first time we'd been together in months and whenever one of us would ask if the other was tired, the answer would be, "I can stay up a little longer."

Soon, we were watching the sun break in the east.

I wish I could have told her that I believed in her, and that my heart ached for her, and that she made me happy and sad all at once. I wish I could have told her that her dreams and her hopes meant the world to me, even when those dreams didn't include me. I wish I could have told her how much joy she brought into my life and that I would always love her no matter what.

WE TOOK A good long shortcut across the wide-open green of the park that night before I left for the Army. We stopped to sit on the swings for a time and she watched me ride down the slide. I did it standing up to show off. At exactly 4:00 A.M., just as the city had timed it, and exactly one hour before I was to get on the bus that was to take me to Fort Benning, the water kicked on and Tammy and I found ourselves stuck. It was either a one hundred yard dash in retreat or three hundred yards to stay our course home. I grabbed Tammy's hand to pull her forward, but she didn't budge. Instead, she pulled me back hard. Pulled me straight into her arms. Pulled me tight. Tight enough that I could feel her trembling and that's when she said, "If you want to grab me and run..." She backed away just enough to brush a stray curl from my eye and then pulled me close again and whispered something that would haunt me forever. "If you want to grab me and run, do it now and don't ever stop." I could feel the warmth of her cheek against my ear as she held me there, and there in each other's arms we stood—I'm not sure for how long—letting ourselves get soaked in those sprinklers as they splashed up the twilight around us.

I LIVED FOR a time in a little hole of an apartment. The little hole of an apartment had a large mirror on the wall and a little hanging bulb to give me light. The walls were of cinder and the bed smelt of death. The refrigerator made a noise, but that was okay—the noise kept me company. I had a duffel bag too that was packed with everything I owned. I had only one more task.

FROM ACROSS THE street, I had watched them celebrate. It was a festive occasion, all pretense of innocence lifted. They even hung a large banner over the door—"WELCOME HOME, ERIC!"

I had followed Dusty Fist and Don the Itch from the little convenience store by the bridge all the way up Douglas, watched them hop out and pop champagne in the drive. There at the door was Eric, who ran down and gave them both big hugs. Now was the time, while they were all together—this was the only chance I would get. It was perfect, a coming together of frayed ends, the four years past, a tapestry only now fully revealed. I would be an avenging angel, I would right this wrong.

UNDER THE HALO of the hanging bulb, kneeling at the foot of my rotting bed, I assembled my pistol and loaded six rounds. The magazine slid gently into the grip, giving it perfect balance and weight. I eased the receiver back, breath bated, to feed that first round of ammunition into the pipe—beautiful, simple, and clean.

My destiny was chosen for me. It had been from the start.

There was only one way in and one way out...

I was born to serve and protect and this was the way.

I rose and found my reflection one last time in that big cracked mirror and I liked what I saw—time had chiseled away, carving muscles across a sturdy frame. This was the strongest I would ever be, the freest, the most determined, and for the first time in what would come to be a short life, I knew exactly what I was supposed to do. I would wear black and the jungle boots that landed me jump after jump. I wouldn't need a holster. From here to the end, the pistol would never leave my grip.

I rose and that is when I heard a noise behind me and saw her reflection coming out of the shadows. It was hot for an autumn night and I had made the mistake of leaving the door wide open. "Where are you going?" she asked.

"To a party," I smiled.

He was right behind her, emerging from the shadows of the stairwell. "If this is what you really wanted," he looked to my pistol, "you would have done it all ready."

"Wasn't it enough to watch her suffer, wasn't it enough to toss her away." I said. "Wasn't it enough that he came back and did what he did to her two days later? But now?" I said. "Now they celebrate, and that will not do."

The determination and strength that came from the hopelessness would guide me past my parents and out the door, I convinced myself.

"You're right," my father said, blocking my path. "You are right."

My mother stepped up behind him. "But to even consider revenge—"

"Not revenge—Justice!"

"Just think of what this would do to me and your father."

"You and—?" I took a step back. "This has *nothing* to do with *you*!"

"I know you wish you could go back and take her place," my father said, "and that is an incredible burden to carry."

They were circling me to keep me from the door.

Oh, how I wanted to hate them.

"To have someone love you, no matter what, do you have any idea what that's like?"

"Oh, baby, you don't think we know." My mother reached out to me.

"Don't you pretend!" I shouted. "Don't you dare! Because she was the only person who ever told me—ever in my life!"

"What?" My mother pleaded, "What did she tell you, baby?"

"Oh, God!" I raged. "That she *loved* me!"

A pained look crossed both their faces and both began speaking at once. "You really think she ever—oh, but why didn't you ever—how could you possibly think—you don't think *we* love you?!"

"It doesn't matter," I said. "They threatened you. And they threatened others…and that will not do." My eyes went hard upon the door. Once I was past them, I would be moving fast and wouldn't stop until it was done.

"Okay," my father said, "if you have to go—go."

My mother looked to my father in horror.

"But don't you lie to yourself," my father said, "up until this very moment you have given those people the one chance they never gave Tammy—you've shown them Mercy."

"No, I haven't!" I shouted. "Don't you say that to me!"

"Your heart is broken." My mother came at me again. "And they've pressed you—they've pressed you so hard—but you're too strong."

"Don't you say that!"

"We *have* called the police," my father said. "If you leave here now, they *will* stop you. You won't make it over there. They'll do whatever it takes to ensure that. They *will* put you down before you even get close."

"But it isn't right!"

"It's not, we know, but you'll find another way, baby, you always do."

"SHE WAS RAPED!!!"

"We know, baby…"

"SHE WAS MURDERED!!!"

"We know…"

THE HOMECOMING

The harder I tried, the looser my grip became. I held onto it with everything in me, but I had no strength left.

"What if he does it again?" I tried.

"But what if he doesn't?" my mother said. "It's okay to fear that and it's okay to be powerless and to need people in your life and to forgive yourself and to let yourself be loved. It is. That doesn't mean you love her any less."

"Just let it fall," my father whispered his way up behind me. "Let the pistol fall. Let it fall and give us your hand. That's all you have to do."

I looked to my mother. I looked to my father. I looked to my pistol.

"So futile, isn't it?" I said and as I said it, the pistol fell. "If not him, some other murderer, and I can't do anything to stop it."

At that moment, I surrendered to the weight of a heavier burden—the weight of forever separation, of myths and dreams broken, of gods and heroes falling from the sky and crumbling to dust. Everything I had ever believed, ever dreamed, ever hoped vanished once and for all, and I fell soldier-crushed to my knees. "She should be here right now and I just want to touch her one more time and I don't understand any of this."

My mother Grace took me in her arms and held me for I'm not sure how long and then my father lifted me to my feet and helped me to the door.

PART V

ACCEPTANCE

WE WERE STUCK at a red light when the caravan of honking cars rolled past. The Yankton Bucks had won a sudden-death homecoming victory. It was a time for bonfires. It was a time for celebration.

I found my Zippo. It was in my jacket, engraved with **Fiat Lux**, which meant, "Let there be light."

I was in the back seat of my parent's car, clicking that Zippo open and clicking that Zippo closed, when my thoughts returned to those sprinklers and how we could have run away. I stared at those cars rolling past on their way over the bridge, their taillights trailing red into the darkness, a darkness that would offer its full embrace to the tiny town this night.

Of the five stages of grief, the final stage, acceptance, is always the worst, for it is the ache that lingers. It has been said that for every soldier who lies bleeding on a battlefield, on the other side, a son returns safely home. It was a quiet war, a war of secrets and lies, and now it was over. This night a soldier died on the battlefield. This night a son returned home.

Nights as still as this were to be expected in the whispering season, when the air cooled slowly as the days winnowed down, and the only sound heard was a gentle wind strumming high through the pines. Snow would come soon and the sojourn of the geese would last only a day or two. The seasons would pass one into the next, and along the way, the geese would make their return. Death and rebirth, this was the way of the world, an insignificant little rock spinning through the expanding blackness.

We yearn heavenward, and when fortune shines, we bask in its glow with no thought of the clouds that loom. When it storms, we brave ourselves up the best we can, because in the end, we just don't know…and maybe, just maybe, not knowing is the great adventure.

There are no easy answers—that much is certain.

The only trick I know is to listen, not when *I* am weak, but when I am strong, to those around me who might be suffering and in need. We must hear their cry and reach out our hands. It is the least we can do and the best way we can love, because in the end, we only got each other, and together, just maybe, we can grab up hope, and with hope held firmly in our hearts, and in our hands, most importantly in our hands, we can find the way to carry on…

THE END

THE HOMECOMING

Marc Merrill was born and raised in Yankton, South Dakota. Upon graduation from high school, he served in the 82nd Airborne Division as an Infantry Paratrooper. Reaching the end of his tour of duty in 1994, he received several decorations and an honorable discharge. He attended the University of South Dakota, graduating Summa Cum Laude with a double major in English and Theatre. From there he went on to attend the prestigious School of Cinema and Television at the University of Southern California, earning an MFA in writing for cinema and television. He spends his time between Los Angeles and South Dakota, writing, directing, and acting for stage and screen. This is his first novel.